The Alympa Chronicles: Starlight

Book 1

R.L. Stanley

To Our Worshipfulness, Our Highnessness, Our Princess, Our General.
Thank you.

CONTENTS

PROLOGUE

"Why are we on this miserable moon anyways?"

"*Talik*," Jhama warned, eying her scaled crewmate as they sloshed through the stifling, half-flooded streets. "I'm not playing this game."

"Of all the places to put a fueling station, they pick this *gotso* rock," the taller man continued, ignoring his companion. "You would think they'd choose a place friendlier to living things."

He blinked quickly, film-like lids gliding sideways across reptilian eyes in an attempt to wipe away the wetness slowly blinding him. It didn't work. He scratched at his uniform next, a low, hissing growl bubbling deep in his throat at the waterlogged feel of the damp fabric against his skin. It was almost as suffocating as the air.

"Look at this! I'll have to change as soon as we board. I feel like I just showered in my clothes."

Jhama watched him evenly, debating whether or not to let herself get sucked in and finally relenting when her partner stumbled through a particularly dirty puddle and loudly swore.

"I thought your species came from a tropical planet, Talik," she commented innocently, and he glared, struggling to wipe the mud from his boots and the bottoms of his pants.

"I'm from the temperate regions, Jhama. Temperate! Not this boil-in-your-own-air climate—"

A sudden, deafening hiss cut him off as a vent across the narrow street clanged opened and released a plume of white-hot steam into the already oppressively muggy air. The two officers quickly backed away, the dense vapor uncomfortably heating their skin through their clothes.

Talik considered the offending grate for a moment before looking back to his friend, resigned and exhausted.

"I hate this place."

Jhama smirked to herself and patted the officer's damp shoulder.

1

"Don't we all?"

He rewarded her teasing with yet another doleful, disgusted hiss.

"Temperate regions, Jhama," he repeated in the tone of one quickly nearing his wit's end. "*Temperate.*"

She sniggered, but deep down she pitied her coworker.

She couldn't blame him for his discomfort. Othlu's farthest moon really wasn't the most pleasant destination. Its jagged surface was pitted with volcanic steam vents that—when combined with the vapor byproducts of the mining facilities and cramped workers' towns clustered around them—exponentially increased the humidity. Its nine hours of intense daylight then turned the nigh-uninhabitable rock into a sauna as the sun's heat merged with the trapped warmth of the vents and the factories beneath the thick atmosphere. Each breath yielded more water than air, and Jhama briefly gave thanks for the lighter gravity. She couldn't imagine struggling to walk in addition to fighting to breathe and feeling the hot, heavy air pressing down on her skin.

She shivered involuntarily at the mere thought of what that world would look like and reached up to her ear, brushing aside light orange hair and touching the small, hearing-aid-like device barely visible in the canal. These earwigs were a nice step up from their old gadgets; the bulkier earpieces had been knocked off their heads way too often.

"Avery Byrone," she recited and paused as the line connected, shooting Talik a quick smile that faded as a voice filtered through the static in her left ear.

"What's up, Jhama?"

"Hey, Byrone," she returned. "What's the timeline?"

"We should be done refueling soon. I'd start heading back before the captain sounds the return."

"Gladly," Jhama sighed in relief, wiping the sweat and water from her brow with her sleeve. "It's disgusting out here."

"Well, yeah," the engineer's voice replied like it was obvious, "it's the far moon. It sucks."

"Thanks for the support, L.C.," she said dryly, using the man's rank abbreviation as a ribbing nickname. Her partner rolled his eyes, no doubt guessing the general gist of what their superior had said. "Talik and I'll head back now. Tell the loading bay to keep an eye out for us."

"Will do. Oh man, Talik's with you? The poor guy—he's from his homeworld's temperate region, right?"

"Yeah," she began, playfully side-eying her companion, "he keeps mentioning something about that." Talik shot her a dirty look, and she smirked again. "See you on board, sir."

"See you on board."

Jhama reached up and tapped her earwig again, closing the channel, before gently elbowing Talik and pointing at the alley they were about to pass.

"Come on." She paused, retying her ponytail in an attempt to get her hair higher up off her neck and shoulders. "Byrone said we should head back to the ship now."

"They're done refueling?"

"Almost." She tugged on his sleeve, pulling him after her into the even more cluttered and narrow backstreet. "Come on."

"This is a tight fit," Talik muttered, looking at the dripping and steaming pipes running up the stained metal walls that crowded them on either side. "Is it just me or is it even hotter in here?"

"It's not just you. It must be the pipes." Jhama gingerly stepped over a toppled barrel oozing of some sort oily substance and wrinkled her nose at the sludge dripping from her black boots. "*Ugh,* what is this stuff?"

"I'm not even thinking about it."

"Good idea." Jhama reached out towards the dark, slimy wall to balance herself and jerked her hand away with a sharp hiss of pain.

"Jhama, you okay?" Talik asked, gently grabbing her shoulder.

"Yeah," she said tightly as she cradled her hand to her chest. Her blue skin was raw and glistening with violet blood. "Just burned myself on a pipe. Watch yourself, they're *really* hot."

As the two of them picked their way through the alley, cautiously watching their feet and taking care to not touch the walls, it started to rain. The drops were large and uncomfortably warm, and the blue-skinned woman tried her best not to think about how filthy the water had to be. The alley was nearly pitch black, its gloom pierced only by the amber-red lights mounted to the walls high above them. The caged, oblong bulbs were placed about every twelve feet, and their height, combined with the distance between them, offered very little guidance in the dark.

"Could this get any worse?" Talik grumbled, just before tripping on something with a loud clang and crashing hard into Jhama's back.

"Talik!" she yelped, barely managing to catch herself and her friend on the edge of the dumpster he'd no doubt stubbed his toe on.

"Sorry!" he whispered and quickly released his tight grip on her arms once his feet were under him again. "I can't see in here…I think I tripped on the corner of a dumpster or something."

Thought so, she sighed and hauled him forward once more.

"Come on," she scolded. "You're leading the way this time. I don't want you mauling my arm with your talons again."

"I can't wait to get off this rock," he grumbled, squinting up at the offending sky. The red lights reflected off his scaled features like the oil on the water beneath their feet. "Of course it had to start raining. This moon wasn't horrible enough already."

Jhama looked up with him as they continued walking, absorbed in their mutual disdain for the smog-filled atmosphere. And with their attention fixed decidedly elsewhere, neither noticed the shadow peel away from the wall behind them.

Navy blue uniforms, Corps emblem embroidered on upper arms. Silver eight-point star with a gold comet circling it in a diagonal orbit angled at their backs.

The corner of the shadowy newcomer's mouth twitched with the faintest trace of a sinister sneer.

My dear Ren's crew. He pulled the cowl of his heavy coat lower over his face. *Finally.*

"Quit whining, Talik," the woman said playfully, looking forward once more. The tall, dark-clothed stranger remained unnoticed behind them, quickly closing in. "Couple more blocks, and we'll be back on board—nice and dry and cool."

Yellow shoulder padding—low ranking officers. Ensigns. Perfect.

"Oh, I never thought recycled air would sound so nice," Talik sighed blissfully.

Jhama laughed and pushed him forward a little faster.

"You and me both, so let's pick up the pace, yeah?"

Now.

Talik heard the third set of steps first.

Initially, he thought it was just the sound of their sloshing footfalls echoing off the walls, but when they suddenly grew louder and faster than either of their gaits, he quickly spun around, hand falling naturally to the weapon at his hip.

A tall figure was behind them, charging them, almost on them—

"Jhama!"

The shorter woman turned on instinct, her gun half-drawn from its holster when the assailant's hand slammed harshly into her throat, viciously silencing her and knocking her back into Talik at the same time. She could hear her partner's panicked voice through her coughing and the sound of his weapon falling into the water beneath them.

"*Gotso!*"

The stranger kicked her own weapon from her hand next with a painfully heavy boot before stomping down on her knee, twisting the joint and sending her harshly to the ground as she cried out in pain.

"You, stay down there," a gravelly voice snapped

To her horror, Jhama found herself frozen in her kneeling position, gaze fixed at the disturbed water beneath her as she struggled to catch her breath. In her limited field of vision, she could make out the stained, calcified hem of their attacker's water-repellant coat, but nothing else.

Talik staggered back a few steps, eyes wide, and quickly reached for his earwig.

"Oren—"

The dark cowl swung to face him.

"Quiet!"

Talik's voice promptly died in his throat, and the officer struggled to make a sound, any sound at all, and found he couldn't.

"Talik?" Jhama called, voice spiked with panic, and he dove for his fallen weapon, only to have his terrifying opponent grab him by the throat and slam him back against the wall with a gloved hand.

"You, shut up, too!" he barked over his shoulder to the blue-skinned woman and quickly looked back at Talik as the uniformed man pulled back a fist to strike him in the head. "Stop!"

Talik's yellow eyes widened, narrow pupils dilating as much as they could, as he found he was just as frozen as his coworker—one taloned hand clutching the straps and fastenings across the front of the man's coat, the other drawn back in a fist. His breathing was harsh and erratic, the only outward sign of his panic. The man before him took in a deep breath, tipping his head back slightly before tilting it side to side.

Stretching, Talik realized with bizarre, terrified detachment as he stared. *He's stretching.*

"See, wasn't that easy?" the stranger asked, peeved, before grabbing Talik's fist and pulling his arm to his side. "Though it should hardly be a surprise. Oren always did seem to pick a feisty crew." Next, he all but tore the crewman's hand from the front of his coat, returning it to his side, as well. "Your two fellow crewmates I ran into earlier today were just as difficult."

He stepped back from his victims, heaving a sigh and rotating his shoulders, and Talik was finally able to get a good look at whoever this man was. He was narrow-shouldered despite his tall height, gangly, Talik supposed, beneath the heavy clothing. The clothing…it was odd given their location. Not the water-repellant part, that was to be expected. It was the weight, the complete coverage it provided. It had to make it unbearably hot, hard to breathe, and the paralyzed ensign realized that was probably why he kept sighing and taking such heavy breaths. The gloves, the gloves were probably so he'd leave no fingerprints, the deep cowl to hide his face.

Whoever this man was, he didn't want to be seen. He wanted to leave no trace. And that meant…

Talik swallowed hard.

That means he's probably going to kill us.

The man slowly crossed his arms and smiled to himself beneath the hood.

"I suppose you're trying to profile me right about now, aren't you, boy? Like a good little officer," he teased and turned to look at Jhama. "No need." He walked forward, his splashing footfalls and the scared breaths of the partners the only sounds in the alley. "I'll be telling you exactly who I am and what I want, particularly from each of you." He knelt beside Jhama and tucked her hair behind her ears where it had fallen into her face. "You may speak only to answer my questions. Tell me, what's your name?"

"Jhama Assora," she answered obediently, mouth dry. Why was she answering? She didn't want to answer, didn't want to tell him anything. So why was she *answering?*

"Position, rank, and specialty?" the man continued, clearly enjoying her mute panic.

"Security officer," she heard herself say, and her heart pounded in her chest. "Ensign." Jhama swallowed painfully, her voice a hoarse whisper as she finished responding. "Extraction."

"Excellent." The dark hood turned to face Talik once more, but he remained kneeling by Jhama's side. "What about you? Remember, same rules apply—no speaking unless spoken to. What's your name?"

"Talik Omarik."

"Position, rank, and specialty."

"Security officer, ensign…ordinance specialist."

The man chuckled darkly to himself, standing and walking over to Talik with an almost swaggering gait.

"Ordinance?" he asked, delight gleaming in the single word.

"Yes," Talik bit out.

"Oh," the man grinned, reaching out and patting Talik's face. The trapped man flinched as his captor's gloves briefly caught on the gill-like, spiked ridges running along his cheeks and jaw.

"*You*, Mister Omarik, are my new favorite person." He turned away from his latest assets, wandering a little ways down the alley and laughing to himself. "*Ordinance*. My, how lucky I've been today!" He pivoted on his heel, and Jhama squeezed her eyes shut as she heard him walking back toward them. "Well, I suppose I should tell you my name now since we're going to be partners in crime for your foreseeable futures. It's more fun that way, I suppose. For me, not you, of course," he added with an almost sadistically apologetic tone. "Because while you'll know exactly who I am and what horrible things I'm going to have you doing, you won't be able to tell anyone or do anything to stop it."

Move, Jhama thought to herself, struggling to rise from her kneeling, bent-over posture. *Move, dammit, you have to move. Say something!*

She remained still and silent. This stranger's words, his commands, kept her bound.

Above her, Talik watched their tormentor, his previous discomfort with the weather forgotten in their new, horrific situation. The man walked up to him, standing deliberately toe-to-toe and cocking his head slightly to the side.

"I'll tell you my name, and then I'll tell you what I want you to do. How does that sound?" Talik tried to give his best glare and was unsurprised when the man laughed at his efforts. "My name," he continued, and the ensign was sure he was giving him a feral, twisted grin again, "is Jon Bledsoe. But you can call me Jon."

On the ground, Jhama tensed. Or rather, she would have if she'd had any voluntary control over her own body.

No, she thought wildly, heart pounding mercilessly and breathing picking up until she was nearly hyperventilating. *No, no, no, no—*

Above her, Jon smirked and slowly turned to look down at her. There it was...the fear. The fear and desperation he'd come to miss so much.

"It seems Miss Assora knows me better than you do, Mister Omarik," he said, returning to her side with a painful, predatory slowness. "Do you know who I am, Jhama?"

"Yes," she whispered, shivering.

"And I assume the way I overpowered you now makes sense?"

"Yes."

"*And* given that you are familiar with my name, my reputation, and my abilities, I assume you can guess the general reason why I'm here, speaking to you and your partner?" he asked, voice overly sweet as he gestured back to the man still immobile against the wall. There was a long pause, and Jhama took a deep, shaking breath.

"Yes."

Jon rolled his eyes and looked at Talik.

"Is your friend always this evasive when answering questions? That was rhetorical, don't reply." He returned his focus to Jhama. "And?" he prompted. "What is my reason? What's my *endgame?*"

"To kill—"

"My brother, yes, very good!" He patted Jhama's shoulder with a smile. "We're already on the same page, and we haven't even started discussing the details. Isn't that impressive? *Now,*" his gentle touch changed into a painful grip on her shoulder that would've made her cry out in pain if she could've, "here's how we're going to do it. You will—"

A faint computerized voice came from the communication device nestled in the woman's ear, cutting Jon off. His expression darkened.

"Did you send a distress signal?" he growled, and Jhama hurried to answer.

"No, i-it's the return call. Our ship is done refueling. We have to board for takeoff." He still didn't seem convinced, so she tried to elaborate and was relieved to find that she could still speak. "It's an automated message. No one's actually talking to me. We...we're still alone."

Jon looked at Talik for confirmation, shadowed face expectant.

"Is she telling the truth?"

"Yes."

"Well, then, it seems we've been interrupted." Jon got to his feet and paced a little in the tight space before coming to a decision. "Perfectly alright." He looked between his two victims. "Stand up, Miss Assora, and face me."

Jhama slowly, painfully got to her feet, taking care to lean most of her bodyweight on her uninjured knee. She wanted nothing more than to spit in this man's face but, seeing Talik still invisibly pinned to the wall and remembering their helplessness, thought better of it.

She'd find a way out of this for them later.

"Good, now go stand next to your friend, Mister Omarik. I really don't want to have to keep turning between the two of you. And do not even think about trying anything, or I will be most...displeased." She silently obeyed him, standing close enough to her crewmate that their shoulders pressed together. It was the smallest amount of comfort she could give.

Their captor noticed.

"How cute," he said dryly, before continuing. "Since we're short on time, I'll contact you through different radio frequencies on the lower communication bands with further instructions. Listen daily for messages and follow them *precisely* the way I say. You'll have to sift through a lot of static, but you'll find them. Do you understand?"

"Yes." Talik whispered, and Jhama echoed his response.

"Good. You will not tell anyone what happened in this alleyway. You will not tell anyone about the messages you have received or are to receive. You will not do anything at all to alert anyone of your, hm, let's call it your new employment. Including any overly distressed thinking—I know you have that pesky mind reader as your deputy chief of security, and I would hate for him to ruin our plans before they even begin.

"If you need to explain injuries or justify why you're lurking near somewhere you shouldn't be or looking into something you have no reason to, make something up. Oh," he added, reaching out and gently grabbing Talik's chin, "and do make sure it's convincing. You can't look like someone's coercing you, so make sure you blend in with the locals. No one should suspect that you're up to anything, let alone sabotage."

The two ensigns' stomachs plummeted, and a cold sweat broke out over Jhama's skin.

Sabotage? What in the galaxy is he having us do?

"I see you're starting to appreciate the severity of your situation." Bledsoe smiled to himself, an eager fluttering filling his chest. After so many years, it was all finally coming together. "Coordinate your stories and never, under any circumstance, say my name to anyone else. Not even to each other.

"You'll tell no one of your missions. You'll do as I command. And before you execute our plan—the *final* stages of our plan, mind you," he added in an aside, putting a hand on each of the officers' shoulders, "not the phases you two will be carrying out to build up to it, I want you to give Ren a message. Tell him his brother sends his regards." He clapped their shoulders once before shoving them viciously down the alley. But without his permission to move, they simply pitched forward, crashing into the dumpsters and oil drums on their way to the dirty, flooded ground. "Return to your ship now. Don't dawdle."

He laughed as he watched the young ensigns shakily help each other up, holding onto one another as they retreated as quickly as possible down the alley. His cackle was a chilling, haunting sound that cut both to their bones, and Talik swallowed bile at the stranger's parting command. His lilting, patronizing tone was more menacing than anything else he'd done or said.

"Make me proud."

"Run," Jhama gasped, finding herself able to speak once more, and pulled frantically at her friend's uniform. "Talik, *run*, come on!"

He didn't wait to be told a third time.

Jon Bledsoe continued to laugh as he watched his two new, final sleeper agents flee around the corner. In retrospect, he had kicked the girl's leg rather hard. It would impede her ability to be the best asset possible, though not for long. Ren's damn doctor would see to that. He heard voices behind him and looked over his shoulder to see more people filling the sidewalks, all clad in the same uniforms as Talik and Jhama.

Reporting back to ship.

He lightly dusted off his clothes, wiping some excess water from its slicked surfaces and making sure his cowl was pulled low over his face before joining the crowds.

It's been seventeen years since I've seen the old girl.... It would be nice to see her again. It'll make destroying her that much sweeter.

A few of the people he passed on the street spared him a glance. Like Talik, they found the heavy coat and gloves strange but quickly dismissed him as they returned to whatever conversation they'd been having before. A hot, sticky wind wound through the narrow streets, and Jon flinched at the touch of it against his face, expression turning into a scowl and a low growl bubbling in his throat. That sensation, it reminded him of—

"REN!"

Ren's giant of a first officer was on him in an instant, tackling him back—where had she even come from—and Bledsoe howled in pain as something razor sharp slashed down his face, blinding his left eye, tearing into him, sending blood everywhere, coating his skin in a hot, sticky—

Jon slammed shoulders with someone, and the memory was lost, replaced with a burly, furious miner grabbing a fistful of his jacket at the base of the hood.

"Hey, idiot, watch where you're…"

The miner's angry threat died in his throat as the moron's cowl fell back just enough to reveal a grotesque web of scars across the left side of his pale face, including a blind, fogged eye beneath the worst of the healed gouges. Gray-streaked hair hung to his shoulders, the oily strands framing his angular, ravaged features.

He looked familiar….

"You've seen enough, *idiot?*" the stranger snarled, teeth bared, and grabbed ahold of the worker in turn, pulling him close enough to speak into his ear. "You will let me go and forget you ever saw me."

The miner's harsh, confused expression cleared immediately. And without another word, he loosed his grip on Jon's hood and continued on his way, leaving the man to pull his cowl over his head once more and resume following the steady stream of blue uniforms back to their ship.

The memory of that night so long ago when it'd all gone wrong, when Ren had betrayed him and sicced his first officer on him, had set him on edge. That rage, that *fire*, was back in his gut, and he took in a deep, steadying breath. He couldn't draw any more attention to himself, not even here. That miner had almost recognized him.

You were thorough, Ren. You made sure my face was on every planet, moon, and station, Jon thought bitterly as he stepped into another alley and hurried through. The shipyard was around the corner. *Just like you said you would.*

A block ahead of Jon, Talik and Jhama were running back to their ship, terrified and soaked to the bone. Every time they tried to talk about what had happened, their voices stuck in their throats. The words refused to come. And it didn't take Talik long to figure out what Jhama had already known about their attacker—this mysterious Jon Bledsoe.

Mind control. Was that even possible? He'd never heard of an alien people who could do that, and because of Jon's outfit, he'd been unable to pick out any defining features to identify his species. He adjusted his grip on Jhama's elbows, trying to help her keep her feet under her.

"Are you okay?" he asked breathlessly, and she nodded.

"Yeah. Yeah, I'll heal. You?"

"What *happened?*"

His voice was unintentionally harsh, scared, and Jhama tried to find the words, or even *a* word, that she could use to try and give him answers. She found only one would rise easily to her lips, so she settled on it. Talik would have to connect the dots himself.

"Alympa."

There was a brief moment of confusion on his face, but as Jhama watched, his expression shifted, eyes widening with shocked horror.

"Alympa?"

"Yeah." She gave a small hiss of pain as she put too much weight on her knee. "Hope-forsaken planet…we keep forgetting it can spit out monsters."

She looked up in relief as they rounded the street corner and were met with a massive, oblong vessel. She bore a resemblance to a bullet of old or perhaps an insect of some kind—a sort of beetle. Her silver surface reflected the lights of the city and the other ships around her, and not for the first time, Jhama noted she had a good name.

Starlight.

"I don't…" Talik broke off, upset. The words had fallen silent on the tip of his tongue again.

"I know. We have to though." Jhama grabbed his hand tightly, not caring about the pain it caused her burn. "I'll find a way to get us out of this. Don't worry. We *won't* hurt anyone. I'll make sure of it."

Talik looked down at her with wide, scared eyes.

"Promise?"

"Yeah," she whispered, gently squeezing his hand. "I promise."

The two people slowly approached the loading ramp at the side of the vessel, and Jhama waved ruefully at their two fellow security officers standing watch.

"Hey, guys. We're a little early."

"Jhama, what did you do?" one of them laughed, disbelieving and gaping at their soaked friends. "We were only here for two hours!"

She effortlessly echoed their laughter, shaking her head with an embarrassed smile.

"We decided to take a shortcut through an alley, and I tripped over an oil barrel," she explained, hating how easily the lie fell from her lips and how helpless she was to stop it. "Burned my hand on one of the pipes when I fell, banged my knee, pulled him with me—"

"She's just a graceful dancer, isn't she?" Talik finished, rolling his eyes. "If you guys could sign us in, I'll help her to Doctor Balok."

"Yeah, of course," their crewmate said easily and waved them on as his partner registered the two ensigns on the boarding roster. "You two get squared away. You *know* Sprit will have your hide if you're out of commission because of a refueling stop."

"Don't remind me," Jhama groaned playfully.

But as Talik helped her limp across the threshold of *Starlight's* bay, fellow officers laughing at her false clumsiness, she felt nothing but an overwhelming urge to scream *stop us*.

Of course, no one did. They'd done their jobs well. There seemed to be nothing to stop.

Checking everyone back in only took ten minutes. *Starlight's* captain prided himself on his punctual crew, and today was no exception. The takeoff and flight sequences were just as quick, and soon, the ship was powering up with an earth-shaking rumble, rising from the landing pad as its gears retracted into its belly.

Everything went smoothly, without a problem...perfectly.

In the shadow of a nearby alley, Jon watched the silver, glittering vessel rise higher in the sky, his features bathed in the pale blue light of *Starlight's* external engines. His plan was in motion. All four of his sleeper agents had gotten aboard without a hitch, and soon everything would fall into place.

At last, Ren, he thought to himself, subconsciously reaching up to touch his scars as the dual points of *Starlight's* engines receded into the polluted sky. *At long last I'll be able to return the favor.*

Jon pulled back his coat sleeve to reveal a metal cuff covered in an electronics board and other strange components. He flipped a few switches, pressed one final button, and disappeared in a flash of light.

He had work to do.

CHAPTER 1

Undisclosed Location

Rin wasn't sure where she was.

Her head ached and throbbed, particularly behind her ears, and her eyes seemed overly sensitive to any kind of light, including the soft, diffuse glow at the seams of the walls and ceiling above her. Her vision was blurred and doubled, swimming with dark blotches and tiny points that glittered like metal shavings. It was cold in here. Or was it? She wasn't sure if it was cold, now that she thought about it, even though she could feel herself shivering, swaying slightly on her bare feet.

Where...

Her thoughts were woolly, distorted like her vision and thick and heavy like the tongue in her mouth. She felt half-asleep, submerged in water, until suddenly, a bright light flashed in her face like the bulb on a camera. She tried to take a step back, flinching. However, her body seemed quite content to stay where it was, and her startlement registered as nothing more than a slightly more noticeable sway backwards.

In her confused state, she didn't notice the hand that balanced her, taloned fingers pushing at her shoulder to get her relatively still again. She thought she could hear voices though, strange voices, speaking a language she'd never heard before. It was guttural, hissing...almost like a reptile, actually. She let her eyelids pull themselves shut once more.

The alien who had balanced Rin turned to look at the other two in the room with him in disbelief. Like Talik, spiked ridges adorned his jaws and cheeks, but they also ran in rows down his skull, arching from his forehead down to the base of his neck.

"How much did you give her, Cerik?" he demanded. This human looked pale despite her light brown complexion, and the last thing he needed was sick merchandise.

The man behind the camera-like device aimed at the girl shrugged, and his partner quickly followed suit.

"Don't know, Chief. Kaus and I weren't on her abduction team," Cerik said, preparing the camera for another take. "Probably a big dose, though. She's human. You know they don't like getting snatched. Or being operated on," he added with a laugh.

Chief grunted, turning back to the girl behind him. She was young, probably eighteen to twenty human years old, relatively fit beneath the nondescript gray jumpsuit they'd changed her into, and average height and build. She'd bring in a good price. The long, dark hair that hung to her mid-back would probably be cut by whoever bought her; it would only get in the way of labor or whatever else her owners had her do. The only thing that concerned him was the fogged look in her doe eyes, the overly vacant expression on her oval face.

On the one hand, it meant she was compliant, truly incapacitated by the sedative, but on the other, it didn't make for the best holophoto.

He reached out and casually lifted her hair away from her ears, looking at the cochlear-like implants curving behind them.

"Surgery looks neat as always," he observed, letting her hair drop back into place. "Are they turned on yet?"

"Not the translation function, sir, per protocol. Even if they were, though, she wouldn't understand us. She's still too out of it."

"Keep it that way." He started to leave the small room, throwing the duo one last order without turning to look at them. "And make sure she doesn't fall over next time you take a picture. I don't want her bruised for the auction."

There was a second blinding flash, a pause, and then a semi-loud thud.

"Kaus, you moron, watch it!" the photographer snapped. "Get her standing up again, come on. We don't have all day."

Chief rolled his eyes and shook his head as he left the chamber and closed the door behind him.

"Idiots."

He had an auction to run. He didn't have any time to waste sitting around supervising his less skilled catalogers. As he walked down the halls towards the larger room where his patrons were waiting, he took stock of his appearance, making sure his nails were relatively clean and his clothing was straight. There were quite a few high rollers at this particular auction, including a new face that he'd been assured through a trusted contact was a deep-pocketed resource to tap.

What was her name, again, he wondered as he reached out and pushed open the heavy metal door before him. *Madame Ilota, that's right.*

Immediately, he was greeted with a front of color and conversation. He was still quite proud of how he'd turned the storage hangar into a tastefully decorated and upholstered space. The stage at the end of the room was particularly well done, equipped with holoprojectors so they could display the lots without the hassle of making them physically cooperate.

As he made his way through the crowded room, shaking hands and greeting people when appropriate, he kept his eye out for this Madame Ilota. Their mutual friend had given him a picture to positively ID her with when the time came. She was Ethonian with bright red hair and her species' trademark green, camouflage-mottled skin. And her eyes... she had the most striking eyes Chief had ever seen. They looked like molten copper, fiery and dangerous. She wouldn't be too hard to pick out, and quite suddenly, he spotted her. She was standing near the wall beside the refreshments table, looking rather bored.

She was shorter than he'd imagined. Actually, much shorter, he realized as he drew closer. She'd only come up to his shoulder, if that. Unlike the rest of the buyers, she wasn't dressed in robes or gowns to display her wealth. Instead, she was wearing what honestly looked like a black, stylized pilot's jumpsuit, though the top was a high collar tank instead of a bulky long-sleeve. It hid her curves well but prominently displayed the muscles in her arms almost like a threat, and Chief found himself scrambling to try and remember what she did for a living.

He quickly realized that his contact hadn't said.

"Madame Ilota," he greeted, effortlessly switching from his native tongue to common-speak once he was close enough.

She turned to face him, expression cool and expectant. The soles of her sturdy boots gave her a few more inches to work with, and with the help of her thick, wavy hair pulled off her shoulders in some kind of updo, the top of her head was somewhere near the height of his chin.

"I'm Chief—this is my auction. It's a pleasure to have you here. We're always eager to meet new faces in the markets," he continued, taking in her empty and unadorned hands. They seemed quite rough and calloused. Whatever business she was in, it was physical. "I see you don't have anything to eat or drink. Could I get you something more to your liking?"

"Thank you for the offer," she said, graciously shaking his hand and giving him a smile he noted only faintly reached her eyes. "But I'm here for business, not pleasure, Chief."

He gestured to her garb as she let go of his hand.

"I can see that. Quite an interesting fashion choice given the event and your fellow buyers."

She gave him that strange, unreadable smile once more.

"What can I say? I dress for practicality, not the occasion."

Her voice was smooth with an element of danger in its even, lilting tones, and for a moment Chief was afraid of her. But then again, anyone who was at a black market slave auction wasn't to be trifled with.

"A woman after my own heart," he said, briefly inclining his head. "Is there a particular property you're interested in? A particular type you're looking for?"

Madame Ilota made a vague waving gesture with her hand before letting her arms cross over her chest once more.

"Someone...versatile," she said, finally settling on a word. "Strong. Ideally, I'd be looking for a human." She shook her head, a wry sort of smile pulling at her lips. "But they're hard to come by, as I'm sure you know. Not many people want to risk the trip to black site systems. Not since the Corps increased their surveillance in the areas." She eyed him carefully, like she was measuring him up, and her smile turned a little more flirtatious; the challenge in her eyes glowed a little brighter. "I've heard rumors you're not as easily intimidated."

Chief laughed, crossing his arms to mirror her posture.

I like this woman.

"Your rumors, Madame, are more or less true. I'm not intimidated. I'm paranoid." He picked a drink from the table beside them and took a sip. "And only the paranoid ones successfully evade the Corps. How do you think I can host auctions as high end as this?"

She cocked an eyebrow, expectant.

"So, are you saying my trip will be worth its risks and expenses?"

"I have a few specimens you may be interested in," he replied with a wolfish smile, and her expression relaxed. She started to walk away, brushing past him as she went.

"Well, then. I look forward to your show," she said lowly with a smile identical to his before weaving her way into the crowd.

Only once she'd vanished from sight did Chief realize he still didn't know what exactly her work was. She wanted humans, though, and she seemed confident she could handle the notoriously willful species. He shook his head wonderingly as he returned to his other patrons. Whatever she did, she was the boss. He could respect that.

He pulled his transceiver from his belt and opened a channel.

"How are we doing, Cerik?"

Back in the holophoto room, Cerik pulled out his own radio.

"Fine, Chief. We just wrapped up the photos for our final lot, that human girl you saw. All we've got to do now is bring the files to the projectors."

"Please tell me you two didn't bruise her any more than you already had," he said dryly, and Kaus winced. Cerik just rolled his eyes.

"No, sir. I made sure Kaus didn't let that happen again."

"Good. I have a potential buyer already set up for her. Make sure you show her early—not first, but early. Within the first five at most."

"Yes, sir." The channel closed, and Cerik gestured to the unsteady, half-conscious girl as he packed up the last of his holophotography equipment. "You heard Chief. We'll send her out third. And would you get her sitting down?" he added just as Kaus nudged Rin back into a balanced position for a sixth time. "I don't want her falling over while we're gone and splitting her head open or something."

"Yeah, yeah, whatever."

Rin found herself suddenly sitting down hard on the ground, and the painful jolt was enough to snap her out of whatever fog she'd been hovering in. Or at least, partly snap her out of it. Things seemed a little sharper now than they had been. Noises were a little clearer, the details around her a little less blurred. It was nowhere near perfect, but it was something. A quick, lopsided glance around the small, bare-walled, cell-like room told her she was alone.

What the hell happened?

She wearily closed her eyes and tried to focus on the last thing she remembered.

Driving home. She'd been driving home, that was it. She could see the highway speed limit sign in her head, her headlights reflecting off the painted metal. It had been…what time had it been? Oh, right. It had been 11:14 pm. She'd glanced at the dash clock when her engine started having trouble. It'd just died on her, no warning, no smoke, nothing.

She felt herself sway dangerously to the side and quickly opened her eyes, sluggishly catching herself with an overly pliable hand on the ground beside her. Was this concrete? She squinted at the floor, head pounding. It felt slightly warmer than concrete, somewhat softer, too. And what was she wearing? She picked at the coarse fibers of her gray pants with her free hand, perplexed, but still too out of it to truly panic just yet. These weren't her clothes.

Why was her head hurting so much, especially her ears? And what was that faint electronic sound? It was an odd warbling noise, barely there below the surface, but definitely there. She slowly reached for her ear, wincing as instead she accidentally poked her cheek. She reluctantly lowered her hand. Maybe it would be better if she waited until she was more coherent before prodding at her ears again.

Her car had stopped. That's right. She'd pulled it over to the side of the street, and it was late enough at night that that particular stretch of highway had been empty, abandoned in the middle of the woods except for her. She'd gotten out of her car next—wait no. She'd tried to call someone. But her phone was dead, like her car. The power was just suddenly...gone.

What on Earth had happened next?

She disjointedly rubbed at her eyes and blinked hard a couple more times. Her vision was clearing up, and the fear was starting to register through the drugs in her system.

She'd gotten out of her car. She'd gotten out of her car to check the engine, to see if it was something she could fix. And then—

A sharp, phantom pain split open the back of her skull, and the tang of asphalt settled on her tongue like some sort of bad aftertaste.

She'd been hit on the head. Someone had come up behind her, hit her on the back of the head, and then there'd been a sting in her neck, like something biting her. Everything went fuzzy after that. Fuzzy and impenetrable save for a foreign language, harsh and cold and rasping, and rough hands pulling her every which way while people took photographs of her and shoved her around.

Oh god. Her heart pounded in her chest, adrenaline filling her veins as the picture started to come together. *I was abducted. I was taken. They're probably traffickers, oh my god—*

Her rising panic was interrupted by the sound of the heavy door unlocking five feet away. She could hear muffled voices speaking that same odd language behind the opening metal, and she shuddered. It had to be her abductors coming back.

Oh god. Think. Think, think, think—you're too out of it to fight, you don't know how many there are or where you are. Her mind raced through several different options, different scenarios and plans, before finally selecting one. *Play drugged. Keep looking out of it. Don't let them know you're waking up.*

She quickly slumped back to her original boneless posture, keeping her gaze unfocused on the floor. Mercifully, her hair fell in her face as she moved, hiding her quickly shifting expressions.

Control your breathing, she silently whispered, squeezing her eyes shut. *Control your breathing. Play drugged.*

Her breathing slowly evened, and next she forced her face to regain its previously slack and vacant expression. Someone was walking towards her, saying something that sounded a little angry, frustrated. She really hoped they weren't trying to talk to her. She couldn't understand anything they were—

She gave a small, startled yelp as a rough hand grabbed ahold of her chin. His nails were long and sharp, digging painfully into her skin, and his hand, it felt weird, *leathery.* The stranger tipped her head back so she was forced to look up at him, and as soon as she saw him, her heart stopped.

This has to be a bad trip. I'm seeing things. This can't be real.

She was looking at an alien.

That was the only way to describe him, to explain his scaled skin, his snake eyes, the ridges and spines adorning his features. His clothes were a mix of textures and dull colors: earth tones, yellows, greens. He seemed to be waiting for something, some kind of response, but Rin couldn't make a sound. She was frozen, through and through.

The creature snarled, baring narrow teeth that had been filed into jagged points.

"I said get up!"

Cerik looked at the wide-eyed, terrified girl in Kaus' grip and rolled his eyes.

"Kaus!" His partner looked at him and shrugged in a what-do-you-want way, and Cerik just shook his head and pointed at the girl. "You didn't turn on her translators."

"Those damn...come here," he growled and reached for the girl's ears. "Every time."

Rin's breathing grew ragged, heart jumping into her throat as long nails scratched against her ear, but she couldn't bring herself to flinch or push him away. She could only sit, paralyzed with fear and no small amount of twisted confusion, as he finished whatever he was doing. He finally let go and backed away a few paces, waiting, and just when she was starting to wonder what exactly was supposed to happen next, a long, sharp beep sounded directly in her ears.

She gave another yelp and clapped her hands over her ears, and her eyes widened as she felt some kind of implant behind both of them.

What the hell?

"Hey!"

She jumped and looked up at the alien in front of her. Another had joined him, and while they looked practically identical to her human eye, the newcomer was dressed in reds and blues. The two men— could you call an alien a man, she wondered—were blurry again now that they were further away, and the world was still a bit unsteady. But the adrenaline and fear were quickly taking care of that.

"Don't touch those," reds-and-blues said, gesturing to a small hole in the side of his head as he spoke that she assumed was his own ear. She slowly frowned, now even more alarmed, as she continued to stare at him blankly.

His mouth hadn't moved right.

The words she'd heard and the words he'd said hadn't matched up.

"Those are translators," he continued. "They convert any language into your native tongue, so no pulling the 'I don't understand' card. Is that clear?"

She just stared, struggling to wrap her head around what was going on.

It's a bad reaction to whatever drug they gave me, she told herself, shaking. *That's it. That's it, this isn't happening. This isn't real.*

Cerik shook his head as the human slowly drew her legs up to her chest and wrapped her arms protectively around her knees. She still looked pretty out of it, though that could've been the shock of seeing aliens. At least she wasn't attacking them. More than a few humans had had that response.

"Okay, she's not completely here, yet," he mumbled, turning to his friend. "Just get her on her feet and take her to the prep room. Chief will handle it from there. I gotta take the first product to the stage."

Prep room? Product? Stage?

Rin watched reds-and-blues leave, noting the slight limp in his right leg. That was one opening for her. She moved her focus to yellows-and-greens, and her stomach flipped. He just looked angry, immovable.

"Alright, come on. Get up." She hesitated a second too long, and he stepped forward menacingly. "Up, or I drag you out there by your hair!"

Rin moved as quickly as possible, slowly coordinating her limbs until she was unsteadily kneeling. The world spun viciously, and she choked back bile as her migraine returned with a vengeance. Standing was apparently still out of the question.

"I don't have time for this," yellows-and-greens hissed and stepped forward, grabbing her elbow and hauling her to her feet. "Come on!"

Rin made a small noise of pain as her pulse throbbed behind her eyes, and she quickly pressed her hand to her mouth to stop herself from throwing up. That was the absolute last thing she needed right now—puking on one of her more pissed off abductors.

"Smart move, human. Let's go."

Human.

There was no way he was an alien. Aliens didn't exist. They abducted people in *The X-Files* and B-rated horror movies. He wasn't an alien.

Then why make the distinction of human?

She struggled to match the man's pace, trying to keep her weak legs under her as he practically dragged her along beside him. He wasn't sparing her a single glance, seemingly unconcerned with the fact that she was this close to losing what little food she had in her stomach and splattering it on his boots instead. She tried to look around at what she passed, but any kind of movement made her nausea worse so she settled on keeping her head down and moving her feet quickly enough. She'd take stock of her situation and plan her next step once she was sitting down again or at least standing still.

Meanwhile in the main room, Chief had finally managed to wrangle all of the patrons into their seats and was currently showing them the holographic images of his second piece of merchandise. The first had sold relatively easily, and this one was shaping up to be no different. Both had been big, bulky specimens—good for physical labor or security. Once he'd gotten the bidding down to two or three people, he had his staff bring the actual item out for inspection. Like the first sale, one of the patrons withdrew his bid after a closer look, though this time, the man had said something about how the product had an "unpleasant look" in his eye, even under all those sedatives.

Chief was about to roll his eyes and call the client out on his nonsense, but then he saw Madame Ilota in the second row. She had that vaguely bored expression on her face and gave him a pointed look before focusing back on the stage.

He'd let the bidder's cheapness slide just this once. He quickly wrapped up the sale and ushered the purchased lot and its buyer off the stage. It was time to move on.

"This next lot is particularly special—a species in high demand for pretty much anything you can think of. A human. Our *only* human at this auction." Immediately, there was a murmur of interest, and Chief saw Ilota sit up straighter in her seat. He gestured for the projectionists to put up the holographs of the girl and smiled at the increased interest at the sight of her. "She is eighteen to twenty human years old, five feet and seven inches tall, and weighs one hundred and thirty-five pounds. She's from her planet's more northern regions, meaning she's had good exposure to cold weather as well as hot and humid environments. She's in good health, physically fit, and has so far been surprisingly obedient. I will let you interpret that as you will."

There was a ripple of laughter. A docile human was either a blessing or spelled trouble, and they all knew it.

"Bidding will open at half a million."

CHAPTER 2

Immediately, half the room's hands went up, and Chief smiled as he increased the price and the response stayed strong. This was why he risked trips to black site systems. Humans brought in a lot of money, easily tripling the cost it took to catch them in the first place. Besides it was another way to stick it to the Peacekeeper Corps, to highlight their utter uselessness, their defanged state. They couldn't even keep up the black site cordons, let alone track an underground slave market.

The bidding went on for several minutes, the price for this one human climbing higher and higher until finally he'd narrowed it down to three clients: a prominent arms dealer; a rising, high-end drug designer; and, he noted with odd satisfaction he couldn't explain, Madame Ilota. The woman raised her hand, and he pointed to her.

"I believe it's time you let us see the lot in person now," she said with that same pointed lilt to her voice.

"Of course, Madame Ilota," he answered and waved her and the other two bidders towards him. "If the three of you would like to come onto the stage, I'll have my men bring her out now."

Madame Ilota nodded easily, rising in a fluid motion and reaching up to fiddle briefly with her left earring, squeezing it slightly. They were her only piece of jewelry—two bronze, button-like circles that caught the light like drops of amber. She quickly moved her hand back to her side, and Chief filed the motion away as a tell, a crack in her armor that betrayed either nervousness or excitement. Her two competitors were nothing special. He knew their profiles, their portfolios. They didn't have the funds to match Ilota, so all of this was really more a matter of pride and posturing than anything else—a competition of status.

As his bidders made their way to the stage, he lifted his radio.

"Kaus, bring out the human."

Rin fought the urge to look at her keeper with scared eyes at those words, and instead kept herself pliant and unfocused beside him. She could hear people shuffling around her, could see bizarre shapes and colors out of the corners of her eyes, but she didn't dare look around just yet. Kaus was still keeping an annoyingly close watch on her. All she could tell was that the people were all in the same gray jumpsuit as her, sitting or standing in that dazed stupor she was still pretending to be in.

"Coming, Chief." Kaus' taloned grip tightened on her arm above her elbow, and soon she was being dragged along once more.

Keep looking down. Keep shuffling, stay off balance.

Miraculously, her senses had returned to her almost in full by now. But while her vision was no longer blurry and her head pounded a little less, her hearing was still slightly distorted by that electronic baseline. She was becoming worried it was inescapable, part of whatever those implants were. She could tell through her hair and peripheral vision that she was being pulled along a hallway, and it was all she could do to remember not to keep up with yellows-and-greens too easily.

They were approaching a metal double door now, and despite its thickness, Rin could hear a buzz of conversation and noise just beyond the barrier.

She quickly recalled what her current escort's friend had said.

Chief will take it from there. I have to take the first product to the stage now.

Whatever was beyond those rapidly approaching doors, Rin was one hundred percent sure she wasn't going to like it. But just before they reached the terrifying threshold, yellows-and-greens yanked her sideways towards a smaller, unobtrusive door instead.

"*Not* that way," he snapped, ignoring how she nearly tripped and fell at the sharp change in direction. "You're going on stage."

Rin's heart raced painfully in her chest, each pulse throbbing in her temples and roaring in her ears. As his taloned hand grasped the doorknob and twisted it open, she reflexively dug her heels in and pulled back.

You're not *taking me out there. You're not—*

"Come on!" Kaus barked, jerking her forward, and she crashed into him, briefly losing her balance before he hauled her upright once more. This small hallway was dark, and Rin could only just make out a short flight of stairs before them. "Bidders are waiting."

Bidders?

Her thoughts were interrupted by another callous yank forward, and she winced as she accidentally stubbed her toe and missed a few steps in the dark. Yellows-and-greens seemed to have no trouble at all, and she wondered just how many times he'd walked up these stairs, dragging someone along with him. Based off his annoyed indifference, probably more times than he could count. They quickly reached the last step, and Rin was finally able to see that the room, if it could be called that, was so dim because a heavy, black curtain was blocking off its exit.

Stage, she realized. *This is the stage.*

Kaus pushed her forward, pulling the blackout fabric out of their way. Light hit Rin full in the face, and she winced, turning her head away and raising a hand to her eyes as she was paraded blindly onward. She hadn't realized just how dark off-stage had been until they stepped out here in the open, and she slowly lowered her hand as yellows-and-greens pulled sharply on her elbow, bringing her to a stop. It could have been her imagination, but she thought she heard people whispering around her. Reluctantly, she opened her eyes to look at whatever was in front of her, and her overworked heart raced to a crescendo before stopping completely.

"Oh god," she whimpered, the words nothing more than a paralyzed exhale mute to anyone but her.

Dozens upon dozens of eyes looked up at her with open interest and desire; dozens upon dozens of eyes on just as many faces that were absolutely, definitively, not human: fur, scales, vibrant colors, stripes, spots, antennae.... Where was she? Rin felt herself begin to shake, the tremors barely noticeably at first before becoming violent, and her stomach viciously roiled, sending her doubling over and—

There was a chorus of disgusted gasps, and Rin squeezed her eyes shut, trying to ignore the sour taste in her mouth.

"Ugh!" Madame Ilota looked at the arms dealer, unimpressed by his outburst as the man lowered his hand from his nose. "That's damaged goods, Chief," he scowled and pointed at the girl. "I thought you were more honest than this."

"I assure you, she is in perfect health," Chief insisted, making a placating gesture with his hands while tilting his head to the mess at the girl's feet. "She's just overwhelmed. You all know how humans get."

There was an awkward pause as one of Chief's staff quickly cleaned up the mess of vomit, glaring at Rin as they did.

"I don't care what lies you use to cover your hide, Chief," the arms dealer pressed, glowering. "She's clearly not well. Look at her!" Chief shot Cerik a dirty look where the cataloguer was setting up the next lot's holographs at the projector, and the man defensively shrugged.

"I'm withdrawing my bid. You two can fight over her," he added in a displeased aside to Ilota and the drug dealer before storming off the stage.

Rin watched him leave through the strands of hair hanging in her face, still keeping up her hunched, unsteady posture.

This is an auction.

"I assume the two of you are still interested?" Chief asked, forcing himself to remain businesslike. "I assure you, she is in good health. We *did* have our doctors look her over. I…will admit she was dosed a little heavily with a sedative when she was taken, but she apparently put up quite a fight."

Ilota responded to his rambling by making her way towards Rin, an unreadable light in her eyes, and the remaining bidder quickly followed her. The girl watched the two people draw closer and tried her best to size them up. The one with eggshell blue skin was tall and thin and dressed in dark red robes. He looked like a scholar or a priest of some sort, easy to overpower or run from. It was the woman who worried her. Rin took in her muscled, yet comparatively short stature, and practical clothing. Like Chief, she got a distinct air of danger off of her, a kind of intimidating mystery. If the human was going to make a run for it, the woman would be the one to get away from first.

"I'll look at her first, if you don't mind," scholar-priest said quickly, stepping in front of the redheaded woman and drawing a sharp glare from her. Rin closed her eyes as the man's gloved hands grabbed her, examining her hands before reaching for her face and looking at her teeth, mouth, and eyes. "Seems healthy enough."

Ilota rolled her eyes, grabbing scholar-priest's shoulder and yanking him away from the hunched girl.

"Thank you for reiterating what we've already been told twice," she said dryly, drawing a few laughs from the people watching. "Now let the *actual* bidders take a look."

She turned her copper gaze on the girl, grabbing the human's chin with one hand and turning her head to the side so she could examine the implants. And Rin found that while her motions were brusque and harsh on the surface, her actual touch was surprisingly gentle.

"How long ago did you put these in?" Ilota asked, looking over her shoulder to Chief. "I need to know how much post-operative care I'll need to invest in."

"Two days ago. My staff assured me the procedure went smoothly. They're state of the art—brand new, never-before-seen prototypes."

Ilota tuned out his boasting and roughly lifted the girl's head just enough so she could look into her eyes. She was hiding it well, but this close, Ilota could plainly see the human's fear and confusion. Could see her ragged breathing, feel her shaking beneath her touch. But most of all, she could see the spark in the back of those dark eyes.

Humans, the Madame thought proudly and allowed herself a smile. The faintest frown flickered over the girl's face at the strange change in her expression. *They're the galaxy's greatest con artists.*

She let go of the girl's chin, pushing her back slightly as she did so, and reached up to her earring once more, squeezing it twice this time as she turned to Chief.

"I have to agree with my partner's ingenious deduction," she said with a shrug. "She *is* quite healthy." Chief let out a bark of laughter at her sarcastic words, and the drug designer flushed. "I'll raise the price to six million."

Outside the hangar—hidden behind an outcrop of boulders in the yellow, dense fog of the planet's noxious surface—Lieutenant Lewis Holt quickly touched his earwig. His expression was grim beneath his gas mask.

"Commander Matzepo just sent her signal." He lifted his rifle to the ready position and quickly rose from the team's crouched position to a standing one. "Ensign Assora, with me." Jhama quickly stepped up beside him, her heart pounding. "The rest of you follow in formation. Remember, they have seven guards on the rooftop, so use scanners. Cover your partner and shoot only when necessary. Covert as far in as possible."

The fifteen *Starlight* officers reached up and pressed a button on the sides of their gas masks, and a display flickered to life across the glass. It quickly pointed them in the direction of the storage hangar, highlighting the distant points where the auction guards were stationed. Without another word, the strike team started across the lifeless, rocky surface, Jhama making sure to stay close to her superior's side as they advanced. Their heavy boots were all but silent on the ground as they ran, weapons held at the ready and senses alert and straining through the fog. Holt glanced at the timer in the corner of his facepiece. ETA thirty seconds. Commander Matzepo had better be ready for them to come blowing down the door.

Back in the auction house, "Ilota" sighed heavily, the timer in her head slowly ticking down from thirty seconds as the scholar-priest drug designer made a counter offer at six and a half million.

"Seven million," she said almost lazily, checking her short nails to give herself something to do. There was a long silence, and she fought the urge to punch the drug lord when he countered her. *I'm just trying to run out the clock here, why do you have to keep making this more complicated?*

"Seven and a half."

Twenty seconds to go. Good enough.

Ilota sighed and remorsefully turned to the auctioneer. The lilt in her voice evaporated, replaced instead with a sarcastic drawl.

"Sorry, Chief," she began with a smile that was overly apologetic. She walked over to the human and grabbed her shoulder, shaking her a little. "While this has been fun, I'm afraid I'm going to have to draw our little bidding war here to a close. The human's coming with me."

Twelve seconds.

"The bidding's not done yet!" the drug designer protested, impressively offended, and Rin looked at the woman grabbing her. Her smile was back, and suddenly the human had a very bad feeling about all of this.

Outside, Holt and Jhama stepped over two fallen guards, fastened four charges to the wall of the auction's storage hangar, and backed away to a safe distance.

"The biding *is* done, and she's mine," Ilota said simply, giving him a too-sweet smile. "By the way," she continued, to Chief this time, "my name's not Ilota. It's *Commander* Sprit Matzepo." Chief's eyes bugged out, and Sprit grinned that wolfish grin that'd had worried him before. "You should *really* vet your new clients more carefully."

Before Chief could react, could call his guards or attack the undercover Peacekeeper in their midst, the wall behind his patrons exploded. Noxious gas flooded the room, sending everyone screaming in different directions, and a group of people in blue jumpsuits and gas masks stepped through the smoke and rubble in an arrowhead formation.

"There my people are," Sprit sighed, still grinning, and turned to the human beside her as she fished her standard issue earwig from her pocket and slipped it into her left ear.

Now, Rin thought. *Now, now, do it NOW.*

"Come on, kid. Auction's ov—"

Rin pivoted on her heel as fast as she could and brought her elbow smashing into the green-skinned alien's face with a loud crunch of breaking bone. The woman cried out in pain, stumbling backwards and falling off the edge of the stage to land in a painful heap on the floor. Without breaking pace, the human turned tail and ran, body-slamming the scholar-priest into Chief as she went and toppling them both off the stage as well.

"Djienn!" Sprit shouted, gritting her teeth and gripping her broken nose. *Oh, I'm going to have so much blood on my clothes when this is over.* She reached for the back of her head and groaned as she felt the bump already rising there. *Not to mention one hell of a headache.* Half-blind with tears, she quickly pulled herself to her feet and climbed back onto the stage in time to see the girl vanish behind the curtain. "Wait stop! Human, get back here!"

Run, the human thought blindly. *Run, run, run—*

Rin threw open the side door and yelped as she sprinted full speed into someone. She tried to push away from them, but their sharp-nailed hands held her tight, and she looked up into the person's face.

Reds-and-blues.

"I thought you weren't as out of it as you were acting," he growled, and Rin felt her hope quickly vanish as she started to freeze up again.

Limp, you idiot, he has a limp!

She promptly kicked his right knee, forcing the joint to bend at an unnatural angle, and her hope surged back to life. Reds-and-blues went down like a sack of potatoes, crying out in pain and clutching at his wounded leg, and Rin bolted. Fleetingly, she wished she was wearing shoes. Getting out of here would be so much easier, wherever *here* was. She'd figure that out later. All she had to do right now was run and find someplace to hide. She turned the next corner at a full sprint and screamed as she came face-to-face with five of those reptile-looking people.

Turn around, her mind ordered, imagined voice jumping an octave as she came to a scrambling stop. *Other way, other way—*

She ran back the way she'd come for fifty feet, turning a few corners, but came to another stumbling halt as ten more reptile people exited a door at the end of the hall ahead of her. Unlike the Tarikians behind her, these wore heavy, leather-padded uniforms and gas masks. Rin helplessly backed away, eyeing the metal clubs hanging from their belts. Those looked too much like stun batons.

She decided she'd rather take her chances with the five people behind her over the group heading toward her now and quickly spun on her heel, rounding one of the corners she'd just turned at full tilt. She was running out of space between the two fronts, running out of options, and she dashed to a closed door, frantically pulling on the locked handle to no avail.

"Come on," she begged, voice shaking and rising in panic as the group of five turned the corner to her. "Come on, come *on!* Open!"

The metal just rattled in time with her jerks, and she pushed away from it, breathing heavily. She knew the group of ten was closing in, and the group of five was only eight feet away now—

Something slammed into her from behind, and Rin went sprawling to the ground, cheek striking painfully against the concrete floors. She groaned and dazedly twisted onto her back, blinking stars from her vision. There was no one around her. What the hell had just happened?

Her answer came soon enough.

There was a cry of pain as the lead slaver jerked back, hands at his nose as if he'd been punched square in the face. His partner's head wrenched to the side, and he quickly put his hand to his mouth, eyes wide as he spat out a fragment of a tooth. And Rin watched in complete and utter astonishment as the two traffickers suddenly went down like they'd been hit with an invisible right cross and knee to the gut. As soon as they were on their knees, their heads snapped to the side, one after the other, like they'd been clocked with a round-house kick, and they slumped sideways, out cold.

The three reptilians behind the unconscious bodies came to a stop, quickly backing up and looking around for the attacker only to arrive at the same conclusion Rin had.

There wasn't one to be found.

And before they could figure out how to attack what they couldn't see, the fallen leader's gun was drawn from its holster, seemingly levitating in mid-air, and fired.

Rin screamed as each man's head snapped back with a burned hole dead between their eyes, and their bodies dropped to the cold floor like felled puppets. She quickly scrambled to her feet and screamed again, throwing her arms over her head as the gun turned to face her.

"Damn Tarikians...what?" a woman's nonplussed voice asked only to continue, this time mildly annoyed. "Oh, *djienn*. Galaxy's sake, human, I'm not here to shoot you!"

The disembodied gun dropped to the floor with a loud clatter, and Rin watched with wide eyes as the air before her shimmered like a mirage until a redheaded, green-skinned woman with a bloody and possibly broken nose stood before her. Her hands were raised to her shoulders, and the human realized with a jolt that it was the lady from the auction.

"I'm here to help," she said in that same exasperated tone.

A thousand different responses raced through Rin's head: you just tried to buy me; you just killed three people; dear *god*, you're an alien; et cetera. But before she could decide on which one to use, the group of ten arrived.

"Get down!"

The green woman grabbed Rin by the arm and yanked the human behind her, snatching the gun from the ground and firing at her new opponents in one fluid motion. Her first four shots struck home easily, thinning the oncoming crowd, and she shoved the girl down the hall.

"Go. Go, run!" Sprit glanced over her shoulder as the human hesitated for a fraction of a second before fleeing. "I do hope that's not a dead-end hall," the officer muttered before taking a deep breath and vanishing into thin air again.

The gun fell to the ground in her wake, useless. She *really* should have listened to Lieutenant Holt and brought her specialty weapon on this job. Having a gun that camouflaged with her would have been really helpful right around now.

Oh well, she mutely sighed, easily evading the blind fire her targets were randomly laying down the hall. *I'll make do with what I've got.*

She snagged a stun baton off a goon's belt and jabbed him in the belly with it, holding it there long enough to knock him out before dropping it and sidestepping a wild, shot-in-the-dark punch someone threw in her general direction. She flicked her earwig on as she righted herself, sweeping a few strands of hair out of her face.

"Holt, what's your ETA?" she asked, just as she poked another man in the eyes and delivered a blindingly fast punch to his throat that left him on the floor gasping and rubbing at his swelling face.

"Commander?"

She rolled her eyes at her deputy's uncertain response, voice turning acerbic.

"To come and help me out, Holt," she snapped, ducking another punch and kicking a knee in. "I'm a bit pinned down here trying to get the human!"

In the main room, Holt gestured for Jhama and another one of his strike team to follow him.

"I've got a lead on you, Commander," he said, adjusting his gas mask's display to show a blueprint of the facility. "ETA two minutes."

"Well, hurry," Sprit grunted, ramming her head up into one of Tarikians' chins before shoving his dazed form into his partner. "I can only do so much hand-to-hand—"

She broke off with a sharp cry of pain, flashing briefly into view before turning invisible again, and clapped a hand over her arm. Another shot blew out part of the wall just above her head, and she quickly ducked, retreating down the hall. It was time to go. As she ran, she tilted her hand back from the plasma burn on her upper left arm, wrinkling her nose at the smell of scorched skin and the red blood coating her palm.

"Commander, are you okay?" Holt's voice called.

"Yeah," she replied tightly, reapplying pressure and trying to ignore the sting. "Someone just got off a lucky shot."

"Are you sure, ma'am?"

"Just my arm, Holt," she reassured him, gritting her teeth. "It's a flesh wound. I'm fine."

"We'll catch up with you soon."

"Yeah, well, you better hurry," Sprit sighed as she rounded a corner and slowed to a stop, letting herself flicker back into view. "I caught up with the human." At the sound of her voice, Rin spun around, releasing the handle of yet another locked door at the end of the hall.

"More trouble, commander?" Holt asked.

"You could say that." Sprit turned to face the way the two of them came. "We just ran out of hallway."

"We're coming, ma'am."

There was a tense note to Holt's voice, and Sprit gave a wry smile.

"So you keep saying. Oh, one more thing, lieutenant. Remind me to always listen to you from now on."

"Commander?"

"I could *really* use an invisible gun right now." Before Holt could respond, she lifted a hand to her earwig. "I'll see you soon, lieutenant." With that, she closed the channel and turned to her charge. "None of the doors are open, huh?" The girl just stared at her silently, and Sprit rolled her eyes as she saw the distance she was keeping between them. "Would you relax? I'm not gonna hurt you. I've got enough to worry about with these Tarikians without you going all bug-eyed on me."

Rin watched the woman carefully. Her arm was bleeding, almost like she'd been shot, which was good news for Rin. It'd make it easier to get away, though was getting away the best option? The woman had been using words like lieutenant. Maybe her best bet was to stay with her....

But what if this was some kind of insurgency or a different crime ring? In that case, staying definitely wasn't her best choice either.

She'd stay with her for now, Rin decided. Whoever she was, she could take out the weird lizard people. Once she got them out of here, then Rin would make a run for it.

Sprit narrowed her eyes as the human continued to watch her with dark, unblinking eyes.

"Whatever you're thinking, I don't like it," she muttered, and the girl looked away, crossing her arms tighter. Soon, both could hear the approaching footsteps of the remaining Tarikians, and Sprit rolled her shoulders, wincing as the motion pulled at her damaged skin. "Well, here goes nothing." She glanced at Rin. "I'd sit in that corner if I were you."

Rin quickly and quietly moved to the spot Sprit was pointing to, and as she sat down, she realized she was at least partly hidden in one of the door's thresholds. She nervously drew her knees up to her chest, preparing to cover her head at the first sign of those *Tarikians*. Satisfied the human was as out of the way as possible, Sprit faced forward and promptly faded from view just in time for the remaining six—no, seven, the one she'd poked in the eyes was back and looking *really* angry—traffickers to come around the corner.

She'd take poked-eyes out first, she decided with an unseen, feral smile. For old time's sake.

Rin jumped and pressed further into the shadow of the threshold as, without warning, one of the Tarikians slammed into the wall head-first and dropped senseless to the floor, seemingly of his own accord. That green woman was good, Rin had to admit as she watched the others lumber around with inaccurate swings in an attempt to find their assailant. But her relief as another one of their opponents was downed with his own stun baton quickly faded as two of the more heavily armored aliens broke off from the rest and started towards her.

Oh no.

Rin scrambled to her feet and backed away to the end of the hall.

"Stay away," she whispered, voice shaking, and jumped as her back hit the corner. Grinning at her predicament, the two monsters continued to close in, and Rin felt a new wave of fear-spiked adrenaline surge in her chest. "I said stay away!"

Sprit looked over her shoulder at the shout, heart skipping a beat.

"Hey!" she shouted, elbowing the nearest slaver in the face before stepping out of the disjointed fray. One of the two goons closing in on the human looked back at her, and she turned visible once more, fists clenched at her sides and eyes burning. "Get away from her."

"You deal with her, I'll get the human," the taller one growled. His partner turned to face Sprit while he continued to corner his boss' escaped property. "Get over here!"

He reached for her, going to grab her by her throat. Rin could only watch in panic as he drew closer, vaguely aware of Sprit's fight with the others in the background. There was nothing for her to do, no way out of—

Bite him.

Rin lunged forward, grabbing onto his forearm, and sank her teeth viciously into his hand. A horribly bitter taste filled her mouth as the man screamed and tried to pull her off of him, and finally she pushed away, coughing and spitting black blood into her palms as he howled in pain. He stumbled back and glared at her, cradling his hand to his chest. His face was a contorted mask of pain, and after another furious scowl, he started forward once more.

"Oh, you little—"

His words were cut off with a loud thunk, and he pitched forward to reveal Sprit behind him, looking a little too pleased with herself. She gave the prone body a smirk and twirled the stun baton in her hand before letting it clatter to the floor between them.

"Well, that was fun."

Rin sighed in relief, sagging back against the wall. That had been too close.

"Don't look so relieved, human; we're not done yet," Sprit warned, and Rin wearily looked at her protector as she turned to face the remaining four Tarikians. One immediately drew his gun and aimed it at them, and the officer slowly lifted her hands to her shoulders and stepped in front of the girl. They'd gotten this far; she wasn't going to let the kid get shot now. "Easy, spikey."

"You are cornered and injured," he growled, clearly pleased with their work. Sprit made a noncommittal sound in the back of her throat and shrugged, as if the fact was debatable. "Give us the human."

This is it, Rin thought, her breaths growing shaky. *She's gonna turn me over to save herself—*

"Hmm…don't think so."

Rin looked down at the shorter woman before her, stunned. The Tarikian seemed equally taken aback, and he tried repeating himself.

"Give us the human!"

"And, *again*, I don't think so."

"I will shoot you if you don't give us the human! It belongs to us!"

"Well, actually, *she* belongs to *herself*, but that's neither here nor there," Sprit returned and made a dismissive waving gesture with her hand, wincing as her injured arm protested. "Anyways, what *is* relevant is that if you shoot me, he'll shoot you."

"What?" the Tarikian asked thoroughly confused, and Sprit pointed behind him with a taunting expression. Slowly, the traffickers turned around and immediately found themselves staring down three blasters.

"Put your weapons down," Holt ordered. "Now."

His voice was soft and even with the slightest bur of an accent that sounded almost Earthly to Rin, and a shiver ran down her spine at the near-familiarity. It sounded like Spanish or Russian and at the same time nothing human. This must have been the lieutenant the auction lady was talking to. He was on the taller side, maybe an inch short of six feet, and he was so far the most human person she'd seen. In fact, he could have passed as a white man except for the green-tinged ivory spines adorning his face in symmetrical, delicate patterns. His hair was a bit ragged, like he'd cut it himself—greying blonde and somewhat longer on top, a dusky brown underneath.

But despite the slightly disheveled haircut, his uniform was pristine. It was a navy blue jumpsuit like the ones the two younger people flanking him wore, except his shoulder pads were blood red. His gun hand, Rin noticed, was also infinitely steadier than the others'. He could have been carven of stone. And those eyes…those steel eyes betrayed nothing, and Rin had the distinct impression that he was looking right through her.

"Nice of you to join us, lieutenant," Sprit began, lowering her arms. "You bring a couple extra masks for us? The air is starting to get a bit sour."

"Assora," Holt ordered, tilting his head towards Sprit and Rin.

Jhama reholstered her weapon and unclipped two spare gas masks from her belt, tossing them down the hall to her superior. Sprit caught them and nodded her thanks as she pulled hers over her head and handed the other to the human.

"I trust you can figure out how to put that on."

Rin awkwardly pulled the glass and synthetic material over her head and mimicked Sprit as the officer twisted a knob at the bottom of the mask to start the airflow.

"Now that we're all comfortable," Sprit continued once she was sure the girl was breathing properly, "I suggest you do as my deputy says and put down your weapons."

"There are only three of you armed," the Tarikian said, eyeing the situation carefully. "And four of us."

Sprit rolled her eyes and crossed her arms, visibly annoyed.

"If you think your three friends can draw their weapons *and* take us all out before we drop you, you are very mistaken," she replied. There was a tense pause as the slaver adjusted his hold on his gun and shifted his weight from foot to foot. "Come on, don't be an idiot."

He eyed her carefully before finally speaking.

"You are unarmed and injured," he said rationally. "That human is useless. The only threats are those three, and two of them are green— their hands shake." He slowly shifted his aim to Holt. "That means *you* are the only threat." He gave the lieutenant a smile filled with jagged, broken teeth. "So, which of us is the faster shot?"

Holt considered him for only half of a second.

"I am."

It was said so simply, so matter-of-factly, that it took the Tarikian a few moments to find a response.

"Suppose we put that to the test—"

Rin jerked back into the wall as Holt fired, and all hell broke loose.

The Tarikian hadn't even finished hitting the ground yet before the second ensign took out the other slaver beside him. Immediately, the third trafficker lifted his blaster in a panic and aimed for Holt.

"Sir, get down!" Jhama shouted.

Holt instantly dropped to his knee, giving the woman a clear shot over his head that ended the firefight in a split second. He watched the body as it fell and looked back to his subordinate.

"Good shot, Assora."

"Thank you, sir," she said with a shaky smile and offered a hand to pull him to his feet. He gratefully took it and looked to where the last man was fighting what appeared to be thin air. The human was still plastered to the wall behind them, watching and waiting for an opportunity to run. "Commander Matzepo seems to be having fun."

Holt shook his head, sighing, and drew his weapon.

"Um, sir?" Jhama asked, watching with some alarm as he took aim at the flailing Tarikian. "Sir, what if you hit Command—"

"I won't, ensign," he said simply and pulled the trigger.

The plasma bolt struck home, and the Tarikian collapsed.

A fraction of a second later, Sprit rematerialized and slowly turned to her lieutenant. A long, uncomfortable silence dragged out between the two officers, and Jhama and the other ensign shifted nervously.

This was not gonna go over well.

"You almost shot me," Sprit finally hissed. "You almost *shot me!*"

Holt reholstered his weapon and moved to check the Tarikians for any life signs and restrain the ones who were still alive.

"I knew precisely where you were, ma'am," he said calmly, and Sprit stormed towards him, throwing her hands up in the air.

"Oh, I'm sorry," she began, sarcasm dripping off her words as her volume slowly increased, "I didn't realize mind reading let you see invisible coworkers, my mistake!" The irony vanished, replaced by fury. "You almost shot me, Holt!"

Holt stood, clasping his hands behind his back. Behind them, Rin slowly started edging along the wall down the hallway. They were all distracted. She could work with this, could make her getaway now.

"Commander," Holt began, this time apologetic, "I—"

"Don't do it again!" Sprit barked, poking him hard in the chest. Holt nodded, keeping his eyes deferentially lowered and his voice soft.

"Yes, ma'am."

Sprit sighed and closed her eyes, stepping back from the lieutenant and running one hand through her hair as much as she could.

"*Djïenn*, you damn near gave me a heart attack, Holt!"

Almost past them, Rin thought, heart pounding in her chest.

"I apologize, Commander. I should have told you what I was going to do."

Just a little farther…

"Yeah," Sprit agreed, snatching Holt's gun from his holster given her unarmed state and adjusting the setting without breaking eye contact with him. "You really should have."

And, still holding her lieutenant's gaze, she quickly aimed the gun at Rin and pulled the trigger.

CHAPTER 3

"*Commander!*" Holt cried indignantly as the human convulsed and fell to the ground. Sprit switched the safety on and tossed his gun back to him, and he quickly stowed it back in its holster.

"It was on stun, Holt, relax," she said and rolled her eyes as she passed the two gaping ensigns to continue checking and restraining the slavers.

Holt made a helpless gesture between her and the unconscious girl, and Sprit could just make out the barely visible *what the hell* expression he was trying so hard to hide.

"I'm sorry," she continued, equal parts annoyed and sarcastic once more, "did *you* want to keep chasing her around?"

"Commander, respectfully, she is a scared girl—"

"She broke my nose!"

"Is there a problem here?" a new voice asked, and the four officers immediately turned around.

Unlike the rest of them, this newcomer wore a black jumpsuit with silver shoulder pads. He wasn't tall, but he wasn't short either and had somewhat broad shoulders and a well-muscled frame. An intimidating, powerful presence irrelevant to his stature radiated from him, and Holt quickly squared his shoulders, hands clasping behind his back. Sprit did the same, though her posture was infinitely more relaxed, nearly lazy.

"Captain Oren," the lieutenant greeted.

"As you were, Holt," the man returned, nodding once to him before looking expectantly at his security chief.

Sprit waved his opening question away and turned back to what she was doing.

"No problems, sir, just a disagreement on our methods."

"The disagreement being I do not support shooting humans, sir," Holt said pointedly, and Sprit shot him a dirty, betrayed look as their captain turned to her, hands slowly resting on his hips.

"Shooting humans?" he echoed, voice dangerously innocent, and Sprit crossed her arms.

"Captain, I used the lowest stun setting," she protested, gesturing to the girl sprawled on the floor near the wall. "Holt's making it sound much worse than it is!"

"Oh no, I think you're doing that all on your own, Sprit," the man replied and motioned for Jhama to come over. "Ensign Assora, I want you and your crewmate to take the human aboard *Starlight* and bring her to Doctor Balok. Tell him she's an abductee, he'll know the proper protocol."

"Yes, sir."

The two ensigns quickly moved to pick up Rin, and Oren called after them.

"One more thing." He paused to give Sprit a warning glare, and she shrugged defensively. "Make sure he knows Sprit decided it was a good idea to shoot her with a blaster on the lowest stun setting."

"Yes, sir."

As Jhama and the other ensign picked the girl up, Rin gave a soft groan and forced her eyes to open halfway. She felt groggy, weighed down, almost like she'd been sedated, but not quite. This hurt more, as if all of her muscles had viciously seized up before relaxing. Through the fog, she could see the two yellow-shoulder-pad people looming over her, and she felt one of them pick her up under her arms and knees. And as they stood, a dizzying and somewhat nauseating experience, she caught sight of Sprit and Holt—at least that's what she thought their names were. There was someone else with them, someone dressed in black. As she was carried past the trio, she got a better look at the newcomer, and what she saw sent her fully over the edge into that waiting darkness.

His skin was a vibrant, clay-like red color, and even beneath the gas mask she could see his irises were an impenetrable black to match his pupils. Two narrow, ragged white strips marked each cheekbone, curving slightly with the angles of his face but largely running parallel to his straight, dark brows. He was entirely bald save for a small, dark goatee that had no moustache accompanying it, and when Rin looked to where most people would have hair, she was met with the sight of two ram-like horns. Or, rather, what was left of them. The bones were thick and heavily ridged, starting as dark brown-red near the base and slowly growing lighter until the very tip where they faded back ever so slightly into that dark tone once more.

Only the left horn remained, curving backwards from his forehead near his temples to end in a dulled tip behind delicately pointed ears. The right horn was shorn off close to its base, leaving behind a jagged end and a mess of web-like scars across that side of his forehead that branched down over his brow to partially frame his right eye.

As the two ensigns carried Rin past him, he looked down at the girl. And when he spoke, his voice reverberated in her chest, deep and melodic like wind through the mountains. And while those eyes and that scar-marred face filled her with fear, that voice brought with it an irrepressible and undeniable calm that washed over her.

"We have a lot of work to do."

With that, Rin slipped back into unconsciousness.

Oren tracked the senseless girl with his eyes for a little longer, brow furrowing in concern. He looked to Sprit and pointed after the human.

"Was that Tarikian blood all over her mouth?"

"Yeah," she said, jutting her chin towards one of the bodies at the end of the hall that the ensigns had restrained. "She bit that one's hand. I was pretty impressed by it, actually. How'd you find us?"

"I followed the trail of bodies," Oren said simply and sighed. "We have quite a mess to clean up." He started down the hall and gestured for his officers to join him. "Sprit, get on the line with your teams. We have to make sure all the abductees are found and brought to Balok as well. Once he's cleared their health, we'll collaborate with them to get everyone back home."

"Yes, sir," she acknowledged with a quick nod and started off.

"Sprit!"

"Oren," she replied with a quick about-face and expectant expression. At his unimpressed look, she cleared her throat. "*Sir.*"

"Apologize to the poor girl for shooting her when she wakes up," he said sternly, and she scoffed in disbelief, pointing down the halls in the direction the ensigns had carried Rin.

"She broke my nose!"

"I don't care if she was the one who shot you, Sprit," he returned dryly. "*Apologize.*"

Sprit groaned and rolled her eyes.

"Yes, sir," she muttered. Amusedly shaking his head, Oren reached out and gently lifted her chin.

"Now, go get patched up." There was a kindness in his eyes, and she gave him a small smile as he gingerly touched her wounded arm. "We can cover it from here."

"Yes, sir." She fleetingly touched his elbow in return as she left, reaching to her earwig and starting her orders. "Alright, response teams one and two, set up a ray wall at the strike team's entry point and begin the air filtration process. I want to get that noxious gas out of here as soon as possible. Team three, I want you to assist the captain in finding the…"

Oren sighed as her voice finally faded down the hall and put a hand on Holt's arm.

"Let's go find the rest of them, lieutenant. You lead the way."

"Yes, sir." Holt took in a slow, deep breath and closed his eyes.

Center yourself. Hear the whole base—everyone, crew and hostiles.

Oren's mouth pressed into a tight line as he saw Holt flinch. He always worried about the man when he did this, no matter how many times the lieutenant told him he was fine. Holt took in another deep breath at the onslaught of thoughts in his head, the cacophony of easily fifty largely unfamiliar people thinking separately.

Eliminate our crew. They're irrelevant. One at a time, the minds of his coworkers quieted, buzzing there at the edge of his consciousness like a radio on the lowest volume setting. *Eliminate the Tarikians and their patrons. Don't look for anger, viciousness, or indignation. Look for the confusion.*

Oren crossed his arms over his chest and shifted his weight on his feet, watching his deputy security chief with concerned eyes. There was a slight furrow to his brow, and his breathing seemed unnaturally slow. Then again, it always seemed unnaturally slow when he did this.

Closer…almost there…

"Where am I?"

"Where's momma?"

"What's going on—"

Holt's eyes snapped open, and he took in a quick, short breath.

"You got them?" Oren asked, waiting as his officer took a moment to rub his eyes and catch his breath.

"Yes, sir. This way." They set off at a quick pace, Holt leading the way, and the mind reader cleared his throat. "Their thoughts are very faint…fogged and confused. But they are there."

"Good man," Oren said, clapping him on the back only to immediately hiss in pain as several small, sharp points stabbed his palm.

"Careful, sir, I've got—"

"Spines on your back, yes, I've just remembered," he groused, rubbing his palm against his pants in an attempt to ease the stinging. "Don't you usually warn me before I do something like that?"

"You've given me express orders on several occasions not to read your mind, captain," Holt began, sounding like he was only half-paying attention. "Not to mention I am a little...preoccupied..."

"What's wrong?" Oren asked as the taller man slowed to a stop in front of him. "Holt?"

"I'm having difficulty following them, sir. They're going quiet," the man muttered, looking around them like he was trying to pinpoint the fading thoughts. "Why are they going—"

The first scream tore through Holt's mind with no warning, and he gasped, hand pressing against his throbbing forehead as he doubled over slightly. Distantly, he felt his captain's hands on his back and arm.

"Holt? Holt, talk to me."

More screams started to fill his ears, panic that wasn't his rising in his throat, and Holt forced himself upright once more, quickly shoving the abductees' thoughts back.

Compartmentalize. Don't get overwhelmed.

"They're killing them," he finally said, voice sounding a little hoarse to his ears, and immediately started running, chasing the few minds he could still find. He flicked on his earwig. "Strike team. I've found the abductees, rendezvous with me."

Behind him, he could hear Oren echoing his command, and he pushed the base's noise back into static, focusing instead on the rapidly fading screams and confusion. He would get there in time. He had to get there in time; there were at least three small children still alive.

It took him only fifteen seconds to find the door, a few members of his strike team joining him from the main entrance. The room was just down the hall from the auction stage, and he quickly drew his weapon, Oren a fraction of a second behind him.

He couldn't hear them anymore.

"Ensign Omarik, door," Holt ordered, even voice betraying none of his inner turmoil.

Talik quickly kicked the metal door in at the handle, wasting no time on checking if it was locked or not. And immediately the Tarikian crewman turned away with a gagging sound, hand against the glass of his gasmask over his nose and mouth in a vain reflex. The rest of the strike team wasn't far behind him.

Holt just stood there, staring with a blank expression at the room before him. It was long and narrow, completely gray and cold. The air inside was the slight yellow color of the outside atmosphere, making it a little difficult to see through.

But not difficult enough to hide the bodies.

"Djienn," he heard Oren breathe beside him, his voice heavy with remorse as he slowly returned his weapon to its holster. "We were too late here. I want two of you to stay with me. I'll call in Balok's people to deal with this, and once they arrive, you can go back to your posts. The rest of you return to your other assignments."

There was a mumbled chorus of 'yes, sir' and 'yes, captain' as everyone went their separate ways. Oren sighed and put a heavy hand on Holt's shoulder, carefully avoiding the spines this time as he pulled him back from the doorway.

"They must have gassed them with air from outside," Holt heard himself explain as he pointed to the series of open vents on the ceiling. "Turned off the filtration system."

"We were too far away to help, lieutenant."

Holt gave a robotic nod and holstered his blaster, finally turning away from the twenty-five bodies crammed into such a tight space. He'd counted ten children. Oren watched his crewman aimlessly walk away from him a few feet down the hall, a dazed look in his eyes.

"You okay, Lewis?"

It was as if a switch flipped at the sound of his first name. Holt immediately straightened his posture, that unflappable façade dropping over him once more.

"Fine, sir," he said, turning to his captain. His hands automatically went behind his back and clasped together at the base of his spine. His gaze seemed unfocused, seeing through the walls around them. "More suspects are trying to escape through the transport hangar, but Lieutenant Commander Byrone has the doors locked down so they—"

"Lewis," Oren tried again and caught his officer's arm as he tried to walk away. Holt looked at him with wide, unreadable eyes.

"I *am* fine, sir. This is not the first time we have lost civilians," he said simply, pulling from his captain's loose grasp to continue on his way. "I have traffickers to interrogate."

"*Holt.*"

Holt stopped in the middle of the hall, nails digging into the palm of his right hand for a split second before he turned to face his captain, expression guileless.

"With your permission, sir."

Oren looked at him, tired and pitying beneath his gasmask. Lewis was brilliant. He kept a cool head under pressure, took care of the people under his command, and was the ace up Oren's sleeve when it came to strategy due to his mind reading. But *Starlight*'s best-kept secret was that he was also the most stubborn crewmember on board. And the captain knew he wasn't going to win a fight with him on this.

"Go," he said, tilting his head down the hall. "Keep me informed."

"Thank you, sir."

Oren turned back to the kill room and watched as the remaining strike team members started to record and collect the bodies, lining them up in the hall so Doctor Balok's people could get to them more easily. Mournfully, he took in the ages and species of the people before him and shook his head. There were children in there.

He subconsciously reached for the scars around his horn, running his fingers over the spidery marks, and wondered briefly if their small, innocent minds had been the one's Holt had heard screaming.

———

"Alright, we don't know how many people we're going to be receiving or what condition they're going to be in, so I want this entire medbay in crisis mode," Balok announced, hurrying through his work space with a bundle of blankets in his arms. "We may have people with hypothermia or even hyperthermia or perhaps serious wounds. So, we need to establish a triage station—oh! We should also have a quarantine room ready. We don't know where the abductees have been or what they've been exposed to—"

Two of the chief medic's nurses watched as the man tore through the space, picking up and putting down what seemed like a million things at once and giving a thousand different instructions to the room at large. The taller of the two leaned over to her violet-skinned partner.

"Dalia, is Balok always like this on jobs?"

"It's not usually this bad," Dalia admitted, stepping back slightly to avoid getting hit by something else the doctor was moving. She looked up at her furred coworker with a knowing smile, galaxy-filled eyes glittering with amusement. Her voice dropped to a conspiratorial whisper. "I think he just gets excited with the big ones."

"Gehmra!" Balok called from beside one of the hermetically sealed quarantine rooms, and the furred woman immediately looked to him. "Could you assist me with prepping this room for decontamination?"

"Yes, doctor, I'll be right there. Wish me luck," she whispered in an aside to Dalia and gingerly entered Balok's chaotic fray.

"Dalia!" The remaining woman looked over her shoulder to where a fellow nurse was pushing a cart of bandages, antiseptic, and sterile field generators. "Can you help me set up triage and wound care?"

"Yeah, I'll be right there."

This was going to be an intense shift.

Within the next few minutes, Sprit's security teams started bringing in Tarikians and patrons who'd been injured during their arrests. No one spoke to them beyond getting basic information about pain levels, types of injuries, and pre-existing conditions or allergies before they started any treatments, and Balok noted with pride that at least his people were being professional. He knew from experience it wasn't easy to treat traffickers with respect or even provide them with the best care possible; they were some of the lowest criminals they came across in this kind of work. But medical officers were out here to do a job and do it well, regardless of their patients' moral depravity.

Ten of their thirty beds were now occupied, and he looked around the large, elliptical room. No one seemed to be running out of materials just yet, and his doctors, nurses, and medical assistants seemed to be able to handle the current patients by themselves.

"Hmm," he hummed and sat on a nearby stool, fingers tapping restlessly against his white-clad knee. "I suppose I'll wait for the abductees, then."

He hadn't been sitting for more than a few seconds when the large glass doors leading into the medbay slid open with a quiet hiss to reveal Jhama Assora and another ensign, who quickly departed once he was sure the human was safely in his coworker's arms.

"Could I get some help here?" she called, and Balok immediately got to his feet, hurrying over to her.

"Is this the human?" he asked, gingerly helping her carry the girl over to the quarantine room. "Oh, do be careful with her neck! Keep her head steady."

"Yeah," Jhama grunted, shifting her hold on the lanky human to try and support her lolling head a little better. "Commander Matzepo shot her with a blaster on the lowest stun setting."

Balok looked up at her, horrified.

"She did *what?*"

"Captain figured you'd want to know."

"Well, I certainly do," he replied, still perturbed. "But I'd also like a word with Sprit about her behavior as well." He hit a button on the wall with his elbow, and the quarantine door slid open, letting them shuffle inside. "Let's set her on the bed here."

Jhama hefted the girl up and set her down on the mattress a little harder than she'd originally intended, and Balok looked at her disapprovingly as she clumsily tried to re-align the unconscious girl's limbs and largely failed.

"I can take it from here, ensign," he grumbled, shooing her away towards a wheeled stool in the corner. "Sit there, I need to clear us of contaminants before I let either one of us out of here." Far more gently than Jhama, he folded the human's hands on her stomach and slipped a pillow under her head, making sure her long hair wasn't caught on anything or pulling uncomfortably on her scalp. "There we go, that's better," he said with a smile and gently patted the girl's shoulder. "We'll have you up on your feet in no time, young miss."

He crossed the square room to the panel on the wall and entered a few different codes. A low droning whine filled the air and a front of pale green light slowly panned across the room twice before turning off. A stream of data and biological scans popped up on the wall panel, and Balok scrolled through it, humming to himself with his small, ever-present smile pulling at the corners of his lips.

"Well, our human looks completely healthy. No contaminants and no trackers embedded in her aside from those hearing implants…." He trailed off, pulling up another scan. "Oh, looks like we have a problem here," he began. "Ensign, it appears you picked up something from our guest—a small insect humans call *ticks*. They're quite fascinating, really. They latch onto your skin and then draw out blood—"

"Oh, doctor, I *really* don't need an entomology lesson," Jhama interrupted apologetically and not unkindly. "How long will decon take?"

"Oh, not very long at all," he said, waving her concern away as he pulled a pair of tweezers from one of the drawers next to her. "All we'll need to do is remove the little guy and make sure he didn't give you any infections. Such as what they call Lyme disease, that's a nasty—"

"Balok," Jhama said loudly, and he looked at her, oblivious.

"Yes, ensign?"

"Could we start decon? I have to get back to work."

"Yes, yes, of course." He gestured for her to undo the top of her uniform, and she quickly unfastened the four asymmetrical buttons that ran down the left side of her chest. As she shrugged the jumpsuit top off her shoulders and pulled her arms free, Balok approached with the tweezers.

"I'll have to pull the tick from your skin…. The scan showed that he was somewhere near your upper arm—there he is! He's hiding under the hem of your under-armor there. Allow me."

Jhama watched as he slid the tip of the tweezers under the sleeve of her tank top and pulled out a small black insect.

"That's it?" she asked, and Balok nodded, beaming.

"Miraculous, isn't it? Something this small can cause so much—"

"No, doctor, I mean, that's it for decontamination?"

"Ah. Unfortunately, no," he said, placing the tick in a small vial and pulling a syringe from his pocket. "I'll give you this injection to eradicate any potential illness this small fellow could have given you. It'll be thirty minutes before I know you won't have a reaction to it," he explained, prepping the shot as he spoke. "May I?"

"Please."

Balok gently took her arm in his hand and stuck the needle into her shoulder, injecting its contents and withdrawing the sliver of metal as quickly as he'd inserted it.

"There we go, all done," he smiled, patting her hand. "I'll be back in a moment to continue looking at our human. Sit tight."

There was another swish as Balok opened the door and exited the room, and suddenly, the small space was very quiet. Jhama let out a long, slow breath and cleared her throat, looking over the unconscious human. She'd gotten a good look at the girl carrying her over here, but just sitting here with her was a little uncomfortable.

"Sorry about him," she finally said, if only to fill the silence. "He's a bit intense and, uh, scattered. But he is a good doctor, I promise." The human obviously didn't respond, and Jhama pulled her uniform back on, shaking her head. "I'm talking to a sleeping person."

At that moment, the door slid open again, and Balok re-entered, this time carrying a small examiner's bag with him.

"Alright, I'm going to make sure our guest isn't injured in any way the scans missed. It would be very helpful to me if you stayed as far out of the way as possible," he added apologetically. "I know this isn't the most conducive space for that." Jhama nodded, and Balok waited as she moved her stool right next to the threshold and out of the way of any of the supplies and drawers. "Thank you."

A few minutes passed in relative silence as Balok bustled around the small room, humming as he treated stray scrapes and bruises along the girl's feet, knees, elbows, and hands. The skin around the hearing implants was slightly discolored, too, probably from post-op bruising. It was nothing a little bit of antiseptic and various boosters wouldn't help, though, and Balok made sure to clean around the cochlear-like devices especially well. He had to give it to the Tarikians; they *had* gone to a good surgeon to get these installed. Unfortunately, though, based on the data he'd gathered from her scans, there was no removing them without also rendering the girl deaf. And while the underlying electronic nature to everything she would hear would take some getting used to, Balok had no doubt that she would adapt; it seemed to be the human motto. Everything was going well. Until…

His humming cut off as he checked the inside of the girl's mouth.

"Oh dear."

"Is something wrong?" Jhama asked and sat up a little straighter.

Balok gently let the human's jaw close and looked up at the ensign, a sad light in his eyes.

"I'm seeing signs she was in cryofreeze." His perpetual smile turned pitying and empathetic. "Based on the deposits on her teeth, I'd have to say for about eight months."

Jhama closed her eyes, letting her head thump back against the glass door.

"Missing persons rule," she said softly, and Balok looked back to his current patient. "She can't go home."

"No," he agreed, gingerly placing a hand on the human's shoulder once more and squeezing. "She cannot."

The main doors opened with a distant swoosh, and Jhama looked through the glass wall to see Sprit walking in, left arm cradled against her stomach. Immediately, two nurses converged on her and tried to lead her to a bed across the room, but the security chief had other ideas.

"Wait, is that where the human is?" she asked, pointing towards the quarantine room Balok and Jhama were in.

Dalia followed her gesture and nodded.

"Yes, ma'am, but we should really treat this burn and your nose—"

"Yeah, yeah, do that while I'm sitting over there," Sprit interrupted, hooking a nearby stool with her foot and kicking it across the floor so it rolled to a stop about four feet from the door. She slowly took a seat and let herself cave in, bracing her forearms on her knees.

"Are you alright, commander?"

Sprit looked up at Jhama's static-tainted voice. The ensign was holding down the quarantine room's intercom button, and they exchanged wan smiles.

"Just a little sore and beat up, Jhama. How about you?"

"I was bitten by a human insect, ma'am."

Sprit snorted and sat up as Dalia returned to fix her nose.

"Sounds par for the course with humans," she chuckled and winced as the nurse cleaned the blood from her skin. "Gently, please, Dalia."

"Sorry, ma'am. Some of this has dried on."

"I'll get it later," she sighed, and the nurse shrugged, preparing some tape strips and applying them over the bridge of Sprit's nose. "How's the human doing?"

"Since you *stunned* her?" Balok's voice called through the intercom, and Sprit winced again. "Remarkably well, though, as I was telling Ensign Assora, it seems our guest was in cryofreeze for eight months."

Sprit groaned.

"The missing persons rule..."

"We came to the same conclusion," he said, opening the door and stepping out. "Now, what nonsense did you get yourself into this time?"

Sprit pointed to the door he'd just walked through.

"The human elbowed me in the face."

"Huh." He looked back at the still-sleeping girl. "Well, that explains how she got that bruise." He turned back to the security chief, now wholly unamused. "I assume that's also why you deemed it appropriate to *shoot* her?"

Sprit was about to open her mouth to argue, right hand resting on her hip while a second nurse started worked on her left arm, when one of her other ensigns walked in. Omarik, that was his name, she recalled. He was solemn and worn down, eyes downcast and shoulders stooped. Immediately, Sprit's playful demeanor vanished, and Balok gave them some space as the man walked over to her.

"What happened, ensign?"

"They killed all the abductees, ma'am," he said softly, taking care to keep his words just between them. Sprit closed her eyes and bowed her head, fist clenching against her knee. "Spoiled merchandise or something like that. Lieutenant Holt will know the specifics once he's done interrogating the Tarikians and customers they caught at the hangar."

"Djienn," Sprit sighed, looking up at the ceiling for a few moments before turning her focus back to the shaken young man. "That human is the only survivor, isn't she?"

Talik glanced at the quarantine room, and Jhama lowered her gaze.

"Yes, ma'am." Sprit shook her head, unable to fathom the news he'd just given her. "Where should we put the bodies?"

Sprit looked at the second nurse treating her arm, and he shrugged.

"You should ask Balok," he offered. "Our morgue probably won't hold them all."

"I'll do that then," Talik said with a curt nod to Sprit. "Ma'am."

"Thanks for the report, Ensign Omarik," she said absently, heaviness settling in her very bones. "Once you sort out the morgue situation with

CHAPTER 4

"How is she?"

"As well as can be expected," Balok replied, not looking up from his tablet. "You'll have a full report on her within the hour."

Oren crossed his arms a little tighter over his chest as he watched the sedated human through the glass door of her room.

"No lasting injuries?"

The doctor looked up at him in mild annoyance.

"No, none," he repeated, carefully enunciating as if he were talking to a child, "and you will have a full report on her within the hour." Oren shot him an unamused look, and Balok defensively held up his hands. "Apologies, I forgot you don't appreciate my humor."

"*Balok.*"

"Yes, yes—my *sincere* apologies this time, captain."

"What is it with my crew deciding to get snarky with me today?" he muttered, and Balok joined him, still scribbling away with his stylus.

"It was a hard assignment," the doctor said absently as he transcribed some of the bio readings from the quarantine room panel. "And we all take out our frustrations in different ways. Though," he added, glancing at his boss before returning to his report, "if it was Sprit, that's simply her being your sister."

"She can't stay professional for *one* job," Oren muttered, and Balok hummed his consensus.

"She can't stay professional at all. But that's what makes her Sprit, wouldn't you agree?"

"She's my security chief, Balok," Oren replied, exhausted. "She needs to step it up." The doctor side-eyed him curiously.

"Do you know where Commander Matzepo is at this moment?" he asked a little too innocently as he turned back to his work.

The captain frowned.

"No," he said slowly. "Should I be worried?"

"Hardly," Balok said dismissively, returning to his desk and looking at something beneath a microscope. "She's in the loading bay talking to her security teams about this last assignment." He straightened and continued writing on his tablet. "We've already gotten some counseling service requests from the strike members who were with you and Lieutenant Holt when you found the bodies." He gave Oren a proud smile and pointed at him with his stylus. "She's taking care of your crew quite admirably. You should give her more credit."

"I know," he sighed, pulling up a stool next to the doctor. "She's just always going to be that wild, troublemaking little girl to me, though."

"Well, that's hardly fair to her," Balok chastised, still not paying complete attention. "You should send her on her way to another ship if that's the case."

"You know no one else would take her. She's too…off-book, shall we say?"

"Hmm, I suppose," Balok replied vaguely. "Though—"

An automated voice suddenly spoke in Oren's ear, and he apologetically held up a hand to his chief medical officer.

"Lewis Holt."

"Sorry, incoming message."

"No worries, captain," the doctor assured him as the man got up and walked away, finger resting subconsciously on the earwig.

"Holt, what do you have for me?"

"I've just finished the interrogation with the lead Tarikian. He goes by the moniker Chief."

"Does he have any more people or other contraband items hidden away?"

"No, sir. And he was the one who turned off the filtration system in the room the abductees were in."

"Well then, we can charge him with twenty-five counts of murder in addition to trafficking and visiting a black site system." It was a small victory, but Oren would take it. "Did you get his associates' names?"

"Yes, sir," Holt readily replied. "We also have a rudimentary shipment schedule, though it is likely to change now that we have dismantled Chief's arm of the operation."

Oren nodded to himself, hand resting on his hip as he stared at the floor.

"You've done good work, Holt. Now, go get some sleep. You can fill me in on the rest in your full report tomorrow."

"Thank you, sir."

Oren closed the channel and returned to his post outside the girl's quarantine room, pensively silent.

"I see you're still having Lieutenant Holt use his abilities for interrogations," Balok called a little stiffly, and Oren groaned under his breath.

"They murdered twenty-five people last night alone, doctor," he said, turning to face his medic. The man's smile had vanished, replaced instead by a displeased frown. "Look, I understand your concerns, but Holt is no different than a truth serum or a lie detector." The doctor was still looking at him with an unmoved expression, so he pressed on. "With people like this, we don't have the luxury of time. You know that. They could've had more people locked away somewhere, more kids. They could've been transporting guns or other even more deadly weapons that could be fueling the class wars on Alympa. They could've been moving *Encarta*, doc, for galaxy's sake!"

Balok's eyes flashed dangerously at the mention of the violent, primitive species from Jaeda.

"Those hypotheticals are all well and good, but where do you draw the line?" the doctor challenged softly, holding his captain's gaze with an impressive steadiness. "Where do you draw the line with who falls under your category of people like this?"

"I'm not a tyrant, Balok," Oren replied in the silence that followed. "I'm not ordering Holt to pry into their minds or drive them insane. I am *not* Jon Bledsoe." Balok looked down a little guiltily. "All I ask him to do in those interrogations is see if they are lying. He reads the thoughts they all but broadcast to him, and the information he gets from them you'd find in a comprehensive personnel file."

Another long quiet filled the room, and Balok slowly rose, joining his superior at Rin's door.

"My apologies, captain. I did not mean to insinuate anything about your character."

"No. No apologies," Oren sighed, turning with the man to look at their human. "You're just doing your job…looking out for the crew."

"How *is* Lieutenant Holt?"

Oren scoffed and shook his head wonderingly.

"He says he's fine."

That well-worn smile returned easily to Balok's face, and he crossed his arms and rocked back on his heels.

"Of course he does," he chuckled. "The boy's as stubborn and resilient as a whilden, Oren." He looked from his captain to the unconscious human. "If he says he's fine, then trust him."

Another silence overtook them, this one more amiable.

"How long until the sedative you gave the human wears off?"

"She'll be back with us any minute now." Balok clipped the stylus to the edge of the tablet, satisfied with his work. "Do you know who you'll want to go in and talk to her first?"

"Sprit." Oren's response held no hesitation. "She's had the most contact. It'll make communicating as easy as possible given the girl's current circumstances."

"I agree," Balok said, patting the horned man on the arm and heading for his desk to set down his report. "Should I send for her?"

Oren returned the familiar touch with a small smile.

"If you could. I have to give my report to the Galactic Council about what happened."

"Oh dear," Balok muttered, and Oren made an unenthused noise of agreement as he headed for the medbay doors. "I wish you luck with that conversation."

"Thank you, doctor."

"Any time, captain," he called and sighed, smiling to himself as he heard the medbay doors open and then shut a few moments later. He reached for the intercom panel on the wall above his desk and pressed a button. "Loading bay."

"Connected."

"Sprit, it's Doctor Balok. May I speak with you for a moment?" He waited a few seconds and beamed as the Ethonian's voice finally came through.

"Hey, doc. Tarikians giving you trouble?"

"I should be asking you that. The last one was discharged into your care ten minutes ago."

"Of course. Then what's up?"

"The captain has requested that you report to medbay."

Sprit groaned and let her forehead thump against the bulkhead.

"Am I still in trouble for shooting the human?"

"No, though *please* refrain from shooting the people we're trying to rescue in the future." Sprit grumbled again, and the doctor continued. "It *is* about our guest, however. I'll be seeing you shortly."

"Wait, Balok!" The security chief growled in frustration as the physician closed the channel. "You couldn't be more specific than that?" she sarcastically asked the intercom. When no response was forthcoming, she turned back to her waiting security division. "You're dismissed. Remember!" she added, raising her voice as they started to depart, and they all looked back at her. "We did the best we could on this one. And we managed to save one person. We could have saved no one." A few people looked down, eyes shining and faces pained. "I know that doesn't seem like a lot, but trust me. You'll all have one day when you save no one. If you're lucky, it'll only be one day. And on those jobs, that one person you saved makes all the difference." Sprit waited another moment before shooing them towards the doors. "Now go on. You're dismissed for real this time. Get outta here."

She watched everyone slowly file out into the surrounding halls and gave Holt a wry smile as he walked over to her.

"What's their mood, Lewis?"

"Largely the same as before your speech, ma'am" he admitted.

"Damn," Sprit hissed, hands resting on her hips. "I really thought that'd help."

"It did help some of them, commander," he reassured her, and she made an indecipherable noise in the back of her throat. "Just…not the majority."

She gave him an annoyed look.

"You're really the bearer of good news, aren't you?"

Holt cleared his throat and deliberately looked away from her into the clearing space of the loading bay.

"If that is how you choose to take my feedback, then yes, ma'am."

"Oh, you are so lucky I have somewhere to be right now, lieutenant," Sprit muttered and stormed off at her deputy's frank, questioning expression. "No! No, I'm *not* getting sucked into your fake innocence, Holt! I see what you're doing!"

The loading bay door slid open and shut, leaving Holt standing awkwardly alone with an utterly perplexed expression.

"I was…simply being polite, ma'am…."

———

Sprit wasn't in the best mood when she walked into the medbay for the second time that day. She was tired, she was sore, and she wanted nothing more than to retreat to her quarters and crash for the night. It had been a *long* day.

Unfortunately for her, she wasn't going to get any of that.

"Ah, Commander!" Balok called, grinning at his desk, and quickly shoved his half-eaten, dehydrated nutrition bar into his pocket as she approached. "You've decided to join us!"

Sprit looked around the empty medbay and gave him a confused, slightly frustrated look as she held her arms out at her sides.

"Who's us, Balok? We're the only ones here."

"Our human's waking up," he said around his mouthful of food and gestured to the quarantine room. "I meant for you to get here a little sooner so we could coordinate what you'll need to talk to her about—"

"Talk to her?" Sprit echoed in disbelief. "Balok, I'm not going to talk to her!"

"Nonsense," the doctor interrupted, waving her words away as he got up and started herding her towards the room. "All you'll have to do is figure out her name and her age and explain her new situation."

"Oh, is that all?" the security chief snapped, digging her heels in in a vain effort to halt her forward movement. "Balok, come on! I *shot* her!"

"Which makes this the perfect opportunity to patch things up between you two," the doctor explained patiently and continued to propel the shorter woman forward. "Come now, she doesn't bite. Though, I suppose she does throw elbows."

"*Balok*—"

"Captain's orders, commander," Balok pressed, leaning his considerable weight into her back. "Now, let's go. She's not going to stay asleep forever."

"Oh, of course this was Oren! Was this because I didn't call him sir at the storage hangar?"

"You'll have to bring that up with him," he answered reasonably as he opened the door and gave Sprit a firm push that sent her stumbling into the room. "Have fun!"

"Balok!" she yelped, immediately regaining her footing and turning back to the door. Scowling, she hit the button on the jamb, but instead of opening the door, the panel just made a discordant sound. Sprit glared at the doctor through the glass, and the man shrugged, lime-green eyes suspiciously innocuous. Her expression turned stony, her voice equally unamused. "Balok, unlock the door."

"Captain's orders, commander," he repeated and pointed behind her with an entertained smile before retreating to his desk without another word.

"Balok, come on!" she shouted after him, all but whining.

When he continued to pay her no mind, she growled in frustration and turned around hard, slamming her back into the glass.

What did they even expect her to be able to *do?* She could already feel the start of a migraine building behind her eyes. This human was quickly becoming the bane of her existence—

Sprit froze.

The girl's hand had just moved.

"Alright," she breathed and cautiously moved to the stool Jhama had vacated about half an hour ago. "Okay, human. Let's not do anything rash. Does that sound good?" The girl's fingers slowly curled against the sheets and her brow furrowed ever so slightly. "I'm going to take that as a yes." Sprit slowly sat down on the stool and uncomfortably cleared her throat. "And now we wait."

One deck above them, Lewis Holt was meditating. Or rather, trying to meditate. He'd attempted to get into the right headspace in his quarters, but the constant activity in the hall and the loud, distressed thoughts of the rest of the crew hadn't helped his efforts. But here…

He slowly opened his eyes to watch the wall of stars stretching out before him—multi-colored, innumerable, and reassuring in their steady constancy. A gentle calm washed over him.

Here, he might actually have some luck. He shifted from his kneeling position to a more comfortable cross-legged one and let his hands rest loosely in his lap. Mercifully, the two officers who'd been on the observation deck before him left when he entered, exchanging brief, respectful nods with him as they departed. Holt never would have asked them to leave. He was too polite for that. However, there seemed to be a general consensus among the crew to always give the lieutenant some space, and for that, he was thankful.

He redirected his focus to the wall-sized window before him, to the brilliant points of light consuming the view like spilled glitter. He absently rubbed the hem of his pant leg between his fingers and let his eyes drift half-shut once more. After a few slow, deep breaths, he began reciting his decades old mantra.

Center yourself. Hear the whole ship, everyone…crew, civilians, and arrestees.

One hundred and eighty-five minds surged to the forefront of his own, overwhelming his senses with their chaotic ramblings of varying intensities and volumes. Their individual thoughts were indecipherable. It was deafening, headache inducing, painful, and Holt continued to breath evenly through it, his expression carefully composed.

Eliminate the crew on deck five, moving from bow to stern—

The observation deck door hissed open behind him, shattering his focus, and he opened his eyes fully, blinking a couple times. Three small children ran in, giggling and elbowing each other before coming to a sliding, hushed stop behind their leader's thrown-out arms. Wide eyes stared at the deputy's back in over-dramatic alarm.

"It's Holt!" the little girl running point whispered in panic. "Run!"

Instantly the children fled, pushing past each other to get to the door.

"*Shh!*" their leader hissed, swatting frantically at her younger companions. "Run, go!"

There was another swish of the metal door opening and closing, and the room was quiet again. Holt sighed and refocused his attention.

Eliminate the crew on deck five. Bow to stern.

The mental noise from the loading bay and most of engineering dialed down to a near-imperceptible volume in the back of his mind.

Eliminate deck four...

The officer quarters, brig, mess hall, and remaining sections of engineering faded from his immediate attention, joining deck five in static.

Eliminate deck three....

More crew quarters, the medbay, the boiler room, and auxiliary control fell nearly silent.

Eliminate deck one.

The remainder of the crew quarters, the firing range, and gym joined the other decks in that barely-existent bandwidth at the edge of his mind. Holt stayed at that point for a while, letting himself get acclimated to the reduced volume. Now came the final step—the deck he was on. He was so close to reaching that peace he so desperately needed.

Eliminate the bridge...department offices...armory...conference rooms...

Deck two fell quiet one section at a time until the only room left was the observation deck, the only mind his own. His unfocused gaze continued to watch the stars slowly drift, feeling oddly detached from the world around him. The ship was still and quiet. Not silent—it would never be silent for him ever again. But everyone else was forced down to a volume of one, a faint buzz of thought that constantly continued in the background. His own thoughts were the only ones remaining at the forefront of his mind, and the relative peace sent shivers down his spine. He could barely remember the days when it used to always be like this...sorting the voices without effort. Until—

His eyes opened fully and his heart rate empathetically picked up as a new voice, a new mind suddenly woke. It was scared and small, on the verge of tears.

"Where am I? What's happening? What...where..."

It was the human.

Holt released a long, slow breath and carefully got to his feet, joints creaking in protest. Reluctantly, he filed the girl's mind away with the others on board. It wouldn't do for him to get distracted again. Even now, he could still recall pieces of the abductees' final thoughts as they'd been killed, could bring their voices back to life, simmering below the surface. With a last glance at the vast, star-filled expanse, he straightened his uniform and went back to work.

Rin woke up suddenly this time. The world seemingly rushed at her all at once, and she sat up fast with a loud, harsh gasp that quickly turned into a coughing fit as her sharp inhale caught in her throat.

"Holy djienn!" Sprit half-shouted and nearly fell off her stool, catching herself on the door beside her. The human immediately looked to the yell's source, and fear jolted through her at the sight of the auction lady.

Run.

Frantically, Rin pushed herself back on the bed, only to retreat too far and fall off the narrow mattress, and Sprit watched with wide eyes as the girl's flailing arm caught the edge of the cart beside her and toppled the whole thing, scattering scanners and other non-invasive equipment across the tiles alongside her with a loud, rattling crash. The moment she hit the floor, Rin scrambled back into the corner behind the bed, completely out of view of the door.

A long silence stretched out, broken only by the human's ragged breathing and the frantic beeping of the vital signs monitor.

"Everyone okay in there?" Balok called, and Sprit made an uncertain face as she debated her response options.

"Let me get back to you on that, doc," she finally said as she slowly scooted her stool towards the other side of the bed.

"Well, her monitors are telling me her heart stopped and she's no longer breathing," Balok returned. "Something I should know about?"

"No, uh," Sprit glanced at the disconnected wires draped across the mattress, "she just ripped off her leads when she fell out of bed."

"Fell out of bed? I sent you in there to *talk* to her—"

"Yeah, I'll fill you in later, Balok," Sprit interrupted, finally clearing the foot of the bed. The human stared up at her, shaking, with wide, terrified eyes. "Um…hello there."

Rin continued to stare at the woman before her, breathing hard. It hadn't been a bad trip. There was an honest-to-god, green, camouflage-skinned and copper-eyed alien in front of her.

"You're, uh, you're safe. We're not gonna hurt you or anything like that," Sprit began and indicated the small room around them. "This is our medbay, or rather this is a quarantine room. The door's right there if you want to leave—wait. Wait, no the doors are locked, um, ignore that."

Seeing the increasingly panicked look on the human's face, Sprit quickly backtracked.

"Wait, no. No, no, I don't mean the doors are locked like *that*, we're not keeping you prisoner here or anything," she said with a nervous, awkward laugh, struggling to explain herself while Balok grimaced at his desk. "Balok just locked *me* in here," she explained in a tone that said that this was an everyday occurrence. "Balok's the doctor, by the way," she added in a quick aside, pointing at the glass door. "I think you met him already—lime green eyes; curly, burnt orange hair? Anyways, he locked me in here because I didn't want to talk to you." She broke off as the human's eyebrows slowly traveled higher up her forehead, pale expression growing more confused and stressed by the second. "That's…not any better, is it? Wait, give me a second here."

Sprit finally stopped her rambling, hands steepled over her mouth.

What to do, what to do, what to do—

"English…"

"Sorry?" Sprit asked and looked at the human in surprise. The girl cleared her throat and repeated her barely audible whisper.

"English…you speak English." The girl frowned, shaking her head a bit like she was trying to clear it. "No, I…I *hear* English—"

"Oh, yeah," the woman interrupted and gestured to her own ears. "Those are you translators."

Rin's heart skipped a beat in her chest as she remembered the metal she'd felt behind her ears, and her hands flew to the implants, immediately trying to scratch and pry them away.

"No! No, no, no, don't do that!" Sprit yelped, hurrying towards the girl and jumping as the human screamed and kicked at her, automatically moving her arms into a defensive position over her head.

De-escalation training, idiot, she silently hissed and slowly backed off, her hands at her shoulders. *Calm down, will you? Just…I can't believe I'm saying this…just act like Holt.*

"I'm sorry," she said as she slowly sat down on the floor opposite her. "I guess you're pretty freaked out, huh?"

Rin slowly uncovered her head to look at the shorter woman. She'd changed her clothes, she noticed. Now she was wearing one of those navy blue jumpsuits like everyone else, except her shoulder pads were a light blue. The woman pointed to herself.

"I'm Commander Sprit Matzepo. But you can call me Sprit."

Rin noticed the movement of Sprit's mouth matched the pronunciation of her name, and the small detail brought a modicum of comfort to her. It was short-lived though, and Rin's hands slowly moved back to her ears.

"I *really* wouldn't pick at those, kid," Sprit pressed, reaching out and touching the tiled ground between them. "They're surgically implanted, so you've got some bruising. Besides, if we took them out or if you somehow managed to rip 'em out—which, just so you know, wouldn't work, so *please* don't try—you wouldn't understand anything anyone says to you." She paused uncomfortably. "And you'd be...deaf. Which, you know, isn't a big deal," she hurried to assure her. "We've got lots of aids and ways to help you acclimate to deafness."

Not a big deal?! Rin thought wildly to herself, heart pounding almost painfully behind her ribs.

"But," Sprit continued, carefully keeping her voice even and calm, "you're gonna be getting used to *a lot* of new things real quick in the next few weeks. It would be nice for you to not have to add learning common-speak to your to-do list."

The human just stared at her warily, her hands tightly balled into fists in her lap.

"Well," Sprit began diplomatically when she saw the girl wasn't going to offer anything else, "we can talk about that later with Balok if you'd like." She gestured to the girl. "So. I'm Sprit. What's your name?"

Rin took a moment to look at the woman before her—really look. She'd been right about the kindness in her rough touch at the auction. Even now, she was somehow gentle behind her unrefined social skills and over-all prickliness. Besides, so far Rin had stayed safe with her. And Sprit hadn't handed her off to someone else like Rin had thought when she'd first woken up here. Not to mention those navy blue uniforms did look official.

And ultimately, what else could she do?

"Rin," she finally whispered and slowly let a leg straighten out from where her knees had been pressed against her chest. "My name is Rin Cooper."

CHAPTER 5

"Rin," Sprit echoed, giving the girl her pirate smile. "Now we're getting somewhere. Where are you from?"

"Montana," Rin answered after a long pause, her voice hesitant and soft-spoken. But then she frowned. "I mean, Earth? Um…"

"It's okay," Sprit laughed, dismissing her uncertainty. "We're familiar with Earth, though Montana is new." She leaned against the side of the abandoned bed. "How old are you?"

Rin didn't respond. She could feel her throat closing up on her as her heart renewed its pace, and Sprit sighed and nodded to herself.

"Tell you what," the security chief began, tapping the floor between them again. "We'll play a game. I give you a bit of information about me, and then you can tell me the same thing about you. That sound good?"

Rin glanced at the mottled-green hand resting on the tiled ground between them, and Sprit slowly withdrew her arm.

"I guess I'll start off by telling you where I'm from. Seems only fair, right?" Sprit said, and Rin looked away. "Okay, so I'm from Dokrai. It's this massive city on Ethonius, *but* I'm also a foster kid. So, I was mostly raised by Trozerans in a remote village called Sahmot. That's, uh, actually where the captain's from."

She's a real life alien. Rin squeezed her eyes shut and took in a long, slow breath to try and calm her turning stomach. *Oh my god, she's a real life alien talking to me about real life planets and—*

"Now I guess we move on to our new question, right? Let's see…." Sprit paused, trying to remember what she had asked next. "Age! There we go. In standard time—oh." She broke off with a disgruntled noise. "I suppose I should explain standard time. In space, we have twenty-eight hours a day, two hundred and eighty days a year, forty days a month, and seven months a year. That way, we're all on the same schedule between destinations."

Sprit gave the silent, confused girl a wry smile.

"It takes some getting used to. So, in standard time, I'm forty-four years old. Now, you—how old are you in human time?"

Rin took a deep breath, picking at the hem of her scrubs shirt.

"Seventeen," she whispered, and Sprit had to lean forward to catch the near-silent word.

Her eyes filed with pity.

"Djienn, those Tarikians were way off. You're practically a kid." She leaned against the bed, her heart heavy. "You had your whole life ahead of you on Earth…. Any ideas about what you wanted to do?"

Rin felt her voice stick in her throat again, all the information she'd heard overwhelming her as she tried to process everything. Why was this woman talking like Rin was never going home? Why was she giving her all this information, what did she need to know all of this for? She felt bile rise treacherously in her throat and quickly covered her mouth with a shaking hand as she heaved.

"Oh no," Sprit muttered, eyeing Rin with a mixture of distaste and concern. "We're not doing this again, are we?" Rin squeezed her eyes shut as she felt herself dry heave again, and the security chief scrambled to her feet. "Okay, I'm getting a trashcan, *please* don't throw up on the floor again."

There was a brief rustle of movement, and Rin shortly felt something hard and cold tap her arm in a rather insistent, urgent way. She jumped, finding herself face to face with a wastebasket that Sprit was holding out to her from over the side of the bed, and the commander shook it a bit as an indication for her to grab it.

"If you're gonna throw up, please do it in here," she said, expression pleading. "After the day we've just had, I don't think the medbay staff needs any more cleaning up to do."

Rin snatched the receptacle from Sprit's hands and doubled over it as she threw up nothing but acid, groaning as the bile seared her throat and mouth. On the bed, Sprit made an empathetically disgusted face.

"That didn't sound fun."

Rin looked up at her with weary and bitter eyes, and Sprit grinned.

"That's an expression I'm familiar with, that one right there," she said, pointing at the human's drained face. "That's the 'I'm gonna kill you for making a stupid comment' face. I get that a lot, especially from my deputy. You know, he can be very sarcastic for a guy who stands on cere-mony all the time."

"Lieutenant," Rin whispered hoarsely over the trashcan, and Sprit raised a surprised eyebrow.

"Yeah, that's right," she said. "He's the lieutenant I was talking to at the compound, the one with the spikey face and bad haircut. His name's Lewis Holt." There was a knock at the door, and both of the room's occupants looked to see Balok standing there with a towel and a glass of water in his hands.

"I've unlocked the door, commander," he called, lifting the two objects slightly with a reassuring smile directed at Rin. "If you could take these off my hands, they're for our young guest."

Sprit got off the bed and opened the door, taking the offered items with a small scowl.

"You better not lock this door again when you leave, Balok," she warned, and the man beamed.

"Wouldn't dream of it, commander. Now, if you could ask—"

Sprit closed the door in his face and returned to Rin's side of the bed, holding the towel and glass out to her.

"Here. It's water, don't worry."

Rin set aside the trashcan and gratefully accepted the towel, cleaning her mouth and marveling briefly at the softness of the fabric against her skin before quickly downing the glass. The cool liquid eased the burning in her throat, and Sprit righted the toppled instrument stand beside them as Rin awkwardly looked for a place to put both objects down.

"Here." The officer took the damp towel and empty cup from Rin and placed the items on the newly available metal tray. "We create our own solutions." She sat back down on the ground, this time a little closer to the human. "So, you're seventeen, you're from Montana...what were you doing with your life?" Rin still hesitated, and Sprit tried again. "Look, if you tell me what you did, I'll tell you what we do out here."

"I...I worked in a nursery."

"Oh, children?"

The human pulled a face.

"Plants."

Sprit nodded to herself, amused.

"Don't like kids, huh?" Rin shrugged defensively, and the woman smirked and shook her head. She really was sticking to the one answer, one question exchange. "Well, you held up your end of the deal, which, I suppose, makes it my turn. I'm sure you noticed how everyone on board wears a jumpsuit uniform and that we use words like commander and lieutenant." Rin nodded hesitantly. "Well, that's because we're a very...I like to say 'specific' kind of ship. You see this?" She pointed to the logo stitched into her sleeve, and Rin leaned forward slightly. It was an eight-point star with a comet circling it. "That's *Starlight's* emblem. All of our uniforms have this patch on it; it's our identifier within the Peacekeeper Corps. And, well, I guess that segues nicely into what we do out here. We're…peacekeepers? That's not helpful…oh! Think of us as the space version of your FBI."

Rin's seemingly perpetual frown deepened.

"How—"

"We're familiar with your FBI," Sprit interrupted. "The point is, we handle the big things: murder cases with more than four victims, on and off-world mass casualty events, biochemical and terror attacks, critical hostage situations, and, in your case, illegal trafficking and black market trading." She paused, waiting for a reaction.

The one she finally got wasn't quite what she was looking for.

"Why are you familiar with the FBI?"

"That's a side detail, don't focus…you're just gonna keep bringing it up, aren't you?" Rin gave her a nod with an *obviously* air to it that made Sprit laugh. "Alright, we've, uh, had some exposure to humans."

Excitement flared to life in Rin's chest, reflecting in her shining eyes and straightening posture.

"There are other humans?" Sprit looked down at the hopeful, eager note in Rin's voice. "Can I see them? Talk to them?"

"I…" The commander sighed, her heart growing heavy in her chest. "We've only come across one live human in the last two decades," she began, and something nauseating settled in Rin's gut. There was a pained light in Sprit's eyes, sorrow hidden in the lines of her face. "His name was Daniel. He…he died last year."

"He died last year." Died is such a sanitized way of saying it, Sprit thought bitterly, missing Rin's soft "oh" as the officer lost herself in the memory of that ill-fated mission.

"Anyways," she said, mentally shaking free and forcing an offhanded smile, "Daniel liked to say we were the space FBI. But our *official* name is the Peacekeeper Corps. There are sixty-seven vessels like ours in the fleet that operate in basically every corner of this galaxy. And we are pretty good at what we do, so."

She was greeted with another silence, but this one wasn't as painful as the others had been.

"Are you like a flagship?" Rin asked tentatively, and Sprit snorted, the sound quickly devolving into side-holding laughter.

"Flagship?" she cackled, wiping at her eyes, and Rin felt the corners of her mouth twitch upward at the infectious sound. "Oh, child, we are *so* not a flagship." She breathed deeply a couple times to gather herself only to start laughing again, her arms crossing over her stomach as she doubled over.

"Flagship," she snorted and finally sat up, calming down enough to speak. "We are the *hottest* mess in space, Rin," she finally sighed, wiping tears from her face. "Our chief engineer hasn't spoken to his sister for a whole year, sixty percent of our crew has little to no experience, and honestly, I'm not a hundred percent sure I'm not in here because I sassed the captain after shooting you earlier today."

Immediately, Rin's relaxing expression tensed again.

Sprit winced.

"I haven't actually apologized for that yet, have I?" she asked, and Rin mutely shook her head. "Well then, I'm sorry for shooting you. I was having a bit of a bad day."

"*You* were having a bad day?" Rin returned sullenly and instantly blushed as Sprit jerked back in surprise.

"Would you look at that!" she said, with a grin. "You're sassy, too. We'll get along great." Despite herself, Rin gave a small, scoffing laugh and mirrored the alien's smile. "Yeah, I suppose you were having an infinitely worse day than I was at that auction."

Suddenly, an image surfaced in Rin's mind of vague shapes wearing the same gray jumpsuit as her in the waiting room.

"The others..." She instinctively reached out towards Sprit a little as she spoke, and the officer grew somber once more. "There were others."

"They didn't make it," Sprit told her gently and took a chance, reaching out. Her hand settled carefully on the human's knee, and she felt Rin flinch beneath her touch. But the girl didn't pull away. "The Tarikians, well, let's just leave it at they didn't want us getting our hands on their 'merchandise.'"

Rin looked down at her lap, her eyes drawn to where Sprit's hand was resting on her knee.

"I'm the only one?" she asked softly, and Sprit gently squeezed the girl's leg.

"Some days that's how it goes." She nodded towards her. "How are you ears feeling?"

Instinctively, Rin reached up, running her fingers over the smooth metal grafted into her skin. She'd forgotten they were there.

"Bit sore," she admitted.

"But you're hearing alright?"

"There's this sound..."

"Is it a bit like an electronic base?" Rin nodded. "That's part of the implants. A few people aboard use similar models. Eventually, you'll get used to it, and you won't even notice it anymore," Sprit assured her, but Rin still seemed unconvinced.

"But…how will I explain them?"

Sprit frowned.

"Explain them to whom?" she asked, and Rin looked at her like she was insane.

"…Anyone." When Sprit still looked lost, she elaborated. "When I go home."

Oh boy.

"Uh," Sprit floundered, looking to the empty doorway for help. "I don't…"

She gave an invisible sigh of relief as her earwig announced *"Balok Itoya"* in its computerized voice.

"Commander," the doctor's voice began, "perhaps it would be best to leave that conversation to the captain when he returns. I could use this time to get more detailed scans of her."

"Let's talk about that with my captain when he comes back, Rin," Sprit covered, withdrawing her hand from the girl's knee. "Now, uh, if it's okay with you, our doctor would like to take some more scans to make sure you're completely healthy." Rin suddenly looked cagey again, and she hurried to reassure the human. "No, it's fine. These scans are completely non-invasive procedures, and I promise you Balok is utterly harmless."

"Could…could you stay?" Rin asked softly, and Sprit nodded.

"Yeah, of course. Now, what do you say we get you back in bed?"

Rin gave a hollow smile and cautiously took Sprit's offered hand. It was rough and warm, battle-hardened, and the Ethonian pulled her to her feet with ease.

"Okay, you can just sit on the edge of the bed. I'll take the stool." As they took their positions, Sprit opened the door to shout to the desk. "Doc, we're waiting on you!"

"Yes, yes, I'm coming," a voice grumbled good-naturedly, and Rin watched with wide eyes as a heavy-set, middle-aged man walked in, all smiles and practically radiating comfort.

He had a smattering of tear-shaped freckles under each eye, and his skin had a ruddy, very tanned complexion to it. His wild mess of pale auburn curls only added to his overall youthful air, and Rin realized as she looked at him that those brightly colored eyes were somehow even more unsettling than they had been before now that she was more coherent.

His irises were a darker green with a blur of black lining that would have been pupils in anyone else. For Balok, however, his "pupils" were that lime green color instead, the circles large and almost completely dwarfing his darker irises. Within their circumferences were his actual pupils—three per eye.

He gave her a wide, toothless smile, and held out his hand.

"Hello, Rin. I'm Doctor Balok Itoya," he began, vigorously shaking Rin's tentative grasp, "but please feel free to call me Balok or doctor or any variation of those two that you'd like."

"O-okay," Rin stammered, and Sprit shot Balok a look to tell him to tone it down a bit. He either ignored it or didn't notice.

"Alright, well first off," he started, setting his bag down on the bed next to the wide-eyed girl, "I'm going to take a head to toe scan, and then I'll move on to more system specific exams. Does that sound okay?"

"Uh," Rin began, eyeing the many different scanners with open distrust. "I…"

"If it makes you feel more comfortable, I can perform the scans on Commander Matzepo first," Balok offered a bit too enthusiastically, and Sprit immediately sat up straight, giving the doctor a look that clearly said she was going to kill him when this was all over. "Well, like you said, commander, they *are* non-invasive procedures."

Sprit looked between the grinning doctor and the silently begging girl and groaned, rolling her eyes.

"Fine. It's not like I had my physical last week or anything."

"Splendid!"

Sprit threw Balok a doleful look at his loud, excited voice, and Rin smiled despite herself as the woman grumpily joined her on the opposite side of the bed.

"Alright, alright. Let's just get this over with."

———

Oren Galaxa had a headache.

No, it wasn't a headache. It was a migraine.

The captain gratefully sank back into his bed, supporting his head with a lopsided stack of pillows. He hadn't had a headache like this in months, which, he reluctantly admitted, was a miracle. But today…today was just one of those days. He sighed heavily and massaged his temples, replaying the report and subsequent hour-long conversation he'd just had to endure with Galactic Council President Lokar.

"Because I didn't already have enough bureaucrats trying to tell me how to do my job," he mumbled to no one, running his hands over his face before letting his arms thump down to his sides.

Starlight was treading on thin ice, and Oren knew it. They'd actually been having a good run for the last several months, successfully heading a few serial murder investigations before being transferred to their current assignment. Sprit's undercover operation had taken longer than they'd expected to get into full swing, but once it had, everything fell into place nicely. Byrone actually talked to his sister, for crying out loud. Sprit even cooperated with Holt long enough to plan and execute a flawless storming of the warehouse.

Well...flawless until the end. President Lokar had had a *lot* to say about how the job had ended, and he reluctantly reviewed the end of their heated conversation in his head.

It definitely could have gone better.

"Oren. I won't deny that you're a good captain, one of our best. And you've frankly been blessed with Hanali'a as your first officer. But the rest of your crew—"

"They're just as good as Han and me. They just need the time to get there."

"Time?" The politician's voice cracked with disbelief and static over the radio link. "Oren, you've had your ship for seventeen years, and you had a good crew until you rotated your staff for who knows what reason. Nearly all of your current officers hold ranks far above or in some cases below what they should. Case in point, your chief engineer is a lieutenant commander who's barely been serving long enough to qualify as a lieutenant!"

"Avery Byrone is a technical genius, Lokar," Oren returned, quickly losing his patience. "And what he lacks in experience he makes up for in promise. *Djienn*, he redesigned our entire energy network so we run more efficiently than any other ship in the fleet!"

"He's thirty-three."

"Hardly a child," the captain bit out, an awkward pause following.

"Alright then, what about the other end of the spectrum? Your deputy security chief is still a lieutenant after how many years? The man's forty-nine—"

"Lewis Holt's situation is unique, Lokar. I know you're *fully* aware of that fact," Oren replied with remarkable restraint, hand curling into a fist on his desk.

"What about your sister? You assured me she would calm down."

"Commander Matzepo is still a work in progress after all this time. I admit that," Oren continued, his tone carefully controlled. "But her unconventional approach has its merits. And when it doesn't, that's why I keep Holt as her second-in-command. They balance each oth—"

"And your doctor?" the voice challenged.

Oren's whole demeanor turned cold.

"Careful, Lokar," he warned, voice low. "Now you're treading on ice as thin as mine. Balok's illness will not be debilitating for another seven years—"

"But it eventually will be, and it is terminal." Lokar paused, his tone easing up slightly. "Oren, you have an assortment of characters on your ship. You approach things in inventive ways, and I respect that. But there comes a time when you have to admit you've made one too many mistakes. That last human you let stay on board? Daniel?" Oren looked down at his desk and ran a hand over the scars on his head. "Don't think I forgot about what happened to him *or* the fact that you didn't press charges against his killer. On the contrary, you kept her employed!"

"I won't discuss Lieutenant Anthia Acoua, Lokar. I made my decision concerning her a year ago, and I stand by it," the captain said firmly and took a deep, calming breath. "Lokar, listen. Let us handle the girl's relocation. Let us brief the Corps on the Tarikian underground. We *can* do our jobs."

"Fortunately for you," Lokar finally said after a long pause, his voice dripping with displeasure. "I have no say in this. Your recent record has easily impressed the Corps, enough to overlook the dirt in your past. But know this. If you mess up like you did on this last job one more time—"

"Sir, no one could've anticipated that outcome," Oren interrupted, finally done playing civil. "My crew did the best that they could, given the situation. I'm very proud of them for that, and, with all due respect, they don't need politicians like you beating them to death over it. We know we made a mistake. There are twenty-five civilian bodies in our morgue right now reminding us of that fact. We are aware. And you can be sure it won't happen again." A long, ringing silence dragged out between the two men, and Oren ruefully shook his head. "If there's nothing else, Mister President."

Lokar's reply was stiff and bitter and a godsend to Oren's ears.

"You're dismissed, Captain Oren."

Yeah, in reflection, he'd really stepped in it that time.

I'll have Hanali'a test the waters, see how much trouble I just put us in, he thought tiredly, eyes half-opening as he attempted to will his migraine away. *Can't be worse than last year.* He stopped and thought back to the words he and President Lokar had exchanged. *Okay, maybe it could be. I'll smooth this over somehow. It's just been a…very…long day.*

His headache was just starting to abate when his intercom chimed, and he reluctantly sat up, hitting the button beside the speaker inlaid into the wall at the head of his bed.

"Oren," he greeted, bracing his hands on his knees and looking up at the ceiling.

"Captain, we're ready for you in medbay," Balok's voice answered, and the captain stood up, stretching his back.

"Be right there, Balok. Oh, and doc?"

"Yes, captain?"

"Have something ready for a migraine, would you?"

"Of course, captain."

"Thank you, Balok. That'll be all." Oren turned off the intercom and headed for the door, shrugging the top of his jumpsuit back on over his under-armor as he went.

This day didn't look like it was getting any shorter.

"See? It wasn't that bad," Sprit said, sitting back down on her stool while Rin sat on the edge of the bed, gently swinging her legs back and forth. "And I told you Balok was harmless."

"He's…" Rin trailed off, trying to find the right word to describe the boisterous, sociable doctor.

"Intense?" Sprit offered, and the girl nodded.

"Yeah, that's…" She smiled softly at her swinging feet. "That's one way to put it."

"He grows on you. I notice you're talking more now," the woman pointed out, and Rin looked up.

"Well, what else am I going to do?" she replied, expression slightly more open but still carefully guarded.

"Fair enough." There was a distant hiss, and Sprit leaned forward to look over the now-open threshold of their room. "Hey, Oren."

The tired man lifted a hand to her in acknowledgement, and Balok looked up from where he was uploading Rin's scan results to his computer for further analysis.

"Another migraine?" he greeted cheerily. Oren grunted in response, and Balok beckoned him over, reaching into the med cabinet and withdrawing a couple of pills. "Here. You'll feel better in a few minutes, as you well know."

"Oren?" Rin asked, and Sprit turned to her.

"He's our captain. He can be a bit intimidating on first sight," she admitted. "He looks scary, but I promise he's just a big softie."

"You...talk about your captain like that?"

Sprit chuckled, an affectionate and distant light touching her eyes.

"Remember how I said I was a foster kid on Trozer?" Rin nodded. "Oren's family took me in and adopted me after a few months, which makes him my brother. Though let me tell you, sometimes he's more like a tired dad," she said with a smirk. "I can be a truly awful sister sometimes."

"I think it would be more accurate to say you manage to be a good sister sometimes."

Both Rin and Sprit looked to the doorway, and Rin's heart skipped a beat as she recognized the horned and scarred man from the warehouse. Sprit's smile turned into that broad, pirate grin of hers.

"You know you love me for it," she teased, absently tapping his leg.

Oren gave her a small smile that softened his ominous features and clasped his hands behind his back.

"Normally, I do. But when you get me into trouble with President Lokar..." He trailed off, and Sprit had the grace to look at least a little ashamed.

"Sorry, captain," she muttered, and Oren gently cupped the back of her head. Quite suddenly, Rin felt like she was looking at two much younger versions of the people before her.

"Don't worry. It wasn't *entirely* you," he assured her, and his hand moved to her shoulder in that same familiar way he'd tapped her elbow in the warehouse. "Han and I will deal with the fallout. We'll be fine."

A pointed silence followed in which Oren tilted his head to Rin, and Sprit quickly stood up.

"Right." She cleared her throat, wiping her palms on the sides of her pants. "Rin, this is Captain Oren Galaxa," she introduced, gesturing first to the Trozeran and then to the human. "Captain, this is Rin Cooper of Montana."

"Rin?" Oren echoed, extending his hand to the girl, and Rin took it as she nodded. His skin was rough like Sprit's but didn't seem as warm. "An interesting name."

"My mom chose it," she replied quietly and dropped her gaze uncertainly as she released his hand. "Said it was my dad's friend."

"Well then, your father's friend has an interesting name," he replied easily, and the girl allowed herself a small smile.

Sprit was right. The captain did seem a lot less scary after he spoke to her, though the black uniform, scars, and broken horn still didn't help him out very much. There was something about him.... Something tired and worn in those eyes that said he'd seen some things.

"Well, Rin—may I sit?"

Rin nodded, scooting over on the bed until she reached the head of the mattress, and Oren gave her a brief, toothless smile as he took his position at the foot of the bed. He angled his body towards her, trying to make his posture as unintimidating as possible. Surprisingly, it wasn't that hard, Rin realized. His stature wasn't that imposing on its own.

"I assume that Sprit answered most of your questions?" Rin nodded. "Good. Is there anything else you wanted to ask?"

Let's talk about that with my captain when he comes back, Rin.

"Um," Rin began softly and cleared her throat. "When...when can I go home?" She looked up at the two people before her hopefully, and something flipped uneasily in her stomach as Sprit looked down and Oren's open expression grew muted. "I-I want to go home."

"Sprit," Oren said lowly, turning slightly towards his subordinate. "Could you give us a moment?"

"Yes, sir."

The playful, sarcastic levity was gone from her voice, and Rin watched with growing concern as the woman turned to leave. She gave Rin a quick, apologetic smile as she closed the door behind her, and the room fell quiet for a few moments. Rin slowly shifted her focus from the empty glass door Sprit had vanished through to the uncomfortable man beside her. And, inexplicably, she felt angry.

"I want to go home," she repeated, a hard note entering her warbling voice. Oren was now looking at her with open pity.

"Let us handle the girl's relocating," I said, he thought bitterly and hid a sigh. *Well, I sure got what I asked for.*

"I know you do," he began, easily keeping his voice calm and neutral. He'd had this conversation more times than he'd ever wanted. "But I'm afraid that we can't do that." Rin stared at him, uncomprehending, and he continued in the bluntest way he could. "I'm afraid we can't take you home."

CHAPTER 6

"What?" Rin blurted, heart frozen in her chest. "Why?!"

"Rin—"

"Why?" she all but shouted, heart suddenly restarting at a break-neck pace. She felt caged in, terrified. Outside, Balok grew sorrowful as Sprit tensely crossed her arms over her chest.

"Rin," Oren repeated placatingly and mentally reviewed all the information Balok had given him outside, quickly calculating his next step. "You were kept in cryofreeze after your abduction. It's a process of—"

"I know what cryofreeze is. I've seen sci-fi movies before," Rin interrupted, voice shaking with a bewildering swirl of emotions. Oren simply nodded, refusing to rise to her bait.

"Okay." His voice was infuriatingly calm and sympathetic. "Based off Doctor Balok's readings and the Tarikian records we found, you were taken from your home almost ten Earth months ago."

"So? I-I have to get *home*—"

"Rin." She stopped talking, and he continued. "You were abducted. That leaves no traces, no explanations." She unblinkingly held his gaze. "You've been gone for ten months," he repeated, trying to get his point across as gently as possible. "They no doubt think you're dead by this point. If we bring you home now, what will you tell them? How will you explain where you've been?"

Rin looked down, picking at the hem of her shirt.

"Are..." Rin cleared her throat and clenched her trembling hands in her lap, willing them to be still. "I can *never* go home?" When she looked up at Oren, he could see nothing but that anguish he'd seen in black site system abductees time and time again. And his heart broke for her.

"I'm sorry," he said sincerely. "Truly, I am."

"My grandmother, she's all alone," Rin pressed, dangerously close to begging. "I'm all she has. I can't leave her alone!"

"Rin—"

"She'd never give up on me!" she interrupted, fully pleading with the captain before her. "You don't know her. She's still looking for me!"

"You *cannot* go home." Oren winced at the louder, harsher edge to his voice and sighed. Rin quickly looked back to her feet, her shoulders stooping. Her legs had long since stopped swinging, that air of innocence lost. Now, she just looked small and washed out in the room's cold lighting. "We have people you can talk to about this," he continued, far more gently than before, "to figure out what comes next."

His heart twinged painfully at the hollow, defeated expression on the girl's face as she looked up at him.

"Can I at least go back to Earth?" she asked, the words hopelessly hopeful, and Oren turned away from her, leaning forward to brace his forearms on his knees.

"We've…tried that with other people similar to yours," he said softly, deep voice rumbling in his chest. "It's rarely worked out."

"But *why?*" Rin's voice shook, and she felt herself lurch dangerously close to tears. "It's my *home——*"

"Because planets like yours are small places that are intimately connected, Rin." He paused as she wiped at her eyes and took in a deep breath to counter the rising tears. "Someone somewhere will eventually see you. And you'll have some impossible explaining to do."

Oren was trying. Rin knew he was. He'd treated her kindly, spoken gently. But there was no making this better.

"I just want to go home," she whispered, her voice finally shattering. She pulled her feet up onto the mattress with her and drew her legs up to her chest, burying her face in the bony tangle of knees and arms.

Oren sighed and reached out to touch her arm only to think better of it at the last second. Reluctantly, he pulled his hand back to his lap and stood up.

"I'll leave you alone now, Rin," he said softly. The girl gave no indication that she'd heard him.

He waited a few moments before heading to the door, watching the human with pitying eyes. This was going to be a rough transition, but they had experience with it. He could think of a few colonies off the top of his head where she might fit in. He'd just have to convince her that it wasn't the end of the world.

"Balok will be outside if you need anything. Don't hesitate to ask."

The door slid open and shut, and Rin was alone with her thoughts.

Outside, Oren groaned and pinched the bridge of his nose as he rejoined his two waiting officers.

"That didn't sound so good," Sprit muttered as he sat, and he wearily shook his head. "It was an impressive amount of shouting for her."

"She's understandably upset," he said and waved his sister towards Rin's room. "You may want to go talk to her."

"Yeah, captain, will do." She clapped a hand on his shoulder as she headed off to the quarantine room, and Oren turned to Balok.

"Did anything come up on her scans?" The doctor's expression remained rather grave, and Oren groaned again, leaning against the edge of the desk at Balok's elbow. "We just can't catch a break, can we?"

"No, it seems we cannot," the medic agreed, reaching for the computer's touch screen and quickly pulling up information. "Here's what I've found…."

Rin looked up with red, watery eyes as the door slid open, and Sprit gently knocked on the jamb.

"Can I come in?"

Rin scooted over to the center of the bed in reply, resting her back against the wall behind her, and Sprit took the silent gesture as an invitation. She eased the door shut behind her and silently joined the human on the narrow mattress, their shoulders touching.

"Do you want to talk?" Rin mutely shook her head, her composure wavering. "Okay. Is it alright if I just sit here?"

Rin looked at the woman beside her, taking in her empathetic half smile and relaxed posture. Everything radiated comfort and safety, and as Rin thought back to everything Sprit had done so far, aside from shooting her, she found herself nodding.

"Great," the officer said, and they promptly lapsed into silence.

They sat that way for a long time, Rin tense and shaking while Sprit was wholly at ease, until finally it was too much. The woman jumped as the girl suddenly started sobbing, her hands helplessly touching the implants behind her ears as she rested her forehead against her knees. Sprit sighed.

"You're okay," she said gently, tenderly tucking Rin's hair behind her ears and out of her face. "You're gonna be alright."

She gently rubbed circles into the girl's quaking back, noting with concern that she could trace out every bone of her spine and ribs. The crying continued, and after several minutes Sprit finally wrapped her arm around Rin's shoulders. Tentatively, she pulled the girl close, and Rin let herself move with the motion, allowing her knees to fall into Sprit's lap and doubling her arms over her stomach as she cried harder. She buried her face into Sprit's shoulder and tried to block out the world.

"You're okay, Rin," she repeated softly, and her heart broke as the human tucked herself into her smaller frame. "I promise this is all gonna work out just fine, kiddo."

Rin closed her eyes and focused on the slow heartbeat beneath her ear, trying to find comfort in the somewhat familiar sound and the touch of soft fabric beneath her cheek. This she could ground herself in. With her eyes closed, she could pretend that Sprit was just human, that she was safe somewhere on Earth waiting for her grandmother to come pick her up from this nightmare. But the moment her eyes opened....

Sprit sighed and held the girl tighter, moving one hand up to gently run through Rin's hair.

Yep, the adult thought dryly. *This is definitely part of my job description.*

Outside, Oren was looking at his chief medical officer incredulously.

"You have got to be kidding me, doctor."

"On the contrary, I'm being utterly serious," Balok replied, pointing to the screens. "This genetic anomaly is spread throughout her entire system. It's not just a fluke. Admittedly, we only have ten human specimens to compare them to—"

"Balok, don't call them specimens," Oren interrupted, hand going to the bridge of his nose once more, but the doctor just kept talking.

"Well, regardless, I'm confident enough to say I don't believe Miss Cooper is nearly as human as she thinks she is."

Oren eyed the man carefully.

"How confident is confident enough?"

Balok looked at him in mild affront.

"I am as confident in saying that she's not human as I am in saying that you're Trozeran." Oren gave him a reprimanding look, and Balok grumbled. "Oh, alright. If she *is* entirely human, and mind you, that is a rather large if, then she's first in a new line of human evolution, which is an astonishing privilege to witness—"

"Which is more likely?" Oren interrupted, holding up a hand to stem the increasingly excited rambling. Balok reluctantly pulled himself back on track.

"I'm inclined to say interspecies, *but* you never know," he said with a surreptitious smile. "Expect the unexpected."

"Don't I always on this ship?" Oren muttered under his breath.

"A sound practice, to be sure," Balok agreed, and the captain gave him an unimpressed look. "Well, you said it yourself, we tend to be an accident-prone vessel," he continued defensively. "I'm sure Lokar backed us up on that assessment."

"Don't remind me." He sighed and ran a hand over his scars. "And speaking of Lokar, I have to go talk to Hanali'a." He started towards the exit. "Tell Sprit when she's done in there that she's housing the human—the whatever she is—until we sort this mess out."

"Yes, sir," Balok said, closing the files on their mysterious guest's genetic anomaly. Oren stopped just before the main doors and looked back to the doctor.

"And Balok?"

"Hm?"

"Let's keep this parentage information to ourselves for now."

Balok respectfully inclined his head.

"As you wish, captain. My lips are sealed." He gave a toothless grin to prove his point, and Oren shook his head as he left.

His crew really was at a different level of ridiculous today.

Back in the quarantine room, Rin was finally starting to calm down. That or she was running out of tears, Sprit wasn't sure which it was. Either way, she was slowly quieting, and the redhead retracted her arm as the teenager pushed away from her to sit up.

"You feeling a little better?" Rin morosely shook her head. "Hey. It can't be all bad, right? I mean, look around. You're in *space*. You're going where no—well, few—humans have gone before."

Rin scoffed and scrubbed at her sore eyes, clearly unimpressed.

"I don't *want* to 'go where no man has gone before.'"

"Fair enough," Sprit sighed and awkwardly scratched the back of her neck. "I suppose I wasn't exactly happy when they moved me to Trozer, either."

Rin gave no reply to her personal insight, and Sprit inwardly groaned as they went quiet once more. Now what?

The Ethonian absently drummed her fingers on her leg, trying to think up something else to offer. She came up empty. But just when she was about to tap out and get Balok in the room, Rin's stomach let out a loud growl. The girl instantly flushed and found something of immense interest in her shirt hem. Sprit, on the other hand, was ecstatic.

Food. I can handle food.

"You're probably hungry, huh?"

"A little," Rin reluctantly admitted, not looking at Sprit.

"Want to get something to eat?"

That would mean leaving the room, even leaving the medbay, Rin realized. Her stomach flipped nauseatingly, and she looked at the main doors through her glass threshold with no small amount of trepidation.

"Sure?"

"Great." Sprit hopped off the bed, rubbing her hands together, and Rin cautiously exited after her. "Hey, Balok, I'm taking Rin to get food."

"Have fun," he replied without looking up from his screens, and his two guests were almost out the door when the doctor seemed to register what had just been said. "Wait, what?" He looked up and spun his chair around. "Commander!"

Sprit turned back at his admonishing shout.

"What?"

Balok scoffed and pointed to Rin.

"I would think she'd like some clothes or at the very least *shoes.*"

"Oh, right." Sprit opened one of the tall cabinets lining the wall and pulled out some spare uniforms, flipping through them until she found an ensign's that was roughly the girl's size. "Hey, catch." She tossed it to Rin and, as the human fumbled with the navy jumpsuit, hung the others up in the closet again. "You can change in the quarantine room. Just hit the small white button on the doorframe, and the glass will tint."

She watched the girl retreat to the room they'd just left, feeling Balok staring at her bemusedly from his desk. She crossed her arms, side-eyeing him.

"Taking our barefooted, scrub-clad human to the cafeteria without having her change…. It really has been a long day, hasn't it?" he teased. Sprit scowled.

"You have *no* idea how draining it is to keep acting like Holt. Don't judge me," she hissed back, and Balok frowned, nonplussed.

"Now, why would you go do a thing like that?"

"Because *Sprit* made her scream and freak out!" she said, jerking a thumb at the now-tinted door. "Holt's always been better at handling this sort of thing."

"Well, Oren asked *you* to take care of her, not Holt," the doctor said pointedly with a reassuring smile. "I'm sure he had his reasons for that. Now that she's adjusted a bit, why don't you try being you?"

"That…won't go over well."

"Suit yourself," he shrugged. "By the way, she'll be staying in your quarters for the foreseeable future."

"What?! Balok—"

"*Captain's* orders," he said with that mischievous smile as he walked to the closet and pulled out a pair of black canvas shoes. "Who knows, you may find you enjoy having a roommate again."

"Not really!"

Before they could argue further, the door slid open and Rin walked out, pulling a little uncomfortably at the sleeves of the uniform.

"Too tight?" Balok asked, handing her the slip-on shoes.

Rin shook her head as she sat on the floor to put them on.

"It's just a little loose."

As soon as she was done, Sprit offered her a hand and pulled her to her feet.

"Alright, now we're ready to go." She propelled the human toward the door. "We'll see you around, Balok."

"Have fun," he called, paying attention as he said the words this time, and waved goodbye to his two patients. He sighed contently as the door swished open and closed and turned back to his computers. "Well, the two of them will certainly enjoy themselves." He looked with a broad smile at the tick in the sealed vial at his elbow. "Wouldn't you agree, my little friend?"

Rin looked around with wide eyes, heart in her throat.

"So right now, we're on deck three. The medbay, which is where we just were, is at the bow of the ship under the bridge," Sprit rambled, unsure of what else to do with her guest. "These rooms we're passing here are crew quarters, and actually most of those are on this deck."

Rin wasn't listening. The people they were passing—the wide variety of skin colors and textures, horns, hair, fur, baldness, multiple limbs, ridges and spots, no noses, no eyes, several eyes, no mouths, sometimes combinations of all of the above—they all transfixed her with a sense of wonder and horror at the same time. Some of them, they looked almost human. Others...others looked like they were wholly alien with features that were more similar to insects or amphibians or in some cases large cats like lions and jaguars. And Rin was overcome.

"The cafeteria is on the deck below us, so we'll have to get to the lift at the end of the hall," Sprit continued, grabbing Rin's elbow and pulling her out of the way as someone left his quarters, carrying a crate of wiring and spare parts.

The girl almost gasped, her breath freezing in her chest.

It was one of those lizard people, those *Tarikians*—

"Hey, Ensign Omarik," the redhead greeted, briefly waving as she continued to pull Rin on their way. "He's harmless, kid, relax."

"Hello, Commander," Talik returned, heart racing as he tightened his grip on the box in his hands. *That was close. I have to bring this to Jhama.... I finished my part of the transmission....*

"Not *all* Tarikians are bad, Cooper," Sprit admonished, shaking her head as Talik rushed past them down the hall. Rin flushed and looked down. "I mean, some of them are jerks, like the traffickers you met, but every species has those people."

They rounded a corner, and the woman groaned, coming to a stop and touching Rin's elbow.

"I forgot the boiler room was this way." She turned to Rin. "Oh well, might as well show it to you. Okay, kid, that door up ahead is the boiler room. It's where we keep our back-up life support generators and our water heaters, tanks, and pumps. We route all piping and valves through there from engineering, too. And it's very loud. And hot. And a little on the humid side." She laughed at the human's uncomfortable expression. "Yeah, you and me both. Come on."

Rin felt something uneasy building in her gut as they approached the heavy, imposing glass door at the end of the hall. It was easily six inches thick, reinforced with what looked like steel. There was no handle or knob that she could see, only another one of those panels like the ones in the medbay, except this one also had a keypad. That uneasy feeling continued to grow, the hairs on the back of her neck standing on end as they finally reached the barricade of a door.

"It's soundproofed," Sprit explained as she entered her authorization code. "That way people can actually talk to each other and sleep on this deck." She paused before she entered the last digit. "Fair warning, the noise kind of hits you like a wall when you open the door."

"Why the passcode?" Rin asked, rubbing her arms to try to get rid of the crawling sensation. Sprit waved her unspoken anxiety away.

"It's just a security measure. Like I said, the room's got our back-up life support generators and water processing and distribution systems."

She entered the last number of her code, and the door swung open. Immediately, Rin winced, clapping her hands over her ears as a sharp whine emitted from her implants. Her partner grimaced at the din, unaware of the piercing sound the human was hearing.

"Yeah," she said loudly, quickly walking in with Rin behind her. "I warned you."

As soon as they were out of the way, the door swung shut quickly, and Rin looked at the surprisingly large hexagonal room. Each wall had one of those heavy glass doors, and the space was filled with tanks, pipes, and large squares with multiple different warning labels on them that she couldn't read. She assumed they were the generators. Like Sprit had said, it was very hot. She could see condensation running down the sides of some of the metal panels, along with wisps of steam at some of the seams and vents. It was a cacophony of tarnished chrome and uncomfortable heat, and Rin could barely hear her footsteps on the diamond plate floors as Sprit quickly pulled her through the space to the door at the far end of the room. A few people waved to the commander as she passed, but she was too focused on getting out of there to notice.

"Almost out," she shouted as she quickly entered her code again into the interior panel, and the door promptly opened. Gratefully, the two stepped outside. Rin slowly lowered her hands from her ears as the heavy door closed behind them, and the world was a more reasonable volume once more.

"Do you *always* have to go through there?" Rin asked, rubbing the skin around her implants, and Sprit shook her head as she started off down the hall once more.

"No, there are other routes, but I'm used to taking this one." The human hurried to catch up, falling into step beside her. "It's the shortest to the lift, and I've got places to be." Sprit noticed the girl was close enough that their shoulders bumped with every step, and her dark eyes were fixed on the floor.

She's probably just a little nervous.

And the woman had to admit, it was impressive Rin hadn't crashed into any of the crew passing by. Yet. She should keep an eye on that.

They reached the lift, and she pressed the down button.

"Okay, so the cafeteria is right after engineering once we're on deck four," she said.

The girl absently nodded, engrossed in her surroundings, and her focus shifted down the hall to her right where it turned out of view.

"What's down there?"

"Auxiliary control," Sprit answered, following her gaze. "If anything happens to the bridge, we can control *Starlight* from there."

There was a soft *ding* as the elevator arrived, and the doors opened to reveal another alien—this one pushing a cart of metal boxes. Rin nearly jumped, and her heart leapt into her throat at their tentacled face and thick, trunk-like limbs.

"Lieutenant," Sprit greeted and pulled Rin out of the way by her elbow as her subordinate exited the lift.

Her slower-moving crewmate nodded to her, and Sprit stepped into the lift behind them, pulling her stunned, gawking roommate after her. She pressed the icon for deck four and leaned back against the wall as the doors closed, and they started to descend.

"I can think of a few foods for you to try out," she offered, and Rin looked at her with wide eyes. "I promise I won't grab anything too spicy or too bitter or sweet or anything for your first meal. Maybe some kind of bread or fruit."

"Uh, s-sounds good," she said softly, and Sprit smiled.

They came to a stop, and the doors opened with another soft *ding*.

"Alright, last stretch."

Sprit led the way into the hall, Rin following practically at her heel. They were nearing a large glass segment of wall on the hall's right-hand side, and the girl's mouth opened in a soft gasp as she saw what was on the other side, far below them. Slowly and breathlessly, Rin broke away from her guide and approached the guardrail that lined the viewing panel, and Sprit watched the human gingerly rest her hands along the metal bar as she gazed into the bustling room beneath them. Slowly she joined her, leaning forward with her forearms crossed on the railing.

"Welcome to engineering."

Four massive cylinders stood in the middle of the hangar-sized room, each one housing an immense coil. Strange, blue light pulsated from the tubes' interiors, reflecting off the many catwalks and access platforms that extended around them and marked the upper reaches of the space. Dozens of large monitors and complex computer consoles lined the walls opposite and below Sprit and Rin, and scores of people supervised their data and readings. They were all dressed in the same navy uniform, but the shoulder pads varied—yellow, green, red, white, and blue. The narrower walls at either end of the large chamber were covered in piping and wiring, and Rin wondered if any of them ran to the boiler room or maybe auxiliary control. Unlike the former of those two places, the glass of the observation wall wasn't ridiculously thick. In fact, it was probably only half the depth, and Rin realized she could hear a faint sound thrum in time with the coils' pulsating light beyond the transparent barrier.

"What're those coils?" she asked, pointing, and looked to Sprit.

"Internal engine components; they're our beating heart. See, we have an FTL, or faster-than-light, drive with seven traveling and three docking and maneuvering speeds. It's actually fueled by…" She trailed off as Rin's confused frown deepened and gave a quiet huff of laughter. "You know what? You don't really need to know how it works." She leaned closer to the glass and looked up to the room's ceiling. "*But*, if the mood ever does strike you, you can always ask our friendly neighborhood engineer for some more detail."

She lopsidedly grinned and waved at something near the ceiling.

"What are you—" Rin broke off with a yelp as a lanky person suddenly dropped into view, bracing himself on the glass with one hand.

Sprit just laughed, clapping Rin on the shoulder as she gave a careless salute to the upside-down young man. Like everyone else, he was in a jumpsuit, though his was a little stained and had white shoulder pads. He mirrored Sprit's grin and waved to the two of them before touching his earwig and speaking into it. Rin gaped at him, fascinated.

Sprit touched her own comm device as the tinny voice announced *"Avery Byrone."*

"How's engineering looking, Avery?" she asked.

"Like she's perfect, Sprit," their upside-down companion replied and effortlessly moved a little lower onto the glass like a gecko before righting himself so he was eyelevel with his guests. "We've had no problems with the energy supply we picked up from Othlu's moon."

"Good. We don't need any more problems today, am I right?"

"Yes, ma'am," he laughed and then looked at Rin. Sharp, painful sadness knifed through him as he quickly placed the out-of-place teenager as human. "Hi." He waved to her, keeping his knees and other hand firmly pressed against the glass.

Cautiously, Rin returned the gesture, and that brilliant smile lit up the engineer's face once more.

Avery looked about as human as Holt did, Rin noted, except his skin was marble-white, without blemish. His inky black hair matched his monochrome eyes—eyes that, Rin noticed, had no discernible irises or pupils and almost glittered in the ship's lighting. He had no other alien features to him except for a dark, charcoal-colored, narrow ridge that adorned his features in a continuous contour, like a ribbon. It started at the bridge of his nose, rising in a V-shape to end in parallel points at his temples before running back down to his ears where they branched once more. One trail ended shortly after, just below his cheekbone, while the other continued behind his ear and vanished below his collar. Rin couldn't be sure, but it seemed to be made of layered scales—almost like miniature plates of armor.

Avery returned his focus to Sprit.

"Can I talk to her?"

"Yeah, hold on." She pulled her earwig out and wiped it off on her sleeve before handing it to the girl. She took it, nonplussed, and Sprit pointed to the young engineer. "Avery wants to talk to you."

"Oh, uh..." She uncertainly lifted the device to her ear and put it in—her fingers hovering by it, ready to rip it out at a moment's notice.

Avery just continued to smile, the expression sincere and reassuring. He knew how alone she was feeling as a human stranded in space, thanks to Daniel. And, also thanks to Daniel, he knew one of the best ways to make her feel a little better.

"Hello, there."

Rin's eyes widened. His mouth—it'd matched the words he'd said.

"H-hi," she stammered, slowly smiling. "You speak English!"

Avery nodded, quickly trying to pull words from his memory.

"Yes, I learned some from a…friend." Once more that sadness hit him, and he cleared his throat. "What do you think of *Starlight?*"

"It's…" Rin paused, her relaxing expression faltering a little. "It takes some getting used to."

"Well, I promise we don't bite." Some shouted Avery's name from below, and he turned to look down, leaning away from the glass and letting one arm hang at his side. "Be right down!" He looked back to his superior and the girl. "I'll see you two around."

With that, he stood up and, as Rin watched, gaping, walked along the wall—completely horizontal and disobeying the laws of gravity.

"*What?*" She pulled out the earwig and turned to Sprit, demanding an explanation with her stunned expression. "How is he…*what?*"

Sprit just laughed, taking the earwig from her dazedly extended hand and putting it back in.

"Avery can manipulate the gravity field around his specific person if he so chooses. It's really quite helpful for his career field. He gets repairs done two, three times as fast as his more experienced counterparts."

"Wait. You." Rin pointed a wavering finger at Sprit as the still-laughing woman put an arm around her back and guided them towards the cafeteria. "You can turn invisible. I remember now, at that auction place, you turned *invisible.*"

"Nah, I just camouflage," she returned off-handedly. "There's nothing as fancy as invisibility here, kiddo." She squeezed the girl's shoulder. "Now come on. Let's actually get something to eat."

CHAPTER 7

Sprit looked at the human hunched over on the edge of her bed. Rin had her head in her hands and her elbows on her knees, pointedly avoiding the older woman's stare.

"Well, *that* didn't go so well, did it?" Sprit asked sarcastically, and Rin apologetically flinched. "Lesson learned—don't take people new to aliens into a loud, crowded cafeteria full of aliens."

"Sorry," Rin groaned, looking up as Sprit nudged her with a plate of food. The officer had managed to snag it from the mess hall while hurrying Rin back out into the hallway with several apologies and rueful, forced smiles to her startled crewmates.

"Don't worry about it," the woman chuckled. "It was honestly one of the more entertaining things I've seen in a while." She dragged her desk chair over and sat down in front of the girl. "I don't think I've seen that many people simultaneously choke on their food and go to draw their weapons before."

"I didn't *mean* to scream! I just turned around and that tentacle guy from before was right there, and—"

"Rin, Rin," Sprit interrupted, halting her rambling with a laugh, "it's *fine*. Don't worry about it." She indicated the food. "I figured you might like that. It's some bread and this fruit called *iyelno*. It's very juicy, so watch out when you bite into it. It tends to splash. The inside is practically water, but it's very high in electrolytes and other ions. The skin's not that bad for you either, but it is a bit tough."

Rin picked up the rough-skinned fruit, running her fingers over the pale green and brown surface.

"Is it sweet, bitter, or…?"

"Sweet. Go on, give it a try."

Rin cautiously bit into the peach-sized fruit, finding that she had to bite down a little harder than she'd originally expected to break the skin. But once she did, a bunch of liquid sprayed out, and she gave a small yelp as it splashed over herself and her host. She gratefully accepted the napkin Sprit handed her and wiped herself off.

"Like I said, they're a bit messy."

"It's good," Rin smiled, taking a second, more cautious bite of the iyelno.

"The bread, I've been told, is the same as your Earth bread, though Daniel always said it was on the sour side." She sat back and watched as the girl ravenously ate the plate of food. "It's been a while since you ate anything, huh?"

"I…I guess nine months?"

There was a long, awkward silence.

"You know what, I'm gonna go get you more food." Sprit stood up and headed to the door. "Don't get into more trouble while I'm gone."

Once she'd left, Rin took the opportunity to look at her new quarters a little more closely. It was surprisingly spartan given Sprit's personality. Everything was neat and orderly, from her immaculately made bed to her pristine bedside table and desk. If she opened the sliding closet and bathroom doors, Rin was almost positive it would be just as carefully laid out as the rest of the room. She made her way over to the nightstand and gingerly picked up a small metal object that looked a bit like a coaster. There was a small black button on its edge, and as she pressed it, a white holographic image projected above the disk. It looked a lot like those three-dimensional laser crystals she'd seen a few times back on Earth. It took a moment for her to place the people in it, but once she did, she was quite surprised.

It was Oren and Sprit, both of them much younger. They were clad in combinations of leather, metals, fabrics, and, in the case of Sprit's hair, feathers. The security chief couldn't have been more than thirteen years old, but much to Rin's surprise, Oren didn't seem that different. Yes, there was something more youthful to his eyes—fewer creases at their corners, a noticeable lack of scars on his forehead. Both of his horns were still intact. But despite the holophoto being at least thirty years old, the passage of time just didn't seem all too visible on the captain, and Rin wondered just how long Trozerans lived in the first place. He was giving Sprit a piggyback ride, and the teen's arms were wrapped around his horns, pushing him slightly forward and off-balance. They were grinning at each other over Oren's shoulder, caught in an innocent and pure moment, completely unaware of the photographer.

Rin pressed the button again and set the deactivated device back in its place.

Next, she moved to the two doors along the wall just inside the entrance, curiosity getting the better of her. Her host had pointed them out when they'd walked in, saying generally that they were her bathroom and closet without actually specifying which was which.

She picked the one closest to the main door and found that it was a manually sliding door, unlike the entrance's. The metal glided smoothly on its tracks to reveal a closet full of a haphazard combination of civilian and work clothing.

"Probably a good idea it's a manual door," she muttered, thinking aloud as she went to close it again. "It would suck to not be able to get dressed because the power's out."

But just before she shut the closet, she caught a glimpse of something metallic glinting through the fabric. Frowning, she pushed a few of the hangars out of the way—some things, it seemed, were universal—to see what it was.

Her heart stopped.

"Oh my god," Rin blurted, quickly shoving the clothes back where they belonged and closing the door.

"Anthia!" Sprit's voice shouted in the hall, and Rin looked to the bedroom door with a jolt of panic. "Tell Oren I'll be a little late. I'm almost done sorting out our guest situation."

Rin quickly returned to the bed, sitting down on the mattress just as the door opened and Sprit rejoined her.

"So, I grabbed some grain-based pudding stuff and some assorted berries, I guess? I'm not quite sure what I grabbed, but it looked good, so." She shrugged and held the plate out to the girl. Rin gratefully took it, and Sprit frowned slightly as she took in her tense posture and skittish air. "You looked in the closet, didn't you?"

Rin looked up, torn between relief that she didn't have to bring it up herself and fear over the woman's response.

"I was trying to see which was the bathroom, and I picked the wrong one," she explained apologetically, speaking nearly too fast for Sprit to follow. "You have *a lot* of guns."

Sprit crossed her arms defensively.

"Well, they're not *all* guns." The human listened in fear-tinged bemusement as she picked at the mystery food Sprit had grabbed. "Some of them are knives and stun batons and other stuff, but that's beside the point. I'm the *security chief*, Rin. I test new equipment out, and I keep my own personal arsenal because you never know when you might need it."

"So, rule number one of living here is don't—"

"Go into my closet, yeah," Sprit finished with her and pointed to the small, dark curtains above her desk. "And I probably wouldn't look out that window for a little while, at least not until you're acclimated to the whole aliens and space thing."

"Out there?" Rin clarified, pointing. "Is that—"

"Space? Yep. Oh! There's an observation room on deck two that I could take you to tomorrow if you like. It's certainly one way to get into the whole space travel thing." Sprit walked to her desk and turned on the terminal, going through the touch screen interface at a bewildering pace until she reached the display she wanted.

"Sorry, I'm being a rude host," she said without looking to her disoriented guest. "It's just my shift started ten minutes ago, and I need to put in my log that I'll be late.... There we go." She finished what she was typing before closing out of the windows and turning around. "Okay, if I take any longer, the captain's gonna kill me, so I should get going."

She opened one of her drawers and pulled out her belt and holster, strapping both around her body and making sure that her weapon was still secure. Rin watched with wide eyes as she opened the closet and pushed her clothes out of the way to pull something out from the back corner. She turned to the human, waving the item in her hand.

"See? Knife."

Sprit quickly knelt and pulled up the hem of her pants, slipping the blade into the scabbard sewn into the inside of her boot. Once she was sure it was secure, she stood up and did a quick inventory, touching her ear and glancing back at her desk as she muttered to herself. Satisfied, she looked at her charge and gave a brief afterthought of a smile.

"Okay, well, do you need anything else? I'm due up on the bridge, and I'll be gone for the next seven hours."

Rin stared for several long moments in silence, trying to think of something to say.

"Uh...I...no?"

"Okay, great. Um, there are cups in the nightstand drawer, and you can get water from the sink in the bathroom. Try not to wander, but if you do and inevitably get lost, just ask the computer how to get back to my room, and you'll be fine." She left in a whirlwind, and Rin was left sitting there on the bed, dumbstruck. Suddenly the door opened again, and Sprit leaned over the threshold.

"By the way, if you decide to get some sleep, which I do recommend, watch out for the knife I have taped to the back of the headboard. See you after work."

Rin listened to her running footsteps retreat down the hall as the door closed and took in a long, slow breath before carefully releasing it.

"She's a little crazy," she whispered to the empty room.

The silence seemed to agree with her.

Oren idly checked the time on the arm of his captain's chair as the bridge doors swished open behind him, and Sprit hurried over to her station to the left of doors as she entered. A few of the other officers smirked to each other, hiding laughs behind tactfully raised hands.

"Sorry I'm late, captain," she said breathlessly, tying off her braid as she finished redoing it. "I was just getting our human guest settled."

Oren turned his chair slightly so he could look at her.

"How is she?"

"A little better, sir," she said, turning on her security displays. "She just finished eating."

"Good." He began swiveling his chair back to its original position but stopped. "And for future reference, commander, if you're tending to a guest, you can miss your entire shift for all I care. However, I expect you to notify me if—"

"I'll be late—yes, sir," Sprit interrupted, finally catching her breath and giving him a brief flash of a smile. He stared at her disapprovingly, and she cleared her throat. "Sorry, sir. Won't happen again."

"I would hope not." He faced forwards again and gazed at the stars beyond the transparent wall of their bridge. "Lieutenant Acoua, could you fill Commander Matzepo in on our shift schedule?"

Sprit turned in her seat to look at the woman at the station across the room from her. She looked exactly like Avery, except instead of ridges she had spots of the same charcoal gray color that followed the same path. Her hair was drawn into a tight bun that sat low at the back of her head, and unlike her brother, there was a stern, cold air to her. She rotated her chair to look at Sprit, her posture stiff and imposing despite her small stature as she adjusted her headset.

"We'll rendezvous with *Horizon* and Captain Tzo in a couple hours, ma'am. You should tell your people to get the auction arrestees ready for a prisoner transfer."

Sprit nodded, quickly pulling up her log and entering the event into the daily schedule.

"Where's the ship taking them?"

"Prison colony on Anvers to await trial."

"Thanks, Anthia." Sprit tapped her earwig. "Lewis Holt."

"Yes, commander?" her deputy's voice answered momentarily, and she smirked.

"That was fast. I thought you were off duty."

Immediately, Oren turned around to look at his sister.

"Is Holt still awake?" he demanded, and Sprit cringed. "I *told* him to get some rest."

"Yeah, you're busted, Holt," she muttered under her breath, and her deputy nearly groaned. "Captain knows you didn't go to bed."

"I...was *about* to, ma'am, I just—"

"Oren Galaxa," his earwig interrupted, and in his quarters, Holt tiredly pinched the bridge of his nose and set his reports to the side.

"Yes, sir?" he answered, hoping his annoyance wasn't audible.

"Lieutenant, go to *bed*," Oren ordered, exasperated. "Sprit will hand off the assignment to one of the other security officers."

Holt felt a distant urge to roll his eyes and took a deep, diplomatic breath instead.

"Understood, sir."

"*Bed*, Lewis," the captain repeated before closing the channel and giving Sprit a pointed look warning her not to try anything.

Once he was facing forward again, Sprit cautiously turned to her console and lowered her voice to a whisper.

"You still there, Holt?"

"Yes, ma'am."

"Complete prison transfer to *Horizon* in two hours. Got it?"

"Yes, ma'am."

She closed the channel and subtly glanced over her shoulder to see Oren watching her, thoroughly annoyed.

"Really, Sprit?"

"He was already awake!" she said defensively and quickly pressed on when her boss opened his mouth to argue. "Oh, come on, you *know* he wasn't gonna go to sleep."

Oren grumbled to himself and faced forward again.

"Everyone's a mutineer, today," he sighed, shaking his head. "Alright, commander, go *properly* brief your deputy." Sprit nodded her thanks and quickly re-contacted her subordinate. "Anthia, I want you contact Tzo and tell her she'll be dealing with Lieutenant Holt."

"Yes, sir," she said flatly and entered a few lines of code into her station's computer. "*Horizon,* this is *Starlight.* Come in." She adjusted her headset as she waited for the signal to connect. "I have them, sir." Oren nodded absently to let her know to proceed and half-listened as she spoke in her brusque tones. "*Horizon*, this is *Starlight*. You'll perform the transfer with Lieutenant Lewis Holt at our ship's..." she trailed off and looked to Sprit, who flashed her four fingers with her right hand, "deck four docking port on our starboard side. Are we still expecting you in four hours?" There was a pause, and Anthia nodded, writing some information down with her stylus. "Understood. We'll see you at zero two hundred hours, captain. *Starlight*, out."

Oren frowned and turned to his communication's officer.

"I thought we were meeting in four hours."

Anthia answered without turning to face him, typing quickly.

"They handed off their prior pick-up to another vessel, sir. They'll be here in two."

"Alright, then," Oren sighed and let his chair swivel back into its resting position. It had been a very, *very* long day, and it didn't seem like tomorrow was going to be any shorter. "Let's get moving, people."

At her post, Sprit grimaced and reopened her channel with Holt yet again. She was turning into Anthia with how many calls she was making this shift.

"New development, commander?" Holt greeted, and she made a disgruntled noise in confirmation.

"How'd you know?" She immediately stopped, expression going flat. "Dammit, Holt, stop psychically eavesdropping!"

"I cannot help it, commander," he replied with admirable patience. "The captain is quite annoyed by the change in schedule."

"I'll let him know to think quieter, then," she returned sarcastically and was about to close the channel when she remembered the point of the call. "Anyways, as you are *evidently* aware, our timetable was moved up to the next two hours. Process our guests, get their files in order, and get ready to move them to the deck four starboard docking port when Tzo arrives."

"Yes, ma'am."

"*Sprit*, Holt. For the last time, my name is Sprit."

With that, she closed the channel on him, and Holt sighed, shrugging his uniform back on from where he'd pulled the jumpsuit down to his waist, and got up from his desk. He really had been planning on trying to get some sleep this time or at least meditate a little more thoroughly. But there were some days this job just decided to pile it on, and apparently it was one of those days.

He left his quarters and tried to ignore the ghosts in the corners of his mind, especially the ones with children's voices.

Back in Sprit's quarters, Rin was bored out of her mind. She didn't think that would have been possible, given she was on a space ship, but here she was. Her hostess had told her not to look out the window, not to go wandering, not to go in the closet—which Rin was fully okay with *not* doing. Her attempt to use the computer terminal had ended in complete failure when she and the machine came to the mutual realization that neither spoke the other's language. So that left her awkwardly sitting on the edge of Sprit's bed with an empty glass in a drawer and nothing to do. She wasn't particularly tired given all the sleeping she'd apparently been doing, and she was understandably ramped up given her current surroundings. There seemed to be no middle ground for her.

"What am I supposed to do in here?" she whispered, tapping her fingers on her knees, and finally came to a decision. She might as well get some water.

She got up, opening the side table drawer and pulling out the glass as she headed towards the bathroom. Like the closet, it had a manual sliding door, and she pulled the metal smoothly along its track.

It wasn't all that different from a bathroom on Earth, she noted with pleasant surprise and walked through the small space to put the cup under the steel faucet. Water immediately started flowing, and Rin gave a small smile at the familiarity of a motion sensor sink. She moved on to the rest of the bathroom, entering the faucet-less shower and wondering exactly how water got out until she saw the holes in the ceiling. Gently, she closed the stall's glass door and was about to exit the bathroom when she noticed double doors in the general area of where she was fairly certain the closet was in the main room.

Remembering the extensive weaponry she'd seen before, Rin gingerly opened one door just enough to see inside and promptly closed it again.

"Yeah," she said to the empty air as she quickly left the bathroom, "that's where she mounted all her guns. And…other things."

She sat on the edge of the bed and drank her water, eyeing the curtain over the porthole window with slightly narrowed eyes. That was space out there. *Infinity.* An endless void filled with burning gas and rocks hurtling at nearly incomprehensible speeds—

I'll build up to it eventually, Rin decided and fell back onto the bed to stare at the ceiling, empty glass lying on the mattress next to her.

Holt cleared his throat, and immediately all of the gathered security officers fell silent, looking at him expectantly.

"Thank you," he began softly and lifted his tablet as he continued. "We are meeting with Captain Tzo's *Horizon* to transfer the prisoners to Anvers. However, they are running ahead of schedule so they will be here in two hours. We need to have a full roster and complete paperwork by the time they arrive for all seventy-five of our prisoners." Holt paused as he heard a few groans. "I appreciate the time constraint, but we must do our best to meet the deadline. The sooner these people are off our ship, the sooner we move to a new assignment, which I know you are all eager to do. Commander Matzepo will not be joining us for the transfer, so I will be in charge. Are there any questions?"

There was a chorus of "no, sirs" and general negatory sounds.

"Very well." He tucked his tablet under his arm and pointed with the other towards the cellblock. "I assigned each of us three inmates. Complete their paperwork and processing if it has not been done already, and once you finish, send your reports to me. Dismissed."

Everyone immediately checked their tablets for their list of inmates, and Holt frowned as he watched them go.

"Has anyone seen Ensigns Omarik and Assora?" he asked, pitching his voice just loud enough that everyone could hear him. They stopped and turned to him.

"Uh, I think Jhama said something about feeling sick, sir," someone began uncertainly. "She said she lost her mask for a bit when we raided the warehouse and inhaled some of the atmo. Didn't sit too well with her, so she's taking a shift off."

Holt frowned, reviewing the raid in his mind. He hadn't heard anything like that, hadn't sensed any panic from Ensign Assora that she no doubt would have felt in that situation. Could he have missed it, he wondered?

No. No, he would have felt that. He had been keeping a close eye on the rookie. Still frowning, he made a quick note on his tablet.

"And Ensign Omarik?" There was no response, and he looked up at his people. "Has anyone seen Ensign Omarik?"

"No, sir," someone else finally answered. "I think I saw Talik tinkering with something in engineering, but that was about an hour ago. Sorry, sir."

Holt sighed, the forceful exhale and his annoyance carefully hidden.

"Very well." He gestured for everyone to get back to work. "I shall speak with them once we complete the transfer. As you were."

And as he quickly walked to register his assigned inmates, he did his best to ignore the snickering thoughts and whispers around him.

"Oh man, Talik and Jhama are in *so* much trouble," someone muttered to his coworker, on the edge of laughter. "They've got the reader after them."

"Are you *insane?*" his friend hissed, smacking his arm as Holt walked by ten feet away. "He can *hear* you!"

The lieutenant's pace momentarily faltered, but he quickly regained his indifferent gait, shoulders squared and posture stiff as he left the anteroom for the cells. Behind him, he could feel the rueful and embarrassed air radiating from his two fellow officers.

They were right, though, he admitted. Ensigns Omarik and Assora had some answering to do, because he knew for a fact that Jhama *hadn't* lost her gasmask in the raid, and Talik was far too professional to just not show up for a shift. In fact, they both were. He paused just before the cellblock hall and looked down. He didn't want to do this, never liked doing this, but something didn't feel right. Something twisted uneasily in his gut, and his resolve hardened.

He slowly closed his eyes and breathed, deep and even.

Where are you?

He didn't have the time to do a deck-by-deck sweep, so he listened to the ship as a whole, prodding and feeling for either ensign's mind. And just when he thought he was going to come up empty, he found them. They just seemed preoccupied, thinking about the last mission like most of the people on board, yet his discomfort increased.

Something still wasn't right.

"Sprit Matzepo," he said, touching his earwig. Something like anxiety bubbled in his chest, and he pushed the crew's thoughts to the periphery of his own mind. The relief was instant.

"Holt, what's up?"

"Commander, did anything happen to Ensigns Assora or Omarik on the raid?" he asked without any preamble.

On the bridge, Sprit frowned.

"No, they were both fine," she said, confused. "I mean, Jhama was a little shaken up after losing everyone except the human, but I talked to her." She paused, her eyes narrowing. "Holt, is there something I need to know?"

"I am not sure, ma'am," he admitted reluctantly, taking a quick, deep breath. "It's probably nothing. I will make sure we get these transfer reports to you soon."

"Holt."

He paused, hand hovering at his ear.

"Yes, commander?"

Sprit hesitated, chewing on her lip.

"I trust your instincts. Keep an ear to the ground," she finally said, gears turning in her head. "Let me know the moment nothing becomes something."

Holt nodded curtly.

"Yes, ma'am."

On the bridge, Sprit sighed, leg bouncing restlessly at her station.

"That's never a good sign."

She glanced at the young, wiry ensign hovering near her console and smiled half-heartedly.

"It's nothing, Lucien," she assured him gently. The dark-skinned man gazed at her, unswayed, violet eyes coaxing her to talk. "Look, I promise, kid," she lied more insistently. "It's *nothing*."

"Your leg's bouncing," he said dryly, pointing at her moving append-age with an unimpressed look. Immediately, she forced her leg to go still, and their helmsman snickered.

"It's *nothing!*" she repeated, laughing at his persistence, and pushed him towards his station at the front right corner of the bridge. "Go on. Mind the helm, or you're gonna crash us."

"Jora's watching it for me," Lucien returned playfully, but followed her order anyways.

Sprit watched him return to his station, his gait as carefree and inno-cent as ever as he tapped the shoulder of the ensign who'd briefly taken his place when he went on break. And as she watched them trade places, she felt two pairs of eyes boring into her, sending her skin crawling. She shifted her gaze and found Anthia and the captain both looking at her, somber and, in Oren's case, expectant. She took a deep breath, her hands clenching and relaxing on her still knees.

"It's nothing, sir," she assured him. "Holt just has a feeling."

"A feeling? Did he get anything other than that?"

"No, sir. But I told him to keep an ear to the ground."

"*I* told that man to get some rest," he sighed, running a hand over his head and intact horn. "He's jumping at shadows."

"Yes, sir."

They turned back to their stations, but still Sprit could feel someone staring at her. She subtly looked up at Anthia's console and found the Feralan was still watching her intently, those black eyes completely un-readable. The security chief ground her heels into the deck to make sure neither leg started bouncing again and went back to work.

Jhama took a deep, uneven breath and kept her eyes fixed on the steel plated floors. Talik hadn't been able to stop pacing, not since the message had come in. And while she knew he'd be falling apart under any other circumstance, she also knew that he couldn't now. Not in this living hell they were in.

"Talik," she tried again, but he just held up his hand in an unmistakable gesture for her to shut up. "Talik, *listen* to me—"

"No!" he shouted, rounding on her and immediately clapping a hand over his mouth, his expression of desperate anger morphing into one of horror. "I-I'm sorry. I'm sorry, I didn't mean…I didn't…"

"It's okay, Talik," she whispered, reaching out and grabbing ahold of his hand. "I'm sorry, too." She gently pulled him over to sit beside her on his bed and held his hand in her lap, squeezing tightly. Her eyes filled with tears that would never fall, and she looked at him with agonizing guilt. "I made a promise to you on the moon. And I can't keep it."

He tightened his grip on her hand in turn and closed his eyes.

"It's not your fault," he whispered back. "It's…it's not *our* fault."

Jhama swallowed hard and looked out the window across the room, watching the stars stream by as they continued along faster than light.

"We'll be meeting *Horizon* soon," she said softly. "Finally getting rid of those auction scum." She gave a hollow scoff. "How messed up is it that we're facing this, and all I can think about is our job? Our *real* job? What it'll feel like to put those traffickers away, to get some justice for all those people they killed—"

"Those people we couldn't save," Talik corrected, his cracking façade growing firm once more. "All the people *we* couldn't save. *Won't* be able to save."

Jhama took in a slow, deep breath, her free hand curling into a fist in her lap. Something was tickling the back of her mind—some kind of way out. She just couldn't quite grasp it, and she looked at her friend.

"Say that again?"

"The people we won't save, Jhama. There'll be so many people we won't be able to save, that *we* k…." The word died in his throat, and he tried again, scowling. "That we'll have *as good as* killed."

Her grip on Talik's hand loosened, and she slowly looked back out the window.

"Were you in the loading bay after the raid, Talik?" she asked, strangely distant. "When Sprit gave her debrief?" Her friend looked at her oddly, but nodded. "Do you remember what she said?"

"No. I was too busy thinking about those kids…."

"She said we still saved one." Jhama continued to stare out the window at the passing stars, completely zoned out. "She said we still saved one when we could've saved no one. And that we'll all have one day when we save no one." She felt Talik pull his hand from her grasp so he could cradle his head, his elbows braced on his knees. She just continued to watch the stars. "And she said…she said that on those days, that one person you save makes all the difference."

"What does that matter? We'll save no one, Jhama. *No one.*"

Think like the Wetworker, Jhama ordered herself, squeezing her eyes shut and sniffing hard. *Think like Anthia.*

"I can," she whispered, her eyes still closed, her fist still clenched on her knee. Talik looked at her in a painful mix of relief and shock.

"You can't tell me," he said quickly. "Don't tell me anything, Jhama, you know he'll figure it out somehow."

She nodded sloppily, dragging her hand across her nose and eyes.

"I won't," she said firmly, forcing herself to stay calm. "Just leave it with me."

"I-I can't. I *have* to keep it."

"No. No, you don't," she told him, looking him in the eye and holding his hand with a vicious strength. Her voice shook with the fervor of her words. "I've been playing it over and over in my head, Talik. You don't need to keep it with you. We both needed to keep it secret and make sure it works, and you needed to build it, place it, and power it on." She shook her head, a tortured smile pulling at her lips. "But it said *nothing* about you having to keep it the night before." She squeezed his hand. "Please. Leave it with me."

When Talik still hesitated, she pressed on.

"I can save at least one. We won't break any of his rules. But I can save at least one."

Talik looked at her for a long time, both of them shaking and on the verge of breakdowns they weren't allowed to have for fear of attracting unwanted attention. He took in her determined, resolute face and her fierce grasp on his hand. He took in the fire in her star-lit eyes.

"You can save one?" he asked, just to make sure, and she nodded.

"I can save one. More than one if I do this right."

And looking at her, Talik believed it. He forced himself to let go of her hand and unsteadily got up, an intense rush tearing through him as he walked to his closet and opened it to pull a large metal box from its recesses. His hands shook as he held it close to his pounding chest and turned to face his partner, his expression now as hardened as hers and his eyes just as aflame.

"Take it." He held it out to her, and she slowly stood. "You take it, and you save them."

"Don't worry." She took the heavy container from him and pressed the cold metal close to her chest. "This promise I can keep. Now, go. Cover for me."

CHAPTER 8

Talik sprinted as fast as he could to the brig, all but pushing past people on deck four to get there. Jhama was taking care of the package. Now it was time to re-establish normalcy, to cover their tracks.

"Holt is going to kill me," he panted, throwing an apology over his shoulder as he stepped on someone's foot. "I am so late."

"No, he won't," Jhama returned over his earwig, biting her lip as she carefully worked on tweaking their assignment. She adjusted the angle of her desk lamp and tried again. "He's too polite for that. Sprit, though, Sprit will kill you."

Talik groaned, tilting his head back as he ran.

"*Gotso*, how are we supposed to cover this one up?" he hissed.

"Just come up with something convincing," she said nonchalantly. "Like—okay, here. I was feeling upset about the auction raid, about how we weren't able to save the abductees and all those kids. And you, being the good friend you are, you decided to stay and comfort me."

"And we just *didn't* tell them?"

"I can't come up with everything, Omarik!" she retorted, setting her tool down as she spoke.

"Talik, Holt and Sprit are looking for you!" someone shouted after him, and Talik groaned again, squeezing his eyes shut.

"I am *aware*, thank you!" he returned ungratefully, and his coworker laughed in the quickly growing distance. "Okay," he huffed, refocusing. "I got it. You didn't want report that you weren't coming in because you were ashamed."

"*Ashamed?*" she asked incredulously, carefully resuming her work.

"Yeah, I mean, Holt *experienced* all of them dying, right?" he pressed. "And he's back at work. You felt weak, and I got wrapped up trying to comfort you and get you to come to your shift."

"Eh," Jhama said after a while with a shrug. "I can work with that. Nice thinking. Remember, believe it's true, and it will be."

Talik turned the corner to the brig and yelped as he ran into someone full force. It was like sprinting into a wall, and before the Tarikian could fall over, the crewman grabbed his elbows and pulled him back to his feet.

"Oh, I'm *so* sorry," he rambled, still gasping for breath. "I'm late for my shift, and I…." He trailed off as he finally regained his balance and looked up at his accidental victim. And once he did, he gulped and let go of the man's arms like he'd been burned.

"Lieutenant Holt. Sir, uh…" he stammered and belatedly stood at attention. The man continued to stare at him almost impassively. "I am so, *so* sorry, sir."

"It's…quite alright, ensign." Talik shifted uncomfortably on his feet, struggling to maintain eye contact. "Perhaps now would be a good time to tell me why you are late, Ensign Omarik, and why your friend Assora is not with you. It is very unlike either of you."

"Uh, yes, sir," Talik began unsteadily, glancing guiltily over his shoulder before looking to the floor. They'd become too good at this. "Jhama was just…she wasn't feeling well—"

"Ensign, if you are going to attempt the gasmask story with me, I should tell you I know it isn't true. I conferred with Doctor Balok—"

"No, sir!" Talik interrupted, looking horrified and then instantly ashamed. "No, she told the others that because…" His voice wavered and broke, the perfect lie. He glanced around them carefully, as if making sure they wouldn't be overheard. "Can I speak to you in confidence, sir?"

Holt frowned slightly, but acquiesced. All he could feel from the ensign was empathy, a drive to comfort, and intense guilt. They'd been thinking about the auction mission when he'd heard their minds earlier, and he was starting to get an idea of why.

"It was just those kids, sir," he finally said, standing at attention and holding Holt's intense gaze. "She'd never worked a job where we lost so many kids, not at once, sir. And you know that's especially hard for her."

Holt continued to hold eye contact with him until he looked down.

"Are you saying you were comforting her, ensign?"

"Yes, sir. I was trying to get her to go to our shift."

Holt hesitated, carefully studying Talik. His emotions and thoughts rang true. Perhaps he had been wrong. Perhaps he had been, as the captain had so eloquently put it, "jumping at shadows."

"Why did neither of you let Commander Matzepo or myself know you were going to be late or that she was not going to attend shift?" he asked, deliberately keeping his tone impersonal. Instantly, Talik looked uncomfortable, and Holt frowned as the man scratched at his collar. "Ensign Omarik?"

"She...she was ashamed, sir," he finally explained. "I told her that was ridiculous, but...."

"About what, ensign? The mission?"

"No, sir, about...she was ashamed because you felt them all die." He had perfected the look of guilt, the discomfort at sharing such personal information about a peer to a superior. "You felt them die, even the kids, sir, but she knew you'd still be at your post. She didn't feel them die, she just saw the aftermath, but she still couldn't do what you're doing, and she felt that she should have been able to—"

He broke off as Holt held up a hand to stem his rapid stream of words. Neither said anything for an uncomfortably long while until Holt stepped aside and gestured to the brig.

"I believe you have some catching up to do," he said simply, and the ensign gratefully hurried inside. "Ensign Omarik."

Talik paused guilelessly on the threshold of the brig anteroom.

"Yes, sir?"

Holt hesitated and subtly glanced around to ensure they were alone.

"Jhama." Talik blinked in surprise. The lieutenant never used anyone's informal name. What was going on? "Is she okay? Is she alright by herself?"

Well, now Talik was thoroughly caught off guard.

"Yes, sir." Still trying to wrap his head around the out-of-character inquiry, Talik respectfully inclined his head. "I'm sorry we broke protocol, sir, it won't happen again."

Holt reassumed his professionalism and clasped his hands behind his back.

"I would hope not, ensign," he said gravely and hesitated. "Perhaps you should schedule an appointment with a counselor as well."

"Oh, I-I'm fine, sir, really," he began but stopped when Holt continued to watch him with those unsettling, unwavering gray eyes of his. "Okay, sir. I will."

Holt nodded once and knelt, picking up the tablet Talik hadn't even noticed he'd knocked out of his hands when they collided.

"Oh, let me get that for you, sir," he said in an embarrassed rush, going to pick it up too late as Holt already started standing again.

"I believe you have missed enough of your shift already, ensign," he said pointedly with what, for a split second, was a near-playful light in his eyes. "Especially given that I completed *both* Assora's work and yours."

Talik gave a rueful smile.

"Thank you, sir. Like I said, this won't happen again."

Holt watched the man retreat and tucked his tablet under his arm before walking down the hall. He tapped his earwig.

"Sprit Matzepo."

"Holt, what have you got?"

"False alarm, commander," he said, glancing over his shoulder to the brig door as he rounded the corner. "I apologize. It seems Ensign Assora will be requiring psychiatric services, nothing more. She won't be reporting for her shift, but Ensign Omarik arrived."

Sprit heaved a heavy sigh of relief.

"Good," she breathed, slouching in her seat. "That's good. Well, not for Jhama, but it's good it wasn't something worse. How are the reports coming along?"

"I'm bringing them to you now, commander."

Sprit closed her eyes and smiled, letting her head thump back against her chair.

"Holt, there are times I remember why I tolerate Oren keeping you around," she grinned. "Today's one of those times."

"I'm glad you feel that way, commander."

"Oh, see, now you're making me regret it. Get up here with those reports. *Horizon* will be joining us shortly. Sprit out."

"Jumping at shadows?"

Sprit looked at Oren and fought the urge to scowl at his knowing, near-invisible smirk.

"Not a word," she growled warningly, and he turned away with a self-satisfied chuckle.

"Sir, *Horizon* is hailing us," Anthia interrupted, fine-tuning the connection with one or two subtle turns of a few dials. "They reached the rendezvous point, and they're advising us to drop out of FTL."

"Tell Tzo I know how to pilot my own ship," Oren grumbled, and Anthia went to transmit the message. "Acoua!" She turned to him, as stern as ever. "I *know* you know that wasn't a real order. Just tell her we'll be there within the next couple minutes."

"Yes, sir."

Lucien snorted at the helm, and Oren eyed the young man intently.

"Mind the helm, Ensign Trinidore," he said, and the kid grimaced at having been caught. "I doubt *Horizon* would appreciate it if we crashed into her."

"Yes, sir. Sorry, sir."

The door opened, and Holt walked in, handing his tablet to Sprit and waiting as she quickly pulled her stylus from behind her ear and signed off on each file. Oren sighed, contentment settling in his bones. Things were going well.

"Start the rendezvous protocol," he ordered.

———

In Sprit's quarters, Rin quickly snapped out of her half-asleep daze as the persistent hum of the engines changed pitch. It was subtle, but enough to get her attention. As she finished waking up, rubbing the sleep from her eyes and sitting on the edge of the bed, the ship imperceptibly continued to slow down, and she realized she hadn't really noticed they were moving in the first place. It was impressive. Finally, she felt them come to a gentle, effortless stop, and the engine's dull hum faded to a barely-present buzz.

"Why'd we stop?" she muttered and, despite Sprit's warning, made her way over to the window above the security chief's desk. The fabric was heavy and black between her fingers and felt oddly like denim, and as she drew it away, she braced herself for what lied beyond it.

Only to be greeted by a metal hull.

"What the…"

She leaned a little closer to the glass, climbing up onto the desk and leaning over the computer console so she could get a better look. The metal looked unpolished and weather-beaten, and its rustic, red-bronze color made Rin think of old weather vanes and stripped cars. Whatever it was, it was only fifteen feet away, and she quickly realized they must have pulled up alongside another ship.

The passing noise in the hall suddenly increased, and Rin gingerly climbed off the desk, taking care not to kick the computer as she did. Once her feet were solidly on the ground, she walked to the door and paused, considering the button before her.

"Aliens," she whispered, closing her eyes and crossing her arms tightly over her chest. "I'm on a spaceship with aliens. There are *aliens* outside." She took in a slow breath. "No freaking out. *No* screaming."

She resolutely opened her eyes and pushed the button.

The door slid open, and the first thing she saw was a sea of blue. Six rows four security personnel across were walking by, clearly on high alert with their weapons free. Suitably intrigued, she cautiously leaned over the threshold, bracing herself on the doorjamb, and looked to the front of the column. That man with the bad haircut and the spines on his face was leading them, and she shuddered as he glanced over his shoulder and instantly made eye contact with her—as if he'd known precisely where she was.

Concern seemed to flicker briefly across his face, and she thought she saw his gray eyes shift focus to the rest of the column behind him. Curiosity getting the better of her yet again, Rin followed his gaze.

Her heart froze, and her blood turned to ice.

She gasped and stumbled back into Sprit's room, suddenly nauseous and light-headed. It was the Tarikians. It was the people who had abducted her—who had drugged her, defiled her, and taken her away from her home. Without her in the threshold to trip the motion sensor, the door shut, and she shakily sat on the ground, back against the wall.

Her heart was racing now, making up for the few seconds it'd been stopped, and she felt an overwhelming panic flood over her.

The Tarikians were going to take her again. They were going to take her and actually sell her this time. She shouldn't have trusted these strangers—these people with names like Sprit, Oren, and Balok. These people who had horns and turned invisible and did god knows what else. She could feel herself starting to hyperventilate as the memories of her abduction and the auction assaulted her once more, and she was about to get up and run to the bathroom when there was a sudden knock on the door.

"Miss Cooper?" a man's voice called, with the slightest burr of a nearly familiar accent. Rin froze and pressed back against the wall. "Miss Cooper, I can assure you there is no danger. They are fully restrained." She eyed the door warily, fear oscillating between abating and growing. "We aren't letting them go, and we aren't letting them sell you, ma'am."

Ma'am? The idea of being called ma'am almost made her laugh.

"We're transferring them to another vessel which will take them to a prison colony, Miss Cooper. That is all."

The faceless voice on the other side of the door said nothing else, and Rin stared at the sealed threshold with no small amount of turmoil.

I can assure you there is no danger.

She stood and tentatively opened the door again. Whoever had been talking to her was long gone, and Rin was about to place the benevolent stranger's voice when one of the passing prisoners lunged at her, teeth bared in a grotesque snarl.

"Human!"

He roared the word like a vile curse, and Rin stumbled back as the Tarikian security officer she recognized from earlier in the hall with Sprit shoved the prisoner back into place.

Reds-and-blues, she realized, harsh adrenaline surging through her as she placed the manacled alien's clothing and aggravated limp. *Oh god, it's reds-and-blues.*

Talik turned to the human once he was sure the trafficker wasn't going to give him any more trouble, and his heart ached.

"Are you okay?" he asked, moving towards the shaken girl with an open, sympathetic expression, only to have the door close in his face. The ensign sighed and reluctantly returned to his post along the moving column, side-eyeing reds-and-blues and purposely ignoring the way the criminal snarled at him.

Damn traffickers. They're all the same.

In Sprit's quarters, Rin was lying in the Ethonian's bed, her arms wrapped tightly around the pillow tucked under her and her face buried in the squishy material.

God, she just wanted to go home.

Holt and his people stood expectantly just outside deck four's starboard docking port. Tzo's transfer team would board any second, and the lieutenant could feel his colleague's eagerness to get these particular criminals off their ship. He understood the urge, the reason behind the intense wait for the docking door's status light to change from red to green. Sentient traffickers were among the hardest felons to deal with. The idea of buying and selling *people*...he knew some found it hard to comprehend.

But little surprised him anymore.

"What fancy ship's taking us?" the Tarikian, Chief, drawled, clearly not concerned in the slightest with his current predicament. "I hope it's state of the art."

"Tzo Runner's *Horizon,*" he heard Talik reply, and Chief instantly quieted. "I'm positive she and her first-rate crew will make your stay most hospitable."

His words dripped with spiteful sarcasm, and while Holt appreciated the intent behind them, they were hardly professional.

"Ensign Omarik," he warned, still facing forward, and Talik looked down. "We do not interact with the prisoners."

"Sorry, sir."

The docking door light suddenly turned green, and depressurized air hissed from the slowly opening seals. Holt calmly clasped his hands behind his back, the rest of his security team following suit where they were either waiting with him or watching the prisoners. After about ten seconds, the docking port finished opening, and immediately Captain Tzo stepped through the steam-like gas. Holt knew it wasn't hot. Its gray tint came from the pressurization fluid used, not the temperature, but Trozerans always did like to make an entrance. Not that he'd ever say that to his captain's face.

Or *hers*, for that matter.

Tzo Runner was talking before she'd even crossed the threshold, melodic, deep tones of Trozeran rolling off her tongue at a rapid-fire pace as she swept aboard and directed her own crew towards *Starlight*'s prisoners. A thick, dark brown cloak hung from her warrior's frame, brushing at the heels of her heavy boots as she moved and fastening about her shoulders with a thick leather cuff and bronze clips that attached to the straps of her bodice. If Holt were to guess, the mantle was probably made of Trozeran sealskin—the pelt of an animal she'd killed on a rite of passage expedition as a teenager.

"Captain Tzo," he greeted, and she immediately turned her focus on the officer.

"Lieutenant." Her irises were a hard, uncompromising black like Oren's, and a long, claw-like scar ran down her left temple and jaw, narrowly missing her carotid before ending near her collarbone—another hunting souvenir, no doubt. "It's been a long time."

She shook the mind reader's hand with a firm grip, and he nodded respectfully.

"Yes, ma'am. Unfortunately, Commander Matzepo could not join us."

"And neither could my brother, it seems," she muttered, looking up in the direction of the bridge two decks above them. "Tell him I'm disappointed in his priorities. It's not often I get out this way."

"I...do not believe that would be appropriate, ma'am," Holt said hesitantly, and Tzo just laughed.

"No, I don't suppose it would be, reader." Holt's jaw clenched ever so slightly at the nickname. "Do you have the transfer paperwork?" He quickly handed the tablet over, and she passed it in turn to her first officer. "See? We handle important matters ourselves, Holt," she said in a pointed aside to the deputy.

"I'll be sure to pass that along to my superior, ma'am."

"Oh, don't bother," she responded off-handedly, walking down the line of inmates and taking them in one at a time. "Sprit will only take that as a challenge to somehow do even less the next time I see her." She gave a small smirk, the expression perfectly suited for her weather-beaten and fine-boned features. "And to think, I got all dressed up for my siblings," she sighed in mock disappointment and gestured to herself. The decorative white paint adorning her jawline, cheeks, and forehead in carefully drawn patterns had clearly been applied within the last hour at most.

"Yes, ma'am."

Tzo rolled her eyes at his formulaic, neutral reply.

"You're no fun, Lewis. Hasn't anyone told you that?"

"Routinely, ma'am."

Tzo scoffed and turned around as her first officer, Roiz Lazarus, returned and handed her Holt's tablet.

"We downloaded everything, Runner, and are processing it now."

"Good. Get them on board, Lazarus." She returned Holt's property to him and started down the line of prisoners. "I've got a brother to see."

"Uh, Captain Tzo, I don't believe he's expecting you," Holt began, moving to go after her, but she just pointed him back to the transfer with a bark of laughter.

"It's *my* ship he's dealing with, lieutenant. He knows to expect me."

Holt watched her go and quickly tapped his earwig.

"Oren Galaxa."

Rin was back at the door.

It wasn't like she had anything better to do in here for *five hours*. People watching would have to do, and besides, she felt a little stupid for freaking out earlier. This was her world now, for better or for worse, and it was time she got used to it, she told herself firmly.

It was turning out to be easier said than done.

The sounds beyond the metal seemed quieter than before, so she assumed the prison transfer was either done or happening further down on the deck. Not that many people would be passing by around now, which made it the best time to attempt a round two.

"Okay, Rin," she exhaled softly. "Let's try this again."

She pressed the button and carefully stepped into the open threshold. No one.

The hall was completely empty. It was almost eerie how quiet it was, and Rin shifted uncomfortably on her feet. She had been bracing herself for at least *someone*, and this was a bit unsettling.

Then, she heard the footsteps. They were heavy and quick, filled with intense purpose, and Rin leaned over the threshold to look down the still empty hall. Whoever it was, they were approaching from that direction, and a peculiar uneasiness came over the girl.

And that was when *she* rounded the corner, long cloak curving about her moving limbs like water.

She was reasonably tall, maybe a few inches taller than the captain, but definitely the same species. Her hair hung in scores of long, dreads down her back, starting from just between and behind her horns. Unlike Oren's, her horns were slightly smaller and curved closer to her scalp, though both were intact and even looked like they were polished. Strips of leather wound around the bases of the exposed bones in an intricate braid and tied off at the base of her skull, holding her thick hair away from her neck and face. A single, ragged strip of white, almost pinkish, skin ran across her broad nose, starting and ending on each cheek.

She wore a long, deliberately tattered skirt of a rich turquoise color over baggy, dull red pants. An antique, Earth-like revolver gun hung at her hip in an aged holster, and her half-gloved hand rested naturally on the butt of the weapon, giving her walk a fatal, predatory gait. Her ornately engraved armor bodice had six small sheaths sewn into the stiff leather, three per side; each held a light, expertly crafted throwing knife that Rin had no doubt this strange woman could use with devastating accuracy. A red, long-sleeve shirt nearly as frayed as her skirt hung from her arms and shoulders, looking ready to fall off her body by design. Rin wondered for a moment what point the ratty fabric had, given it's near disintegrated state, until the lady passed her doorway. Her scarred skin and the brute muscle of her arms were clearly visible beneath the thread-bare cloth, and Rin was suddenly reminded of Sprit's outfit when they had first met.

Subtle, physical intimidation.

And if the striking woman had taken the human's breath away just walking by, the girl's heart came to a stuttering stop when the Trozeran abruptly looked at her. A shudder wracked her body at the intimidating contact, and Rin cautiously stepped back into Sprit's room, mirroring the warrior's unblinking gaze until the door slid shut. And quite simply, the moment was lost.

"Who was that?" Rin asked the empty room.

As usual, it had no answer.

CHAPTER 9

Oren didn't turn when the bridge door hissed open behind him.

"Hello, Runner," he said absently, continuing to read the report in his hands. "Did you have a safe voyage?"

"Galaxa," she returned, walking into the room and making her way purposefully towards her brother. "What do you think? Without incident, as usual." Lucien watched uneasily from his station as the woman put her hands on the top of his captain's chair and leaned forward to speak directly next to her kinsman's ear. "I've always been the better pilot."

Oren looked up from his report to the viewscreen, still ignoring her.

"Ensign Trinidore, tell me—how many accidents and at-fault delays have we had since you took over the helm?"

Lucien looked between the two Trozerans anxiously. He felt like he was about to step into the middle of something messy, but he couldn't just *not* answer his captain.

"Uh, zero, sir?" he answered tentatively, and Oren nodded.

"That's correct. Now, how many records have we broken?"

"Two, sir." His expression was apologetic as he continued, and the Trozeran woman eyed him dangerously. "Record times on completing a transit route and navigating the singularity asteroid field in Sector 049."

Oren looked at Tzo over his shoulder and shrugged.

"If we're taking credit for our helmsmen's flight skills, I have to say, Tzo, I was under the impression *I* was the better pilot."

A long, explosive silence dragged out between the two people that nobody except Lucien seemed to care about until finally, Oren started chuckling. Tzo bowed her head, letting it rest heavily on his shoulder as she started laughing as well. And the helmsman watched in complete confusion as Oren got up and tackled the taller woman in a bone-crushing hug that she returned with equal enthusiasm.

"It's good to see you, brother," she sighed, pulling back from him and reaching up to grab his horns in her hands.

He reciprocated the action, touching his forehead to hers by gently tugging on her horns, and smiled as he closed his eyes.

"It's good to see you, too."

They stood that way for a few moments before Oren broke their contact, shifting his grasp from her horns to her shoulders.

"How is Sahmot?"

"Mother keeps us all in line. You know how she is," she said conspiratorially and then immediately looked to Sprit's empty security station. "Speaking of mother, where is our sister?"

"I believe she hid in her room when she heard you come aboard," Oren joked dryly, sitting back down in his chair and picking his report up once more. Tzo smirked but immediately grew intrigued.

"Did I see a human in her quarters on my way up here?"

Oren grunted an affirmative.

"Only survivor of the people you're taking off my ship."

She crossed her arms, expression somber.

"Gas?"

"You've seen it before?" he asked and looked at her curiously.

"New tactic," she confirmed. "We've seen it a couple of times."

"It's barbaric," Lucien muttered at his station, and both Trozerans looked at him.

"Trafficking is a barbaric business, helmsman," Tzo said simply. "Do not expect its methods to be any less so." The twenty-year-old stared at his console in silence, unmoved. "Helmsman." He looked to her, and her tone grew lighter. "If what you and Oren said is true, you're good." She gestured to the viewscreen to where the bow of her own massive vessel was just barely visible. "If you ever want a career change, contact me. My crew would be honored to have one of the Madak People guide us."

"I, uh…" Lucien trailed off, floundering, and Oren smirked at his report as the young man blushed. "Th-thank you, ma'am. I will, uh, I will keep that in mind."

Tzo clapped Oren on the shoulder.

"Stellar crew as always, brother, if somewhat unexpected. Where's your first officer, though?"

"Hanali'a is resting. She just got back from testifying at a long trial at headquarters." She made a noise of empathetic disgust.

"Give her my love and tell her mother misses her company."

"She'll be glad to hear that."

"Good. Now, I'm going to find our sister." Tzo started leaving the bridge, and Oren scoffed, returning to his tablet report.

"Good luck with that."

———————

"Lazarus, look at me. Is this my joking face?"

"No—"

"Then don't ask if I'm joking!" Sprit snapped in irritated Trozeran, shooing the man off towards *Horizon*. "Go get me a copy of the transfer reports with Runner's signature on them."

"Little Matzepo," the first officer grumbled, blue eyes twinkling as he walked away. "Still the fiery boss of everyone."

"Damn straight," she called after him, and he threw her an obscene gesture as he returned to his ship for the requested paperwork—all seventy-five files of it. "I know you want to say something, Holt."

Behind her, Sprit's deputy blinked innocently, his head cocked to the side like a puppy.

"Ma'am?"

"Oh, come on," she pushed, turning to him with crossed arms. "It makes you uncomfortable—my casualness with Tzo's people."

"Hardly, ma'am," Lewis said, expression open and yet neutral at the same time. "I expect First Officer Roiz has known you since you were ten years old. Some camaraderie is to be expected."

Sprit raised her eyebrow and smirked, relishing the opportunity to push her deputy's formality buttons.

"You do know he just told me to go fu—"

"MATZEPO!"

Holt winced ever so slightly at the bellow down the hall, and Sprit's smirk turned into a grin. She turned around slyly and shrugged at the woman marching towards her with playful aggression.

"Runner!" she greeted with that same cheeky smile. "Is this old rust bucket yours?" she continued in mock surprise, putting a hand over her chest for extra drama. "*I* thought your ship was top of the line."

The captain growled and picked up the shorter woman in a bear hug, swinging her around in a circle a few times before setting her back down on dizzy feet. As she had with their brother, she reached out and held Sprit's head in her hands, pressing their foreheads together while Sprit gently held Tzo's horns in return. Respectfully, Holt backed away, giving them space and directing the *Starlight* officers instead. In the background, he could hear the two women speaking in quickly escalating Trozeran, catching up on however many months or years it had been since the sisters had last seen each other. He wouldn't deny them their time.

He knew family came first.

"Lewis." Holt turned to Roiz as the man exited the docking port, and accepted the offered tablet with a questioning look. "Tzo's signed copies of the transfer papers. Sprit asked for them. Or rather *demanded* them."

"I see," Holt said, missing Roiz's amused smirk. "Thank you, sir."

"You don't joke often, do you, Lewis?" Roiz asked, watching the man pour over the tablet to ensure everything was in order. Holt looked up at him blankly.

"Should I, sir?"

The Trozeran cocked an eyebrow.

"No, I suppose you shouldn't."

Behind them, Sprit dissolved into peals of laughter before rejoining Tzo in animated conversation.

It took five hours for Tzo's crew to get everyone properly situated. To anyone who didn't know better, who didn't know the ins and outs of bureaucracy and cross-organizational transfers, those five hours would've seemed absurd.

It unfortunately wasn't.

"Only five hours to jump through Peacekeeper hoops? Impressive," Sprit admitted, shaking Roiz and Tzo's hands respectively. She turned her attention to her adoptive sister as they walked down the hall towards the docking port. "Extend my compliments to your crew. They did good work today."

The captain nodded, smiling.

"I'll do that. I'm sure they'll love to know Little Matzepo approves of them," she added in a ribbing tease, and Sprit not so lightly punched her arm. "How *professional*. Now, if you don't mind, we need to deliver our guests to their new home. Give Oren my love."

"Of course, Tzo."

Roiz hung back a several feet from his captain and Sprit with Holt, reaching to shake the deputy's hand before stopping himself.

"Ah, you don't touch others," the first officer chuckled with a self-deprecating shake of his head. "My apologies, I'd forgotten."

"Don't worry yourself, sir."

"How do you say it, give me a moment to remember." Roiz paused and then bowed shallowly. "May the Creator bless your journey," he recited, keeping his gaze averted, and Holt inclined his head in return.

"And yours."

"Holt, leave him alone!" Sprit called walking over and herding Roiz away from her deputy. "You're too formal, come on."

"It's always a pleasure to see you, Sprit," Roiz smiled, cupping her face briefly. "Until next time, Little Matzepo."

"Until next time, Lazarus."

Sprit watched the last Trozeran leave and waited as the docking port's status light changed from green to red. She tapped her earwig.

"Oren Galaxa...yes, sir, we've got a red status light. You're clear to pull away on our end."

She waited there for a minute, Holt next to her. They'd dismissed the rest of their security teams since it was the end of shift, and she wondered briefly why the man was still beside her. Before she could dwell on it, though, she heard the whir of motors that told her *Starlight* was retracting her docking ramp, and she gave wistful smile.

"Oren Galaxa."

"Yes, sir?" Sprit said, answering the earwig's chime a bit too absently, and on the bridge Oren sympathetically smiled.

"Go get some rest, Sprit. It's been a long day, and you deserve some downtime."

Sprit's wistful smile turned into a grateful one.

"Yes, sir."

"And Sprit? Tell Holt to go to bed. *Please.*"

Sprit laughed.

"Yes, sir." She closed the channel and looked at her cohort. "Captain says actually go to bed this time."

For a moment, Sprit thought she saw Holt smile.

"Then I take my leave, commander. Good night."

She watched him walk away and smirked as she called after him.

"It's morning, Lewis!"

He stopped and turned back to her, hands still firmly clasped behind his back.

"So it is. Good morning, then, commander. I hope you rest well."

"You, too, Holt." He wordlessly resumed his departure, and Sprit shook her head and rolled her eyes. "I'll break him one of these days...."

Rin had finally found a way to entertain herself. She hadn't done this since she was a kid, but at least it was something. She wasn't even sure *why* it was fun. Maybe it was the head-rush when she sat back up. Maybe it was seeing things from a different perspective. Maybe it made her feel like a bat. All she knew for sure was that right now, hanging upside down off the side of the bed was the only thing keeping her sane. It was also stretching her back out quite nicely—

The door slid open, and Sprit stopped, staring at her alien roommate in bafflement and resignation.

"Well, I have to say, this is new."

Rin immediately sat up and braced herself on the wall and mattress as the blood rushed from her head back into the rest of her body.

"I had nothing to do," she said in swift, bleary justification, and Sprit snorted, kicking off her shoes and nudging them under the foot of the bed. Next, she unclipped her belt and dropped it and the full holster in their assigned desk drawer.

"You could've gone exploring or talked to the computer—"

"The computer and I don't like each other," Rin interrupted, and Sprit frowned, absently unbuttoning the top of her uniform.

"It's a *computer*, what could possibly...." She trailed off. "It doesn't speak English."

"No. It doesn't."

Sprit shrugged her uniform off her shoulders and pulled her arms from the sleeves.

"I'll see about asking Avery to re-install the ship's human interface systems," she said, smoothing out her now-exposed underarmor shirt. "But I'll do that in a few hours when I'm not ready to fall over." Rin awkwardly looked away as Sprit yanked off her uniform, leaving her in shorts and her tank top. "Oh, come on. I *know* you've seen more skin than this in your life." She reached into her closet and pulled out a well-worn pair of capris and a loose t-shirt. Both were dyed and decorated in a way that reminded Rin of the strange woman who walked by, and she looked away again as Sprit stripped and finished changing.

"Who was that woman? The one with the horns who looked like the captain?"

"Oh, that was Tzo. Tzo Runner," Sprit answered from the recesses of her shirt as she pulled it over her head. "She's Oren's birth sister and my adoptive sister."

"Was she the captain of that ship we pulled up next to?"

Sprit nodded tiredly and entered her bathroom, quickly brushing her hair out from its tight braid and putting it back up into a ponytail before cleaning her teeth. Rin continued speaking

"I guess it runs in the family, huh?"

Sprit yawned as she walked back into the main room.

"Yeah, I suppose." She rubbed at her eyes and groaned. With her adrenaline gone, her exhaustion was hitting her full force. "Ok, Rin, it's technically morning, but I'm super tired, so I'm going to just crash."

"Oh. Here, sorry." Rin stood up, but Sprit pointed her back down.

"No, no. I'm fine sharing the bed with you." Rin still hesitated, and Sprit sighed. "Look, I'd say you could sleep on the floor with a pillow and blanket, but look at the floor. It's metal; you're not gonna sleep at all. Just share the bed with me tonight, and I'll put in an order for a bunk bed when I wake up. Deal?"

Rin nodded.

"Okay, then, come on." Sprit climbed into bed and dropped face-first into a pillow, foregoing blankets or sheets as usual. When she spoke, her words were muffled. "We can go eat lunch in the cafeteria tomorrow. It tends to be the least crazy meal."

"Okay," Rin said softly, gingerly getting into bed and lying ramrod straight on her back next to the alien.

"Computer, lights off." The room was plunged into darkness, and Rin immediately held her breath, seized by a crushing sense of anxiety at the heaviness of the black. Sprit must have heard her sharp inhale, because she sighed. "Computer, lights at one percent." A barely perceptible glow lit up the room, and Rin immediately began breathing more easily. "I'll ask Avery for a night light, too." Rin tried to relax a little, and Sprit muttered to herself, probably thinking that the pillow was hiding her words. "This is why I don't do roommates...."

"I'll try not to get abducted next time," Rin muttered back, twisting onto her stomach. Sprit immediately lifted her head up from the pillow.

"You and your damn bionic ears," she huffed before shoving her face back into the plush fabric. "You should turn those things off when you sleep if you don't like white noise, by the way."

"Uh, how do you—"

Sprit reached for Rin's right ear and pressed a small white button just at the base of the implant. Instantly, the world went silent on that side, and Rin felt a heady sense of peace wash over her.

"Want me to get the other?" Sprit asked, but Rin shook her head.

"If something happens, I want to be able to hear," she said softly.

"Makes sense," Sprit said with a shrug and dropped back onto the mattress, shoving her spare pillow and blanket at the girl with a blind hand. And somehow, within a few seconds, she was snoring.

Rin carefully turned her head so that her still-functioning ear was pressed into the pillow and pulled the blanket around her. It was warm and comforting, soft as anything she'd ever felt. But she still couldn't fall asleep. She was too tense, waiting for something to happen—but exactly what, she wasn't sure.

And then, Sprit's arm landed heavily over her back, thrown there in her unconscious shifting. It was such a small thing, such innocent contact, *human* contact. In the dark, not looking at her, Rin could pretend the alien, the Ethonian, the entirely unearthly, was human.

She carefully nestled a little closer to Sprit, closed her eyes, and let sleep take her.

On *Horizon*'s bridge, Tzo Runner was quiet. Pensive. One leg crossed over the other as she sat in her chair—chin resting on her fist, her elbow propped on the arm crossed over her belly. She was distant, preoccupied. Roiz Lazarus silently approached her left side, his voice low when he spoke.

"Is something wrong, Runner?"

She took a deep breath and adjusted her posture, crossing both her arms over her leather-protected gut. Her elbows rested carefully on her chair's armrests. When she spoke, her voice was as quiet as his.

"It's just a feeling." The hairs on the back of her neck stood on end, and she turned ever so slightly to Roiz. "Contact Matzepo. Ask her if the Priestess has spoken—anything at all. Tell her I need guidance."

"Yes, Runner."

He quickly departed to contact his captain's mother, and Tzo crossed her arms a little tighter over her uneasy stomach.

It's just a feeling.

In her quarters, Jhama exhaled slowly as she finished tightening the last screw. She put her tools back in their allotted spaces in her kit and carefully placed the device back in its metal box.

"Talik Omarik," she said flatly, finger resting against her earwig.

"Jhama?"

She gave a ghost of a smile as she stared at the stars before her with an otherwise empty expression.

"You can take it back whenever you're ready," she said softly, careful to keep her voice down. "It's still completely functional."

"Thank you." His grateful fervor made her stomach turn uneasily.

"Don't thank me."

She closed the channel and carried the box to her closet, hiding it in its recesses. Talik would pick it up soon. And then, his part in this would end. She returned to her desk, resting her hands on the cold surface as she watched the stars beyond her window. A cold fire filled her heart, and she glared at the darkness and the distant points of light.

"I win this round, bastard."

Six hours later, Jon Bledsoe's final order for the first phase came in. Talik and Jhama had been gathered around his desk since their shift ended, constantly scanning the lower band channels until they finally found the short message. It was a higher frequency than normal, and Jhama chewed her lip. Maybe Lieutenant Acoua would find this one. Feralans had notoriously good hearing, and this message would no doubt cause some *very* small disruptions to the main channels.

"What's it say?" Jhama asked flatly, unable to bring herself to look at her friend.

"Mister Omarik," Talik read, "at fourteen hundred hours, attach the package to engineering portside wall and execute. Gas the room first. Do not keep people out of danger."

"That's lunch hour," Jhama said in the silence that followed, picking at her sleeve. "There'll be fewer people in there."

"Are you sure you—"

"I *will* save at least one," she interrupted firmly, staring at him with a harshness that he was almost certain belonged to Lieutenant Acoua.

"Why are you looking at me like the Wetworker?" he asked, giving her a forced smile and a laugh that came off more nervous than amused.

She stared at him silently for a few moments before forcing herself to speak in that same detached way.

"Because my plan hinges on not saving you." Talik's gaze slowly changed from looking at her to looking through her. "I'm sorry, Talik."

"No, it's...it's fine." He cleared his throat and looked away from her, back to the computer screen. "You should go. You've got an hour to distance yourself from me."

She gently squeezed his shoulder.

"I'm sure I'll see you soon," she whispered and stood up to leave. "Goodbye, Talik Omarik. It was an honor serving with you."

He looked up at her and smiled sadly.

"It was an honor serving with you, too." She was about to open the door when he continued. "Keep messing with him, Jhama." She looked back at him, and he gave her a half-hearted smile. "He's *really* gonna hate it."

"I plan to," she said with a smirk, her old self for a precious moment.

She quickly left, head held high and heart pounding, and Talik began prepping the package in his closet. It was the last time either would see the other alive.

On the bridge, Anthia frowned and adjusted her headset. There was something there, turning the constant static into a burst of staccato notes and warping the main frequencies. It was barely noticeable, but it was there—repeating on a loop. Working quickly, she created a new folder on her computer and quickly pulled a recording of the odd fragment. She'd probably have to find a decryption algorithm once she filtered out all the other frequencies on top of it. And while she was almost certain it was a coded message, she was absolutely positive that whatever it was, it wasn't supposed to be there.

"Sir, I've found something odd on our communications channels."

Oren turned to Lieutenant Acoua, one eyebrow raised in a silent request for her to continue.

"I'm not sure what it is, but it could be a coded message on one of our lower band frequencies. All I know for sure at this moment is that it's a repeating pattern that shouldn't be there."

The captain quickly got up and approached her station.

"Let me hear it." He waited as she went to pull off her headset and hand it to him, but she stopped. "What is it?"

"It isn't there anymore, sir." She frowned slightly, adjusting a few dials. "I still have the copy I made, but it's gone on our frequencies."

"More shadows?" he asked softly, and Anthia stared intently at her screen.

"No, sir. It's more likely that they stopped broadcasting. I'd stake my reputation on that." She pulled up the copy she'd made and handed her headset over to her captain, watching him closely as he slid it on under his horns. "This isn't a shadow, sir. Someone's talking, and they don't want us to hear."

A dark look crossed Oren's face, and he handed the headset back.

"Notify Sprit and get to work on deciphering the noise. I want to know what's being said and who's saying it."

"Yes, sir."

He returned to his captain's chair as she started the tedious process of filtering out the interfering static and isolating the lower frequency channel. He steepled his hands over his nose and mouth, elbows resting on the arms of his chair. He could hear Anthia talking to Sprit over the comms, explaining the situation to her in quick undertones.

The hairs on the back of his neck stood on end.

CHAPTER 10

Sprit groaned softly to herself and reluctantly sat up as she switched off her earwig. Six hours of sleep wasn't bad; wasn't good, but it wasn't bad either. Oh well. She'd just get up, deal with whatever mess this was with Anthia, and then go back to sleep. As long as it didn't pan out into something even bigger, because if it did, she was sorely tempted to just go to Balok and ask for a sedative to take her out. Let Holt deal with the chaos of whatever this new mess was. She needed *sleep*.

After all, *she* was the one who'd organized and headed a *successful* sting operation in an underground trafficking ring. And she was the one with a human roommate. She had a lot on her plate, that was all she was trying to say.

"Computer, time?"

"Thirteen hundred hours."

Rin started awake at the electronic voice and pushed herself into a sitting position against the headboard.

"Good morning," Sprit yawned, climbing over the human's legs to get out of bed and grab another uniform from her closet. "Here."

She tossed a skirt and shirt at her roommate without really looking, and Rin sleepily caught them both. The fabric was oddly thick but still soft—dark blue with embroidered leaves and bird-like creatures in reds, oranges, and greens along the hems of both garments.

"It's the only thing I've got in here that's big on me, so it might fit you," Sprit explained, quickly pulling off her pajamas.

Rin followed suit, half-asleep.

"Thanks."

"Hey, so I have to meet up with Anthia and probably Holt today to talk about something that happened." She took her holster out of her desk drawer and put it on, still hurrying around the room in her socks. "But we can go eat first, have them meet us there."

"Oh." Rin yawned again as she pulled Sprit's shirt on. "Okay."

"Really?" Sprit asked, turning to the girl in surprise, but then rolled her eyes. "You're still half-asleep. No wonder you're not uncomfortable with this yet." She quickly ducked into the bathroom and returned with a hairbrush. "Here." She sat down on the edge of the bed next to Rin and quickly brushed the girl's long, straight hair, ridding it of its few tangles before quickly braiding it. "Your hair's really soft," she muttered absently as she tied it off with a strip of leather.

"Thanks?"

Sprit laughed and patted the girl's back as she got up.

"Come on. Put on your shoes, and let's get going."

"*Sprit Matzepo.*"

Anthia touched her earwig, turning her seat towards the security station where Holt was sitting.

"Commander," she greeted, and Holt immediately looked to her.

"Good morning to you, too, Anthia. Rin and I are heading to the cafeteria if you and Holt would like to join us to talk about whatever it was you said we needed to talk about."

Anthia minutely shook her head, irritated.

"Commander, it's sensitive. I really think it would be irresponsible to talk about it in the cafeteria."

"Well, *obviously* not the sensitive stuff, Anthia. Come on, I'm not an idiot. Just bring the data, and we can look it over there. Figure out our plan of attack, see what we're dealing with."

Anthia frowned, clearly displeased, and turned to her station.

"If you think it's best, commander. I'll join you shortly." She disconnected and glanced back to Holt. "Lieutenant, your boss wants to see us in the cafeteria to discuss our problem."

"Is the cafeteria the best place for this conversation, ma'am?" he asked, getting up nonetheless and following his coworker to the lift.

Anthia looked forward, expression somewhere between flat and annoyed as the lift doors closed.

"It is to her."

Holt deliberately pushed the deck four icon, diplomatically avoiding her bitter reply and hoping she wouldn't notice.

She noticed.

"*This* is quieter?"

"Look, kid, *Starlight* has a hundred and ten people aboard. There's always noise in here." Sprit steered her roommate towards a table in the corner that was closest to the door but still facing the room. "I can wave our guests down from here. Besides, it's the quietest table, which I know isn't saying much." She side-eyed the human as the girl sat down, and smirked. "At least Lieutenant Cathla isn't here this time."

Rin flushed furiously.

"I didn't *mean* to scream at him—"

"Relax, Rin, I'm joking," she snorted and clapped the girl on the shoulder as she walked towards the buffet table at the other end of the room. "I'll be back with food!"

Rin sat there nervously, tapping her foot. She was starting to regret turning her implant back on. There were so many different conversations going on, and she felt like she could hear all of them. And then the smells of all the different foods, the colors and shapes of all the different people—it was all so much. Maybe she could try and sneak away back to Sprit's quarters. That'd be nice. It was quiet in there, and only one alien came in at a time.

She was about to throw in the towel and try to find her way back to Sprit's room on her own when the main doors slid open and two people walked in. She recognized one instantly as the lieutenant Sprit had been working with at the auction, but the other—the one who looked like that nice engineer she'd talked to, Avery—she hadn't seen her before.

She looked mean, Rin decided. She had a permanent semi-scowl on her face, a general air that dared people to come up to her. In fact, Rin noticed that the crew she passed seemed to scoot their chairs closer to their tables—deliberately avoiding contact when the black-eyed woman approached but watching her back with fearful eyes as she left.

Oddly, Holt seemed perfectly at ease beside her.

Rin awkwardly waved, leaning slightly over the table to get the duo's attention, and both caught her gesture at a somewhat frightening speed. She swallowed hard and sat back in her chair.

"Uh, hi. Sprit's getting food," she awkwardly greeted as the two people joined her at the table. Anthia sat down without a word, immediately opening a file on her tablet and attaching her headset to the device, but Holt hesitated.

"Miss Cooper," he began, and she blinked in surprise.

"*You*. You were the one behind the door."

He respectfully inclined his head.

"I apologize for frightening you during the transfer. It was not my intention." His gaze was still firmly averted from her face, and despite herself, Rin wanted to smirk at his proper demeanor.

"It's okay. I scare easily," she offered, letting herself give that small smile she'd been feeling.

"May I join you?" he asked, still keeping his eyes downcast, and Rin frowned, confused.

"Um…"

"He needs permission to interrupt your space," Anthia brusquely cut in, not looking up from her work. "Just tell him yes so he can sit down."

"Oh, um, yeah. Sorry, I mean, yes. Yes, you can join me."

Holt bowed shallowly to her and pulled out the seat across from her, and Rin took advantage of his closeness to get a look at his face.

His horns, or whatever he called them, reminded her of the paint on Tzo Runner's face. The small, nub-like spines ran in a boomerang-esque pattern around each eye, on both sides starting above an eyebrow and curving around the outside of his eye-socket to end in a point just under the midpoint of his cheekbone. They were small at the start of his brows, at most half an inch, but by the time they reached his cheeks, they shrank until they were no more than an eighth of an inch high. Another row of the same spines ran down the sides of his face from his temples to the middle of his jawline, once again growing smaller as they descended. The path of the ivory-like bones seemed to curve back towards his ears slightly as they crossed his cheekbones before slanting forward again to end at his jaw, lining up with the ending of the spine ridges around his eyes.

Those eyes…there was something unsettling about those eyes…

Eyes that were staring back at her.

She cleared her throat and looked down at her lap, distracting herself with the hem of her shirt.

"Well, this is a merry bunch," Sprit drawled, and Holt and Rin both looked at her. "Did Holt bow to you already?"

"Uh," Rin floundered, feeling herself start to blush again, and Sprit snorted.

"Don't worry, he does it with everyone. You just learn to roll with it." She hooked her foot around the leg of her chair much like she had in the medbay and pulled it out as she set the trays of food down. "Okay, Rin, I grabbed you some dowpi soup." She slid the corresponding tray over, and the human curiously picked at it with her spoon. "It's a dish from chef's home planet that's somewhat like stews from Earth. I also grabbed some more of what you had last night in case the stew doesn't work out."

"Thanks."

Sprit noted with relief that the girl's half-smile seemed genuine and then moved on to her crewmates.

"Holt, I got you your root tea, and Anthia I got you black coffee."

"Commander, that wasn't necessary—"

"Take the tea, Holt, it won't kill you," she playfully snapped, continually nudging his arm with the mug until he took it from her.

"Coffee?" Rin asked curiously as Anthia snatched up the drink.

"Yeah, we, uh, figured out how to replicate the earth process with a similar bean from the Feralan homeworld. Anthia basically runs on the stuff," Sprit explained and dropped into her seat as she ate what looked like oatmeal. "So, Rin. This is Lieutenant Commander Anthia Acoua. She's the ship communication's officer and Avery's older sister...Anthia. *Anthia.*" She reached out and gently tugged one side of the woman's headset slightly off her ear. "I'm trying to introduce you, get your head out of your tablet. Say hello."

The woman paused the audio file and stiffly looked up at Rin.

"Hello, Cooper."

"Uh, it's actually Rin," the human started correcting, but Anthia was already putting the headset back on and resuming her work. Sprit just rolled her eyes.

"Don't take it personally, she's a sociopath." She jerked her thumb at Holt next. "This is Lieutenant Lewis Holt. He's my deputy chief of security and head of our tactical division for the obvious reason of he can read...minds." She stopped as she fully looked at her partner. "Seriously, you two?!"

Holt immediately looked up from where he was carefully writing some ciphers on a napkin. Anthia continued working, stealing his notes from him without even looking.

"Sorry, commander, did you ask me something?"

Sprit sat there at a loss for words for a second, and Rin giggled.

"No. No, I didn't ask you something, Lewis," she finally answered, shaking her head despairingly. "I *was* trying to introduce you to Rin, but *no.* No, I guess we're just jumping straight into work."

"My apologies, ma'am," Holt began, going to set his pen aside but stopping when Sprit directed him back to his writing.

"No, it's fine. Just keep doing what you were doing, I'll talk to our human on my own." She fought a smirk as Holt sat there, caught in her passive-aggressive reply and unsure what to do, until she finally relented. "It's fine, Holt, seriously. I know you don't do socializing."

"Ah. Thank you, ma'am."

"As you can see, they're a right pair," Sprit sighed, mirroring Rin's amused smile as she went back to her food. "How's the stew?"

"It's…okay?"

"Yeah, Daniel said that, too. Well, actually, he said—" Sprit suddenly stopped talking, raising a hand and tilting her head slightly to the side in that way Rin noticed everyone did when they got a message through their earwig. "Balok, what is it?" There was a long pause, and Sprit took a deep breath. "Okay. I'll send her over once she's done eating. How does ten minutes sound? Okay. Bye, doc."

"Does Balok want to see me?"

Sprit looked at the human and nodded.

"Yeah, he just wants to go over some test results with you. Nothing to worry about." She turned to her coworkers. "Okay, so what's going on with our frequency issue?"

Rin drew one leg up onto the chair with her as she ate, watching the officers with poorly veiled interest. Anthia threw her a distrusting look before pulling off her headset and speaking.

"Without saying anything sensitive, I noticed some patterned noise in one of the higher lower band frequencies. It was causing distortion to the main channels. I managed to get a copy of it before it stopped, and I gave it to Holt for a second opinion." She spun the tablet around and slid it to Sprit. "He agreed with my call."

"Which is?" Sprit looked to Holt, and he indicated the screen.

"It's deliberately patterned, shall we say, ma'am?" he offered, lowering his voice a little bit. "We can't say much more and still avoid sensitive information."

Sprit grew serious, picking up the headset and tablet and listening for herself. Anthia and Holt absently sipped at their drinks, and Rin finished up her stew. It was actually pretty good.

"Any luck with usual ciphers?" Sprit asked after a few minutes, and her partners shook their heads. "Seriously? How many have you tried?"

"Several," Anthia replied, intentionally vague as she side-eyed their human guest.

Rin glared back at her and continued eating.

"Most likely, it's unique," Holt explained, "established between the two parties in an earlier correspondence."

"Holt knows some archaic ciphers we don't have in our databases," Anthia added, taking the tablet back from her commander and putting her headset on again. "He's writing them out for me, and I'll see if I can match patterns."

"Good." Sprit finished the last spoonfuls of her lunch and set the empty bowl on her tray. "Engineering has a few programs we can use as well if you haven't tried that already."

"Kick the results down to my quarters," Anthia said and set her mug next to Sprit's bowl as she stood up. "There are too many eyes and ears on the bridge." She collected Holt's completed cipher napkins and stiffly inclined her head to her superior. "Ma'am."

"See you, Anthia."

Rin watched the small, tense woman depart and once again noticed how everybody shrank away from her path.

"She scares everyone," she said, and Sprit followed her gaze.

"Yeah, like I said—she's a sociopath. Don't get me wrong. I love her. But there's a reason some people call her the Wetworker."

"Wetworker?" Rin repeated, alarmed. "As in assassin?"

"She's good at her job, Miss Cooper," Holt said softly, not looking at either of them. Sprit raised an eyebrow in surprise and turned her seat to face her deputy. "She can do what others cannot in…unfortunate situations. We don't give her enough credit for that ability in those moments, I believe."

Sprit grinned.

"Lewis, do you have a crush on Anthia?"

She expected sputtering, protesting, at least some flushing. She didn't expect him to look up at her evenly, with that ever-present, open and yet unreadable face.

"Hardly, ma'am. I simply understand her." He placed his mug next to the other empty dishes on Sprit's tray. "Ma'am, it is currently thirteen fifty."

"Oh, djienn. Rin, you need to get to Balok. Here." Holt passed her a napkin, and she drew a quick map. "This is the way from here to the medbay. Remember, you have to go up to deck three." Rin nervously took it from her and got up from the table. "Don't worry, you won't get lost. Just follow the map. Go on." She watched her roommate hesitantly leave the cafeteria and briefly laughed once the door closed behind the teenager. "She's definitely gonna get lost. Okay, Holt, let's go."

"Shouldn't you—"

"She'll figure it out, she's smart. Come on, let's get to engineering."

Her deputy shook his head and reluctantly followed her out.

Talik took a deep breath and pulled the gasmask over his face. He'd just finished setting up sleep gas canisters behind the grates of the air ducts, including the one he was currently hiding in. Staying as quiet as possible, he checked the time on his watch again—nine minutes—and counted how many people were still in engineering.

Fifteen.

His heart sank.

In her quarters, Jhama knelt before the small shrine in the hall between her quarter's two bedrooms. She clasped her hands before her lips.

"Zhel, forgive me. I've done something unforgiveable...."

"Okay." Rin stepped out of the elevator, turning the map a few different directions before finding the right way. She walked forwards for a while until she saw she was nearing the boiler room and the rudimentary drawing told her to hang a left. "Oh, good. She's not sending me through there."

That room made her skin crawl. She couldn't explain it. It just gave her a very bad feeling.

So far, Rin had attracted several strange stares. To be fair, an unfamiliar human wandering around the halls in a uniform that wasn't hers and her nose buried in a scribbled-on napkin was bound to draw attention. She was almost positive this was Sprit's idea of a practical joke, but she wasn't about to stop someone and ask how she was really supposed to get to the medbay. She was worried she'd throw up her lunch on the unfortunate Samaritan the moment she opened her mouth.

"Just trust the map, Rin," she whispered, hanging another right and almost bumping into someone. "Sorry!" They just kept walking though, and she frowned after the ensign. "How rude."

She continued on her way and, after hanging a final left, sighed in relief.

"There's the medbay." She folded the napkin and tucked it into the hem of her borrowed skirt. "That wasn't so bad."

The moment the door hissed open, Balok looked up.

"Rin, is that you?" he called, rolling back on his stool so he could see past the curtain. Instantly, he lit up, smiling broadly. "It is! Come in." He gestured grandly to the curtained-off bed beside him, and Rin joined him, sitting down on the covered mattress. "How have you been?"

"Uh, fine?" she said hesitantly, watching as he quickly typed at his console and opened several files. "Is there something wrong with me?"

"Oh no, it's nothing like that," Balok assured her. "I just wanted to ask if you've ever had any odd results during your check-ups at home."

"No…should I have?"

"Hm," was all Balok said in return, still typing, and Rin nervously drummed her fingers against her knee. "No," he finally answered, still a little distant. "No, you are in perfect health, nothing to worry about."

"Then why am I here?"

Balok finally looked up and gave that same over-enthusiastic smile.

"Oh, apologies, Miss Cooper. I just needed some more scans. Again, it's nothing invasive, just some more x-ray type lights—that sort of thing. This time I'll be focusing on your circulatory system."

Rin's nervousness died away, and she gave a small laugh.

"You like poking and prodding, don't you?"

"Well, if you were in my shoes, wouldn't you?" he returned playfully and grabbed a couple scanners from the cabinet above his computer. "We don't meet many humans, let alone ones in good shape. You, my dear, are a godsend."

"Glad I could help," she said wryly and let the doctor ease her down onto her back. As she got settled, he powered on the first device. "It's not going to hurt?"

"No more than a ray of light should," he assured her kindly.

Rin closed her eyes and did her best to relax.

Talik kicked open the ventilation shaft grate and climbed onto the catwalk, double-checking to make sure his gasmask was working. Stage one had been pretty easy, he reflected as he stepped over a couple unconscious bodies on his way to the main floor ladder. He slid down the sides, not bothering to use the rungs, and carefully walked around a few more people on his way to the portside wall—the wall that had nothing but the stars beyond it. He didn't have much time left. He gingerly set his duffle bag on the floor and pulled the package and a toolkit from within its dark depths.

Attach with bolts. Make sure it's level. Not too close to those wires and pipes. Careful with it all…don't want it to happen too soon.

He glanced at his watch as he mounted the device.

Thirteen fifty-nine. He had to move fast.

"Rin made it to the medbay, ma'am," Holt announced, gaze slightly unfocused as he mentally checked in on the girl, and Sprit looked up a few decks to where the medbay would be.

"Told you she'd be fine," she said with a grin.

He wisely didn't comment.

"Commander, I was thinking that in addition to trying to decode the signal, we could examine the communications department's short-term archived data. We can determine if any other messages have been sent," he said, slowing his pace slightly so his chief could keep up a little easier.

"That's a good idea. Wait!" Holt started slightly as Sprit grabbed his upper arm and brought them both to a stop about ten feet from the engineering main doors. She gestured back over her shoulder in the direction they'd just come. "I just remembered, I have a decryption tablet in my quarters. It's some untested portable device Avery came up with—you upload the encrypted data, and the program devises new ciphers on the spot to try and crack it." She clapped Holt's shoulder and started backing away. "I'll meet you in engineering. I'm just going to run up and get it."

"Yes, ma'am." They started to go their own directions, but Holt stopped again. "Commander, should I start the programs we have in engineering or wait for you to get back?"

"Uh, just start running them. I won't be long."

"Yes, ma'am."

Holt turned away and resumed his purposeful walk to the engineering doors while Sprit retreated down the hall. He pulled out his tablet as he went, calling up the audio file Anthia had sent him. There were a few possible programs they could use to clean it up some more and get a clearer read on the pattern and data within the frequencies. In fact, he already had a couple of ideas about where to start.

The door to engineering slid open, and Holt looked up and froze.

Bodies. His heart pounded painfully in his chest. His breaths turned ragged. There were bodies everywhere, on the floor, the catwalks, collapsed over the consoles. They were dead. They were all *dead*—wait.

Wait, no, not dead. They weren't dead, they were still thinking—

"No. No, not you, too," Talik whimpered, and Holt looked to him, stunned expression morphing into one of horror. "I'm...I'm *sorry.*"

"T-Talik," the man stammered, ashen. "What..."

The Tarikian glanced helplessly at his watch.

14:00:01

Without another word, the young ensign swung his hand towards the detonator with one final thought, and Holt lunged forward.

May the afterlife forgive me.

"TALIK, NO!"

CHAPTER 11

Sprit's heart plummeted into her stomach at Holt's shout, and she spun around. Lewis didn't shout. He didn't so much as raise his voice.

"Holt, what—"

A deafening boom suddenly shattered the hall, engulfing the door to engineering in flames, and Sprit's temple connected with the wall as the explosion threw her sideways.

Holt. She blindly pushed herself back to her feet, her vision blurring to the point of near-uselessness as the ship's alarms started blaring. *Get to Holt.*

"Lewis!" she shouted and instantly regretted it as blinding pain spiked through her skull. "Help...somebody, we need..." She reached blindly for her earwig, but her bloody fingers found only empty space.

The blast. Must have been knocked loose in the blast. She stumbled over to the nearest PA system panel, catching herself on one of the hall's support beams and slamming her hand on the broadcast button.

"Engineering, code black," she recited, head buzzing and throbbing at the same time. Her voice probably sounded awful and unsteady. "All hands—engineering, code black." She shoved off the wall and shakily headed towards the burning room. She thought she could see a mass of debris across the hall from the door, half-illuminated by the flames, but she couldn't be sure. "Lewis?"

Holt gritted his teeth, breathing in sharp, harsh bursts. He couldn't see anything. Everything was just white *pain*, especially his right leg, at his thigh. Something was crushing down on him, something hot and sharp, and *Creator*, it *hurt*. He couldn't move, it all just hurt *so much*—

"Lewis?" Sprit repeated as she drew closer, and she saw something in the rubble move. And despite the burns and indigo blood, she recognized him. "Oh, djienn. Holt!" She closed the distance between them at a sprint and immediately grabbed the jagged console remains pinning him down. "I'm gonna get you out, don't worry."

"Commander, *don't*—"

———

"And that was your last test," Balok said and patted Rin's shoulder with a toothless smile. "Wasn't so bad, was it?"

"Never is," she replied under her breath, and he beamed.

"You've become quite vocal since we last saw each other," he said with a pleased *humph*. "I must say I quite like this Rin."

She carefully took his offered hand and sat up.

"Anything weird on your tests?"

"Well, I don't know," he said with an honest shrug and ever-present smile. "I haven't had a chance to examine them, yet, have I?"

"Can I go back to Sprit's room now?"

"I don't see why not." Rin sighed gratefully, and Balok raised an eyebrow. "You should start calling it your room if you really want to get back at her for sending you up here with a napkin," he added in a peeved aside. "What kind of host does a thing like that?"

"Sprit," Rin said, and he chuckled at her answer.

"Very true. I shall see you around, Miss Cooper."

"See you, Balok."

Just as Rin slid off the bed, the floor rocked with a muffled boom from two decks below, and she and everyone else toppled over with startled shouts. The lights instantly powered down with the whine of a dying generator, and Rin could feel the ship decelerating in the dark, the hum in the tiles beneath her palms changing pitch. In the following silence, an alarm started blaring, loud and eerie, and the lights flickered back on.

"Balok?" Rin's voice warbled dangerously, and the doctor quickly pushed himself up from where he'd fallen against his desk, his buoyant personality gone. When he spoke, it felt like he was talking to himself.

"That was an explosion."

"What?"

Before he could elaborate, the PA system came to life, and a familiar voice started speaking, hoarse and shaking.

"Engineering, code black. All hands—engineering, code black."

"Alright everyone, prepare for incoming trauma!" Balok shouted, and instantly his staff were moving, pulling out supplies and clearing out beds and rooms.

"Sprit. That's Sprit," Rin whispered, fear rising in her throat like bile, and she shakily stood up. "Balok, what's going on?"

The siren changed pattern and pitch as an automated voice repeated Sprit's words, and the doctor went still in the chaos around him.

"Rin," he said softly, staring fixedly at the medbay doors. "Get out of here. Now."

The human watched wide-eyed as he pulled a trauma gown over his uniform and started running.

Sprit lifted the debris off Holt in a quick jerk, and her gut twisted as her deputy howled in pain, his bloody hands struggling to push the metal off as he reflexively slammed his head back into the wall. As she shoved the offending wreckage away from them, the seared metal burning her fingers, she saw why he was screaming.

"*Djïenn*, I'm sorry!" she cried, kneeling by his side and pressing down with all of her weight on the ragged hole in his right thigh. "I'm so sorry! I didn't realize it impaled your leg. *Djïenn*, that's a lot of blood, okay, um, here." She grabbed his shaking, burned hands and pressed them down over the gaping wound as she took off her belt and quickly buckled it around his leg like a tourniquet. "There. There we go."

"Doctor Balok," he choked out, struggling to regain control of his voice as he grabbed at his leg around her hands. "*Please*—"

"Okay." She gingerly touched his chin, tilting his head up slightly to look at her. "Hey, stay here. Come on." She pulled his arm around her shoulders, trying to ignore how burned nearly every inch of his skin and uniform was, trying to ignore how she was almost certain she could see bone in some of the cuts on his face and arms. And the smell of it all, the smoke and the char…

"Here we go," she grunted and stood up, all-but dragging her deputy with her. "You okay?"

"Y-yes."

She looked down at him, heart racing as his head rested heavily on her shoulder and his legs almost gave out.

"Liar." She started walking forward, and her fear skyrocketed at his disjointed steps beside her. His breath rattled unnaturally in his lungs, and she swallowed hard. "Holt. *Lewis*—"

"There! Sprit!"

Sprit looked up and nearly collapsed in relief.

"Jhama, we need a stretcher!"

"No." Sprit looked at Holt in disbelief, and he weakly shook his head against her arm. "No, the…the others, they need the stretchers." He gritted his teeth and inhaled sharply as Sprit shifted her grip on his wrist. "I can walk, ma'am."

Liar, she thought again.

She waved the approaching response teams towards engineering, and her gut churned at the way Holt sagged against her.

"Go. Go, we're fine."

"Are you sure? We can—"

"We're fine, Jhama, get the others out!" she ordered, voice cracking as she pointed down the hall. When they still hesitated, she took a deep breath and scowled. *Be their commander.* "GO!"

Everyone sprinted past her, and Sprit plowed forward, hauling Holt along with her at her renewed pace. They were almost to the lift, almost there.

She tried to ignore the trail of blue blood she knew they were leaving behind.

The lift opened as another team arrived, and Sprit waved them on again, giving her breathless thanks to the last ensign out who held the doors for them. Once they were safely inside, she hit the deck three icon and sagged against the wall, holding Holt close against her. The small space was silent except for their ragged breathing, and Sprit watched the flashing red light above the door as they ascended.

"What the hell happened?" she whispered as they passed deck four.

"It was Talik." Holt tried to stand up a little more, bracing himself on her shoulder and the handlebar behind them.

"*Talik?* Talik Omarik?"

He let his head thump back against the wall and screwed his eyes shut at her sharp, disbelieving question.

"Holt?"

"It was Talik," he repeated, and she glanced uneasily at his white-knuckled grip on the bar. "It was Talik...."

"Lewis." He blinked dazedly, swaying on his feet. "Hey, don't do this to me right now."

Just as they reached deck three and the doors opened, he collapsed, and Sprit grunted as she caught the full weight of her taller coworker.

"Holt! Holt, come on, we're almost at the medbay." She stumbled out of the elevator, half-carrying and half-dragging her coworker with her. "Come on, you annoying, proper, rule-following pain in the...come on, it's just ten more feet!"

She was almost at the door when it suddenly slid open, and somebody was there, taking the brunt of the weight off her shoulders and helping her inside. Balok. It was Balok, she realized and wiped at her eyes with a bloody hand that she realized was stained red and not blue.

"What happened?"

"I don't know," she gasped as they ran inside, and the security chief caught a brief glance of Rin standing in the corner, shaking like a leaf. "I wasn't in engineering, I was down the hall. He just keeps saying—"

"It was Talik," Holt mumbled, coming back into consciousness as she and the doctor sat him on the edge of a bed and quickly laid him back. "It was *Talik*."

"That. He just keeps saying that," Sprit finished, climbing up onto the bed with Lewis and straddling his legs so she could put pressure on his wound. Her voice was still shaking, though not as badly as her hands, and she sniffed hard. "I don't know what happened."

Rin's breathing was a jagged mess, and she pressed herself further into the corner as more people ran into the medbay, carrying people on stretchers. They were all scorched, raw and bloody, and the combination of hellish sights and smells was making her nauseous.

"Hanali'a," Holt croaked, trying to push himself off the bed, and Balok gently but firmly pressed him back down.

"Lieutenant, you're badly hurt."

"I have to speak with Hanali'a—"

"You can speak with the first officer once you're better, lieutenant. But right now, I need you to lie still." Balok pulled over a rolling tray of different supplies and tools and quickly turned back to his patient. "How is your control holding up?"

Holt turned his pain-filled gaze on the doctor and disjointedly shook his head.

"Put me under," he whispered hoarsely, and Sprit increased pressure on his leg, watching almost numbly as near-black indigo continued to seep through her fingers, mixing with her own red blood. "*Please*, put me under...."

Balok quickly depressed a syringe in the man's arm, and Holt tensed at first, his breathing picking up a little until rather quickly he relaxed and fell unconscious.

"Please tell me that was supposed to happen," Sprit said tightly, and Balok nodded, quickly opening more gauze packets and handing them to her.

"What happened to him?" he asked as she quickly packed her partner's leg and resumed pressure.

"Impaled by debris. I think it used to be a control panel."

Behind them, Rin drew closer, her heart in her throat. And as they continued to speak in rapid-fire medical jargon, exchanging instructions and questions and answers, she looked closer at the patient on the bed.

She wasn't sure who it was from far away, and morbid curiosity dragged her forward.

He looked like something out of a nightmare. She couldn't quite tell what was charred skin and what was just soot and inhuman blood. Balok pulled the overhead lamp down, and Rin blanched as she realized the man had been burned so deep in some places that the bones of his horns were visible deep into his tissue and the bridge of his nose shone white under the infirmary lights.

Horns.

And she realized with a sickening lurch, that it was Holt.

"I think the bleeding stopped," Sprit whispered as she eased up on his leg.

"Somebody get me a regenerator!" Balok said loudly to the room at large, and Dalia ran over, handing him a bloodstained device. He turned it on, slowly moving its red light over the shallower wounds, and Rin watched in horror and fascination as the burns and cuts sealed, the skin gradually regenerating where the light touched. "Casualties?"

"Uh, three dead on arrival, five more in critical condition who we'll probably lose, not including Lieutenant Holt." Balok clenched his jaw, and Dalia continued, "we're waiting on the last seven, but reports say they have moderate to mild burns, so they'll probably make it."

"Do you have a patient?" he asked, and Dalia shook her head. "Then, you're with me. Get a dose of aigren or another neurosuppressant if we're out and prepare the stasis pod just in case."

"Stasis pod?" Sprit echoed as Dalia left. "Balok—"

"I have six critical cases, including Holt," he interrupted, speaking and working quickly. "If I can get him stable enough for the stasis pod, I can move on to other patients who need me."

He set the regenerator down and pulled a sterile field lamp over the bed with one hand while he grabbed a pair of surgical tweezers with the other. Rin inhaled sharply, and Sprit watched unblinkingly as the doctor pulled slivers of metal from Holt's body and called for more aigren as Lewis started shifting, tossing and turning.

"They're starting to wake him up," he said grimly as Dalia returned with another syringe.

"Who?" Sprit asked, and Balok glanced at her before returning to his grisly work.

"The crew. With this much pain and trauma, Lieutenant Holt's mind is struggling to cope *and* keep our thoughts at bay at the same time."

"We just had lunch."

Both officers glanced at Rin for a moment, and the doctor somehow grew even more concerned. She was within arm's reach, watching them work with sickened eyes.

"Rin," he said tensely, "I thought I told you to get out of here."

"I-I just had lunch with him. I just saw him, ten minutes ago."

"Sprit, can you get her out of here?" Balok asked lowly, turning back to his work. "She doesn't need to be here for this."

"Yeah." Sprit carefully climbed off the bed. "Come on, Rin."

The doors slid open again, and two more response teams returned, carrying with them five of the remaining seven patients.

"Take them to the empty beds in the back in order of least to most severe. Make sure the most severe are *closest* to us!" Balok shouted over his shoulder and did a double take as he saw someone else run in with a security detail on his heels. He looked back at his patient. "Captain, you should be on the bridge."

"Hanali'a has the chair," he replied and joined them at Holt's side. As soon as he saw who it was in the bed, he ran his hands over horns and scalp. "Report."

"Fifteen people in engineering, not including Lewis. Three dead, six in critical condition, seven with moderate to mild burns," Sprit recited, clearing her throat and taking deep breaths. "I don't know what happened. Holt just kept saying it was Talik." She put her hands over her nose and mouth, shaking. "I don't—I don't know what happened."

Oren put a hand on her shoulder and pulled her back as Balok set his equipment aside.

"He's as stable as I have time to make him right now. Let's get him in the stasis pod."

Sprit and Rin watched the medbay staff shift Holt onto a stretcher and carry him into a side room. The human felt weightless, ungrounded. She couldn't grab hold of anything, couldn't touch the world around her.

"Sprit, I need you looking over footage in security," Oren ordered. "Find out what happened." Sprit continued to stand there, staring at the room her deputy had vanished into. "Sprit. Commander Matzepo!"

"Yes, sir," she said with a jump and looked at him. "Sorry, sir."

"Get yourself seen to first."

"I'm fine, sir."

Oren looked at her somberly—at the bruise forming at her left eye and temple, the red trickling from her hairline and oozing from her right palm, and the soot and blue blood that was decidedly not hers staining her hands and uniform.

"You're not fine, Matzepo," he said lowly, and she sniffed, dragging the back of her hand across her nose. "Get looked at."

"I can't, Oren," she persisted, backing towards the door and shaking her head. "The others need the attention. *Holt* needs the attention. I just need to find out why Talik did this to us."

She turned away and ignored Oren's calls as she braced herself on a nearby desk. She felt woozy and nauseous, achy almost.

Adrenaline. I'm just coming down from the adrenaline. Nothing more. It can't be anything more.

Her hand curled into a fist on the desk, and her chest burned.

"I've got a bomber to find," she muttered.

Oren watched her unsteadily storm off, feeling far more tired and older than he had moments before. He beheld his crew, his *people*, around him and closed his eyes against the flashing lights and blaring alarms. They were bleeding, suffering. Even now, he could hear them and the frantic medical staff trying to keep them alive. But there was one presence in particular that kept drawing his attention.

"Are you okay?" he asked, opening his eyes and turning to where the human was standing.

She looked so small, and he realized with a pain in his heart that she was wearing Sprit's old clothes. Her outfit, combined with her teary eyes and the medbay slip-ons made her look like a child, and he remembered painfully that she was. She wasn't even an adult yet. He reached out to her, and she took a step back, bumping into Balok's desk and fumbling for his stool.

"It's okay," he said gently and raised his hands to his shoulders, waiting for her to catch her balance. "It's okay."

All Rin could see was the bloody bed where Holt had been laying, the stained white tiles around them, and she quickly reached for her ears, trying to find the small buttons Sprit had pressed last night. She didn't want to hear this. She didn't want to hear the moans and the screams around her, the chaos of alarms and people shouting orders—

"I want it off. I want it off, I don't want to hear, I want it *off*—"

Oren was suddenly by her side, his calloused hands gently reaching for her implants, and the world fell silent. She hung onto his wrists, not caring that she was pressing his rough palms over her ears. She could feel him. She could touch him.

He was the ground she couldn't find.

"It's all going to be okay," he whispered, knowing the sobbing girl couldn't hear him. "You're okay, Rin."

"We just had lunch," she repeated, haunted, and Oren gently, bit by bit, tugged her closer until she finally let go of his wrists and pulled her arms close to her chest as she leaned against him.

"It's all going to be okay," he repeated and delicately wrapped her in his arms, trying to hold her shaking form together.

And while Rin couldn't hear it, she could feel his voice rumbling in his chest beneath her head. Somehow, it brought just as much comfort.

Balok left the stasis pod room and met Oren's eyes over the top of Rin's head. Even from here, the doctor could hear the girl's tears, and if he didn't have a medbay full of people to treat, he knew he'd be right there with her. But he *did* have a medbay full of people to treat, so Balok simply nodded and gave a subtle thumbs-up before returning to the fray to help another patient.

Oren tightened his hold around Rin and sighed in relief.

Holt was alive. Thank the ancestors. At least one of them was alive.

"Come on, Rin," he said gently, and she looked up at him as he guided her towards the medbay door with a kind hand on her back. "I'll take you back to your quarters. You shouldn't be in this mess."

Rin just closed her eyes and trusted that the man leading her onwards through their muted world was taking her somewhere safe.

———

Jhama quickly ducked into her quarters and ran for her computer. She was shaking—torn between rage, fear, grief, and vindictive spite.

He had to have contacted her. She knew he had two other agents aboard. He'd told them so on the moon. He had to know the explosion didn't go off as it should've, that it went broad and not tall, that it didn't take out any engines. That it didn't kill *everyone* inside, only half of them.

He had to know that they'd messed him up.

Heart in her throat, she powered up her computer display and immediately started scanning the lower band frequencies. And almost instantly, she found it.

I know what you did.

She was suddenly light-headed, and she clenched her hands on her desktop to keep from shaking.

Talik failed me. I am sure you will not. Follow the enclosed blueprints exactly as they are written. No alterations by ANYONE. I failed to appropriately specify that last time, I believe.

Jhama scowled at the screen, and her nails began to draw blood.

You will correct your crewman's mistake by the end of the next 28-hour cycle, and place the devices on the first and second engine coils in addition to the hull where your partner set off his device. And remember. You are to leave Ren my message before you detonate, unless of course you're pressed for time and are faced with the choice of either delivering the message or completing your task.

I'm sure you know you should choose the latter course of action. End of message.

The ensign turned off her computer and sat there, staring at her reflection in the dark glass. This was it. She was well and truly boxed in this time. She slowly shifted her focus to the soot and grime streaked across her uniform and then let the foot of her bed claim her attention next. She could almost see Talik sitting there, even though she knew she'd never see him again.

Her resolve hardened. She looked back at her shadowy reflection in the powered-off computer and fought the urge to shatter the image. She found a way out of his last order. She'd find a way out of this one, too.

"Let's go for round two."

She shoved away from her desk and marched from her quarters. She was on the clock now.

Twenty-eight hours and counting.

CHAPTER 12

Balok groaned and eased himself down onto his stool. This hadn't been a good day. He was in pain, exhausted, and ready to find a dark room to lie down in and have a good cry.

He'd lost five of his six critical patients. That meant eight people were dead—including Ensign Omarik, who was apparently to blame for all of this. Sprit had come storming back in about an hour after she'd left, livid and just as blood-spattered as she had been before, demanding to speak to the dead man. The doctor barely managed to follow her near-delirious rant of half-Trozeran and half-common speak, gathering that Talik had gassed the people in engineering and then cut the cameras before he presumably set up and detonated his weapon. Sprit *needed* to speak to the bastard because she was going to kill him herself.

Needless to say, she hadn't taken it too well when he told her the man in question was already dead. And yes, he was sure, because they'd had to identify him through dental records, he was that decimated.

That had been ten hours ago. Ten hours of intense surgeries and last second saves and times of death. Ten hours of trying to save eight lives and ultimately coming up short. Though, he supposed they did save eight lives as well, even if seven of them hadn't been in very grave conditions to start with. The eighth, though...he looked exhaustedly at the recovery room across the medbay from him. He'd taken every possible precaution to quiet the room for its occupant. He'd tinted all the glass, muted all the unnecessary sounds on the vital monitors. He'd even given the man as many neurosuppressants as was safe.

He knew it wouldn't be enough. The world would still be too loud and too raw for a little bit while Holt rebuilt his strength.

Wearily, Balok pulled out his tablet and checked Holt's stats. He was doing remarkably well so soon out of stasis, and the joint effects of the regenerator, more traditional methods of wound care, and then surgery had brought him largely back up to specs, so to say. The only thing that could stop him from getting back to work in the next few hours would be the mental strain and perhaps some stiffness as he finished healing.

"You're made of titanium, aren't you, Lewis?" he muttered, setting aside the screen and slowly getting back to his feet. His joints cracked in protest, and he grimaced. "I, on the other hand, am made of cheap plastic." He limped towards one of the free beds they had and all but fell into it, face-first. "Dalia?"

The violet-skinned woman was by his side in an instant.

"Yes, sir?"

"Wake me up if anyone's status changes," he mumbled, looking up at her through half-closed eyes. "I'm just going to rest my eyes."

"Of course, Balok. Can I get you any..." She trailed off and shook her head as the man started snoring. "Oh, I envy you, sir."

———

Rin sat at Sprit's desk in the dark, staring unblinkingly at the covered porthole window. She'd been sitting there since Sprit had returned in a huff, agitated and unsteady. Her roommate was currently in the bathroom, muttering to herself as she tried to scrub her uniform clean in the sink. She'd been at it for hours, alternating between trying to sleep and rushing back into the bathroom, and Rin had started more than once at the loud bangs that came unexpectedly from the small space. She shifted on the hard chair and tapped her fingers on the desk.

Space was right beyond that dark curtain. *Space*. And, sure, she was probably going to have a panic attack the moment she moved said curtain, but the ship wasn't moving right now and things were blowing up in engineering, so really there was a non-zero chance of this being now or never.

Just do it already.

She lunged for the curtain and yanked it back. And immediately she was breathless. A small, crooked smile slowly crept onto her face.

"I...I could get used to this."

———

Sprit had long ago given up on restoring her uniform. It was beyond hope, utterly ruined, and she'd have to throw it away. But right now she couldn't be bothered to move. She could feel the water soaking into the bottoms of her socks and knew she should probably pick the drenched garment off the floor before its puddle grew any more. But again, she couldn't be bothered. Instead, she was staring into the sink, taking in the blue tint to the white metal. That was blood, she noted with an odd sort of dissociation. That was Lewis' blood.

Amos.

Another wave of desperation, terror, and guilt swept over her, and she gripped the edge of the sink until her knuckles turned white. That name. She didn't know that name, yet it kept coming up, rising like bile in the back of her throat. Amos and a near-unstoppable urge to scream and hide somewhere dark and safe like a closet. A shudder ran through her that she couldn't explain, and she took in deep breath after deep breath, slowly bringing herself back under control.

"What is going on with me?" she whispered, staring at herself in the mirror. She looked gaunt, the dark circles under her eyes even more pronounced than usual. She'd tried sleeping. All that had brought her were disturbing nightmares she couldn't even bring herself to recount; horrible images of dozens of murders she hadn't worked on. Almost every victim had been Xanidian like Holt. She felt her heart start to race as that fear came back with a vengeance, and she clenched her hand into a fist. "Oh, that's *enough.*"

She snatched the ruined uniform off the floor and threw it into the sink, not caring that the throw turned on the faucet. Maybe the running water would clean out the fabric more while she was gone.

"Rin, I'm going to the medbay." Rin turned guiltily from where she'd been looking out the window, and Sprit rolled her eyes as she pulled on her shoes. "Don't look like you got caught doing something wrong. You're fine." She glanced at the field of stars beyond the glass. "Pretty, isn't it?"

"Yeah…but they don't twinkle," Rin said, facing her roommate curiously.

"You're not looking at them through atmosphere," Sprit explained, and Rin looked back at the stars. "You haven't seen the really beautiful stuff, yet."

"What do you mean?"

"That glass filters out certain types of light. You aren't seeing all the stars, yet."

Rin turned to her in disbelief.

"But there are so many of them already!"

Any other day, Sprit would have sat with her and shared this precious moment of someone truly seeing space for the first time. But she had a raging migraine, not to mention that nagging, horrible feeling that something was right behind her, just waiting for the moment to attack her and rip her to pieces. And that *name* and the feelings it dragged out of her and those nightmares—

"I have to go."

Rin looked up at Sprit's brusque change of topic and finally noticed her ragged appearance. She was sweating even though she was stripped down to her underarmor shirt and some loose cargo pants, and the bandage around her right hand was roughly done and already stained with fresh blood. Suddenly, her discovery of stars didn't seem too important.

"I'll go with you."

Sprit made no comment as the girl quickly hurried after her. She felt like there were snakes writhing in her stomach. She just needed Balok to give her something to get over this.

———

"Balok?" Dalia gently prodded the chief medical officer's shoulder, and the man grumbled sleepily at her, burying his face deeper into his pillow. "Balok, your patient's waking up." The doctor cracked open an eye and considered the nurse before him.

"Which patient?"

"Lieutenant Holt, sir."

"Do I *need* to be there?" he asked waspishly, turning his face back into his pillow. "Lieutenant Holt has woken up on his own for forty-nine years now. I don't need to hold his hand." Dalia responded by putting her hands on her hips and staring him down with a raised eyebrow. He looked back up at her and whined. "Alright, I'm coming, I'm coming."

He wearily sat up and wiped at his eyes and mouth as she spoke.

"You got about thirty minutes of sleep." He yawned as he stood, and she pointed to her own bald head. "You…your hair's a little…"

He looked at her dolefully and raked a hand through his orange curls, hoping the half-asleep gesture would be enough to tame the bed-head he was no doubt sporting. She gave him a quick thumbs-up and an equally fast smile and went back to work.

The doctor gathered his tablet and brought up Holt's vitals. It was time to wake up for both of them. He noted with some concern that the man's blood pressure was elevated, and as Balok swiped through the screens, he saw that his heart rate and respiratory rates were as well. He paused on Holt's threshold and looked back at Dalia.

"Did you look at these vitals?"

"Yes, sir," she said easily. "They seemed expected given the trauma he's been through."

"Fair enough," he muttered and entered Holt's room, engrossed in the readings on the bedside panel above his patient's head. His neural activity seemed particularly active in a pattern Balok wasn't quite familiar with, even for the Xanidian, and he looked down at Holt. "Well, you woke me up, lieutenant. Now it's time for you to wake up as well."

Holt groaned softly and turned his head to the side, but remained decidedly asleep. Balok frowned.

"Well, then. I suppose we can take a look at how you're healing up if you don't want to join us just yet."

He set the tablet on the man's bedside and gently started examining the shinier patches of skin on the man's hands, face, and chest. They seemed to be coming along quite nicely. Their color was good with no signs of infection, and the now-sealed cut along the bridge of his nose would heal with only a barely visible scar. He'd be good to go as soon as he woke up. Balok smiled proudly and made a few notes on his tablet.

"Another job well done. You're good as new, Lieutenant."

The Indegloan turned away, and suddenly Holt flinched on the bed, clenching a fistful of the sheet in his hand and yanking it away from his body hard. Balok jumped at the violent movement and immediately turned back to his patient.

"Lewis? Lewis, can you hear me?"

The medbay doors slid open, and Dalia looked up as Sprit crossed the threshold, looking about ready to fall over as Rin hovered anxiously at her elbow. But the woman hadn't made it more than three steps inside the doors before she tensed up, her heart suddenly feeling like it was about to beat right out of her chest. She couldn't get a full breath. Adrenaline that she couldn't explain surged through her so fast that Sprit dropped to her knees, gasping and tearing up.

Run. I have to run. I have to hide—

"Sprit!"

Balok glanced over his shoulder at Dalia's shout only to have his attention yanked back to his patient as Holt's vitals suddenly skyrocketed.

"What in the galaxy? Lewis!" He grabbed the tossing and turning man by the shoulders and shook him hard. "Wake up!"

Holt sat up like he was spring-loaded, and Balok instantly took a few steps back as the man reoriented himself with wide, hypervigilant eyes.

"There you are, welcome back," Balok sighed. "I'm glad to say you're in good health, even if you gave me more than a few scares." The deputy quickly caught his breath, settling back on the mattress in a daze. "Now, I hate to do this, but something happened with Sprit out near the door, and I need to see what's going on."

"Is she alright?" Holt croaked, squeezing his eyes shut, but Balok was already gone. He ached all over, and his head, it kept *pounding*.

"What happened?" Balok called, hurrying over to where Dalia and Rin were hovering around the fallen officer.

"I think she had some kind of panic attack," the nurse said softly, gently helping Sprit back to her feet with the human's assistance.

Balok frowned, nonplussed.

"Is that right?" he asked intrigued, and Sprit shook her head.

"I don't know, I've...I've been feeling weird," she mumbled. "And my head's *killing* me."

Balok turned between Holt's room and where the nurse and human were easing Sprit down on a spare bed.

"Weird how?" he asked slowly, and Sprit looked up at him through squinting eyes.

"I don't know, just...weird. I've been having weird nightmares and thinking weird things, too. Names and faces I don't know, that sort of thing. They're horrible. Gruesome." She braced her elbows on her knees and dropped her face into her hands, wincing as her crudely wrapped palm protested at the weight. She looked up at the man still turning between her bed and another room and grimaced. "Doc, you're moving way too much. You're making me space sick."

"Sorry," Balok said absently, holding a hand out to her as he looked to Holt's open door. "Something...peculiar is happening," he continued slowly, his mind racing and putting everything together as he spoke. "I think I might know what it is. Give me a moment, please." He returned to Lewis' room, stopping by the med cabinet and getting some anti-anxiety and pain pills.

"Lewis, I know you don't like taking these," he preambled, and Holt looked at him curiously, "but I'm working a theory here that has to do with what's wrong with Sprit. So, if you wouldn't mind..." He held the medications out to the man. "They're just anti-anxiety and pain meds for your headache and, well, your nightmares."

Holt slowly took the pills from him, looking baffled.

"I don't understand. I didn't tell you I had a headache, doctor."

"Uh, no, no you didn't," the man admitted, a small smirk pulling at the corner of his lips, "but she has one. And if you take that pill," he pointed at him and then jerked his thumb over his shoulder, "and her headache goes away, then I think we both know what that means."

The deputy paled slightly, and he nervously downed the meds, shifting uneasily on his mattress.

"Well, I shall see if our little experiment worked," Balok said with that same amused smile.

Once he was alone again, Holt looked down at his right leg and carefully traced over the spot where he knew, under the fabric, he had a scar from the debris. He thought back to the moment his commander had ripped the warped control panel off of him, recalled all the sharp edges and gnarled protuberances. It would have been so easy for her to cut herself. Then, she'd thrown all of her weight down on his gaping wound, not caring how much of his blood got all over her damaged hands as she tried to stop the bleeding.

He let his head rest against the wall and closed his eyes, releasing a long, slow breath as his headache began abating.

"You'll forgive me, commander," he whispered to the empty air, "if I hope yours is not going away, too."

"Well?" Balok asked, and Sprit sighed in relief. "I take it that's good news."

"Yeah. Yeah, it's going away." She looked up at the lights. "Did you dim them or something?"

Balok fought back a laugh and wrangled his grin back into a closed-lipped smile.

"Or something," he parroted, and Sprit frowned.

"I don't like that look," she said warningly. "Balok, get rid of that look."

"What's going on?" Rin asked blankly, and the doctor silently held a finger up to them, clearly trying to collect himself.

"Something quite miraculous, actually. It's a scientific breakthrough to be sure. It's never happened before."

"*What's* a scientific breakthrough, doc?" Sprit growled, her question more of a demand.

He didn't respond and instead walked over to the medbay's communications panel and pressed a button.

"Oren Galaxa."

"Oh, don't you dare bring him down here," Sprit warned. "Balok, do *not* bring him down here!"

"Balok," the captain's voice came through. "Is something wrong?"

"Not wrong, per se, captain," Balok said enigmatically, "but an interesting development has just occurred with your heads of security. You and Hanali'a might want to come down here for this."

"Hanali'a, too? Balok, what is going on?" Sprit demanded, but the doctor ignored her.

"It really is quite remarkable, sir," he continued.

"Balok," the captain sighed, "I'm *really* not in the mood for games."

"Oh, it's no game, sir," the doctor assured him. "Besides, Lieutenant Holt is awake, and I figured you'd like to speak with him."

There was a pause, and on the bridge Oren turned to his first officer and gestured for her to join him in the elevator.

"We'll be right there."

"Excellent, sir." The doctor closed the channel and turned to his new patient. She was still glaring at him, and he beamed. "Well, I suppose congratulations are in order."

"Balok, I swear to the ancestors if you say I'm pregnant," she began, voice dangerously low, and the doctor laughed.

"No, nothing like that," he scoffed, and Sprit started to relax. That was, until he continued with a grin. "You, my dear, are married."

The three women froze, each for very different reasons. Nurse Dalia stared at the tiled floor, eyes wide as she bit her lip and barely subdued the urge to grin. Rin was so uncomfortable that it was all she could do to fight off the impulse to laugh.

Sprit, on the other hand, was about to explode.

"I'm *WHAT?!*"

In his room, Holt winced and pinched the bridge of his nose as he sank down in his bed. This was not going to go well.

Oren could hear the shouting as soon as he saw the medbay door.

"This had better be good," he sighed and looked up at his nine-foot-tall first officer. "You have any ideas about what's going on?"

She considered him with her large, shining black eyes.

"I do not." Her voice was deep, with a touch of a rasp to it, and she looked forward—the motion slightly slow, yet graceful. "I'm sure Balok will tell us shortly."

"It's good to have you back, Hanali'a," he sighed, and she gave the largest smile she could—nothing more than a slight curve of her thin, narrow mouth.

"It seems I picked the perfect moment to return. Humans, traitors, and explosions." She paused. "It's been eighteen years since you were this busy."

"I'm aware," he said grimly. "Jon Bledsoe's name has been crossing my mind more often lately."

"Good," she said, and Oren raised an eyebrow. "It means you have not become complacent."

"I'm flattered," he said dryly, and she chuckled, the low sound an almost eerie, clicking rumble in her chest.

"I WOULD REMEMBER GETTING MARRIED."

Oren stopped walking just outside the medbay door's motion sensor range, Hanali'a coming to a halt beside him.

"Did I just hear Sprit say what I think I heard her say?"

"I believe so," she confirmed, and Oren groaned, letting his head tip back as he prepared himself.

"Alright." He looked forward once more. "Let's go deal with this."

Sprit looked to the door as it slid open and immediately scrambled off the bed, pushing Dalia away and leaving her hand half-dressed.

"*No*, Hanali'a, Rin's in here—"

Rin looked up at the sound of her name and froze as Hanali'a and Oren walked into the medbay, and suddenly, she knew exactly why all the ceilings on this ship were absurdly high. She swallowed hard and blinked a few times to make sure she wasn't dreaming. She wasn't sure *what* she was looking at, if she was being honest.

All she knew was it terrified her.

Hanali'a was massive, and not just in height, though she was easily nine feet tall. She was solid muscle. Her body and limbs looked like those ancient Greek statues—sturdy, toned, and fully capable of effortlessly knocking someone across a room. Her fingers were thin and spindly with darker webbing between each abnormally long digit. Her neck was also taller than proportionally normal by a few inches, and it was encased in several rounds of a stiff, deep red fabric that probably helped support her vertebrae. Her skin was gray with a smooth texture that reminded Rin quite a bit of a dolphin despite the dark vessels visible under her skin— rising from under her neck brace, branching into her cheeks, and descending from her hairline into her forehead.

Unlike everyone else on board, Hanali'a wasn't in uniform. Instead, she wore a long, sleeveless garment of that same dark red, though this fabric looked like a type of silk. It almost resembled a robe at the top— the way it crossed over her broad chest with a dark, rich yellow hem along the collar. But instead of flowing down her body, the immaculate fabric was interrupted by a stiff abdominal corset that no doubt served the same function as the neck brace given how tightly it was pulled around her figure—supporting her spine. The robe parted in the front at the base of the corset and draped down to the deck plating, revealing a pair of form-fitting shorts in the corset's same color. Rin could easily see the lines of the first-officer's muscles through the thin fabric.

Her shoulders, elbows, wrists, and knees were encased in more woven braces, but these were finely crafted combinations of the brown leather used in her corset and the yellow fabric of her collar. Her ankles were similarly wrapped in leather straps, as were her toes. Rin could have been mistaken, but she was pretty sure those digits were also abnormally long and possibly webbed, laced together by the dark strips supporting the balls of her otherwise-bare, very calloused feet.

But the part that really terrified Rin, the part that had her standing there, mute and frozen, was her round head and face.

Hanali'a didn't have a normal nose or mouth; both were little more than slits in her skin. Her nose was flat and broad, raised a bit from the rest of her features and sloping into her slightly thicker forehead and brow. The corners of her downward-curved mouth dipped ever so slightly before rising up, creating a small angle that gave her a marginally more fishlike appearance. Her eyes were large like the stereotypical alien humans coupled with "I Want To Believe" posters, but a bit more rounded, akin to circular right triangles. Her ears were nothing more than small holes in the sides of her skull at her temples, and just behind each ear, she had a pair of gills.

Her hair was thick, heavy, and dark, braided in a long train down her back, but despite the weight and size of the braid, she was mostly bald. She only had three large areas of hair on her scalp; the first started at the top of her head, about halfway down her skull, and ran back to her nape. The other two spots of hair were at the sides of her head, just above her ears and gills and also ran back to end with the first cluster. A pencil-thin, shorter braid hung along the right side of her face, held together by two turquoise wooden beads.

This woman...*she* looked like an alien.

Hanali'a blinked—a thin, translucent, white film sweeping sideways across her eyes—and Rin shuddered.

"Han, this is Rin Cooper," Oren introduced, trying to gauge the human's response. So far, she just looked frozen and overwhelmed. "Rin, this is First Officer Kowah'tlanti'omkatua-naloa. We just call her Han or Hanali'a."

CHAPTER 13

Han somberly inclined her head to the wide-eyed girl.

"Hello, Rin."

"Uh, h-hi," she stammered, voice barely above a whisper, and Sprit dropped her head into her hand as Dalia grabbed her arm and dragged her back to the bed to restart the dressings on her free palm.

"Spectacular," Sprit grumbled, and Oren cleared his throat.

"Doctor Balok, I believe you said we had a situation to deal with?"

"Ah, yes." Balok turned to Holt's room and beamed. "Lieutenant, would you care to join us?"

There was a pause and then a rolling sound as Holt slowly limped out of his room, using a wheeled chair as an aid as he crossed over to them. While his headache had abated, his skin pulled painfully in some places where it was still healing, and the memories of his nightmares were still plenty present in his mind.

"You look horrible," Sprit welcomed, and he wearily nodded, coming to a stop and easing himself into the chair once he'd joined the group.

"I feel less than well, ma'am," he agreed and looked up at the captain and first officer. "Captain. Hanali'a." The two officers nodded to him, Han's gesture once again slower. "I apologize for all of this, sir."

"*Apologize?* Holt, you have nothing to apologize for," he said firmly. "Talik was the one who set off that bomb, not you. You even told me there was something wrong, and I brushed you off as paranoid. You have *nothing* to apologize for. I do."

Holt momentarily closed his eyes, breathing slowly through the dull pain in his leg.

"No, it's not that, sir." He glanced at Sprit before looking back to the floor. "It's about the commander's current…predicament, as it were. I'm afraid I have something to do with it."

"Ah." Oren looked at his little sister as Dalia finished wrapping her hand and bemusedly raised an eyebrow. "Did I hear you shouting just a minute ago about being married? You know mother will be disappointed if she missed a ceremony."

Sprit growled warningly.

"I'm *not* married," she spat, crossing her arms. "All that happened was I had a headache that went away on its own."

"And panic attacks and nightmares," Rin said under her breath, and Sprit glared.

"Helping or hurting, Rin?" she hissed, and Oren gestured for her to cool down.

"What does this have to do with you being married?"

"Her symptoms abated when I gave Lewis meds," Balok answered pointedly. Everyone looked at him blankly, save for Hanali'a and Holt, and the doctor grew disappointed. "I take it none of you are familiar with the marriage practices of the Xanidian, then."

"I am," Hanali'a said evenly as Oren frowned.

"The what-now of the *who?*" Sprit barked, sitting up straighter as Holt sank lower in his seat. She looked at her deputy, eyes narrowing dangerously. "Lewis Holt, you better start talking right now."

"Now, commander, it's not his fault," Balok said breezily, pulling up some functional brain scans while Oren and Sprit's eyes grew wider by the second. "This has never happened with an interspecies blood exchange before, am I right, lieutenant?"

"Yes, doctor," Lewis muttered after a very long pause, still avoiding looking at anyone.

"Someone had better start using common-speak very soon," Oren interrupted, and Rin looked between everyone confusedly.

"Should I still be here?" she asked, but they ignored her.

"A few Xanidians, as you know with Lieutenant Holt, have the ability to read minds," Balok explained, looking like a kid on Christmas morning. "But *all* Xanidians are biologically able to form lifelong telepathic bonds with their chosen partners, who are then called bondmates. It's a Xanidian-specific process that involves microbiology and chemistry that I won't get into. *But* it's instigated by exchanging blood with the chosen partner. So, Sprit, when you heroically pulled your deputy from the debris…" He looked between Sprit's bandaged hand and Holt's right thigh, waiting for his audience to connect the dots.

Oren spoke first, brow furrowed in confusion as he put his hands on his hips.

"But you said this was a *Xanidian-specific* process," he said, pointing to Sprit. "Sprit is not Xanidian."

"It is. Or at least it was," the doctor replied, and Sprit looked at him like he was insane. "It seems Ethonians are just as compatible as—"

"I am not telepathic!" Sprit shouted, voice cracking and jumping an octave. "Doc, you should know that!"

"Well, I'm afraid, commander, that I'm more inclined to believe my experiment than—"

"My people's whole biological history?" she interrupted, incredulously. "Balok, I'm *not* telepathic!"

"But Lieutenant Holt is," Hanali'a said calmly, tilting her head to the highly uncomfortable officer. "If your nervous system is in fact compatible with his, the process, as I understand it, could theoretically move forward. It would simply take longer to come into effect, which would explain why you're feeling the effects only now."

—hit him with my pillow as hard as I can, the little—

The fragment of thought flitted through Holt's mind far too clearly to be one of the crew, and he frowned, trying figure out where it had come from and parse its meaning when the firm bed accessory hit him full in the face, making him jump in his chair.

"Sprit!" Oren shouted as Rin quickly fetched the hurled pillow. "Stop throwing things at your deputy!"

"I think the current situation is enough reason to hit him with a pillow, captain!" she heatedly hissed. "This is a massive potential security risk, and he never told me this could happen!"

"It wasn't technically a security risk if it could only happen with other Xanidians," Balok interjected. Holt massaged his temples and screwed his eyes shut as the room grew louder. "He *is* the only one on board."

"Is this a stable link, then, doctor?" Hanali'a asked curiously.

"*That's* what you're thinking about right now?" Sprit gaped. "If it's a stable link? Look, I'm not telepathic! This is just some weird fluke! We happened to have nightmares and a headache at the same time, so what?"

"Think of a number." Everyone looked at Rin, and she repeated herself. "Uh, f-for Holt. Think of a number." He paused for a second and then nodded. "Um, Sprit, what number is he thinking of?"

She rolled her eyes and threw her hands up in the air.

"I don't know, six thousand, seven hundred and forty-one," she spat, sitting back hard against the wall and crossing her arms bitterly. Rin looked at Holt, and the man grimaced.

"What was the number?"

"Six thousand, seven hundred and forty-one," he muttered. Sprit instantly hurled the pillow at him again, and he flinched.

"*Six thousand, seven hundred and forty-one?!*" she shouted, Oren lunging forward and catching the surprisingly heavy cushion before it hit Lewis in the face again. "You couldn't have picked a *normal* number like four? Or thirty-five?!"

"Congratulations, commander," Balok said, beaming at her with a wide smile. "You have successfully read the lieutenant's mind."

Sprit moaned in despair and folded over her legs on the bed, hands gripping her hair in pure exasperation and defeat while Holt shifted on the chair, uncertainty and embarrassment lining his angular body. Oren sighed and shook his head, covering his bowed face in frustration.

Balok, however, looked around smiling.

"Am I the only one who's excited about this new development?"

Before Hanali'a could share her albeit more muted enthusiasm, an aggravated response rose up from Sprit's bed to growl at him.

"*Yes.*" The single copper eye that accompanied the word gave new meaning to the phrase 'death glare,' and Balok hummed sullenly.

"Hanali'a agrees with me," he muttered.

"Now may not be the best time to challenge her," the first officer cut in diplomatically. "Perhaps we should discuss engineering—"

"I guess you're Sprit Holt, now."

Sprit shot up in bed, jabbing a finger in the human's face.

"SHUT UP, RIN!" She twisted around to face Lewis, her expression telling him her next words were an order and not a question. "Is there a divorce?"

"I...don't know, ma'am," he said hesitantly.

"What do you mean you don't know?" she asked in disbelief. "It's *your* wedding custom!"

"Like the doctor said, these are lifelong bonds, and they typically aren't made lightly," the man replied, tone growing tenser as he spoke. "They weren't meant to be broken—"

"Hey, don't get mad with me! You're the one who did this!"

"I'm not getting mad with you, ma'am," he tried, his voice taking on a sharper edge that matched her own. "You are getting mad with me."

"You're seriously trying to turn this around on *me?!*"

"Sprit," Oren said, stepping over to her and shoving the pillow into her lap. "I think he's saying that's *your* anger in his voice, not his. Calm down."

Sprit faced her deputy, and he looked down, breathing deeply. Her disbelief and frustration slowly faded as she took in the way his hands clenched the arms of his chair and glanced at her own white-knuckled fists pressed against the pillow in her lap. Suddenly, she felt guilty. She forced herself to mirror Holt's breathing until she was marginally less pissed off and winced as he slowly relaxed as well.

"It won't...it's not always like this," he told her softly, looking up at her, but then glanced at the people hovering around them. "For my people, this is a very private conversation," he began, and Hanali'a grasped his drift.

"Of course." She gently put her hand on Oren's shoulder, completely dwarfing the smaller man's joint. "We will give you space."

"Yes," the captain agreed. "I'll assemble a proper meeting to discuss what happened in engineering. I'm sure Balok can provide you two with a private room." The doctor nodded in confirmation, and Oren continued. "Hanali'a can take Rin back to your quarters, Sprit."

Rin looked up at the first officer with open fear, but the giant just gave her that odd little quirk of the lips that was her smile.

"Come, Rin." She stepped aside and gestured to the doors, and the human nervously walked forward. As she passed Hanali'a, the woman put her hand on her shoulder the way she'd touched Oren, and Rin was astounded by the weight in her limb. It had looked like such a light and airy motion. "There is no need to be afraid of me," she said amusedly to the girl under her breath. "I'm the last person who would lay a hand on you."

"That's...not comforting," Rin muttered back, and Hanali'a smiled again.

"Are you coming, Galaxa?" she asked, turning her head to look over her shoulder much like an owl, and Rin's eyes nearly bulged out of her head. The captain gently squeezed Holt's shoulder, being careful this time of his spines, and quickly joined his first officer and human passenger in the hall. "Shall I meet you back on the bridge?"

"Yes. Thank you, Han." He nodded once to Rin and gave her a reassuring smile, gently patting the shoulder Hanali'a wasn't already touching. "You're in the safest hands with her."

Rin smiled nervously in return, and he quickly departed, taking a right turn where the girl and his first officer continued walking ahead.

In the medbay, things were very quiet.

"You two can use Holt's room for this," Balok said softly, mercifully easing off his excitement. "I'll make sure you're not disturbed."

Sprit hopped off the edge of the bed and waited for Lewis to stand.

"You good?" she asked sullenly, and he nodded, leaning less on the chair as they made their way across the medbay. "How about your leg?"

"As well as can be expected, ma'am." He felt a flash of irritation in a corner of his mind that wasn't his, and he capitulated. "There is a little bit of pain, but it's mostly just stiff, commander."

Sprit scoffed and stepped back so Holt could enter the room first.

"First, you tell me we're married, now you're telling me the truth. What's next? You gonna start calling me Sprit?" Holt passed the chair off to her and sat down on the edge of the bed. "Djienn, you're really serious about this."

"Commander, there are some things I must discuss with you about our situation," he began, still keeping his gaze steadily averted. "The first is that for all intents and purposes, we share minds. We have a link between us, an ability to share thoughts, feelings, and even dreams at will. But this can also happen against our wills if both parties involved do not have proper training, or…"

"Or they don't know they've been linked," Sprit finished softly, and Holt nodded.

"Yes, ma'am. And I can only imagine that in both cases it's harder for you as a non-Xanidian. I can teach you ways to control the link, to limit what each of us can sense through it, but I'm afraid that there is no fast way to terminate it. It will be an…uncomfortable time."

"That's just perfect. You're saying we're stuck with each other," she grumbled, and Holt nodded again.

"Yes, ma'am." A long silence dragged out between them. "And because of that, I believe we should talk about things you may see."

"Amos." Holt looked up sharply at the name, fear and pain in his eyes, and it was Sprit's turn to look down. "Sorry."

"He was my younger brother."

She swallowed at his quiet explanation, his confession.

"Didn't know you had a brother," she muttered, trying to give him an opening. Holt joined her in looking down.

"I don't anymore, ma'am. He died when we were…very young."

"I'm sorry." She picked at the bandage around her hand. "How'd it happen?"

"Commander," Holt reprimanded, guarded, "if Balok was correct in his diagnosis and you are sharing my dreams, you saw for yourself."

Sprit crossed an arm over her chest and raised a hand to press her fingertips against her lips, subtly trying to settle the wave of nausea that came over her.

"All those bodies, the blood and the screaming," she whispered, neither officer looking at each other. "That was real?"

"Have you ever heard of Davin Colony, commander? Or the Davin Colony outbreak?" was Holt's quiet, measured reply.

Sprit looked up at his drawn, yet resolved countenance and mutely shook her head. He slid off the bed and closed the door, resuming their conversation as he returned to the mattress. When he looked at her, his eyes were cold and flat, and Sprit knew that what he said next was to stay between them.

"It was a Xanidian research outpost with four hundred and twenty-eight people living in it, including staff members' families. My mother and father were scientists, and they'd been transferred there when I was three years old and Amos was one."

Balok turned at his desk and watched the security chief and deputy speak. Rather, he watched Holt speak. Sprit was just listening, nodding where appropriate and shaking her head when it wasn't. And eventually, she put her hand over her mouth, expression one of horror as the lieutenant continued to talk. Her posture caved, and she sank back into the chair, shaking her head and reaching out to touch Lewis before remembering better.

Balok looked away and returned to his chart. He knew the horror story of Davin Colony, had studied it for his work on a couple occasions. He didn't need to watch someone else learn it for the first time.

"Alright, Miss Cooper," he said softly, looking through her scans. "Let's see if this turned up anythi...what have we here?" He zoomed in on her scans and his eyes widened, glittering with delight and excitement. "Miss Cooper," he began, slowly grinning. "You have an entire additional vascular system!" He peered closely at the images. "That's not your lymphatic system or your arteries or veins..." He sat back in his chair, practically glowing. "Oh, this just got interesting."

Hanali'a could feel the human staring at her in the awkward silence of the lift, and the moment she glanced at her companion, the girl looked forward again. It was a little adorable.

"I don't mind you staring, Rin," the first officer finally said, and Rin shifted awkwardly on her feet. "If I were you, I'd stare as well."

"Sorry, it's just..."

"I'm the most alien person you've seen?" she finished, entertained.

"...Yeah."

The door opened, and Hanali'a again gestured for her to exit first.

"Then, stare all you want. It's a brave new world for you."

"I suppose...."

Hanali'a tilted her head curiously as they continued down the hall, her movement graceful and fluid compared to the human's tenser pace.

"You don't seem particularly excited about it." Rin shrugged defensively. "That's okay. You'll find something that'll capture your heart, I'm sure of it. The galaxy is a big place filled with wondrous things. There's something for everyone, and everyone for something."

They walked in silence for a little longer, Rin counting out the three steps she took for every one Hanali'a did.

"I know you're curious," Han said after a bit. "Go ahead. You can ask me anything."

"Are you amphibious?" Rin asked, cringing at the way it came off.

Hanali'a just chuckled again.

"Yes, I am. We don't function as well as we'd like on land, though, hence, the braces and corset," she explained, gesturing up and down her body. "Gravity tends to take a toll on giants."

"How old are you?"

"Two hundred and one." At Rin's shocked expression, she laughed. "If you think *I'm* old, my wife is two hundred and ninety-four. We've been friends of Oren and his mother for a long time."

"So…you've been around a while," Rin began, figuring out how to ask her question. "Does that…have you met a lot of humans?"

Hanali'a considered her sympathetically.

"Three. As I'm sure someone has told you, none of them are with us today." She inclined her head in a gesture of respect, long neck curving like a swan's. "They were all…beautiful souls and so very good."

"Then why don't you interact with Earth? If we're good, why don't we know all of this and all of you exist?"

Hanali'a slowed to a stop, and Rin realized they'd reached Sprit's quarters. The first officer looked at her and gently put a hand on her shoulder again—her unchanged, inky gaze somehow growing gentle and admiring, like an inverse of Anthia's.

"You're such vivacious people," she said almost wistfully, "with such a hunger for creation, innovation, and pushing boundaries. *Discovery* is your passion. It's filled and driven your history." She grew sad. "At least, when it hasn't been tainted by greed or destruction. So yes, the three humans I met were beautiful and good, but the stories they told of their homeworld…. Humans are ready for us. *Humanity* is not."

Subdued and feeling a little insulted, Rin opened the door and was about to cross the threshold when Hanali'a tightened her grip, and the girl looked back up at her.

"I'm not saying there isn't good on Earth or that we're somehow a perfect paradise. We're not. There are evils in space just as there are on your planet—tragedies, injustices, tyrants, forgotten people…. Don't let anyone tell you otherwise. The stars may be beautiful, but monsters lurk between them."

"Yes, ma'am," Rin whispered, suddenly feeling very cold despite the warmth of the large hand covering her shoulder and back, and Han ruefully shook her head.

"I don't mean to frighten you. The galaxy *is* a marvelous place. But like anything, it has its dangers. Don't let the starlight blind you."

With that, Hanali'a left, and Rin watched her glide away like she was walking through water, silky fabric of her robe practically floating around her. She let out a big sigh and entered Sprit's room, returning to the desk and pulling back the curtains once more. The stars still took her breath away. If anything, after Hanali'a's words, they seemed more beautiful.

The first officer had been honest with her. For the first time, someone had been honest about this brand new world instead of giving her platitudes and telling her everything would work out perfectly. Given that engineering had just blown up, everything everyone had told her so far seemed like a white lie to keep her calm.

"Now you feel real," she whispered and settled back to wait for Sprit to return, the galaxy's sky keeping her company.

CHAPTER 14

Oren looked up as Avery ran into his briefing room, disheveled and out of breath.

"Sorry I'm late, sir," he panted, dropping into a seat next to Balok with a huffing sigh. "Engineering's a mess, but we're working again."

"That's what we're here to discuss," he greeted and looked at the officers gathered around the table. "Where's Anthia?"

Avery tensed, and Hanali'a stepped in from the opposite end of the table.

"She believed her presence wouldn't be conducive."

Oren looked at his engineer in a mixture of exasperation and pity. "I thought you two were speaking again."

Avery clenched his jaw and looked at his fisted hands in his lap.

"No, sir. Just once during the sting operation."

The captain sighed and shook his head.

"Alright, I'm assuming one of you two has her data?" he asked his security chief and deputy, and Sprit nodded, tapping the tablet in front of her. "Good. Let's get down to business. Sprit, Holt, fill us in on the message Anthia intercepted."

"Unfortunately, there's no news," Sprit admitted, bouncing her leg. "She picked up the distortion, pulled a recording of it, and then the transmission went dark. We *were* going to check the short-term data archive in engineering to see if we could find more messages and give the cipher programs more input to work with, but for obvious reasons, we can't do that anymore. During the engineering aftermath, Anthia managed to pull just the message from the noise, and she's been running it through every code breaker we've got. But so far? Nothing."

"Our best-case scenario, they were instructions to Ensign Omarik," Holt said, continuing the report, and Avery did a double take as he saw the shinier patches of skin on his face and hands. "Worst-case, Omarik wasn't the only operative on board, and another attack is coming."

"Holt, were you in the blast?" the chief engineer asked, voice laced with concern, and the deputy looked at him a little nonplussed.

"...Yes, sir."

"Where do you think he's been for the last twelve hours?" Sprit muttered, peeved, and Holt blushed ever so slightly, instantly looking down at his lap as Avery uncomfortably cleared his throat.

"Commander," Holt whispered, barely hiding his mortification.

"What?" Sprit looked around at everyone, frowning in genuine confusion. "Did I miss something?"

Oren raised an eyebrow, meeting his first officer's amused gaze across the table, and cleared his throat.

"As you were saying, Lieutenant Holt?"

"Uh, yes, sir. I recommend that we speak to Ensign Jhama Assora. She was a close friend of Omarik, and if she's not involved with this, she may at the very least be able to give some insight into any meetings he may have had or any recent behavioral changes."

"How did this happen without you picking up on it?"

Holt looked down and cleared his throat.

"I'm...not sure, sir. My best guess at this point would be that he was thinking in abstract steps, using coded words for certain ideas like bomb, detonator, or explosives. That way, unless I was following his thoughts intently, I wouldn't have known what he was doing. It would be difficult to maintain, but not impossible."

"So, if there are other operatives and they're thinking like this—"

"I won't find them, captain. Not unless I go, quite literally, person to person and follow their thoughts for at least a few hours each. We don't have that kind of time, sir."

Oren rested his hands on the table, lacing his fingers together and staring into the dark grain of the wood before them. Hanali'a watched him carefully, acutely aware of the tightness in his shoulders and the deepness of his breaths.

"Avery, what have you found on the bomb?" he finally asked, and the engineer held up his tablet.

"I sent you all pictures of the debris I found that I'm pretty sure went to the device as well as a rudimentary blueprint of what the bomb looked like. It may not be a completely accurate, though...." He trailed off and gestured to everyone as they looked through the files. "Well, you'll see what I mean."

"These are used parts," Hanali'a said, looking up, and Balok peered a little closer at some of the images.

"Exactly. We can't trace it. All of those parts are thrown out at the end of the day by whoever is last on shift in each department. He could have been collecting these parts for months or weeks or even days if he wasn't working alone. It's—" Avery scoffed and threw his hands up in the air, "it's genius. It's...pure genius."

"There are even medical supplies in here. Needles and fragments of pliers." He looked up at Lewis. "That explains the slivers I pulled out of you and the others."

Holt didn't look up. Instead, he and Sprit were engrossed in their tablets, turning the same image in the same direction on their individual devices without noticing their synchronicity.

"Sir, the device misfired," he said, and Sprit instantly looked at him.

"I was just thinking that—" She stopped, her surprise turning into anger. "Get *out* of my head, Holt!"

"It was not intentional, commander, I assure you," he replied, voice low but firm. "I would if I could." There was an awkward silence, and he gestured for her to speak, not looking at her.

She scowled but took it.

"As *I* was saying," she began, shooting Lewis a glare, "this explosion should've been big. The people who were unconscious on the catwalks? They shouldn't have made it out with only moderate to mild burns. They should have been scorched like the people on the ground." She turned her tablet screen to them. "You see these panels and the placement of the charges? This is what directed the explosion down and out, which, by the way, is also where our engines are reinforced. The blast panels and consoles? They cover our engine coils everywhere this bomb reached specifically because that's where stuff is most likely to accidentally explode in engineering. But you see these drilled holes over here?" She pointed to a different section of the screen. "This is where those panels *used* to be. This would have directed the explosion up and out as well as down. Nobody would have made it out of there, and at least two of our engines would have gone up, too, no doubt tearing a massive hole in the side of our ship when they went."

"Someone changed the design," Oren said softly, looking at the same image on his own screen. "That would mean it was either Talik or someone else. If it's someone else, we're dealing with a cell on board, but either way, what kind of terrorist does that? Sabotages their own bomb?"

"One who's unwilling," Holt and Sprit said at the same time, and Sprit immediately slammed her hand down on the table, making Avery jump.

"*Dammit*, Holt!"

"That was not my fault, commander," he fired back, barely keeping a lid on the anger and frustration burning in his chest that he knew was mostly hers. Instantly, the anger was replaced by embarrassment, and his superior looked away, crossing her arms tightly over her chest.

"Do you two need a moment?"

"*No*," Sprit snapped as Holt gave his far quieter answer, and Oren looked at her disapprovingly.

"No, sir."

"What is *wrong* with you two?" Avery asked after a few beats of tense and awkward silence, and Balok smirked.

"An unhappy arranged marriage, Byrone," he answered liltingly, and this time both security officers glared at him. "Apologies."

"Alright, before this turns into more chaos," Oren began firmly, and Sprit glowered, "I want to make our goals clear. Sprit, I want you and Holt to find Ensign Assora and talk to her *without* sniping at each other, please. Tell Anthia to keep up the work on the decryption. We're bound to find one that works soon. Hanali'a, I want you to work with Avery and oversee the repairs to engineering. Make sure we won't have any more problems in there. Are we clear?"

There was a chorus of "yes, sirs" as everyone gathered their tablets.

"Alright. Avery, Han, you're both dismissed. I want to speak with the others for a little longer." The two officers nodded and quickly departed, leaving the room mired in an awkward silence. "So, tell me, Holt, are you usually that sarcastic?"

He looked up at Oren with almost perfectly feigned innocence.

"Sir?"

"Where do you think he's been for the last twelve hours?" Oren repeated with a smirk, and Holt faintly blushed. "I know that was your thought, not Sprit's." Before either of them could say anything, he turned to Balok. "You said you found something on Rin's scan."

Instantly, the mood of the room shifted, and Sprit and Holt looked at Balok apprehensively.

"Yes, it, uh…it seems Miss Cooper has another system of vessels running through her." He passed his tablet around. "It follows the paths of her veins and arteries, but it's entirely independent from her cardiac and lymphatic systems. She has to have at least one additional organ, too, that the vessels drain into, but I'm still examining my scans for it."

"What the hell?" Sprit murmured, snatching the tablet from Holt. "What does it do? What's in them?"

"I have absolutely no idea."

Sprit looked up at the doctor dolefully as Holt took the tablet back.

"You sound way too pleased by that."

"She's definitely not human," he explained. "She *is* an alien-human hybrid, and this is my first step in figuring out what her other half is."

Holt handed the tablet to his captain, expression clouded.

"Are you going to tell her, sir?"

"Eventually, I'll have to," Oren said, and something uneasy pulled at the corner of Holt's mind. "But that's not why I asked the two of you to stay for this part of the conversation." He sighed and sat back in his chair, clearly not completely comfortable with what he had to say next. "I've been thinking about Rin's timing in all of this. From her being the sole survivor of the auction to someone suddenly trying to blow us out of the stars using unbreakable codes to her not being entirely human when Earth is not supposed to have contact with our worlds…" He trailed off, and suddenly his intention was clear to the mind reader. "I have a feeling about her, and it's not good. I want her in our sights at all times. No more leaving her in your quarters unsupervised. Wherever either one of you goes, she goes."

Instantly, Sprit's mind came roaring to life.

She's a scared seventeen-year-old girl, you heartless piece of—

"Yes, sir," Holt said quickly, stepping on Sprit's foot in a clear signal to shut up. "We'll bring her to shift with us and keep her occupied."

"Sprit?"

Holt looked at her carefully as Oren waited for an answer.

"Commander, tell him 'yes, sir' and nothing more."

Sprit blinked in surprise at Holt's clear voice in her head. He hadn't even moved his lips, how did he…oh. She looked at her captain, her brother, and nodded stiffly.

"Yes, sir."

"Thank you. I know you're not keen on this," he said gently, "but if I'm right we won't regret this later."

Sprit and Holt stood, the former eyeing her captain with a critical eye.

"And if you're wrong, brother, we definitely will."

For a moment, the Trozeran got such a strong air of Tzo Runner off of her that he had to remind himself who he was talking to.

"You're dismissed, *commander.*" He watched the two leave, and Balok glanced at his captain.

"She is right, you know."

"You're dismissed, too, doctor."

"Very well, Oren," Balok sighed, and soon the captain was left alone with nothing but empty chairs and an empty table, the warnings of his sister and chief medical officer echoing in his head.

Rin was exploring.

Her slightly morbid conversation with Hanali'a had piqued her interest, not to mention given her a bit of a challenge to live up to.

"So," she whispered to herself, drawing a map on the napkin as she walked so she could retrace her steps later. Her words were hesitant, spoken as an afterthought as she scribbled away. "Humans are creative and vivacious...we are...discoverers." She bumped shoulders with someone. "Oh, sorry!"

"No worries, Rin," Jhama called over her shoulder, smirking at the girl as she buried her nose back in the napkin.

The human smiled at the sound of her name, blushing slightly. It felt good to hear someone say her name here. She belonged. She was known.

"Creative, vivacious, and discoverers," she repeated and continued to whisper the words to herself like a mantra as she went.

"Why didn't you let me tear into him?" Sprit demanded as she and Holt walked quickly down the hall. "Rin has done nothing to us!"

"The captain had his mind made up, ma'am. Tearing into him, as you put it, would have only gotten you into more trouble."

"What do you mean more trouble? I haven't done anything!"

"You have a...belligerent personality. Ma'am."

Sprit gaped.

"*I* have a belligerent personality? What about you, you're one of *the* most sarcastic people I've ever met!" She paused. "Of course, I didn't know that until today, but still!"

"I keep those thoughts to myself, commander. Or at least I *try* to."

"Hey, what I said in the meeting was *not* my fault! What happened to your promise to teach me how to block you out, huh?"

"We will get around to that, but we currently have more important things to attend to."

"More important—Holt, we're talking about constantly getting into each other's heads and not being able to work properly." She grabbed his arm and jerked him around to face her. "Stop walking and listen to me! *Djienn*, just actually talk to me for once!" He was tense beneath her hand, and she reluctantly let him go.

"I'm sorry," she muttered. "Just...*talk* to me."

"Once we've found Rin and spoken to Jhama, once we have fixed whatever is going on here, I will teach you," he finally said, voice carefully measured. "Until then, please. Try to temper your reactions. Try to think in a more...orderly fashion. You have a very strong personality. It can be a bit difficult to keep myself separated from you, and I *am* trying my best to stay out of your head, as you say."

"You didn't call me ma'am or commander once throughout that whole speech," she noted, and Holt looked at her evenly.

"Because given the intimacy of our current situation, it makes you uncomfortable. And since I am largely to blame for this, I thought I'd give you that small mercy." He turned to walk away, but she pulled him back.

"But that makes *you* uncomfortable, and you didn't ask for this—"

He jerked his arm away and took a step back from her.

"*Don't* touch me. Please." His words were sharp and harsh, and Sprit felt like she'd just been slapped. "You've no idea how hard it is to quiet this entire ship's thoughts, especially with a bondmate, so *please*."

"I...I'm sorry," she said helplessly. He tensely nodded before walking away. "Lewis. Lewis, where are you going?"

"I'm following Rin, commander. She's a deck below us."

"And we're back to commander," she sighed, rolling her eyes and running to catch up to him. "I'm sorry I keep grabbing your arm. I'm just stressed out right now."

"I know, ma'am." He could feel the woman beside him deflate at the formal term, and he sighed. He understood how she felt, but there was only so much he could change. He needed his rules to keep everything in check.

Sprit watched him as they walked side by side and wondered if he knew she'd just heard all of that.

"Rin doesn't seem to be going anywhere in particular," Holt said, his eyes trained on the floor. "But she's been mapping her way on the napkin you gave her."

Sprit gave a ghost of a smile, following his gaze.

"Clever girl."

Holt suddenly stopped in the middle of the hallway and sighed.

"She got in a lift," he said, tilting his head a bit as he listened. "She's coming to our level for the—"

"The observation deck, yeah," Sprit finished, earning herself another side-eye from her deputy as they started forward again. "Sorry."

Rin was standing in front of a door at the end of the hall that had some kind of label on the wall beside it that she couldn't read. Nobody had come in or out of it, and she couldn't hear any noise from where she was standing, so she assumed it was the observation deck Sprit had mentioned. But if it wasn't the observation deck, she might be walking into someone's quarters or maybe a conference room or something.

"I really wish she'd ask Avery to re-install that human program."

Oh, well. There was one way to find out what was behind it. She reached for the button and was about to press it when she heard two people running towards her.

"Rin!"

She turned around and saw Sprit and Holt jogging over to her, and her roommate smiled a little breathlessly.

"I see you found the observation deck," she panted.

"Oh, yeah, I was just exploring. Like you recommended." She went to go push the button again, but Sprit tugged the back of her shirt.

"I wouldn't do that just yet. The observation deck's kind of a big deal, and we've gotta take you with us to the bridge right now so we won't be able to give this the time it's due," she explained in a rush of words, and Rin stared blankly at her. "We can do it later."

"Uh, okay," she began uncertainly and let Sprit grab her hand and pull her back down the hall to the lift with them. "But why am I going to the bridge with you?"

"Oh, you know, with the explosion in engineering there's some stuff going down, and we don't want you getting caught in the wrong place at the wrong time—"

"The captain feels you would be safest with us, Miss Cooper," Holt interjected, saving both Rin and himself from more of Sprit's rambling. "That's all."

"Oh." She looked at Sprit as they entered the lift. "Why didn't you just say that?"

"It's been a long day," she grumbled, and Holt deliberately avoided her peeved glare.

"But should I really be on the bridge?" the human asked as the doors opened, and they started walking again, this time down a long, narrow hallway lined with several doors on each side. "I mean, isn't that where the captain and all the officers work?"

They came to a stop at the end of the hall, just outside the door's motion sensor range, and Sprit shrugged.

"Well, not *all* the officers," she said and, with that, stepped forward.

Oren glanced over his shoulder as the bridge door opened, and Sprit and Holt walked in, their almost-human trailing behind them with star-struck eyes.

"I see you've found Miss Cooper," he said, and Sprit walked over to his side while Holt steered Rin towards Sprit's seat.

"Yeah, Holt tracked her down. Since she has to stay with one of us, can I just send Holt to find Jhama?" she asked lowly. "He can keep me updated in real time now with whatever this bond thing is and not be overheard by nosy crewmembers."

"Of course." She went to leave, but Oren grabbed her hand. "Sprit." She looked back at him, and he could see the displeasure in her eyes. "I know you don't agree with my call, but please. Trust me on this one." When she still hesitated, he pushed again. "Trust me like we should have trusted Holt."

"That's a low blow," she muttered but nodded all the same, walking back to her station just to the right of the door where Holt and Rin were already seated in the two chairs. She motioned for her deputy to join her. "Holt, come here."

"Commander?" he asked, and she carefully turned her back to the waiting human before speaking.

"I'll stay here with Rin. Can you find Jhama and talk to her on your own?"

"Of course, ma'am."

"No, Holt, *can* you do it? You've been favoring your leg."

"I can do it, ma'am," he assured her and went to leave once more.

"Oh and Lewis?" He stopped, and she nervously tapped her fingers against her leg. "Keep me in the loop with the link."

"It can be a little overwhelming," he warned uneasily. "You're not ac-customed to this kind of communication, commander."

"I can handle it, Holt. Now, go on. Find Jhama."

"Yes, ma'am."

She joined Rin in Holt's seat as he left the bridge and swiveled in his chair to face the rest of the bridge. The girl was staring at everything with wide eyes, especially the viewscreen, and Sprit glanced at it.

"That's still not all the stars," she said with a smirk.

"Are you *serious?*"

At the captain's chair, Oren smiled to himself. It had been a long time since he'd heard that much excitement over the cosmos, except per-haps for his helmsman Lucien Trinidore.

The boy was rather excitable over everything.

"I'm serious." Sprit smirked and then pointed to the rest of the crew at their stations. "So, what do you say I introduce you to the officers you were so worried about disturbing?" Rin flushed, and Sprit laughed. "You know the captain," she said, pointing to the white, high-backed chair at the center of the room. All other chairs, Rin noticed, were black. Oren turned slightly and nodded once to the human, and she waved back. "And you met Anthia." The communications officer ignored them at her station to the left of the door, engrossed in her decryption programs. "Hanali'a walked you back to my quarters, so I'd think that you'd recognize her."

"One would hope," the first officer replied, and Rin tilted her head curiously as she took in the giant's station.

It was set at the front left section of the bridge and was inlaid about a foot into the deck plating. The silver console curved in a U-shape around her with a massive computer screen at the front that she was currently filling paperwork out on, and Rin caught a glimpse of a myriad of different keys, buttons, knobs, and levers on the console's surface in front of the screen.

"I heard you went exploring," Hanali'a continued, and Rin gave a crooked smile.

"Had a reputation to fill, I guess."

The first officer chuckled and resumed working, and Sprit sighed.

"Well, I guess the only person up here you don't know is Ensign Lucien Trinidore. He's our navigator and helmsman."

Rin looked over to the station that mirrored Hanali'a's in position and setup and smiled as she saw someone who appeared to be closer to her age sitting in the black seat. He was slight, narrow shouldered, but probably around her height, as well. His dark, straight hair was pulled into an intricate ponytail that fell to about his mid-back, and his skin was dark brown.

"Lucien!" The young man looked over his shoulder at them, and his eyes lit up. "You said you wanted to meet the human? Well, here she is. Say hey."

Large, black freckles decorated his cheekbones and the bridge of his straight nose, and a blinding smile broke out across his smooth, angular features. He waved eagerly to her, his violet eyes shining in welcome, and his enthusiasm reminded Rin of the engineer, Avery. He seemed eager and excitable, and it made the girl want to smile.

"Hi! I'm Lucien."

"Hi," she returned with a small laugh, and Oren cleared his throat as Lucien started to turn around.

"Mind the helm, Lucien. Rin will be with us for a while, yet."

"Rin. *Rin*," Lucien repeated, liking the sound of it. He grinned even wider. "That's a great name."

"Thanks," she laughed, and Oren loudly cleared his throat once more as the ensign went to turn around yet again. Lucien flinched.

"Sorry, sir."

Sprit snorted and turned back to her console, swinging Rin's chair with her.

"I'm sure he'll talk your ear off later. He's a great kid, real sweet," the security chief said with a smile as Oren continued his orders. "Have you heard from Avery yet about engineering?"

"Uh, no, sir," Lucien replied, glancing over his shoulder to his captain. "I can lay in a course though while I'm waiting."

"Hold off on that, ensign." Oren quickly tapped his earwig. "Avery Byrone...Avery, what's our status in engineering?"

"I can give you level four traveling speed, but don't jump that high cold, sir. If you work us up from the docking speeds, we should be fine."

"Understood. We're going to start soon so make sure your people are on standby. Galaxa, out." He looked to his helmsman who was watching him expectantly. "Work *Starlight* up from the docking speeds to level four traveling, ensign. Don't take us any higher, or Avery may kill you."

"Yes, sir," he laughed, and Rin watched as he pulled up a star chart on his screen. "Where are we heading?"

"Trozer." Everyone on the bridge looked at him, confused. "Put us down in Sahmot."

"We aren't heading to one of the Corps' starbases, sir?" Lucien asked uncertainly, and the captain shook his head.

"I spoke with Lokar and other high ranking Corps officials, and they agree that until we figure out exactly what's going on with us, we should stay away from Corps facilities. Nobody wants to risk that kind of collateral damage."

"But our home is an acceptable risk?" Sprit asked coldly, and Oren looked at her warningly.

"I spoke with Matzepo. She believes the risks are acceptable."

"Of course she does, she's our mother," Sprit returned dryly.

"Wait, I thought your last name was Matzepo," Rin whispered with a frown, but the woman held up a hand to tell her to wait. At her station, Hanali'a looked a bit uneasy.

"We're going to Sahmot, commander," Oren said firmly and looked at the rest of his staff. "Anyone else have any concerns?"

"We follow your orders, captain," Hanali'a answered and turned to Lucien. "Plot a course for Sahmot, ensign."

Sprit grumbled and crossed her arms, turning back to her console.

"He's needlessly endangering them," she muttered and glanced at Rin who seemed to still be waiting for a clarification on the name situation. "Matzepo is our mother's name," she explained. "On Trozer, everyone takes their mother's name as their surname until they've accomplished something they take their last name from. Oren is Galaxa because he's the first Trozeran in the Corps. Our sister Tzo is Runner because she set a new record on our planet for the dokori races when she was just a teenager. As for me...I'm still Matzepo."

"You must have done something," Rin said, but Sprit shrugged.

"I have. Nothing I want a last name from, though." She glanced at the viewscreen. "Hey, you'll wanna watch this."

"Is the course laid in?" the captain asked, and Lucien nodded.

"Yes, sir."

"Good." Oren pressed a button on the arm of his chair. "Attention all decks, we are about to put *Starlight* through her paces to level four traveling speed. Engineering, be on standby." He let go of the PA button and nodded to Lucien. "Take us out."

The pitch of the engines started soft and slowly grew louder.

"Oh, that's weird," Rin whispered as the stars started moving, and Sprit smirked.

"Wait for us to hit the higher speeds." Eventually the ship accelerated to the point where the stars turned into staccato streams of light, and Rin suddenly felt queasy. Sprit glanced at her roommate, expecting her to be fascinated, and frowned. "You all good?"

"Can you get seasick in space?" she asked weakly, and Sprit immediately swiveled the girl's chair back to face the console with her.

"Just pretend you didn't see the stars moving," she said with false brightness, and at his chair, Oren rolled his eyes and shook his head.

Jhama gently set her pliers on her desk and examined the three disguised explosives before her. She knew they'd pack a punch despite their size, and unfortunately, she hadn't been able to alter the designs this time. They would go off as planned, and there was nothing she could do to stop it, though she had managed to figure out a way to explain everything to whoever investigated her. She pulled a metal briefcase from under her desk and opened it, carefully nestling each bomb between her rolled up shirts. She'd had to improvise transportation.

But just as she was about to close the case, the door to her quarters slid open, and Jhama's heart jumped into her throat.

They found out. They found out somehow, thank the galaxy—

"Momma, guess what I learned today in school!"

She effortlessly smiled, hiding her dismay, and turned her chair to pick up her child as she barreled into her lap.

"Hmmm, let's see. Was it about the stars?" she asked, assuming an overly thoughtful expression, and her daughter vigorously shook her head, dark curls falling into her eyes. "What about black holes?"

"Nope!"

"Well, then, I give up. What was it?"

"We learned about supernovas!"

Jhama gasped and grinned.

"What was your favorite part?"

"The reminant nebulas," the girl said carefully, and Jhama smirked.

"You mean the *remnant* nebulas?"

"Yeah. They're so *pretty*, momma, you have to see them!" The eager girl glanced over her mother's shoulder as she shifted on her lap, and her eyes lit up at the sight of the briefcase's contents. "Are those ion measurers?"

"Ion emission regulators?" Mara nodded dutifully, her green eyes fixed on the devices. "Yeah, they are. How'd you know that?" Jhama asked with pride, running her fingers through her daughter's dark hair.

"Mister Byrone brought one in for show and tell day."

"Wow, I'm impressed you remembered what they were called," she said and hugged Mara close. "You're my little genius. Now, momma has to finish up some stuff for work. How about you go tell your dad about remnant nebulas? I'm sure he'd love to hear about them." She gently kissed the seven year old's forehead. "Once I get back, you can show me all sorts of pictures, my star."

"Okay!"

Jhama helped her daughter off her lap and followed her to the door so she could make sure Mara was heading for the shrine in the hall. The little girl quickly knelt in front of it and beamed at the picture of the Assidrian man at the center of all the candles, beads, and flowers.

A small placard read *Zhel Assora—loyal father, husband, and officer.*

"Hi, papa. Momma's busy with work right now, so she wanted me to tell you about what I learned in school today...."

Jhama cautiously closed the door to her bedroom and returned to her desk, pulling up a screen of computer code and quickly finishing up the final touches. The moment a command-override was used on her terminal, they'd see the video file on screen. It was up to them to open it after that. This was it; this was all she could do to work around the instructions she'd been given.

She turned on her computer's video cam and aimed it at herself.

"He said I couldn't tell anyone else about our situation," she began, swallowing hard and looking at her watch. She had fourteen hours left. "He never said I couldn't tell myself, which is what this is. This is the first entry of my personal diary. And the first thing I wanted to say was I did not do this willingly. Talik didn't either. He was a victim, as much as the other people in that room. I was able to sabotage his device for him, without telling him what I altered." She stopped and glanced over her shoulder to where she could still hear Mara talking to her father's memorial shrine. "But there was no one to sabotage my own." She looked back at the camera, resolved.

"So, here's how this all began. That monster found us on Refueling Station 304..."

CHAPTER 15

Sprit was in the middle of going through the latest decryption results when she suddenly heard Holt's voice in her head, as clearly as if he was standing right next to her.

"I have been unable to find Ensign Assora, ma'am."

"Holy, djienn!" she half-shouted, jumping in her seat and startling everybody on the bridge—especially the human right next to her. "Sorry. Sorry, it's just..." She pointed to her earwig with a tight, frustrated smile. "Technical issues."

Oren looked at her dryly, unconvinced.

"Uh-huh."

"Not a word," she whispered and turned back to her station. "Holt, you need to start wearing a bell or something," she muttered under her breath as Rin watched her bemusedly. When there was no response, she cleared her throat and furrowed her brow.

"Link-you needs to start wearing a bell," she thought intently and nearly sighed in relief when she got a reply fairly quickly.

"Apologies, commander. As I warned you—"

"Yeah, whatever. Did you try the school? She may be picking up Mara."

"Mara left on her own. She's in their quarters but doesn't know where her mother is."

"Did you check the observation deck? Today was supernova day in class, so she may be checking to see if it's available for her kid to stargaze."

Holt frowned slightly as he walked down the hall.

"How do you know the school's daily curriculum?"

"Holt, that's not important right now. Did you check the observation deck?"

"No, ma'am. I'll head there now."

Sprit rolled her eyes at his nagging feeling of curiosity and sighed.

"I know it was supernova day because I loaned the class some nebula photos. Are you happy?"

She jumped as Rin touched her shoulder, and Rin flinched as well.

"Sorry," she said and pointed to the captain. "He was trying to get your attention."

"Wait, seriously?" Sprit asked, turning around in her seat.

"I called your name a few times," Oren confirmed. "I take it you're still ironing out the link communication."

"Apparently." She sighed and pinched the bridge of her nose. "Yes, sir, what is it?"

"Have you found Ensign Assora, yet?" The captain frowned as his security chief went stony, staring at him like she was debating whether or not she was just going to get up and leave. "Sprit?"

"I was *literally* just figuring that out with Holt. Do you mind?"

"By all means," he said sarcastically, and she turned back to her console. "Is she gone again?"

Rin peered into her friend's face and then nodded.

"Yeah."

"She's not in the observation deck, commander."

"Well then, ask the department heads if they've seen her. I don't know, Holt, figure it out."

Sprit pulled herself back into the real world and instantly groaned, pressing a hand to her forehead. Her temples were throbbing again, and Rin gingerly touched her shoulder.

"You okay?"

Sprit rubbed her eyes and then squared her shoulders, nodding.

"Yeah, yeah I'm fine. No progress on Assora, though."

Oren watched her carefully, noting the way she winced and slightly squinted.

"Maybe you should see Balok and get a neural suppressor while you and Holt figure out your situation," he said carefully, and Sprit looked at him, lifting a hand to her head again. "You two aren't discussing anything right now that can't be done with traditional means of communication."

"Yes, sir. Permission to leave the bridge, sir?" she asked, clearly on edge given how formal she was being, and he nodded. "Thank you."

"Jhama!" The ensign looked up at Avery where he was leaning over the catwalk railing, and waved.

"Hey, Avery." She held up the case. "I just wanted to double-check our ion emissions and make sure we're balanced. We've still been getting sensor ghosts down in security."

"Yeah, man, knock yourself out."

"Thanks, L.C.," she called, and the man smiled at his nickname.

"Jhama, hold up!" She stopped and waited as he slid down the ladder to join her. Once he was close, he reached out and gently squeezed her arm. "I'm sorry about Talik. I know how…I've been through this before. If there's anything I can do to help, just let me know."

Jhama bit her lip and looked down at the deck plating beneath their boots.

"I'd rather not talk about him, sir," she whispered, and he nodded, sympathetically giving her some space.

"I understand." He swept his arm towards the engines. "Go on. Run your tests."

"Thank you, sir." She watched him to return to his catwalk, and once she was sure he was occupied again, she set to work.

Holt was uneasy. His skin crawled with some glimmering malicious intent that he couldn't pin down, and he stopped in the middle of the corridor, ignoring the people walking around him and giving him weird looks. This was how it had felt before. He quickly turned to his bond-mate's link.

"Commander, there's something wrong."

There was no reply, and he mentally reached out, feeling for that space Sprit now occupied. But all he touched was a strange, dense static, a foggy numbness. He quickly touched his earwig, unease building.

"Sprit Matzepo."

In medbay, Sprit rubbed her arm and absently answered the incoming message as Balok disposed of the needle he'd just stuck her with.

"Hey, Holt. Did you find Jhama?"

"Did you take a neural suppressant?" he asked, and she sighed as she massaged her temples.

"Yeah, I did. Actually, I took a couple. And before you say anything, Lewis, I got a splitting migraine just from that one conversation. I don't think this is gonna work."

"The link probably just needs more time to settle, commander. The headaches will abate eventually." He paused for a moment before continuing. "I'm feeling it again, ma'am."

"I could tell," she said softly, glancing at Balok and jerking her head to the side in an unspoken order to get lost. "Try engineering first. You still haven't found Jhama?"

"No, ma'am."

"Alright," she groaned, getting to her feet. "Keep me posted."

"Yes, ma'am."

Sprit turned to leave the medbay, shooting Balok a dirty look as she passed him.

"If you make so much as one married joke or a 'trouble in paradise' comment, I will get back at you. And it'll be when you least expect it," she warned, and the doctor held his hands up at his shoulders.

"On my life, I wouldn't dream of it," he said with a smile, and she rolled her eyes as she left. "Happy hunting, commander!"

———————

"All done, Byrone!" Jhama shouted, and the chief engineer looked down to where she was standing beside the first and second engine coils. She held up the case again. "All the readings checked out. I'll tell Sprit it's something else."

"Sounds good. Oh, tell Mara I said hi, would you?"

Jhama laughed and nodded.

"Of course. You know, she still remembered the ion emission regulators from when you brought them in for show and tell at school." The young engineer beamed. "Sometimes, I think she's a natural tinkerer like her father." She waved goodbye. "Thanks, Avery."

"You're welcome," he called as he watched her leave, and at that moment his earwig chirped.

"*Lewis Holt.*"

"Holt, what's up?" he greeted.

"Have you seen Ensign Assora?"

"Yeah, she just left. She was checking the ion emission readings."

"I see. Thank you, sir." He went to hang up, but the engineer called after him.

"Wait, Holt! Do I have to be worried about something?"

"I don't know. I feel there's something off, sir, but I need to check first."

Avery sighed and scratched the back of his neck.

"Holt, everyone's on edge right now," he began. "It could just be, I don't know, sensor ghosts. Jhama...she's just wrecked over Talik."

"I thought that last time, too, sir," he said shortly and closed the link only to open a new one. "Sprit Matzepo."

"Holt, did you find her?"

"She just left engineering, ma'am. Did you leave security a standing order to check the ion emission levels?"

"No," Sprit said, thoroughly baffled. "Avery cleared the levels with us hours ago."

Holt immediately started running towards the nearest lift.

"I have to go."

"Holt!"

He hung up and quickly opened another channel as he practically slid into a lift and hit deck four.

"Avery Byrone." The pain in his leg was steadily growing worse, and he gripped the handrail behind him until his knuckles turned white.

"Holt, *what* is going on?"

"Assora had no order, Byrone," he said severely, and in engineering Avery turned to their coils. "She should not have been in there, sir. Is there anything wrong where she was working, anything suspicious?"

"No, I don't see anything. The engines look clean."

The lift doors opened, and Holt ran out as fast as he could, shoving past people and ignoring their confused and concerned shouts.

"Sir, I need you to get everyone out of engineering immediately and drop us out of FTL."

"Holt, they're clean. I'm telling you, there's nothing there!"

Holt tore around the corner and ran up to the viewing wall, bracing himself against the glass. Avery turned to look up to him from the catwalk just below where he was standing and shrugged helplessly.

"Holt, I'm serious, she didn't leave anything—"

"There." He pointed at the narrow space between the engines, where Avery couldn't see from his vantage point. "She put explosives on coils one and two."

"What? Are you *sure?*"

The lift down the hall chimed as it stopped at the deck, and a woman stepped out, her entire posture defeated and crushed. She glanced up from her feet as she walked at the same time Holt turned to look at the sound, and the moment they locked eyes, she froze.

And Holt knew.

"Assora!" He started towards her but stopped again as she held up a small device in warning, her thumb hovering over the small red button. "Jhama," he whispered, "don't do it."

Avery quickly scaled the wall and glass so he could see what was going on, and the moment he saw Jhama standing there with the detonator, he turned to the room.

"Everyone, get out, now!"

Jhama glanced at engineering to where Avery was directing a select few of his people towards the coils to no doubt try to defuse her explosives while evacuating the rest of the crew, and she turned her anguished eyes on the security deputy before her.

"Jhama, give me the detonator," Holt tried again, voice deliberately soft and reassuring. "Everything will be fine."

———

On deck two, another lift opened, and Sprit tore out of it, running as fast as she could for the bridge at the other end of the deck.

"Oren Galaxa," she panted.

On the bridge, her brother raised a hand to his ear. Behind him, Rin had slowly managed to turn her chair around to face the viewscreen with only minimal nausea. She was starting to get used to the idea of stars moving. They still looked pretty like this, like strands of tinsel, and it gave her a slight thrill—

"Sprit, how's your headache?" Oren began, but his security chief instantly cut him off.

"Oren, drop out of FTL *now!*"

He looked at his helmsman and abruptly stood, drawing everyone's attention.

"Ensign, drop out!"

———

"I'm sorry," Jhama whispered.

She clamped her thumb down, and their world flipped over.

Starlight came falling out of faster than light, listing through the abyss with no sense of direction or up or down. Her left external engine was completely extinguished, debris trailing behind it. The faintest glow of blue burned in the core of her right side, but it was nowhere near enough to keep the vessel level or moving on any one course. Her metal exterior groaned and buckled, silenced in the vacuum of space as her heart continued to tear apart deep inside her.

Holt pushed himself up from where he'd been thrown against the wall and pulled his weapon free, aiming at the fiery silhouette before the engineering window. She didn't pay him any attention. She just stared at the inferno below them, and the deputy could sense the torture rolling off of her in waves without even trying.

"Assora!"

She turned to him, her tear-stained face eerily bathed in the red crisis lights as the alarms began sounding. The smaller white lights above each speaker flashed in time with their droning cries, punctuating the space like lightning, and behind them, engineering burned with a thunderous roar. She glanced at her watch and tightly grabbed ahold of the guardrail.

"Brace!" she shouted, and Holt barely managed grab one of the hall's support beams before the deck pitched beneath them again.

The second engine coil was reduced to a flaming husk.

Enough.

Holt quickly aimed and pulled the trigger, but the young ensign was three steps ahead of him, knocking his arm to the side so his shot went wide and slamming into him, head down and shoulder first. They both crashed into the wall with painful force, and the lieutenant blinked stars from his eyes as his skull cracked against the wall and his weapon fell from his hand. Distantly, he caught a fragment of her thoughts.

Roundhouse—

Lewis barely had time to prep himself for her coming kick only to get punched in the face instead, and Jhama swore loudly, cradling her gouged hand close to her chest.

Oh, Holt thought in a daze and kicked outwards, catching her in the stomach and sending her to the ground, gasping for air. He fetched his weapon and holstered it. *Roundhouse punch, not kick. I should have known.*

"Damn your spines and mind reading!" she cursed, and a new burst of thoughts suddenly hit Lewis full force, repeating in an endless litany.

Get Mara, and get out. Get Mara, and get out.

He lunged forward and pinned her down, hands above her head.

"Why?" he half-shouted, ears ringing with the din from the burning room beside them. She just looked at him helplessly, silently crying.

"There's a delay," she croaked, and he frowned.

"What?"

"In there," she whispered, pointing with one of her restrained hands. "It's a minute delay."

Holt glanced up at engineering, at the blackening glass, and his heart stopped.

"You planted a third bomb."

She suddenly brought her knee slamming into his already bruised gut, and he folded over slightly, bringing his face close enough to hers that she could head-butt him. He fell away from her, hands over his bleeding nose, and she quickly pounced, putting him in a chokehold despite her smaller size and struggling to hold onto him.

"Please, stop fighting! I don't want to do any of this!" she grunted, and all Holt could hear from her thoughts was that same mantra of get Mara, and get out.

"I'm afraid I have a favor to return first," he rasped and promptly snapped his head back so hard he heard a loud crunch of bone. Jhama screamed and let go, holding her completely shattered nose as her eyes streamed with tears and her nerves shrieked. Lewis quickly pinned her once more, holding both her hands above her head again and making sure her legs were restrained with his own.

"Where is the other bomb, Assora?" he demanded, eyes blazing in his bloody face.

The ensign just looked at him, and slowly he felt her anguish turn to resignation and grief as he took in her equally bloody features and the deep gouges from when she'd head-butted him.

She knew there was only one reason she was still alive. There was only one reason she hadn't been given the same fate as Talik, why she'd been given the remote detonator. Her jobs weren't over yet. She craned her head back so she could see engineering burn, could see the bodies on the catwalks as those who were still alive either ran to the exits or tried to put out the fires to save coils three and four. She could see Avery standing on one of the higher catwalks, a little singed and worse for wear, but still fighting and struggling to direct his people to safety through the deck four exits. The deck five exits, she knew, would be engulfed in flames.

She was done. She wasn't going to play along with this anymore or continue this cat and mouse charade.

"Please," she croaked, looking up at her superior and hating herself for his bloody features and ragged breathing. She did this. "Save Mara." He frowned, and she tilted her head down the hall. "She's in our quarters. Tell her..." she bit back a sob and gave a watery smile. She'd always known this out existed. She'd just never wanted to take it—for her baby girl. "Tell her I'm sorry."

"What are you—"

Bite him hard.

She sank her teeth into Holt's forearm until she tasted blood, and as he yanked away, freeing her hand, she snatched his gun from his belt and pressed it into his stomach. He froze, and Jhama glanced at the setting, heart aching. He'd had it on stun. She looked up at him with a pitying smile that only increased the deputy's confusion.

"Thank you," she whispered.

She switched the blaster's setting to kill and sighed, still smiling, and Holt caught her final thought amid the newfound peace radiating from her.

I win.

And before he could react, she put his weapon under her own chin, closed her eyes, and pulled the trigger.

"Momma!"

Holt looked up at the child's screech, going cold to his very core.

Mara was standing in the hall, screaming and sobbing with a blanket clutched in her hands, looking so horribly out of place in the red lighting and the blaring sirens. Her blue skin looked purple, and he stared down at her mother in horror. Her fading smile sent chills down his spine, and he shakily felt for a pulse in the flickering light from the flames and alarms.

She's dead, a voice in his head whispered. *No one walks away from that. Look at her eyes. Listen to her thoughts. She's dead. Stop wasting time!*

He quickly got up and ran down the hall, snatching up the girl and sprinting down the hall to her room. Mara continued to scream and cry in his ear, and he pushed down the horrible memories fighting to rise up in the back of his mind.

"This is not Davin Colony," he breathed, elbowing the button outside Jhama's door. He quickly ran in while the door was still opening, stepping over the toppled memorial shrine. "This is not Davin." He carried the girl to her room, set her on her bed and quickly knelt before her. "Mara. Mara, look at me." He gently touched her cheek and guided her heartbroken attention to him. What did Jhama always call her, what was it? "Stay here, my star," he said, trying to hide the sorrow and fear in his voice as he tucked her hair behind her ears and wrapped her a little tighter in her blanket. "It's going to be okay. Stay here."

He started standing up, but the girl grabbed the front of his uniform, her sobs redoubling in volume. He reluctantly kneeled again.

"Mara. My star, look at me." She looked up at him, shaking and crying. "I know you're scared, but I need you to be brave." Creator, he hated himself. He had sworn to never put another child through this. "I need you to stay here. There are others out there who are scared, too, who need my help." He looked anxiously to the door. Jhama had said they only had a minute of delay to work with, and he had a horrible suspicion where the last bomb was. He turned back to the shivering girl. "If you hear a loud rushing sound in the hall, like…like a storm or lots of wind, do *not* open the door. Understand?" She nodded dutifully. "If you hear a storm, where don't you go?"

She solemnly pointed to the door, hiccuping with sobs, and Holt nodded, gently prying her free from his lapel and feeling cold as his touch left a smear of blood on her small hands.

"I'll return," he promised, and she nodded again, still crying.

Forcing himself not to look back, he turned and ran.

"Please," he whispered, heart about ready to pound through his ribs. "Please, don't be where I think it is."

The alarm changed, and he looked up as the ship's automated voice started speaking.

"*Breach imminent. Evacuate engineering. Decks four and five on high alert. Breach imminent. Evacuate engineering. Decks four and five on high alert.*"

As he rounded the corner to the cracked viewing glass, he saw Avery running along the catwalk below him, pointing and shouting. Every fiber of Avery's being echoed what he was screaming, and Holt could hear it clear as day as he came to a stumbling stop.

Charge on the hull.

He looked to where Talik had placed his bomb not a day earlier and saw the small, blinking device a split second before it blew.

He couldn't shout. Couldn't scream. He could only watch in horror as *Starlight*'s hull was torn open, and people were blown into the waiting darkness without mercy. There shouldn't have been that many people in engineering. There shouldn't have been, but this was an honorable crew. And at this moment Holt nearly cursed them for it. These people stayed to save engineering, and now it was their tomb.

The damaged viewing glass before him creaked, popping ominously as it turned nearly opaque with spidering cracks, and suddenly the world went quiet. All Holt could hear was his racing heart, his rasping breath, and the guilty memory of his conversation with Mara at her bedside.

If you hear a storm, where don't you go?

Distantly, he heard the ship's voice.

"*Breach imminent. Evacuate engineering. Decks four and five on high alert.*"

"Don't open the door," he softly begged and closed his eyes as the glass shattered.

The pull of space ripped him through the air, but just as he braced himself for the horrible death that awaited, something caught hold of his wrist, nearly tearing his arm from its socket. He jerked with the whiplash of coming to such a forceful, sudden stop, and his head cracked against a catwalk railing.

Everything went dark.

CHAPTER 16

Oren breathed harshly through the pain as he pushed himself up from the deck plating.

"Avery Byrone," he barked, touching his earwig, but all he got was static. He repeated himself, voice growing sharper. "*Avery Byrone.*"

There was no response, and he turned to Anthia, thanking the stars that she was already back in her chair—typing away before running over to Sprit's station and pulling up the ship's scans. Rin clambered back into Holt's seat beside her and clung to the console, looking ready to throw up or faint.

"Anthia, *what* is going on?"

"Another explosion in engineering, sir," she read, voice controlled and cool, as if she were reading the weather forecast. "Coil one is gone, and there are scattered reports of another bomb on coil two that they're trying to get to and deactivate."

"It hasn't gone off, yet?"

"No, sir, it's probably on a delay to give us more time to try to deactivate it. That way when it goes off, it inflicts maximum casualties."

"Then, tell them to get away!" he shouted, and she turned to him.

"Sir, I can't communicate with them," she said evenly, giving him a look that said to pull it together. "The blast took out engineering's PA system and the earwigs are overloaded, so they're submitting reports on computers. But I can guarantee most of the terminals were destroyed, and the remaining ones are malfunctioning. They're on their own."

"If they have computers, then tell them on the computers, Anthia!" he ordered.

"Sir, they can't sit around and wait for typed orders from us. Engineering is burning. It's gone," she said harshly, and Hanali'a looked at her grimly. When Oren still hesitated, she pressed again. "I was threat analysis before I was put here, captain, so trust me when I say this was thorough. I can sound a hull breach alarm on all decks to tell them to get as far away from engineering as possible, but that's it. Without the PA or earwigs, the people still inside are on their own."

"Okay." Oren took a deep breath, collecting himself. "Ensign, help Anthia at Sprit's station. Keep her updated while she preps the alarm."

"Yes, sir."

Lucien stood up just as the deck pitched again, and he was thrown over the side of his console, landing back-first on the edge of the metal step under him. Pain seared through him, setting his spine on fire as he cried out and grabbed at whatever he could touch. He couldn't move, couldn't breathe—

"Lucien!"

"Coil two is gone, sir," Anthia called as the captain hurried over to the ensign's side.

"Acoua, is there a hull breach?"

"Not yet, sir," she said, working quickly. "But Avery hadn't finished repairing Talik's damage. Given time, this may do us in, but if there's another blast, that wall will rip open like paper."

Oren glanced at her in tense warning as he gently put his hands on Lucien's shoulders.

"Just get that breach alarm going, Anthia." He turned his attention to his helmsman. "Lucien, what happened?"

"My back," he gritted out between clenched teeth. "I landed on the step."

Oren looked over to where Rin had braced herself under Sprit's console, her breathing harsh and her tear-filled eyes wide.

"Rin. Rin!" She jumped and looked at him, shaking. "I need you to come here." She jerkily shook her head and clung a little tighter to the bolts and braces under the console. "Rin, Lucien's hurt, and I have to help Anthia." She still stayed, and he went for the low blow. "I know you're scared, but we helped you when you needed it. Please."

Rin knocked her head lightly against the wall and gritted her teeth.

"Oh, come on," she whispered, squeezing her eyes shut. "Come on, move."

"*Breach imminent. Evacuate engineering. Decks four and five on high alert.*"

She looked up at the ceiling as the alarm sounded, and the words finally galvanized her into action. She crawled from under the console and unsteadily crossed the bridge to the captain's side.

He gratefully squeezed her shoulder.

"Okay, just hold his hand." Rin took the helmsman's hand in hers and winced as he accidentally ground her knuckles together in his grip.

His skin was tough and leathery against hers, and hot, far too hot to be normal. "Lucien, I'm going to lift you off the step."

"I wouldn't do that, sir," he gasped, grimacing. He suddenly looked ashen. "My spine—"

"We need to see how badly you're hurt." He glanced at Hanali'a who was rapidly working. "Han, what are you doing?"

"Sending out a distress call, sir." She kept working as he opened his mouth to argue. "I know we risk attracting whoever is behind all that's happening, but we need help, Oren."

He nodded grimly, pressing his lips together into a thin, tight line.

"No, you're right. Anthia, take over for her. Han, I need you to help me with Lucien—"

The deck rocked with a final explosion, and there was a loud shattering of glass as everyone lost their footing once more. Rin cried out as she struck her head against Lucien's console, and the ensign tightened his grip on her hand even more, gritting his teeth as the movement jostled his back.

"You're okay," Rin whispered shakily and grabbed Lucien's arm, gently squeezing as he went unconscious from the pain. "It's—you're okay."

Oren watched them, guiltily noting her trembling and tears.

"Sir, the hull and viewing wall both gave in," Anthia reported and quickly ran from Sprit's station back to her own. "Engineering is depressurizing along with the halls and several quarters on deck four."

"Aren't the emergency bulkheads closing?"

"No, sir. The explosives must have hit something in engineering, or whoever set them sabotaged internal sensors beforehand."

Oren closed his eyes and took a fraction of a second to collect himself. Everything that could've possibly gone wrong had gone wrong. This was every worst-case scenario, every nightmare…

"We're in a wreck call," he breathed, and Rin looked on in fear as he braced his arm against Lucien's station and took a deep breath. "Here's the plan. Hanali'a, you and Anthia go to Sprit's security headquarters and manually close the bulkheads while I handle the bridge."

Rin looked at the first officer as the captain spoke, hoping to draw some kind of calm from her towering, effortless form. Instead, what she saw ripped her breath from her lungs, and her heart stuttered, trying and failing to regain its rhythm.

"Anthia, you'll need Sprit's authorization code—" Oren broke off as Rin screamed, the sound a raw, hair-raising mixture of fright and horror. She was staring over his shoulder, hyperventilating, her hands pressed over her mouth as she sobbed, and he quickly turned to his first officer's station, filled with dread. "Han?"

He froze.

That shattering of glass in the last explosion—it had been the sound of Hanali'a being thrown headfirst through her console display.

"Han!" He quickly ran to his second-in-command, hands hovering uselessly over her limp body and bloodied head. "*Djïenn*, okay…okay, uh, Anthia, contact the medbay—"

"No," Rin suddenly interrupted. "No, I'm done. I'm *done with this!*"

The captain looked up as she pushed herself away from Lucien and backed towards the door, her breaths turning into wheezes as her expression wavered on the verge of a complete breakdown.

"Rin, it's going to…." He trailed off mid-lie as the human gasped and tensed up. Her eyes went wide, and Oren swore he could see the veins in her neck stand out against her skin. "Rin?"

It felt like her heart and lungs were being compressed. She couldn't catch a full breath, couldn't stop the horrible feeling rising in her throat. This felt like a panic attack, but it wasn't. This was…this was—

"What in the…"

Anthia looked over her shoulder at her captain's shocked whisper and instantly lunged for her tablet.

That human wasn't human.

Rin's eyes were consumed by a bright, brilliant purple glow, and the eerie light was spreading through the veins in her neck and chest, filling her skin with diffuse color. Oren tentatively reached out to her, and her expression contorted in a nearly feral snarl as the strange light burning beneath her skin and blazing in her eyes flared in brightness.

"*Rin,*" Oren warned, backing away, and then jumped as something smashed down hard on the back of her head. The poor girl crumpled to the plating, out cold, and he looked up to see Anthia standing over her with a shattered tablet clenched in her hands.

"What the hell is she?" Anthia demanded slowly, but all the captain could do was shake his head as he pulled himself to his feet.

"We have no idea."

"Fantastic," she spat, clearly displeased, "*sir.*"

She tossed her now-useless tablet to the side, and suddenly, the ship fell quiet. The alarms shut off, the crisis and siren lights went dark, and every console except part of Anthia's instantly powered down. The floor gradually stopped pitching and tilting, and the hum in *Starlight's* bones died away. Several cold metallic thuds echoed through the deck, growing steadily more muffled, until the only sound left was the unsteady breathing of the two conscious officers. The only light that remained was the starlight beyond the viewscreen.

In hindsight, Sprit had never run this fast in her life. Her attempts to use her earwig after the first explosion had rewarded her with nothing but static, but even with the neurosuppressant she'd just taken, she could still catch glimpses of Holt like faint whispers just out of hearing.

"Holt?" she thought intently, struggling to grab ahold of him as his thoughts and emotions grew more chaotic. *"Holt, please tell me you can hear me."*

There was nothing, and she cursed herself for the hundredth time for taking the suppressants. This was not an ideal situation to be in without contact, but she had to make do with what she'd managed to get from her deputy. There were multiple bombs, people were dying, engineering was gone, and the hull was about to give.

"This is a wreck call," she panted, unknowingly echoing Oren.

There was nothing she could do on the bridge, she decided. She had to know what was going on, and the best place for that was in her headquarters. She caught herself on the support beam just outside the security department's door and glanced down at the end of the hall where she could see the bridge's entrance.

"I've got this, brother," she whispered and quickly ran inside to her computer. As soon as she sat down, the second explosion rocked the ship, and she swore as her ribs slammed painfully into the edge of the desk. "Okay. Okay, let's see."

Her fingers moved at a near-blur across her screens and keyboard, and she hissed as the jostling deck caused more typos than she could afford. Finally, she found the data she wanted and took a deep, steeling breath.

Life support systems on decks four and five were both offline, and fire-suppressant systems weren't putting a dent in the inferno currently blazing in engineering and damaging the loading bay. The ship's earwig network was overloaded and non-functional. Helm control was offline, inertial negators were offline, and the combination of those malfunctions explained why they were getting thrown around so much. As for the bulkheads, it seemed the internal pressure sensors had been damaged, too. If the hull did breach, Sprit wasn't sure the depressurization would register, much less if the bulkheads would drop on their own.

Literally everything they needed online wasn't working.

Breach imminent. Evacuate engineering. Decks four and five on high alert.

"Alright, let's do this." She resumed typing. "It's a good thing you don't know I know all the bridge officers' authorization codes, Oren, because you would have changed them on me."

Her immediate concern was establishing control over the bulkheads and the shield generators that covered the outer hull for just this situation—patching breaches. She could repair life support all she wanted, but if there was a gaping hole in the ship, it wouldn't matter how well their heaters and air processors worked.

"Reroute command functions through auxiliary," she narrated as she typed, heart racing. The life support and shield generator icons turned green, indicating they were back online, but Sprit cursed as the bulkheads stayed red. "Oh, come on. Don't do this right now. Let's try—"

Suddenly, she was hit with overwhelming fear that wasn't hers, and the third and final bomb went off.

A split second later the alarm changed.

"Breach in engineering. Evacuate decks four and five."

"Holt," she whispered, her heart lurching into her throat. She felt his fear switch blindingly between horror, pain, and then grim resignation, and she stood up sharply, as if someone else had hauled her to her feet. She could hear the glass shatter two decks below, could feel the pull of space engulf her—no, not her, *him*—and she screamed. "NO!"

The thoughts were gone. The feelings, the sensations that were his and not hers, they were gone. He...he was gone. Holt, her deputy, her friend, he wasn't there anymore. He was just *gone*. The alarms snapped her back into the present, and, numb with shock, she sat back down and resumed working.

"Seal the breach," she whispered, wiping tears from her eyes, and entered Hanali'a's authorization codes instead of hers with Oren's.

She'd have to pull power from everything to get this to work. She watched the deck-by-deck schematics as all unnecessary functions went dark—consoles, lights, alarms, everything but gravity and life support. While everything powered down, she turned her focus to the shield generators and quickly outlined where the breach was. She shuddered. It was massive, and she couldn't help but think of the people who must have died when it happened. She selected the appropriate generators and threw the switch.

"Please, hold," she whispered, watching with bated breath as the pressure slowly stopped falling on the two decks and the bulkhead icon finally flickered green. Without another second of hesitation, she hit the 'deploy' command. Almost everything instantly shut down, leaving her in the dark with nothing more than a glitching screen.

She couldn't tell which was worse, the silence or screaming alarms and neutral computer's voice warning her of their impending doom. She wearily sank into her chair and let her head tilt back as she listened to the domino effect of thuds echoing throughout the ship. The bulkheads were dropping. A brief glance at her screen told her that the shield was still in place over the hull breach, and she forced herself back to the computer. She wasn't done yet.

"We're sealed off," she said softly, opening the life support systems she'd rerouted through auxiliary control. "Time to keep us alive."

And as she worked, she took in the casualties. Six rooms on deck four had fully depressurized. Engineering was all but air-deprived. The loading bay had some moderate fire damage, but it was nowhere near the husk its adjacent room now was. She'd have to sacrifice overall temperature and air processing in order to keep the entire ship alive, and she tensely ran a hand through her hair as her leg started bouncing.

The explosion had killed coil three in addition to coils one and two, which left only coil four functioning with the backup generators in the boiler room, its controls jerry-rigged through auxiliary and the security department. That meant she had limited power to work with, limited options in regards to how to spread their capabilities, and she realized she had only one choice.

The bulkheads had to stay up.

She'd have to implement shelter in place, and as she sent the orders remotely to auxiliary control through her terminal, she let herself think about the consequences of her decision. She knew she was probably condemning some crew on their decks. She knew some people would need to get out of depressurizing rooms or else they'd die, but she couldn't help them. It was either keep everything sealed or open the wrong door and vent an entire deck by accident. The crew quarters' doors were without power, too. They *could* be pried open, but it took a lot of strength, and again Sprit thought about any wounded officers in depressurizing rooms and kept coming back to that horrible choice. The bulkheads *had* to stay up.

She'd figured out how to mostly keep all decks pressurized. The one thing she wouldn't be able to give everyone was heat. Engineering was completely fried, so she wouldn't be able to get life-support functioning in there, but she could in the other rooms on deck four. She could only hope that, with the shattered viewing panel, the laws of physics would warm and oxygenate engineering enough to keep whoever was trapped in there alive just a little longer.

She wanted nothing more than to run to the bridge, break through the bulkhead sealing the room off from the rest of the ship, and get to her brother. But she couldn't. She had to stay here and make sure none of her fragilely balanced systems and safety nets gave out. She slumped down in her seat and watched the screen with determined eyes, bathed in starlight. And then, finally, losing Holt hit her, and the tears started.

The silence was worse, she decided, crossing her arms over her chest and drawing her legs up on the seat with her as the cold began to set in. It left you nowhere to hide from your thoughts.

"The bulkheads shut, sir," Anthia said in the silence that followed, but the captain just stared at his first officer. "Is she dead?"

He cautiously worked his hand between Han's chest and the control board and shook his head. "She's alive."

Lucien weakly groaned and lifted his head from the deck plating so he could see what was going on.

"Oh galaxy," he exhaled, letting his head drop heavily back to the floor. "Is it bad?"

Oren sat down heavily beside his oldest friend, taking in the cuts and small pebbles of glass burrowed into her scalp. Her breaths were nothing more than shallow gasps, and he reluctantly took stock of the room. Rin was still unconscious on the floor, Lucien was out for the count due to the unknown damage to his back, and Hanali'a was likely in critical condition after plowing headfirst through a computer screen. That left him with Anthia. The lieutenant met his gaze with unwavering calm.

"It's bad, ensign," he finally answered, and the young man painfully lifted his head again to look at the human slumped on the floor.

"What...what happened to Rin?"

"She hit her head," Anthia answered, and Oren looked at her, unimpressed, as she approached. "The bulkheads shut," she repeated. "We've got a hull breach, most likely in engineering, but I wouldn't rule out a third bomb elsewhere. The boiler room would be a prime target."

"Anthia, please," he began wearily, resting a hand on Hanali'a glass-decorated shoulder. Anthia continued like she hadn't heard him.

"But since the bulkheads shut and most of our power grid has been re-routed, it's safe to assume Sprit is in the security offices taking care of everything." She shrugged. "She's probably coordinating with Holt."

"No, actually, she took a neurosuppressant."

Anthia scowled, and despite the situation, Oren laughed once at her frustration.

"Why would she ruin a confidential, unhackable link?" she muttered, but neither got any further before Lucien started wheezing.

"Luc?" Oren quickly returned to his youngest crewmember's side and gently held his hand. "What's wrong?"

"It's just…getting a little hard to breathe," he mumbled, and the captain noted the sweat beading on his brow.

"Here, let me see." He gently unbuttoned the man's uniform and pulled it open so he could get a better look without actually lifting the ensign up. His already somber expression grew darker.

"What…what's wrong?" Lucien shivered as Oren gently touched his sides, his hands rough and cool against his skin.

"Your back's swelling, so your binder's getting tighter and making it harder for you to breathe," he explained softly. "If we could cut it off of you, it might make it easier, but that's entirely your choice."

The helmsman hesitated but then nodded.

"Anthia, tell me you still carry your dagger," the captain called. The Feralan replied by lifting the hem of her pants and drawing a long, slender knife from a sheath sewn into the outside of her boot. "Why do I still ask? Alright, Lucien, this may feel cold."

He took the blade from Anthia hilt first and then cautiously slid the razor-sharp metal between the young man's skin and the seam of the binder around his chest. And as he finished cutting the fabric, the ensign immediately sighed, breathing much more easily.

"There we go. How's your back?" he asked, closing Lucien's uniform up. The helmsman grimaced, gingerly resting his hand on his chest.

"Hurts, but I'm not as bad as Han."

The tinkling sound of cascading glass interrupted them, and Oren turned to see Anthia carefully lifting the first officer's head and neck up from where they'd been hanging over the side of the console.

"Anthia, wait!"

He quickly joined her, and Lucien watched as they delicately eased Han from her seat to the ground. Though really, they just pulled her off balance enough that her massive frame slid off the chair and then guided her fall. It was far from graceful, and Oren hissed anxiously as some of her wounds started bleeding more heavily.

"We should wrap those," Anthia said flatly and unbuttoned the top of her uniform, pulling it off so it hung about her waist. She fetched her knife from where their captain had set it down and mechanically took the blade to the fabric, jaggedly cutting it away until she was just left with a pair of pants. "Here." She held it out to Oren. "Use it for bandages."

"You're going to get cold in just the underarmor," he warned but took it none-the-less.

"I'm told I run cold, sir," she returned and then headed over to Rin with a distrusting light in her eyes. "I should wake her up in case she has a concussion." She hesitated, her statement a veiled question, and Oren sighed, eyeing the unconscious almost-human.

"Yes, you should," he finally said and promptly winced as Anthia flicked the girl in the face probably a bit harder than necessary.

It did the trick, though. Rin groaned and slowly blinked, propping herself up on one elbow.

"What happened?" she croaked.

"You panicked and hit your head," Anthia said as she walked away, and the teenager looked to Oren.

"Harshly put, but yes." He sighed and surveyed his work as Rin got up and walked over to him. "Hanali'a's in a bad way. I need to get her to the medbay sooner rather than later."

Anthia looked at him like she doubted his sanity.

"Sir, did you miss my report about how the earwigs are overloaded and the bulkheads are sealed?" she asked acerbically, and Rin softly gasped as she saw the somehow grayer than normal first officer stretched out on the floor. She had strips of Anthia's ravaged uniform tied off around the worst of her cuts, and her eyes were half-open, fixed blankly on the viewscreen. "The bridge bulkhead closed. We're *stuck* in here, sir."

"Stop telling me what we have going against us, Lieutenant Acoua, and start giving me solutions," Oren ordered, volume rising.

On the floor, Lucien looked very uncomfortable, and Rin frowned as she looked at him, specifically his chest. Something seemed diff...oh.

There were transgender people in space, too.

"Sir, the only solution we have right now is *hoping* that someone got Han's distress signal before we went dark and *hoping* that Commander Matzepo can keep us together until then!"

"Lieutenant, be careful how you raise your voice to me—"

"Please, stop fighting!"

The captain and lieutenant turned to Lucien, taken aback by his un-characteristic outburst.

The young man sniffed and cleared his throat.

"I-I can't move without pain," he continued, voice shaking, "Han is...who knows, but she's covered in blood and glass. Rin's scared out of her mind, and I-I'm pretty sure Anthia hit her on the head with her tablet over there, which is several different levels of not okay." Rin crossed her arms over her chest and glanced at the captain, betrayal shining in her eyes as he looked away. "We have almost no power, there's a hull breach, and..." he gave a weak, helpless laugh, "we have no idea who's dead or who's alive or who's even doing this to us." He paused, squeezing his eyes shut and taking a deep breath. "So, I need you two to stop fighting and act like a captain and lieutenant. Sir. Ma'am."

In the long silence that followed, Rin walked over to Lucien's side, deliberately allowing her shoulder to slam into Anthia's as she passed.

"I'm sorry, ensign," Oren finally said and gestured for his lieutenant to go to her station. "You're right, and I'm sorry." He stared at the stars for a few moments and organized his thoughts. "Anthia, find a way to contact anyone else. It's better than doing nothing, and find out what you can still do on that console. Rin, I'm going to have you stay with Lucien while I monitor Hanali'a. Understood?"

"Yes, sir," Anthia said brusquely, and Rin sat beside the helmsman, taking his hand in hers.

"Thank you," he whispered, and she nodded, her reply just as soft.

"It's no problem."

Sitting here, holding someone's hand—this, she could do.

Holt groaned. He had a splitting headache, his left shoulder felt like it had been dislocated, his right thigh throbbed in time with his heart, and, suspiciously, he was still alive to feel all of it. He painfully opened his eyes and was greeted by the sight of Avery's soot-smudged, marble features anxiously hovering inches above his own.

"Oh, thank god," the engineer blurted, collapsing on Holt's chest and unintentionally driving the air from Holt's lungs as he clung to the man's uniform with burned hands. "I thought you were dead."

"As did I, sir," the deputy wheezed.

Avery laughed, fragile and giddy above him, and Lewis wearily let his hand rest on his superior's back.

As did I.

CHAPTER 17

Avery quickly sat up as Holt groaned and moved beneath him. The deputy had forgotten about the number Jhama did on his stomach, and the pain was coming back with a vengeance now that his adrenaline had faded. He hadn't even finished fully recovering from the first explosion, and now here he was with a litany of new injuries. This was just his luck.

"What happened, sir?" he croaked, and Avery gingerly helped him sit up against the blackened wall. "Why aren't we dead? Not that I am complaining."

"Someone got the shield generators on," the engineer said, pointing with a blistered hand to the wall opposite them.

A red, shimmering veil of electrical discharge stretched across the massive hole in their hull, and Holt shivered with more than the cold as he saw the bodies and debris floating just beyond the barrier like some kind of ghastly, frozen graveyard. He ripped his gaze from the horrifying scene and took in the room around them. More bodies were piled over each other on the floor, charred beyond recognition the closer they were to the engine coils. A few people hung over the sides of catwalks, necks and joints at unnatural angles, and the deputy knew that they'd suffered the fate he'd so miraculously managed to avoid when the breach sealed, and they were dropped midair.

"Why am I not dead?" he asked, looking at the shivering man beside him. Avery's black eyes glistened more than usual in the starlight, and the younger man looked away. "Sir?"

"I caught you," Avery whispered, and Holt glanced at the engineer's burned hands. "You know my abilities. I hung on to anything I touched better than…" He glanced guiltily at the ruins around them, to the icy graves beyond the red. "I couldn't catch any of them. I tried, Holt." He turned to his junior officer, begging him for forgiveness. "They were my people, and I tried to grab them, but they kept slipping away and my hands hurt so much—"

"I know, sir," Holt interrupted gently, and Avery dropped his head into his hands, fingers picking at the scaled ridge framing his face.

"Maybe if I hadn't burned my hands on that catwalk railing, then I could've…."

"Sir, may I?" the deputy asked softly, and Avery let the older man take his hands in his own, examining the light burns in the dimness. They weren't bad. The engineer would heal without any impaired mobility.

"But then, the glass gave in, and I saw you." Holt looked up at him, and Avery sniffed and dragged the back of his hand across his nose, unknowingly smearing soot across his cheek and nose. "I had to catch you. After everything you've done for me, I had to catch you." He paused, looking at the horned man a little closer. "Man, you look like hell."

Holt scoffed, going to stand up and quickly changing his mind when the world spun like a centrifuge, overwhelmed with pain.

"Whoa, easy, Lewis." Avery gently pushed him back down. "You're all beat up. I wouldn't be surprised if you have a concussion."

"What happened to my arm and head?" he asked, keeping his eyes screwed shut until things evened out again.

"Oh, uh." Avery suddenly sounded embarrassed. "That's my fault. I dislocated your arm when I grabbed you, and you kind of snapped, like whiplash? You hit your head on the rail there, and you were out." Holt gingerly rotated his shoulder and found he could move it fairly well. "I, uh, reset it for you, but I'm no Balok, so be careful."

"Thank you, sir." Holt half-crawled, half-dragged himself to the edge of the catwalk and looked down. "Is anyone else alive?"

"No," Avery whispered, sitting heavily against the railing beside him. "I checked. Smoke inhalation, suffocation, burning, blunt force trauma, broken spines…they're all dead." He paused and looked down. "Jhama's over there." Holt followed his pointing finger and saw the shock of blue skin and orange hair against the charred floor. "Her body must've been blown out here when the hull breached. I saw the blaster burn under her chin," he continued carefully, and his crewmate seemed to grow distant. "Did you—"

"She did, sir." Holt sighed and looked up to the broken viewing glass above them, but almost immediately frowned as his breath fogged before his bloodied lips. "The temperature…"

"Yeah, we've got no life support in here. The rails and walls are already icing over in some places so I can't climb as much."

"I need to get to Mara Assora," he grunted, pulling himself up by the rail. "I left her in her quarters, and I promised her I'd come back."

"Holt, easy!" Avery quickly stood with him and steadied his wavering balance. "Look, man, you can barely stand up. How do you plan to climb out of here?"

Holt considered the jagged opening above them and nodded.

"You're right, sir." He let himself sag back down to the cold grate beneath them. "You'll have to go on ahead."

"Are you *insane?* You said it yourself—the temperature is dangerously low in here. In your state, you won't last fifteen minutes." The Xanidian eyed him impassively, and Avery groaned in frustration. "Look, what if I carried you out of here?"

"I'll pull you off the wall, sir," the wounded man returned, voice no less gentle for his words. "You can move much faster on your own, and that little girl needs somebody—"

"No. No, you told her *you* were coming back, so she needs *you*," the chief engineer said firmly and pointed to the stretch of wall above them that led to the shattered glass panel Holt had come through. "I create my own gravity field, remember? I can carry you just fine."

"Have you tried carrying something my weight before while doing this, sir?" Avery hesitated, and Holt pushed on. "You don't have super strength, lieutenant commander, and unfortunately *I* don't create my own gravity."

"So, you want to sit here and freeze to death?" Avery barked, voice echoing eerily in the space around them. "Because that's what's going to happen to you, Holt. After everything you've been through, after Davin Colony, after all the missions you've run, after surviving *four* explosions in less than 28-hours, you're gonna freeze to death!" Holt continued to look at him with that same impassivity, and Avery groaned, turning away and grabbing his inky hair in his hands. "Everyone else here is *dead*, Lewis!" he yelled, rounding on the deputy. "They're *dead!*"

Instantly, Holt was hit by the man's guilt, and he sighed, closing his eyes. When he spoke, his voice was heavy with empathy.

"Avery..."

"Everyone else is dead, because *I* didn't listen to you fast enough and *I* didn't get them out sooner, so I'm not letting you die, too!"

Holt looked up at him, evaluating his options. In his core, he felt that this wasn't going to work. But Byrone needed this, even if none of it was the engineer's fault. He let his tense frame relax in resignation.

"Do you really think you can carry me out of here on your back?"

"Yes." The response was hard and fast, no hesitation. "I do."

"Then, I place myself in your hands, sir."

"Why did you knock me out?"

Anthia looked at the human and resumed her work.

"I did what was necessary in the moment," she finally answered, and Lucien scoffed. "Is there something you want to say to me, ensign?"

"I just think you owe her a better explanation than that. *Ma'am.*"

Anthia eyed him carefully at his surly attitude and shifted her attention to the human. The not human. The whatever she was.

"I did what was necessary in the moment," she repeated, her cold voice giving no invitation for challenge. "Any other information is personal and not appropriate for this environment. But I would be glad to fill you in later when we're alone."

"Don't know if I trust you to be alone with me," Rin muttered under her breath, and Anthia looked at her again.

"Then you can have the captain or Commander Matzepo there as a mediator."

"How did she *hear* that?" Rin breathed to Lucien, who was drawing his hand across his throat in a *stop* gesture, and Anthia answered again.

"Feralan females have heightened senses of hearing." She considered the two young people huddled together, and somehow her next words sounded like a threat. "It's what makes me a good communication's officer."

Oren cleared his throat loudly.

"We'll discuss what happened here later, Rin, I assure you. And Luc, I thought you said no fighting."

Lucien and Rin quickly looked down, and the room grew uncomfortable once more until Anthia gave some desperately wanted news.

"Sir, I managed to get one-way communication."

"With who?"

"At the moment, nobody," she said, turning in her chair to him and noting the way his excitement deflated. "We can't send messages out, but we can receive incoming ones."

"So, if someone responds to our distress call?"

"We'll know who they are, sir." Oren sighed in relief and tilted his head back to rest unevenly against the side of Hanali'a's station as he continued to run his fingers through his first officer's long hair in absent comfort. "It's not a lot, but like you said—"

"It's something." He looked closely at Hanali'a, deeply concerned. "Her breathing's more uneven. She's shivering now…."

"She may not make it, sir."

He looked up at Anthia's blunt words, seething.

"Lieutenant Acoua, your *brother* was in engineering. I'd hope you'd be more understanding of the situation right now."

"She's not the only one who may not make it, captain," she said. "Lieutenant Holt was near engineering. We don't know for sure if it's Commander Matzepo in the security headquarters. Balok may have run to deck five to help with evac after the first explosion and been too close to the next blasts. Knowing your crew, they didn't run out of the fire. They ran *in* to try to help. So how many were killed in the flames? How many others by space? There are children aboard, sir. When we tally the names, how many of them won't have made it out? How many will now be orphans or have fewer parents where before they had more?"

Oren looked back to Hanali'a. At some point his fingers had stopped combing through her hair, opting instead to just hold onto the thick tendrils like a lifeline. Across the room, Lucien and Rin had gone very still, holding onto each other as they all shivered in the cooling air.

"She's not the only one who may not make it, captain," Anthia repeated, and the clicks of her nails on her glitching screen soon filled the silence again. "That's all I'm saying."

"You really don't care that Avery was down there, do you?" Lucien whispered. Anthia's typing slowed, but did not stop.

"Not the way you would." The clicks resumed their original pace. "It's a blessing."

As Rin watched her work, she couldn't help but agree. Her gut was in knots just thinking about the possibility of any of her newfound friends not being there when this was all over—Sprit, Holt, Avery, Balok...even Hanali'a. She could barely focus on remembering to sweep her thumb back and forth across Lucien's hand; there was no way she would have been able to function as an officer, and she looked at Oren.

"She's an old friend," she said softly. "Isn't she?"

"She's practically my aunt," he confessed wearily. "Everyone on this ship, they're family. In some cases, literally." Rin watched him gaze at the bulkhead sealing them into the bridge with hate-filled eyes.

"I'm sorry," she whispered, and he sighed. "I've only been here a few days, and I'm scared for them, too."

"We're a good crew, sir," Lucien said weakly with a lopsided smile, and Oren faintly mirrored the expression. "Don't worry about getting to us. We'll get to you."

"He is right about that, sir," Anthia reluctantly admitted, and Oren softly snorted. "We're resourceful, as presumably Sprit has shown."

"You'd think she'd turn up the heat," he said after a few moments of silence and nodded at the viewscreen. There was a glare on the glass that hadn't been there before, distorting the view around the edges like a thin veil of spider webs. "We're starting to ice over."

"Could we die?" Rin asked softly, and Oren looked at her solemnly.

"From the cold? We could, but I have faith in Sprit. She'll keep us warm enough to survive until help arrives."

Anthia side-eyed him but said nothing.

"Are you kidding?" Sprit shouted at the ceiling, glaring at the ship's infrastructure. "You're really pulling this with me right now? You literally aren't running anything except gravity, air, heat, bulkheads, shield generators, and...okay, you're actually doing a lot, but still."

The ship didn't respond, and Sprit growled, looking back at her flickering screens. The bridge heating systems were deciding to choke on her, and she smacked the wall above her computer. Every trick in the book had failed, and she was left with the sickening realization that she may have just sentenced their captain and first officer to death, not to mention Anthia, Rin, and Lucien.

"Come on! Work with me a little, here!" she begged, but again, the ship naturally didn't reply. "Okay, that's it."

She got up and marched to one of the weapons cases, pressing her thumb against the print lock. Thankfully, she'd had the prescience to run these off batteries. As the safe unlocked, she lifted the lid and slowly smirked.

"I've always wanted to try this." But before she could pull the large welder-rifle hybrid from its case, an alarm started beeping on her glitching computer. She glanced at it, exasperated. "Djienn, what *now?*"

But when she actually deciphered the static-filled screen, she nearly collapsed in relief. She could hear herself laughing almost hysterically and then possibly crying, and she let herself sink down to the floor. This was almost too good to be true, and she ran her hands through her hair.

"Ancestors, thank you," she sighed and blissfully closed her eyes. The rumble of another ship's engines slowly imbued *Starlight*'s walls, and she grinned. "Thank you, thank you, thank you...."

Hope was on the horizon.

"You'll forgive me if I don't have complete confidence, sir," Holt began, and Avery rolled his eyes, adjusting his grip on the man's arms where they were pulled over his shoulders and crossed over his chest.

"If you don't have confidence, then it's not gonna work, Lewis."

"Are we relying on psychic energy now, sir?"

"Don't know," the engineer panted as he slowly climbed up onto the railing and planted his left foot on the wall. "You're the psychic."

"Technically, sir, I'm not psychic—"

"It was a joke, Holt," Avery cut in and took as deep of a breath as he could with his subordinate on his back.

"I don't think we've completely thought this through, sir."

"In what way, Lewis?" He put his right hand on the wall and slowly prepared himself to jump and move his other limbs onto the vertical surface.

One...two...

"I am a little taller than you, sir. My weight—"

Three.

Holt tensed up as Avery threw the rest of his weight against the wall, squeezing his eyes shut and instinctively pressing his face into the man's back. They were going to fall. They were most definitely going to fall—

"Well, what do you know?" Avery gasped, painstakingly kneeling and then getting to his feet in a standing position so they were perpendicular to the wall. "I think I've got you in my gravity field." There was no answer from behind him, and he tapped Holt's arm. "Lewis. Unless you want me to pass out, I need you to loosen up. I can't breathe."

Holt slowly opened his eyes and found himself staring at the ceiling over Avery's shoulder as if it was a wall. He glanced backwards and saw the floor far below them but couldn't feel the pull of gravity trying to yank him down, and the engineer winced as Holt's grip didn't relax but rather tightened.

"Don't look down, man," he grunted. "Rookie mistake."

Lewis quickly looked forward again, closing his eyes.

"Could we do this quickly, sir? It isn't doing my nausea any favors."

"You're kind of heavy, Holt," Avery managed, slowly making his way to the shattered viewing panel. "Give me a minute." He paused. "And please don't throw up on me."

Holt gave a quiet huff of laughter.

"I'll do my best, sir." He closed his eyes and pressed his face into the man's back once more, hoping that just not thinking about what was going on would help his nausea abate. But then Avery flinched.

"Ow, Holt, you're digging your horns into my spine." Alarmed, Holt quickly tilted his head back and almost threw them off balance, Avery's arms wind-milling to keep them steady. "Holt!"

"Sorry, sir."

"Just don't move. You're good right there." As the two men watched their escape draw closer, the one walking on the wall cleared his throat. "Speaking of psychic energy, how are you doing?"

"I...it's actually been manageable, sir," Holt slowly said and frowned. "Perhaps the commander's neurosuppressant affected me, too."

"Oh, yeah, what's going on with you two?" The deputy cringed at the change of conversation. "You were all weird in the meeting earlier."

"Commander Matzepo and I exchanged blood," he reluctantly explained. "Apparently, Ethonians and Xanidians are compati—"

"Oh my god," Avery interrupted, laughing. "Oh my god, you two got *married*."

"...Yes."

The engineer kept laughing, and for a second, Holt was tempted to throw him off balance again. But then the harsh thought fully registered, and he gave a small huff.

Apparently, Sprit had already done her part in influencing him.

"Neither of us is particularly pleased with the situation, though, sir, so if you could keep it to yourself..."

"Oh of course, Holt. You never need to ask me to keep something private." Avery took a deep breath and collected himself. "How's the link going?"

"Not very well." The engineer finally topped the wall, and the world righted itself again, dousing Holt in a wave of vertigo. "It..." he swallowed back bile, "it's painful for her at times, highly distracting for us both. We can barely get any work done."

Avery jumped down to the floor of deck four, and his knees instantly buckled, sending both officers crashing to the metal deck plating. In the following groan-punctuated silence, Anthia's brother lopsidedly propped himself up on an elbow.

"Sorry..."

"I stand corrected, sir," Holt rejoined, painfully getting to his feet and offering the engineer a hand. "It seems you could carry me."

Avery took his hand with a breathless smile and uneasily stood, the two men wavering for a moment as they renegotiated up and down. He gently elbowed Holt's uninjured arm to spare his hands any more contact and pointed down the hall.

"Jhama's quarters are that way, right?" he asked, still out of breath, and Holt nodded, cradling his left arm against his stomach. "Alright. Let's go get Mara."

"Thank you, sir."

They set off down the hall, Holt's limp growing more noticeable as they went. He didn't seem to feel it though. His mind was in several different places at once—checking how many minds were left, seeing which people in command positions were still alive, and trying to find Sprit in the link. Every time he reached for that corner of his mind, he touched wool and spider webs, a dense fog he couldn't penetrate. Avery noticed. His partner was distant, and he had to gently touch the man's elbow to let him know they'd arrived at the Assoras' quarters.

"Ah. Could you brace the door, sir?" Holt asked, refocusing.

"Yeah, but I might need you to get it open first. I can wedge myself in there."

Holt nodded grimly and reached out for the door only to stop. His hand was shaking, trembling, and it wasn't because of him. Carefully, he narrowed his hearing to just this room, to just Mara's thoughts.

"Holt?" Avery asked, confused at his sudden stop.

The mind reader's heart sank.

"Sir, we need to be very careful," he said lowly. Mercifully, Avery just nodded, following his lead. "One of the windows is cracking. If we open the door too fast, the pressure change from the hall into the room—"

"Will shatter it, yeah." He met the deputy's gaze and nodded. "We can do this. Don't worry."

Together, the two men slowly eased the door open, taking it a mere inch at a time until it was open just enough for Holt to get through.

"Go on," Avery grunted, quickly bracing himself in the doorway. "I'll hold the door."

Lewis gratefully nodded and ducked under his arms into the room.

Everything was trashed. The last explosion had toppled almost all of their belongings, and he picked his way through the mess to Mara's room. Carefully, he slid the door open and stepped over the threshold. The little girl was still sitting on the bed, pressed into the corner now with the blanket yanked around her shoulders and over her head. Her wide, unblinking eyes were fixed on the nearly shattered portal window opposite her, and he gingerly made his way over to her, afraid that the slightest misstep would create the final crack in the glass and vent the already thin air. He could hear a faint hissing and glanced at the window again. It seemed there was already a small hole in it.

"Mara?" he called, and the girl jumped, looking at him as she shook like a leaf. "It's alright. Come on, my star." He slowly knelt and gestured for her to come over. "It's okay."

Breathing so fast Holt was worried she'd pass out, the girl slipped off the bed, watching the cracking window. The pane was almost completely white now it was filled with so many fissures. The imminent danger froze her, and Holt took a half step forward, stopping when the glass split even more, nearly sending Mara into hysterics. Her thoughts assaulted him, and his heart broke.

I'm gonna die. I'm gonna die, just like momma. The storm happened, and now I'm gonna die—

"Mara, look at me." She glanced at him, and Holt reflected on what a nightmare he must look like—bruised, bloodied, and no doubt pale beneath it all. "I told you I'd return, didn't I?" She nodded mutely. "Now I'm telling you it's going to be okay. You just have to come over to me, very gently. Can you do that?" The girl nodded with the smallest, hiccupping sobs. "Come, my star."

Holt waited with bated breath as the child crept over to him, forcing himself not to look at the glass. Once she was close enough, he picked her up and backed away, not caring about the strain on his shoulder. All he cared about was the glass on the verge of breaking.

"Sir, the window is going to break soon," he called, not changing his painstaking retreat to the door. "As soon as we're through the door, let it shut."

"Got it." Wincing at the pressure the effort put on his burned hands, Avery forced the door open a little more, bracing it with his foot.

And just as Holt entered the foyer, he heard a shatter and a sudden whoosh of air.

"Avery, make room!" Holt shouted, forgoing any formal titles. Mara whimpered and buried her face into his neck as he turned and ran for the door, letting his body hit the ground so he could slide under his friend's raised leg where it was holding the door open. "Clear!"

Avery stepped out of the threshold, and the door slammed shut with a hollow clang. He looked down at Holt, impressed.

"Didn't know you could slide like that, Lewis," he said with a dirt-smudged smile. Holt tiredly let his head thump against the hull plating, hugging the crying child close to his chest. "You two okay?"

"Give us a minute, sir," he sighed and painfully sat up, adjusting his hold on Mara. "I told you it would be okay," he said softly, and the girl tightened her hold on his uniform. "You're safe, Mara."

She pulled back slightly to look into his face, and her tear-tracked expression furrowed as she reached for him with a small hand. She gently touched one of the bruises her mother had given him.

"You're hurt."

"Yes, I am," he agreed. "But I will be alright." She looked over her shoulder to Avery, her eyes immediately drawn to his raw hands.

"He's hurt, too."

"Yes, but he will be alright, as well."

Avery looked between the girl and Holt, completely baffled.

"Are you two talking?"

"It's shock," Holt answered, struggling slightly to get to his feet without setting Mara down. His leg really hated him right now. "She'll think her words for a while but not speak them."

"I want my mom."

Avery knew what the girl had thought without needing to be told. The deputy's whole body seemed to cave in, and he gently cupped the girl's head.

"I know, Mara. But your mother's gone. I'm so sorry. I know how that feels." The girl started crying again and helplessly wrapped her arms around Holt. He gently reciprocated the action and started walking down the hall, talking to Avery as they went. "We should find the others, sir."

"Yeah." His voice was exhausted, threadbare. "We can go room by room from one end of the deck and open doors, see if anyone's trapped and needs help."

Both men stopped talking and slowly came to a stop as a low, rumbling hum filled the air. Mara gave a small cry of fear, clinging to Holt even tighter as he looked up at the ceiling.

"It's okay, Mara," he said absently, rubbing her back. "Is that—"

"That's another ship," Avery confirmed, his whole body relaxing. "Thank god, it's another ship." But then he tensed and looked to Holt. "It *is* a friendly, right?" He watched as his coworker tilted his head ever so slightly to the side, hand stilling on Mara's back, and listened.

When he came back to *Starlight*, Holt closed his eyes and gave a rare smile. When he spoke, his voice was almost pleased.

"Yes, sir, it is definitely a friendly." He opened his eyes and looked at his superior. "It's *Horizon.*"

On the bridge, Anthia was fighting with the half-functioning computer, trying to get a clear image of the incoming vessel's message. And once she managed to clean up as much of the static as she could, Oren was ready to sit down and cry in relief. On the small screen was his sister in her captain's chair, expression somber and simmering with fury on their behalf.

"*Starlight*, this is *Horizon*." Tzo's voice crackled as much as the video feed, but her words were still a godsend. "We locked onto your rotation and are preparing to board. We are aware of your situation and are standing by with medical assistance, emergency supplies, and hull cutters to get through your bulkheads and docking doors. The moment we successfully dock, we'll begin evacuation." Her voice grew softer, eyes shining with sympathetic pain. "You're alright now, Galaxa. Runner, out."

In the silence that followed, Rin started laughing much the same way Sprit currently was just down the hall, and Lucien closed his eyes, longing to join her, but unable to without causing himself pain. Oren looked at them, his hand still protectively resting on Hanali'a's head.

At her station, Anthia itched to transmit their response but satisfied herself with thinking it instead, muted as they were.

Acknowledged.

————————

Tzo Runner watched the wreck approach with unblinking eyes. Her entire posture was rigid, trembling with rage. Those were good people. Those were her *brother's* people. She'd seen them mere days ago, and now they were here—strung out among the stars in a sick mockery of a cemetery. *Starlight* was listing horribly to one side, trapped in a lazy, lateral spin she couldn't stop with her one barely functioning engine, and Lazarus watched his captain's hands clench into white-knuckled fists on the arms of her chair.

"I'll kill him," she whispered, the wrath in those three words hot enough to consume stars. Lazarus leaned closer to her.

"Who, Runner?"

She turned to him. Her eyes burned like coals, and she spat the name from her lips like poison.

"Jon Bledsoe."

CHAPTER 18

Tzo's crew turned to face her as she approached, her steps heavy and quick with Roiz at her heels. Only a skeleton crew would remain to run *Horizon* once they boarded their sister ship, and the captain had to weave her way through the crowded halls to reach the front of her boarding party. Boarding *force* might have been more accurate; there were so many people. A few of her officers stepped back from where they'd just finished cutting through the docking door.

"We ready?" she asked, and the people closest to her nodded, lifting their hull cutters, antigravity stretchers, and other emergency supplies in confirmation. "Good. Kick the door in."

Without a word, two of her bulkier crewmembers stepped up and slammed their full weight against the center of the door, and with a great, groaning creak, the cutout slab of metal crashed to the floor. The Trozerans coughed as their own atmosphere rushed past them, drawn into and flooding *Starlight*'s stagnant halls with fresh air. It was dark as far as they could see, still and silent, and Tzo clenched her jaw. Already, she could feel the derelict chill permeating her brother's ship.

This wasn't good.

"You know your groups," she announced grimly. "Lazarus, take your men, open all the bulkheads you safely can, and bring the people you find aboard *Horizon*. I'll take my team to the bridge and free the people there. Morai, take your healers to the medbay. Doctor Balok may not like our methods, but you make sure he does what you say. The rest of you, start on decks four and five. Our scans determined the explosion came from engineering, so most of the injured will be there."

"What of the dead, Runner?" Lazarus asked softly, and she looked at Morai as she answered.

"Their absence of life doesn't make them any less Galaxa's crew. We bring them home." The healer nodded gratefully, and she addressed her crew at large. "Those who don't have a specific group, go where you are needed. And where you are needed, stay." She took a long, cylindrical lantern from Lazarus and turned on the bulb-like device. "Now, go. Let's do our jobs."

Tzo took the first step aboard *Starlight*, raising her light as she went. Behind her, her crew followed.

"Who goes there?" a man shouted, his voice cracking and rasping at the same time, and Tzo increased her pace until she found the crewman in the dark. He was nearly doubled over, his clearly broken arm hanging uselessly at his side as he shakily aimed his blaster at them. "Declare yourselves!"

"Tzo Runner," she said, holding her hands at her shoulders. "We're here to help."

As soon as the officer saw the army of Trozerans behind her, he relaxed, sagging against the wall and finally letting himself drop to the floor. As he did, Tzo saw the shard of metal buried in his calf.

"Morai, help him," she ordered and joined the healer at his side.

"Please, they're in auxiliary. I was standing guard…"

"Who's they?" she asked, and the man grimaced as the healer began tending to his arm.

"Everyone we could find," he gasped, and Tzo gently grabbed his shoulder. "We started clearing the deck, but we couldn't pass the boiler room because the bulkheads dropped. We need Balok—"

"Leave the bulkheads to us, crewman," she said with a reassuring smile. "We'll get you to your doctor. Now, what deck are we on?"

"Three, ma'am."

"Thank you." She stood and continued down the hall, gesturing for her team and Lazarus' to follow. "Come. We'll climb the lift shafts."

The crewman watched them go, drawing comfort from their tough, hardened presence. There were scores of them, all here to help, and he took in their ranks. Dark eyes glittered on uniquely marked skin, and diversely shaped and curved horns arched over heads that ranged from bald to heavy with hair. He could see their layered, colorfully rustic clothes in bursts under the light of their lanterns, and he took comfort in their vibrantly rich colors. Their step was heavy and firm, thick-soled boots loud on the metal floors, and he noted that none wore a cloak save for Runner. He wearily looked up at the medic above him, taking in the pastel chalk decorating his skin and horns and the necklaces hanging about his neck.

"Thank you," he whispered, and Morai barely had time to catch him before he passed out.

As *Horizon*'s crew made their way through *Starlight*'s decks, the Peace-keepers slowly converged on the Trozerans, gratefully tumbling into stretchers and allowing their friends to guide their dazed bodies to safety. They didn't know what had happened or who was alive or dead. But that didn't matter. Because for now, it seemed the nightmare was over.

———

Mara had fallen asleep.

"That's impressive," Avery said, walking slowly beside his limping friend. The little girl's raven head rested heavily on Holt's shoulder, and the engineer smirked as he saw the slight drool beneath her cheek.

"Not impressive, sir. Just inevitable," Holt said softly, testing her grip on his uniform. Yeah, he wasn't getting out of that soon. He adjusted his hold on her, switching her over to his right arm and letting his left hang at his side. "How is everybody?"

Avery glanced over his shoulder at the voiceless congregation trailing behind them, and his heart grew even heavier. He knew these people. He knew they could smile, could laugh and raise hell. But right now they were just numb—some crying, others holding each other up. They had glimpsed more than a few bodies in the depressurized rooms they tried to open, barely managing to shut the doors against the pull of the vacuum before whispering a prayer and moving on. It was starting to take a toll. A few had collapsed at engineering, unable to handle what they'd seen.

"Still walking," he finally answered and then frowned. "Can't you just read them?"

"That would not go well, sir." Holt tiredly closed his eyes, blindly walking on. "It is all I can do to process my own grief. I cannot handle theirs as well."

"Okay." Avery gently put his hand on Lewis' shoulder and squeezed. "I understand." They walked in silence for a little longer, and he glanced at the names on the small plates outside the quarters they passed. "We've checked these rooms, right?"

Holt opened his eyes and followed Avery's gaze.

"Yes, sir. We'll reach the lift soon, and those of us who can climb can start to head up—"

A loud bang echoed ahead of them, and Holt froze, the crew gathering nervously behind him. He could sense his friend beside him reaching for his weapon, only to find an empty holster.

"What was that?" Avery asked lowly, and Holt cautiously moved forward, holding Mara close as he did. "Lewis, get back here!"

"It's alright, sir," he exhaled as the distant tattoo of heavy boots became clear to everyone else, and a large group of Trozerans rounded the corner, holding long, slender lanterns aloft. "It's Lazarus."

"Lewis?" the leader called, and Holt limped forward, Avery following close behind.

"Hello, sir," he greeted, exhausted, and the first officer laughed.

"Help them," he ordered his men, pointing them towards the small, shaking crowd as he joined the deputy. "You are *iahan*, my friend," the first officer beamed and reached to clap him on the shoulder only to see that Mara was already occupying it. "Oh, who is this?"

"She's...a friend's child, sir. I promised I'd take care of her."

Roiz's relieved smile slowly slid from his face.

"I take it this friend..." Holt shook his head, and the burly man delicately rested a hand on Mara's sleeping head, as if she were glass. "The poor girl...she is *iahan*, like you," he said sagely. "I can feel it."

"What's *iahan*?" Avery asked as he joined them.

"Your closest word is indestructible," Lazarus answered and shook his hand. "You are Avery Byrone, yes? Galaxa's little genius engineer?"

"Uh, I don't know about little or genius, but I am the engineer, sir," Avery said dryly and pointed back the way they'd come. "We evacuated the deck behind us. We don't think there's anyone left alive, but...." He cleared his throat, suddenly choking up. "Sorry, sir."

Lazarus sighed, running his hand over his horns in a manner reminiscent of Oren.

"We feared as much. Don't worry. We'll secure your dead, as well."

"Thank you, sir." Holt turned around as another dull clang echoed down the deck, this time from behind them. "What was that?"

"We're connecting to as many of your docking doors as we can and cutting through. Come. It's time we get you off this ship."

It was another long, silent walk back the way they came, and Holt carefully noted how none of *Starlight*'s crew looked at engineering as they passed by. *Horizon*'s crew on the other hand...

He kept his gaze fixed forward so that he didn't have to see their horrified expressions. Hearing their thoughts was enough.

"Sister!"

Sprit turned around at the shout and sprinted down the hall, tackling Tzo in a bone-crushing hug.

"Tzo, you have no idea how happy I am to see you," she sighed, and the Trozeran scoffed.

"Believe me, I do. You could have been dead." The women pulled apart and quickly headed back towards the bridge as Tzo's team caught up. "How's Oren? And Hanali'a?"

"I don't know. I sealed off the bridge as soon as I could." Sprit took a deep, shaking breath and ran her hands through her undone hair to try to calm herself. "I'm definitely regretting that, now."

"No, Little Matzepo," Tzo assured her, squeezing her arm. "You did the right thing. Let us help you from here."

"I cut through part of the bulkhead already," Sprit said, pointing, and Tzo saw that she'd scored about a quarter of a large circle into the thick metal. "But I'm using a prototype we've never tested before. It takes way too long."

"Well, thankfully, our hull cutters have some parsecs on them." Tzo waved her team towards the door. "Open it. And send a runner for some of Morai's people. We may need help." Sprit sighed as someone left, and she started anxiously pacing. "Are you okay?"

"Yeah," the security chief said quickly, eyes fixed on the bulkhead as the Trozerans carefully cut through it.

Tzo sighed at the lie and put a hand on her sister's shoulder, only for the woman to pull away as she continued pacing. All they could do now was wait and hope that when the metal finally caved, they wouldn't have lost anyone else.

Sprit hated waiting.

"Acoua, I want you to stay with me once we're out of here," Oren ordered as they watched the welded circle in the bulkhead slowly inch towards completion. "Rin, stay with either Lucien or Hanali'a if Sprit isn't waiting out there. I don't want you wandering on your own."

"Yes, sir," the girl said softly and looked at Lucien. "Can I let go?"

"Oh, yeah. Thanks for staying with me," he said with a small smile, and she returned the expression as she released his hand.

"Thanks for staying with me, too."

The constant hissing and popping of the welder suddenly died off, and they turned their attention back to their one entrance and exit. Oren slowly rose and walked over to stand before his captain's chair, facing the door.

Bang. Bang. Ba—

There was a loud crash as the crew on the other side finally kicked in the cut section of the door, and it fell to the ground, still smoking around its molten edges.

"Oren!" Sprit called and immediately ran in, tackling her brother in a hug. "Oh, you're okay. You're alive."

He quickly hugged her back before pulling away.

"Yes, but Han may not be for long." He turned to Tzo's crew as they walked in. "Hanali'a was thrown through her display, and my helmsman possibly injured his spine. They need immediate help."

"Yes, Galaxa."

He quickly touched Sprit's cheek, wiping a stray tear from her skin.

"It *will* be okay." He shifted his gaze over her shoulder. "Someone else wants to see you, I think."

"Rin," Sprit remembered and turned around just in time to catch the larger, running human in her arms. "Oh djienn, are you okay?"

"Yeah, but Hanali'a, she just—her *head*, and then Lucien, his back, he…" Rin found she couldn't quite form coherent sentences, and Sprit tightened her hug around the girl's trembling body.

"I know. I know, I'm so sorry about all of this."

She watched grimly as Anthia and two Trozeran women lifted Lucien onto a stretcher, and the young man instantly paled at the movement. She could see the slight rise of his breasts under his top and realized they must have removed his binder to help him breathe easier—though, given his shallow gasps, she wasn't sure how much it had helped in the long run. Bloodied and broken glass crunched under their feet as they quickly left, and a bigger group of people came in with a large stretcher that the security chief knew was for Hanali'a.

Sprit rubbed her hand up and down Rin's spine and then cupped the back of her head only to have the girl hiss in pain and pull away.

"What is—wait, is this blood?" Sprit asked, holding her palm up for Rin to see, and immediately the human's expression darkened.

"Yeah, Anthia knocked me out with her tablet."

"Anthia did *what?*" she demanded and instantly turned to glare at the lieutenant where she was waiting in the hall beside Tzo. "Acoua!"

"Sprit!" She looked at Oren, seething, and he made a relax gesture with his hands. "We'll *all* talk about it later."

Before she could press the matter further, the six Trozerans who had been tending to Hanali'a quickly walked by, and the words died on Sprit's lips. The first officer looked horrible, like she'd been thrown headfirst through a windshield, and she recognized the strips of fabric tied around her as the remnants of Anthia's uniform. She was shaking badly and breathing in unsettling, rattling bursts.

"Oh djienn," Sprit breathed, watching her go. "Will she be okay?"

"Tzo's healers will do the best they can," Oren answered as he joined them and wiped his bloody hands off on his clothes. "It's up to Han, now. Come on."

He herded his sister and the not-human off the bridge, and Anthia pointedly stepped aside so she was as far from the pair as possible without being rude.

"Brother," Tzo greeted, hugging him and touching foreheads for a split second as they parted. "It's good to see you alive."

"It's good to see you, full-stop," he returned and sighed. Galaxy, he was so sore, exhausted to his core. "What've you heard on your comms? How's the ship? The crew?"

Tzo suddenly looked as weary as he did, and somehow his stomach sank even lower. He hadn't thought that was possible.

"I'm sorry, Oren. No one made it in engineering." The small shred of hope Sprit had been clinging to was suddenly ripped away, and she took in a sharp breath, fighting to keep herself under control.

But then Tzo continued.

"Well, nobody except for Lewis and Lieutenant Commander Byrone. They cleared deck four of all survivors and brought them aboard—"

"I'm sorry, wait," Sprit interrupted, sounding bizarrely pissed off to the gathered people. "Holt is *alive?*"

"Yes. I thought that would be good news," Tzo said uncertainly as Sprit scowled.

"Oh, that little…I've got to go. Sorry, captain," she called over her shoulder as she sprinted off for the nearest connected docking port.

"Poor Lewis," Tzo said wryly, watching her go, but then resumed their bleak conversation. "You have minor to serious injuries throughout your crew, mainly on decks four and five, but also on deck three, most likely due to your boiler room and auxiliary control. I already have Ratho Morai working with Doctor Balok."

"Thank you," Oren began, but Tzo shook her head. She wasn't done.

"You have the most casualties in engineering, and I've instructed my people to move your dead into the nearest intact rooms and then evacuate and seal the halls as they go. We'll conduct a full inventory of who is and isn't accounted for once we start moving, but we have to depart soon. The only power you have left is in coil four, and it's beginning to fail as we speak." The man sighed and looked down, not reacting as Tzo reached out and put a gloved hand on his shoulder. "I know this is a nightmare—a wreck call, as mother says."

"It doesn't feel real," he admitted under his breath.

Tzo tightened her grip and roughly shook him. Her tone was gentle, even supportive in its strange, abrasive manner.

"I know. But I also know who's behind all of this."

That got everyone's attention. Rin watched Anthia step closer, and Oren's brow furrowed slightly.

"Who?" There was a dangerous fire to his whisper, and to Rin he seemed to grow in height and size. "Who did this to us?"

"Jon Bledsoe."

The effect of the name was instantaneous, and not the one Tzo was hoping for.

"This is *not* Jon," Oren hissed, grabbing her by the arm and pulling her down the hall. Anthia and Rin exchanged a distrusting glance before coming to the same decision and hurrying after them. "My people have *died*, Runner, and you're still spinning stories about him?"

"They're not stories, Galaxa!" Tzo snapped, yanking her arm free. "This?" She gestured to the dark surrounding them. "This is Jon, and you know it."

"If it was Jon, we'd already be dead," he growled. "He doesn't play games—"

"Doesn't play games?" she laughed in derisive disbelief. "All he *does* is play games, Galaxa. *Everything* is a game to him, and we're all his pawns. He's had seventeen years to scheme with that twisted mind of his," she continued, chasing after him as he tried to walk away from her. "Do you really think this is beyond his ability?"

"It can't be Jon," he said through gritted teeth, and Anthia and Rin finally managed to catch up to the captains.

"Why?" Tzo demanded at his heels. "*Why* can't it be Jon? He said he'd be back for you—"

"Captains, you shouldn't have this conversation here," Anthia interrupted, planting herself in front of the siblings and stopping them. "There are too many ears—"

"It just can't be Jon," Oren said stubbornly, and Tzo had enough.

Rin started with a yelp as the woman punched her brother in the face, her strike blinding and head-on. Oren loudly swore, stumbling back from her and grabbing his bleeding nose.

"What is *wrong* with you?" he half-shouted, and Tzo started towards him, shoving Anthia out of the way as she tried to step between them.

"When I'm angry with you, I look you in the eyes when I hit you," she hissed, grabbing a handful of his uniform and yanking him close so they were nose-to-nose. "Jon dances in the shadows so he can stab you in the back. This *is* him, and the sooner you accept that, the sooner your people stop dying." She pushed him away and stormed down the hall, shouting back at him without looking. "He's not redeemable, Ren! Or does he have to snap off your other horn for you to get that?"

A tense, long silence filled the space *Horizon*'s captain had left, and Oren let out a huff of air before speaking.

"Keep that conversation between us." Anthia curtly nodded, and he continued, this time addressing Rin more than his officer. "Do not, under any circumstances, repeat the name Jon Bledsoe to anyone."

"Yes, sir," Rin said softly.

The captain put a hand on her shoulder and gently pulled her along with him down the hall. Anthia followed like a shadow. As they went, more and more people seemed to join them from the rooms they'd taken shelter in, and the captain scanned their faces, reciting their names. Each one he placed settled his nerves a little more, and he thought about what Tzo had said.

No. No, this couldn't be Jon, because if it was, things were going to get a lot worse before they got better.

———

Ratho Morai had his work cut out for him.

Every single bed and useable surface in his infirmary was filled with injured people, and his already somber expression darkened as more of *Starlight*'s crew were carried in. As medical staff from both ships frantically tried to address each and every wound, broken bone, and burn, he slowly walked among the patients, asking if they'd been tended to yet or if they needed anything. Mostly, all he got were dazed stares and questions about other people he had no information about, but at least it was contact.

"So, this is your medbay."

"We prefer infirmary, Doctor Balok," Morai greeted, turning to the newcomer. "You can put your equipment wherever you can find room."

"Thank you," Balok said absently and looked around at the medical wing as he shifted his grasp on his examiner's bag, dazed.

The rust-colored walls were lined with dried and bunched herbs and jars upon jars of neatly labeled pills and concoctions. He could see sterile bandages and disinfectant salves in the transparent cabinets and drawers, along with various scalpels, surgical scissors, and other sharps all still sealed in their packaging, ready for use. It was well equipped. But Balok's eyes also highlighted the lack of more modern items, such as animation suspenders and sterile field lamps that would be crucial in dealing with some of the injuries surrounding them. It was missing laser scalpels and precision quality instruments. Morai walked over to stand beside him, easily navigating the maze of chairs, beds, gurneys, and stretchers all filled with wounded.

"You're not yet convinced of our ability to care for your people," he noted and dismissed the doctor's guilty reaction. "No, I understand. But faith healing and herbal poultices have been around for hundreds of generations on Trozer. It hasn't failed us yet, and coupling it with modern medicine has only made it better. Trust us. We know what we're doing." He squeezed the tired man's shoulder and smiled gently. "Your people are our people, and if it helps, I have never lost a life that modern care would have saved in my service as Runner's head healer."

Balok looked at the man in surprise. He was young, younger than most of *Horizon*'s crew now that he thought about it, but there was wisdom to him. Chalky paints in shades of blue, red, and yellow decorated his horns and face in patterns that had to have ritualistic meaning. Broad, colorful beaded jewelry hung at his neck and wrists, and, like the paint, Balok was sure they were ceremonial.

If a Trozeran was this decorated at this age, he had to be good.

"Never," Balok echoed with a ghost of a smile. "Is that so?"

"Never, doctor. Now, come. Your people are in good hands."

As Ratho guided his *Starlight* counterpart to a chair and took note of the man's cut and bruised hands, he caught sight of the mind reader with the child walking past his doorway again. He'd clearly been beaten, and his left arm hung limply at his side, but he hadn't yet come for help. He just kept pacing with the sleeping girl cradled in his right arm, and the healer knew he'd have to go fetch him soon before he collapsed.

Holt still hadn't been able to find Sprit.

Crew from both ships packed the halls until they were nigh innavigable, though his coworkers took up the most space—slumped against the walls and holding onto each other with shaking hands and tired, vacant expressions. His pulse picked up every time he thought he saw red hair, but then slowed almost immediately when it wasn't coupled with copper eyes or camouflage skin. The deeper into the Trozeran ship he went, the narrower the halls seemed to become, there were so many people. Eventually, he gave up and headed back the way he came. Knowing Sprit, she would have stayed at the bridge until Oren was freed. She wouldn't be this deep into *Horizon*. As he went, the dull cramping in his arm returned, and he winced and tried to shift his grip.

"Where are you, commander?" he whispered and grimaced as Mara moved in her sleep and set his tired muscles afire with pain. He couldn't keep this up much longer. He was going to have to stop and get help.

Unseen by Holt, Sprit ran around the corner, quickly surveying the people around her until she saw the back of his head at the other end of the hall. She glowered and started forward, tangle of emotions burning in her gut like a hot poker. That little—who did he think he was, not trying to find her to let her know he hadn't died like she'd thought? She was going to *kill* him.

Okay, maybe not kill him. But a good slap ought to do.

"It's okay," Holt said softly to the still-asleep child. "You're—"

"LIEUTENANT LEWIS HOLT!"

Holt jumped at the loud bellow right behind him and spun around, almost cowering at the same time and lifting his injured arm to cover Mara's head as he moved. And that's when he saw her, standing not two feet away behind him, disheveled and battered. If he wasn't mistaken, he could see remains of tears on her cheeks, and the redness to her eyes only supported his theory.

"Commander," he breathed, voice laden with relief and concern, and Sprit's anger evaporated the instant she saw his bloody and bruised face. He looked *awful*. Her stunned silence broke as he uncomfortably cleared his throat, and she glanced at her raised hand where she'd been about to slap him and then to the sleeping child cradled in his arms.

"Uh." Awkwardly, she lowered her arm and crossed both over her chest. "I see, uh, someone beat me to the punch." She gave a wan smirk at the joke, and Holt painfully returned the expression. She looked at her boots next and uncomfortably shifted from foot to foot. "It's good to see you. Alive, I mean."

"You, too, ma'am." She gave him a look at the formal address, and he hurried to salvage their exchange. "Um, sincerely. But I'd recommend from now on that we refrain from using neurosuppressants."

"Yeah," Sprit said a little too quickly and enthusiastically, and Holt cleared his throat. "That's—it's a good idea. So, uh, what's with the kid?"

"Oh. Assora." He paused as Mara tightened her grip on his uniform. "Her last request was for me to take care of Mara, ma'am."

"Oh. I...I'm sorry." The two stood there, silent and uncomfortable, until Sprit spoke again, pointing to his face. "Have you seen anyone yet? Balok or Morai?"

"No, ma'am, I was..." he paused but continued at her expectant expression, "I was waiting to find you, commander." He shifted his hold on Mara. "I couldn't tell if the link was wrong because of the suppressant or because you'd been...harmed," he finished diplomatically.

Sprit smiled weakly, close to tears as everything began to settle in.

"Me, too." She sighed and wiped at her eyes. "Okay, uh, well, you've found me, so now we should get you to infirmary." She sounded more like she was talking herself through what to do next, and she grabbed his left arm to pull him along.

"Ma'am, don't!" She froze and gingerly released his elbow, and he exhaled in relief. "Byrone accidentally dislocated it when he caught me in engineering. It's still delicate."

"Djienn, what part of you *isn't* broken?" she asked sarcastically, and Holt watched sympathetically as what she'd meant as a joke finally sank in. "I'm sorry," she whispered, stricken as she started to cry. "I'm sorry. I know you don't do this sort of thing, I'm sorry—"

"Commander," he tried quietly, but when she continued to back away, shaking her head in silent apology for breaking down, he grabbed her wrist with his injured arm. "*Sprit.*" She looked up at him, expression comically torn between crying and shock. "Sprit, it's okay."

He gave a silent prayer of thanks as she let him gently tug her to him, and he hugged her as close as he could with an impaired arm and a child asleep on his right side. Sprit guiltily pressed her face against his sternum, hiding her tears in his uniform, and a shudder ran through her as Holt cupped the back of her head, fingers tucking into her hair and gently caressing her scalp. This was the last thing the crew needed to see, she reflected bitterly—their heads of security hugging and crying in the middle of the hallway with an orphan sandwiched between them. But, and she wasn't sure if it was her imagination or the neuro-suppressant wearing off, she could almost swear Holt was okay with this. He was willing to stand here as long as she needed to.

"You're alive," she whispered, and Holt carefully pulled her closer, waiting to see if she flinched at the contact in a mute warning to back off. She didn't. "I thought you were dead. It felt like I could feel the glass break, like I was next to you. It was *horrible*."

Before he could think of a reply, Holt saw Ratho Morai step out of his infirmary, scanning the crowds until he found the security chiefs and locked eyes with the deputy. He held up a first-aid kit questioningly, and Holt gave the biggest nod he could without disturbing either his superior or the sleeping child.

He'd found Sprit. Now, they could rest.

CHAPTER 19

Two steps forward, three steps back.

That's what this felt like, Oren reflected, as he stared down into the vat of fluid Hanali'a's body was suspended in. Two steps forward, three steps back. Every few minutes somebody came in to update him about casualty numbers. One report, they'd be lower than expected, but then the update would come along, and the names would fill page after page, some different from the last list, others the same. Some who'd been thought dead had been found alive, tucked away in the recesses of *Horizon*'s hallways. Other's who'd managed to hang to life for a few hours perished in the infirmary. And Hanali'a...he sat down heavily.

He'd gotten so many conflicting predictions on whether or not she was going to pull through that he'd stopped asking. One moment she'd be stable, the next she'd be falling apart, and then sometimes she'd be like she currently was—wavering dangerously between the two.

"She'll be fine," a voice said stubbornly, and he looked to where Rin was sitting sideways in a chair, her arms crossed defensively over her chest and her head resting against the wall behind her. Her eyes fixed on Hanali'a's watery bed, and he took in the way Rin's legs hooked over the seat's metal arm. He supposed it was the best way for her to get some rest given how cramped everywhere else was.

"If you don't mind, Miss Cooper, I'll steal some of your confidence," he sighed, and she looked at him.

"Only so many things can go wrong," she said, hiding a yawn behind her hand. "She'd be one too many."

"Interesting philosophy."

"Thanks," she mumbled, and her eyes slowly drifted shut.

"What's the next round of bad news, Morai?" Oren asked resignedly as the man walked in behind him, but the healer shook his head.

"It's not that. Runner found something." Oren stood, heart pounding. "She wants you to join her and senior staff in her briefing room."

"What did she find?"

Morai smiled at his earnestness and shifted the blanket in his arms.

"Why would she tell me, Galaxa?" he asked, voice gentle despite its teasing tone. "Go. I'll watch over your first officer and human."

"Thank you, Morai."

He shook the doctor's hand and hurried from the infirmary, nodding to the people who met his gaze and trying to hide his tense concern. His crew had been through enough and thought they were okay now. They didn't need his lack of stoicism to upend everything again.

Morai watched Oren go as he carefully unfolded the blanket and draped the heavy fabric over the unconscious human asleep in the chair. He may have had his hands full, but this was where the healer excelled. Wreck calls were his strongest suit. They'd all be okay.

───────

"What did you find?"

Tzo glared at her brother, radiating displeasure as he came in.

"Please, by all means, start talking before the door closes," she said dryly. "We're *definitely* not discussing sensitive information in here."

Oren ignored her and focused on Sprit, Anthia, and Holt, shifting his focus to the deputy and communications officer when he saw they were the ones wearing the remains of the exosuits. *Starlight's* remaining engine coil had finally given out nearly an hour ago, meaning anyone who went aboard to investigate had to wear the clumsy, heavy environmental suits to combat the cold and fading air. He sat at the head of the table opposite Tzo and folded his hands on its cold surface.

"Well?"

"We searched Jhama's quarters, sir," Holt began, glancing at Sprit. "We found a video file on Assora's computer when we used Sprit's command-override, so I had Acoua pull a copy and destroy the original file. I didn't think we wanted someone else coming across it and spreading the word."

"And what is the word?" the captain asked, and Holt looked down, uneasily picking at the metal cuffs of the exosuit. "*Holt.*"

"You should watch the file," Anthia said curtly, and Oren eyed her carefully at her next words. "After the conversation you had with Tzo, I think it'll get the message across faster than arguing about it."

"Get on with it," he said with a note of frustration in his voice and gestured to the screen above Tzo's chair. "Show us."

Anthia pressed a button, and the screen came to glitching, static-filled life. And the moment Oren saw Jhama's face, his gut sank.

He said I couldn't tell anyone else about our situation. He never said I couldn't tell myself, which is what this is. This is the first entry of my personal diary. And the first thing I wanted to say was I did not do this willingly. Talik didn't either. He was a victim as much as the other people in that room. I was able to sabotage his device for him without telling him what I altered….

Holt looked down as the recording was interrupted by Mara's laugh in the background, and under the table, Sprit reached out and put a hand on his knee.

So, here's how this all began. That monster found us on Refueling Station 304 and cornered us in an alleyway. He was fast, brutal…

"Oh, djienn," Sprit breathed, sinking down in her chair and closing her eyes as the story continued.

He would contact us through encoded lower band frequencies. Each time he did, I hoped Anthia would pick up the distortion. I find myself thinking more and more like her as this goes on—how do I get out with minimal casualties? How do I cheat this game when he's the one with the rulebook?

Sprit's grip on Holt's leg turned painful, yet he remained silent. His attention was fixed on Anthia Acoua, who was so still and so cold as she watched Jhama describe her fate that for a moment he thought she was standing over Daniel's body again. She glanced at him, and he turned his focus back to the video feed.

And I can't say his name. I can't give any kind of personally defining features or facts about him because of what he told us. But Talik and I found there was one word we could use, and if you can't put it together from here, I don't know what to tell you. I guess we're all doomed, then, she laughed, and everyone shivered at the dead woman's gallows humor. *It's one word. I can't tell you how it relates because that's personal information, but…I can give it to you.*

Tzo rose from her seat and crossed the room to stand behind her brother's chair, grasping his shoulders and squeezing hard as he closed his eyes. She continued to glare at the static-filled screen. Both knew very well to whom this word pointed. His hand subconsciously reached up to massage the scars around his broken horn.

Alympa.

Holt took a deep breath and released it slowly as Jhama continued talking, gradually nearing her final words. He shuddered, drawing Sprit's concerned attention.

I'm sorry for everything I've done. I'm sorry for everything I will do. I tried my best to keep sabotaging his plans, but I don't think it's going to work out well for me in the end. So, do me a favor. Send Mara to live with my sister. And then kick Alympa's ass. Ensign Jhama Assora, signing off.

In the long, shaken silence that followed, Anthia raised an eyebrow and sighed, seemingly bored as she crossed her legs. When she spoke, she was dryly matter-of-fact.

"Well, we're screwed."

"How *helpful*, lieutenant."

"You're welcome, sir."

"Would you like to help me?"

Rin jumped slightly as the healer addressed her without even looking. She thought that she'd been faking sleep fairly well, watching him work through nearly closed lashes. Apparently, she'd been mistaken.

"I, uh, don't think that'd be a good idea," she replied, voice gravelly with unfeigned drowsiness.

"Oh, you won't hurt her," he assured her and beckoned for Rin to approach. "She's stabilized. We relieved the intracranial pressure and removed all the shards of glass. Nothing punctured her brain, so she's fine in that regard. We've got a new brace on her neck to help her with the whiplash. She's on pain medications, and we're monitoring her for any signs of blood clots." He gave her another small, secret smile. "She pulled through all on her own. All that's left is for her to stay in the fluid for as long as possible. We've found that keeping people in their element helps their healing along much faster. And in her case, it alleviates the strain of gravity on her body."

He backed off so Rin could come over and look more closely at the first officer. She looked like a child, curled in the fetal position like that with her hair flowing free about her, her eyes closed in such an innocent, relaxed way. Rin peered a little closer and smiled as she saw Han's gills slowly fluttering as she breathed.

"What was that you told Galaxa? She'd be fine because too many bad things had happened already?" Rin nodded, not really paying attention. She was engrossed by the way the first officer who she knew to be a heavy giant looked feather-light, weightless. "That's a rather hopeful take on the law of averages."

"I guess."

Morai tapped her arm with a package of some kind of powder and gestured to the tub.

"You can go ahead and pour this in there. Don't be shy, just put in the whole thing and make sure you spread it around."

He watched as she wordlessly followed his directions, an interested, calculating light in her eyes. Humans, he reflected. All they needed was to keep busy, and they flourished. Admittedly, that could be a generalization seeing as she was only the second one he'd ever met, and she wasn't even fully human.

Come to think of it, he should probably ask her about that.

"So, what's your story?" he asked, and she looked at him, confused. "Sorry?"

"Well, you're half-human, aren't you?" he elaborated as he took the now-empty bag from her and continued to add a few more medications and herbs. "I can sense it in you. You've got something powerful inside that isn't from your human blood. So," he wiped his hands off on his shirt, leaving small trails of tiny leaves behind, "what's your story?"

"I'm…" Rin giggled nervously and deliberately put Hanali'a's basin between them, suddenly very uncomfortable. "I'm human."

"Well, yes, but what else are you?" Seeing the girl's unsettled, caged expression, he hurried to explain. "Oh, I'm sorry if I offended you. I'm very curious about interspecies people. There are fewer genetically compatible species than you'd think, so——"

"No, I'm *human*," Rin repeated harshly, horrible anxiety consuming her insides. "I'm from Montana, I-I was kidnapped by traffickers." Morai seemed to freeze, and inexplicably, her anxiety turned into anger. "I'm human!"

"I…oh, djienn, I'm so sorry. I thought you knew." The young healer quickly backed away, reaching behind him with one hand for the beaded curtain. "I'm sorry. I'll get Balok to talk to you, I…"

Rin thought about the moment everything had gone blurry on the bridge, the way her fear morphed into something bestial she couldn't hold back. There had been something purple clouding the edges of her sight. And suddenly she remembered fear on Oren Galaxa's face as he backed away from her, followed by a painful crack on her skull.

"Sprit! We'll all talk about it later."

All those tests Balok kept running, Oren's request for her to stay with either Sprit or Holt under constant surveillance, Anthia's distrust—

"I'm so sorry," Morai repeated as he hurriedly retreated, and Rin felt something in her chest snap.

"I'm human!" she shouted after him, and for a moment she swore she caught a flash of purple in her peripheral vision. Her voice dropped to a hoarse whisper as she backed into her chair and shakily sat down. "I'm human.…"

"Doctor Balok!"

The Indegloan turned to the healer, brow furrowing in concern at the note of panic in his voice.

"What is it?" A horrible thought struck him, and he quickly met the man halfway. "Is it Hanali'a?"

"No. No, it's your human. Your half-human, I mean," he said in a rush, his voice lowering to a barely audible whisper. "I thought she knew what she was."

"*What?* How did *you* know?" Balok whispered back, voice jumping even in its quieted state. "Never mind, that's not important now. What did you say to Rin?"

"I asked her what else she was, and she started getting agitated—"

"Alright, enough. Just take me to her, please, and send someone to get Galaxa."

As the two hurried off, Avery looked up from where he was sitting beside Lucien's stretcher.

"What do you think that's about?" he asked.

The helmsman lifted his head just enough to see where they were going, and his eyes filled with concern.

"That's where Hanali'a's room is," he said, letting his head fall back down. "I hope she's okay."

"Hey." He ruffled Lucien's undone hair with a bandaged hand and smirked. "It's Han. She's what, two hundred? She's indestructible."

"That's true, I guess."

"You worry too much, Luc," Avery chastised with an easy smile and sat back in his chair. "Everything will be fine."

"I still have to find out why Anthia hit Rin over the head with her tablet," Lucien mumbled, pain medications making his words drowsy and overly relaxed. "Wasn't nice…"

"Wait, Anthia did what?" Avery demanded sharply.

Lucien looked at the lieutenant's brother and gave a micro shrug.

"She knocked Rin out on the bridge with her tablet. Don't know why though." He yawned, and Avery absently patted his shoulder.

"Oh, I'll find out, Lucien," he assured him, dangerously quiet. "Don't worry."

He waited until the ensign was asleep before getting up and leaving the infirmary. He had a sister to talk to.

"So, what's our plan of attack?" Sprit asked, looking at Oren as she helped Holt pull off the remainders of the exosuit. "This is definitely Jon Bledsoe, which means we're in way over our heads."

"You should notify the Corps," Anthia said, and Oren looked at her crossed feet where they were kicked up on the edge of the table with an unimpressed, raised eyebrow. "Runner said I could, sir."

"I did," Tzo admitted, and Oren quickly changed the subject.

"I'll tell the Galactic Council we're heading for Sahmot and appraise them of the situation. We'll repair there, but I want us to stay away from the fleet."

"I'll set up a secure channel, sir." Anthia swung her feet off the table and got up. "May I?"

Both captains dismissed her with a synchronous motion that under different circumstances Sprit would have found entertaining, if not endearing, and Lieutenant Acoua departed. Next, *Starlight*'s captain turned to his security officers.

"I want a full lid on this. Nobody so much as breathes the name Jon Bledsoe, understood?" They both nodded. "Keep an eye out for any kind of unusual behavior, which, yes, is going to be exponentially harder given everyone is out of sorts. But we can't assume Talik and Jhama were the only operatives on board." He hesitated and looked to Lewis. "If possible, I want you to keep an ear to the ground. See if you can find anything your way. But under *no* circumstances do I want you to keep doing it if it endangers you in *any* way," he warned with a pointed look.

"Yes, sir."

"Alright. We have something else we need to talk about, though." He sighed and looked at Tzo. "Could you give us the room?"

"Wow, that serious?" she asked and defensively held her hands up as he scowled. "Fine, fine. I'm going."

"It's Miss Cooper. Is it not, sir?" Holt asked as soon as the door closed behind Runner.

"Yes." He sighed and stood up, pacing the length of the table. "Rin started to...*change* on the bridge." He stopped and braced himself on the back of one of the chairs. "Her alien genes started coming out."

"What?"

He continued, cutting off Sprit's surprised interjection.

"Whatever she is, it's..." He scoffed, a small, wondrous smile pulling at his lips. "I've never seen anything like it before," he admitted. "It was during the explosions. This bright, violet light filled her veins, and her eyes and skin started glowing with it. It was beautiful and...and terrifying, too."

"That was when Lieutenant Acoua knocked her out with the tablet," Holt said softly, and the captain nodded.

"It was the right move. If I hadn't been so caught off guard, I would have done the same." He sighed and massaged the back of his neck. "So now we have another problem—what to do with her."

"Is she stable?"

"For the moment. I—" Someone quickly knocked on the heavy metal door before pushing it open, not waiting for a reply or call to enter. It was one of the infirmary workers, and Oren turned to her, heart sinking as he took in her furrowed brow. "Hanali'a?"

"No, Galaxa." She seemed to hesitate, glancing at Sprit and Holt, and Oren beckoned for her to continue.

"They can hear whatever you have to say."

"It's your human. She's quite…agitated, I think Morai phrased it."

The *Starlight* officers exchanged a glance, and Sprit sighed, dropping the part of Holt's exosuit that she was still holding on the table.

"You were saying about another problem?"

———

Rin looked up the moment Balok walked through the beaded curtain, Morai at his heels, and quickly sized the doctor up. He seemed cautious, reserved, and she clenched her hands tighter around the rim of Hanali'a's basin. Her skin felt like it was crawling, and she swallowed hard, trying to find her voice.

"What am I?"

"Human," Balok answered after a long pause

Her knuckles turned white.

"What else?" she hissed, and the doctor hesitated again.

"Rin, we really should wait for the captain—"

"What else am I, Balok?"

"We don't know."

Rin looked at Oren as he walked in, Sprit and Holt behind him.

"But you knew there was something," she pressed, eyeing them with open distrust and making sure to keep Hanali'a between them. "When did you find out? Was it all those tests you ran, telling me I was fine?"

"Yes." Balok glanced at the captain in a silent question as to whether complete honesty was the best idea at the moment. Oren simply continued. "But only Balok and I knew. Sprit and Holt had no idea until the last twenty-eight hours. We thought you had enough to deal with as it was." He watched the girl's fire slowly burn out, and she began trembling. "Rin, you should sit down."

"How can I not be human?" she whispered, looking ready to throw up.

Oren tilted his head towards the girl, and Sprit walked over, prying Rin's hands from the first officer's bedside, and led her back to her chair.

"That's what we wanted to ask you." Oren paused and half-turned to Morai. "Could you give us the room? Balok can keep an eye on Hanali'a and get you if she starts to take a turn."

The healer simply bowed and left. He was partly to blame for this, so the sooner he left them to talk, the better.

"What can you tell us about your parents, Rin?" Balok asked gently, and the girl looked at him, unsure where to start. "Anything works. Their names, where they were from, what they looked like…anything could help us try to give you some answers."

"I…" She trailed off, crossing her arms defensively and drawing her feet up onto the chair with her. "They were *human*."

"Rin, your DNA is only fifty percent human," the doctor said sympathetically. "One of your parents wasn't."

Rin looked at Sprit helplessly, and the woman gave her a sad smile, reaching out to stroke her hair.

"Come on, Rin. What's your mom's story?"

"She…her name was Myra. Myra Cooper. She died, though, years ago when I was five." She looked at her lap and picked at the hem of her borrowed shirt. "Some kind of brain aneurysm."

"What did she look like?"

Rin looked up at Oren as she answered him.

"Me. Well, except for my eyes and my mouth, I guess." Her fingers absently traced her lips. "They must be my dad's since they aren't hers."

"Must be, Miss Cooper?" Holt asked, frowning, and everyone turned to him. "Have you never seen your father?"

"He left before I was born," she said with another defensive shrug, her tone clearly saying this was a sore topic. "My mom always said he just went away, but my grandmother said he got killed."

"Didn't anyone have a picture?" Sprit pressed, her frown mirroring Holt's as she felt their link begin to clear once more. And she was glad to see they were thinking in their usual lock step. "Hasn't anyone been able to describe him to you? Or tell you his name?"

Rin scoffed, rolling her eyes.

"He walked out on me and my mom. No one keeps photos of you when you do that. Besides, he said he was John Doe, so he was obviously up to something." When everyone stared at her bitter words, she explained. "It's the name we use when we can't identify people. Amnesiacs, dead bodies, coma patients—they're all John and Jane Doe."

"A telling moniker to take on," Oren observed, and Rin just scoffed. "No one remembers what your father looks like?"

Rin shook her head, not really looking at them.

"My grandmother said he was abusive. That he was the reason my mom ended up the way she did."

"What way?" Oren asked gently, and she looked at him guardedly.

"She could barely take care of herself after he left." Her voice was matter-of-fact, but Holt felt the undercurrent of hate running through her. "My grandmother had to take me away from her before I was a year old just so I wouldn't die. She's the one who raised me."

"Did your mother ever talk about your father?"

"No. She'd just get upset." She looked down, clearly uncomfortable. "Then, she'd just say my name over and over again." She pulled her hair from its half-undone braid and ran her fingers through it, absent and subdued. "He wasn't human, was he?" She looked up at them, resigned. "My dad?"

"Probably not, Miss Cooper," Holt confirmed, and Sprit put her arm around Rin's shoulders, brusquely pulling her close.

"Have you ever had any kind of health problems?" Balok asked after giving her a few moments, and Rin shook her head. "No weird growths or anything that your doctors couldn't explain or that you had removed? Or, as a more specific example, no extra organs or vascular systems?"

Rin pulled a face and shook her head.

"No, nothing like..." She trailed off and narrowed her eyes. "Why the more specific example?"

"Well, it seems you have an extra organ beneath your heart," Balok began reluctantly, and Rin's eyes widened at what had to be a painful speed. "And a, uh, an entire additional vascular system. I don't know what's in it, I don't know what it's for, but I would bet it had something to do with how you went 'glowy and purple' as Anthia put it."

"How I went *what* now?"

"I assume it's triggered by an extreme adrenaline response," Balok continued, unfazed as Rin gaped, "but beyond that I have no idea."

"Wait. You're saying she could fully manifest with her next adrenaline rush?" Oren asked in an undertone, pulling Balok aside slightly, and the doctor shrugged. "Someone is trying to kill us, and you're telling me she could transform the next time she gets too stressed out?"

"Well, I didn't know that's what would trigger her reaction, but yes, I'd say that's a fair summary of the situation at hand," Balok returned, and Oren sighed.

"This day keeps getting better and better." He breathed deeply, closing his eyes and thinking hard about all the different variables he had in play right now. "I realize this is not an ideal situation, Rin," he started, but to his complete surprise, Holt interrupted him.

"Miss Cooper, as you probably noticed, we have a situation on our hands that is highly dangerous. Since you have been lied to enough, I am going to give you the truth."

"Lieutenant Holt," Oren warned, but the deputy continued.

"A man is trying to kill us. *Starlight* is not safe right now, and given what Balok just told us and the fact that we don't know what you can do, the captain feels it would be best to leave you with his family in Sahmot."

"What?!" Rin shouted and then quickly forced herself to calm down as she felt her heart begin to race. She couldn't freak out. She couldn't go all 'glowy and purple' right now, whatever that meant. "You can't leave me!"

"Rin," Sprit began softly as Oren glared at his security officer.

"Reading my mind *again*, lieutenant?" he growled.

"Sir, my bondmate was particularly insistent I be the one to break the news to her. And that it be done honestly." Holt hesitated, glancing at Sprit where she was comforting Rin. "And to be frank, sir, she scares me more than you do."

Oren rolled his eyes. He couldn't disagree with the man.

"Rin, we'd come back for you," Sprit assured her. "Once we figured this out, we'd come back for you, I promise. Besides." Here, she smiled. "Matzepo is *fantastic*. She raised me after all, not to mention Oren."

"I met you at a slave auction where people were shooting and trying to kill each other," Rin said slowly. "Since then, you've had four explosions, a whole lot of people have died, and…and *I* scare you?" She gave a breathless laugh, disbelief lacing her words. "Do you have *any* idea how scared that makes *me?*"

Holt looked down, his hands clenching behind his back. The action didn't go unnoticed by either the captain or his sister.

"Holt?" Oren asked, pointedly. "Something else you'd like to say?"

Sprit's expression was far more concerned; she could feel his turmoil. *"Lewis, you okay?"*

"I understand this is terrifying, Miss Cooper," he said delicately, setting aside Sprit's voice in the link, "but believe me when I say it could be much worse. Being separated from others and high stress situations when learning about your own abilities is quite helpful. It leads to far less harm to yourself and others."

"That's not really making me feel any better, Holt," Rin muttered, and Sprit sighed, reaching out and ruffling the girl's hair.

"Don't expect it to. He's not Hanali'a." The security chief looked to the doctor and captain. "It's been a long day. So, if you don't mind, I'd like to call it a night for all of us." She tapped Rin's shoulder and motioned for her to stand as she headed for the beaded-curtain threshold, snagging Holt's arm and pulling him along as she and Rin passed. "With your permission, captain?"

Oren shook his head at the way she was towing the two less-than-comfortable people in her wake and waved them on.

"We'll talk about this more when we've arrived at Sahmot," he said. "Rest easy, commander."

"Rest easy, captain," she returned and promptly dragged her deputy and roommate with her from the room. "Okay, you two, so Tzo gave us a small guest room a couple halls from here, but there's only one bed, so two of us are going to have to take the floor. Holt, I was thinking you'd take the mattress since you've been beaten into the deck plating—"

"*HOLT!*"

Holt started at the volume of the foreign thought in his mind just as something small and fast tackled him around the legs.

"Oh. Your kid's back." Sprit smirked to herself and kept walking, pulling Rin with her. "Meet you there, Lewis."

"Commander—"

"Just follow the link or whatever!" She put her arm around Rin's waist as they walked on.

"Ma'am, that's not how it works," the lieutenant tried, but his superior ignored him and continued down the hall.

"Yeah, while you were gone, Holt adopted a kid."

"What?" Rin asked, nonplussed, and Sprit sighed.

"I shouldn't make fun of him for it," she said, her smile fading as she forced herself to set her dark, coping humor aside. "Mara is Jhama's daughter—the woman responsible for the second attack."

"Oh." They walked in silence for a bit. "Does Holt even like kids?"

"They're a secret joy of his," Sprit whispered back conspiratorially, a smirk playing at her lips. "Don't worry, he'll work it out." They arrived at the door to their temporary quarters, and the officer pulled the heavy metal open. "Home sweet home for the next few hours."

Cramped was a charitable description of the space.

The bed was nothing more than a shelf-like alcove in the wall, a thin mattress its only form of padding along with a few folded blankets and an equally compressed pillow. The room itself was probably only five paces across, and Rin looked up at the vaulted, gradually narrowing ceiling. At least the height gave them some semblance of space. About twelve steps from the door was the other wall, and Rin saw it had a reasonably sized window. She started to walk over to it, but Sprit caught her arm.

"You don't want to look out there," she said gravely. "We're towing *Starlight* just off *Horizon*'s bow. She's little behind us, sure, but she's not a pretty sight." She tilted her head towards the floor and wearily sat down, joints cracking and protesting. "Come on. You can use my lap as a pillow." She pulled one of the two spare blankets off the bed and waved at Rin with it. "Come on. Sooner you're situated, the sooner I can sleep."

Rin eased herself to the floor beside her, noting how *Horizon*'s deck plating was smooth and brown instead of patterned and silver. It would definitely make it more comfortable to sleep on. Above her, Sprit smiled as the girl gingerly leaned over and set her head on her lap, and the older woman absently ran her fingers through her roommate's hair.

"You want your implants off?" Rin shook her head, and the security chief carefully draped the blanket over her. "Alright. Get some sleep."

When Holt finally got directions to their shared quarters, Mara was asleep in his arms again. Apparently, she'd burned quite a lot of energy chasing Morai and the other Trozeran medics around, and the healer was quite relieved to have her out of the way. Unfortunately, the girl didn't want to let go of Holt either, so now *he* had to deal with her underfoot. It wasn't that he hated kids, far from it. His problem was that he needed time alone. Time to recharge in relative peace and quiet. And the kid attached to his hip wasn't going to help with that.

He quietly opened the door to the quarters and stepped inside. It was small, but it would do. Sprit was already out cold on the floor, her head tilted back on the edge of the mattress and her hands resting on Rin where she was lying on her lap. The girl looked up at him as he walked in and offered a small, tired smile before lying back down.

"I hope I did not wake you, Miss Cooper."

"You're fine," she yawned and listened as Holt climbed into bed, carefully negotiating his long limbs in the cramped space. "G'night…"

"Goodnight, Miss Cooper." Holt carefully lied back on the mattress, keeping Mara nestled against his chest and making sure he didn't kick or elbow Sprit in the head as he went down. Jhama's daughter shifted a little, grabbing onto his uniform tighter, but mercifully did not wake up.

Once they were situated, he glanced at the shock of red hair encroaching on his resting place and quietly scoffed.

"Goodnight, commander."

He closed his eyes and tried to sleep, counting the number of breaths the child sleeping on top of him took to his every one.

One...two...three...

———————————

Rin briefly woke a few hours later and glanced at her companions, vision blurred by sleep and exhaustion. She couldn't see very well, but the stars beyond their window gave sufficient light that she could make out enough.

Sprit was quietly snoring, her head tilted back like it had been when she'd first fallen asleep, but her hands had long ago slipped off of Rin's body, finally pulled away by the gentle tug of gravity. Mara was still sprawled over Holt, drooling slightly onto his uniform and no doubt getting an impressive imprint of a button on her cheek. And Holt...

Rin was pretty sure she'd never seen him this relaxed before, despite the bruises and the weak scabs decorating his face. He looked younger, his brow free from worry lines, his mouth not pressed tight in concern. And his hand closest to them...

Rin smiled, small and soft, and went back to sleep.

His hand was nestled protectively in Sprit's hair.

CHAPTER 20

Tzo glanced at her brother solemnly across Hanali'a's watery bed.

"Jon," she muttered, the name poison on her lips, and Oren looked at her. "The High Priestess warned us a serpent was back, Ren. That he'd be wound tight around you before you even noticed."

The Peacekeeper captain ran his hand back and forth along the lip of the basin. His voice was quiet and passive.

"What else did she say?"

"To kill his servants." He scoffed, shaking his head, and she pressed on. "Each blow to them is a blow to him."

"How helpful," he returned, dripping with sarcasm, and Tzo bristled.

"Omarik and Assora tried to *kill* you all."

"They couldn't help it!" he snapped, and now it was her turn to scoff. "And they fought him tooth and nail, Tzo! They fought—"

"Once his slave, always his slave," she interrupted, voice cool but not unsympathetic when she continued. "You know that."

"Stop it."

Another long silence stretched between the twins, and Tzo watched him tap a rhythm out on the metal beneath his hands.

"What's your plan?" she finally asked.

"Matzepo." His reply was quick and firm, and Tzo sighed, putting her hands on her hips and looking up at the ceiling.

"Mother is not guaranteed safety, Oren."

"Jon respects her—"

"No, he respects her *power*," she corrected, pointing at him. "And he used to, back when she was still more influential than he was."

"She's our only choice, Tzo," he said after a long pause, and she shook her head. "I can't let Jon get close to the fleet. With his power, it would be...catastrophic isn't even close."

"But you'll risk our home?" she challenged, eyes blazing, and crossed her arms over her chest. "Our people? Friends, family? You'll risk *them?*"

"He won't attack Sahmot," he assured her for what felt like the tenth time already. "He won't kill the town that took him in, raised him—"

"And a *lot* of good we did!"

Her shouted honesty hung in the air between them, and she looked down, scuffing the toes of her boots against the deck.

"We'll go to Sahmot," Oren repeated after a long pause. "We'll repair *Starlight* there. Tzo, are you listening?" She looked up at him with a bitter glare, and he continued, resting one palm on the water above Hanali'a so his skin just barely brushed the lukewarm fluid. "Warn Trozer's fleet to maintain radio silence with all incoming vessels until they give visual confirmation of their identities and allow us to scan for Alympan life signs. Issue the confirmation protocol as well."

"No trouble, huh?" she asked, dryly, and he looked up at her.

"I'm confident, not naïve." He withdrew his arm from the basin and clasped his hands behind his back. "We take every precaution."

Tzo followed his intense, troubled gaze to their old friend between them. Her voice dropped its command harshness, turning her into his sister once more instead of his colleague.

"How's Han?"

Oren gave a small smile, still watching his first officer.

"She'll make a full recovery."

"Good. I'll give my infirmary staff a raise," Tzo said with a smirk and walked towards the beaded doorway. "See you on the surface, Ren."

"See you on the surface," he returned absently and reached forward to grip the edge of the tub again as she left.

———

Rin was almost positive her jaw was bruised.

It wasn't her fault; it was that kid's. Mara had tried to get up when everyone was still asleep, and instead of being quiet, she managed to knee Holt in his heavily bruised stomach, making him jerk awake in pain. That would have all been fine and this mess would have ended there, but his hand was unfortunately still tangled in Sprit's hair. The security chief woke with a startled, pained yelp as someone pulled hard on her scalp, and her knee snapped up in a reflexive protective move, which, again, would have been *fine* if Rin hadn't been using her lap as a pillow.

"Djienn, Holt, let go of my hair!" Sprit snapped, pawing at where her deputy's hand was tangled in her locks, and Lewis grimaced as he quickly pulled his hand free, taking a few strands with him.

"Sorry, ma'am," he grimaced, awkwardly patting her hair back into place and inwardly groaning as he only seemed to make it worse.

"Quit petting me!" She swatted his hands away and looked at Rin as the girl sat up and scooted away, massaging her jaw with a low noise of pain. "Oh, djienn, did I hit you?"

"You kneed me," she groaned. Yep, that was going to bruise.

"Look at what you did, Holt," Sprit hissed, scowling at the man as he got out of bed, still carrying the girl with him. "Where are you going?"

"Mara wanted to see out the window, ma'am."

Just as he finished speaking, the deck and walls started vibrating more than usual, and the whole ship was seized by violent turbulence. Holt quickly braced himself on the railing against the wall, and instantly, Rin felt herself go into overdrive. Her heart raced in her chest, and her breath came in quick gasps as she reached for the edge of the mattress.

Crashing. They were crashing. They had to be—

"Easy! Easy, Rin, we're just landing," Sprit assured her, gently putting her hands on Rin's back and trying to ground her once more. "We're just breaking through the atmosphere, give us a second." The girl looked up at her in open distrust until, gradually, the ship steadied. Sprit grinned. "Come on. You're not gonna want to miss this."

She pulled Rin to her feet and dragged her over to the window where Holt and Mara were already standing, eagerly pointing below them.

"Welcome to Trozer."

Rin watched with wide eyes as the surface of the red, Mars-like planet drew closer. Massive black oceans covered each of its poles like someone had dipped the planet in an inkwell, and while she wasn't positive, Rin was pretty sure she could *see* the reflections of clouds in the water, the air was so clear. Massive, jagged valleys cut across its middle like old, deep scars, visible from space with astounding mountain ranges capped with snow at its more northern and southern altitudes. The ground was largely the same color as Trozeran skin, Rin realized and took in some of the darker and lighter swaths of land as they passed, drawing ever closer. At first, she couldn't tell what they were, but then she could pick out details.

The lighter areas were cities—adobes and converted tents, thatched roofs and rich colors that matched Trozeran clothing in vibrancy, prints, and style. Everything melded perfectly with the land, seemingly growing out of the earth with the mountains and other natural wonders. Even from here, Rin could tell the planet surface was hot, and she wondered if it would be dry or wet heat. They passed over forests of small, shrub-like trees with near-black bark and variously colored leaves and massive fields of gently swaying green-yellow grass that looked so tall Rin wasn't sure if she'd be able to see over it if she stood in the middle of it all.

"Rin, look over there." She turned to where Sprit was pointing and gasped, putting a hand to the glass. "Those are whilden."

The darker swaths weren't cities. They were massive herds.

Everywhere the animals ran, they created a front of red-orange dust, and Sprit smiled as *Horizon* came low enough that they could make out details of the big beasts. They were around the size of elephants, possibly larger, and covered in thick, heavy fur. Rin wasn't even sure how to describe them. They had massive antlers similar to moose; in fact, they looked a lot like moose, but there was something almost bear-esque to them as well in their bulk and muscle, or perhaps more like bison with the distribution of fur. They varied in shades of brown ranging from ebony to bronze, often with many different tones and gradients on the same creature. A few, she realized, as they came even lower, had white markings around their eyes, snouts, and underbellies.

"And there go the hunters," Sprit muttered, and Rin watched as what looked like massive water buffaloes closed in on the edges of the herd.

"Wait, the buffalo things hunt the moose things?"

"No," Sprit laughed, "we do. The 'buffalo things' are called dokori. We ride them." Now, Rin could pick out the Trozeran hunters on the backs of the water buffalo-esque creatures, aiming spears and bows and other older style weapons. "What can I say? We love our traditions."

"No wonder your family has so many scars, commander," Holt said softly, tightening his hold on Mara a little, and Sprit snorted.

"No, that's from the imoru." She glanced at Rin's questioning, confused look. "You'll meet them later. Maybe," she amended when she felt Holt's brief moment of panic. So, Holt was scared of large carnivorous felines—good to know.

"I believe that is an appropriate fear response, commander."

"Holt, if you've got something to say, say it out loud and not in the link. I'm standing right here. I can take it," Sprit said dryly, much to his chagrin, and Mara giggled. "And there's Sahmot."

They came to a stop a little ways out from a smaller village, and Rin eagerly leaned forward to get a better look only to have her view blocked by rising dust as the ship slowly touched down.

"We should get ready, commander," Holt said softly as *Horizon* rumbled beneath them. "Captain Runner delivered some supplies while we were sleeping—UV block and some lighter clothes."

The two women followed Holt back to the bed, and he sat Mara on the mattress, grabbing few bottles of sunscreen lotion from where they'd been propped against the side of the bed and tossing one to Sprit.

"Thank you," Sprit said in a sing-songy way and promptly squeezed some of the greenish goo out onto Rin's hands. "There you go, rub that in until you can't see it anymore. Trust me, you're gonna need it in our sun."

Rin cautiously spread it over her exposed skin and wrinkled her nose. It smelled overwhelmingly like eucalyptus. As she methodically worked the sunscreen into her skin, she glanced at Sprit and Holt. Sprit had the top of her jumpsuit undone and tied about her waist, and she was already done applying the salve to her arms and chest around her underarmor. Holt meanwhile was busy showing Mara how to put on the UV block. Once he was sure she had the hang of it, he stood up and quickly undid the top of his uniform as well, turning so his back faced his roommates. Unlike Sprit, he didn't wear an underarmor shirt, and Rin followed the spines dotting his bruised skin, tracking their upside down spade pattern along his shoulders and down his flanks to its point at the small of his back. He was oddly muscled for his reserved demeanor, and briefly Rin wondered just how poorly a fight with him would go.

She'd barely managed to get a good look at him before he pulled on a lightweight, long-sleeved shirt and quickly buttoned the white fabric up.

His story had to be an interesting one, Rin decided and then flushed when Holt glanced at her over his shoulder.

Right. Mind reading. She busied herself with the lotion once more.
Good job making things awkward, Rin.

Anthia didn't look up as her brother came bursting into her work area, muttering agitatedly as he swatted at the clinging strands of beads.

"Lieutenant Commander Byrone," she greeted flatly and adjusted the volume on her computer, listening harder to the lower band frequencies. She had to find Jon's transmissions. "Something I can help you with?"

He threw a mass of black fabric at her in response, and again without looking, Anthia caught the garment. She considered the terminal before her for a moment. He was angry. She should pause her work.

Avery watched his older sister closely as she turned off her channels and took off her headphones. And surprisingly, she turned her attention to him. Neither of them said anything, and the man sighed as he realized she was waiting for him to speak first.

"What happened to your uniform?" he asked, gesturing at her without making eye contact.

"I cut it up to use as bandages for Han," she returned evenly and took in the white, full-coverage tunic and pants he wore, including gloves and a veiled hood currently pulled down about his shoulders. "What happened to yours?"

Avery frowned and glanced over his shoulder through the beads to the busy corridors.

"We're disembarking," he said haltingly. "Didn't you feel us land?"

"No. I must've been too focused." She picked up her headphones and slipped them into her underarmor's pocket as she powered down her terminal.

"Did you knock out Rin?" Avery finally demanded in an angry rush, and she looked up at him impassively.

Oh. So that was why he was here.

"You're asking me about something you don't understand, sir," she began coolly, and her brother interrupted her.

"I don't have time for your games, Anthia. And right now, I'm not your superior, I'm your brother. Did you or did you not knock out Rin?"

She waited a few beats before answering.

"Yes." She stood and pulled the tunic on over her underarmor, leaving its hood and veil down. "I have the captain's approval."

"You always have his approval," Avery growled as she removed her boots and the remains of her uniform and donned the black pants next. "That doesn't make what you do right."

Anthia looked at him dryly as she pulled on the dark gloves.

"Collecting another human, Avery?" she asked, only to take a quick step back, guarded once more, as he moved menacingly towards her.

"That is *not* why I'm pissed at you!" he shouted, flushing with the depth of his hurt. "God, that's not—what is *wrong* with you, Anthia?!"

She gave him a few moments to back away and collect himself.

"It was an attempt at a joke." She pulled the hood over her head, adjusting the veil over her face until she could see through the protective mesh covering her eyes. "Too soon, I guess."

She went to walk by her taller sibling, but he grabbed her arm, pulling her back so they were face-to-face.

"It is always going to be too soon, Anthia," he hissed. "*Always.*"

He released her and marched off, pulling the hood and veil over his head in a disjointed way that betrayed his emotion. Anthia waited a few moments before following. That conversation had gone better than the last non-work related one they'd had. It was progress.

———

"We're ready to disembark, Oren," Tzo greeted, coming up behind her brother at the front of the crowded loading bay. "Repair supplies are standing by as well as medical aid. Mother seems to have mobilized the entire town to help you."

He smiled and grasped her shoulder.

"Thank you, Tzo. We'd be dead without you."

"Don't I know it," she sighed and tapped Oren's arm. "Here comes our sister with her extended family." She snorted at his confused face as he turned around, and his expression quickly cleared.

"Very funny," he drawled, watching bemusedly as the shorter woman guided her half-human, bondmate, and tag-along child through the mayhem towards them. "I see you're still in one piece, Sprit."

"Still kicking and biting," she returned wryly. "Though I'm short a few hairs since Holt decided to wake me up by yanking on it."

"Again, commander, I apologize—"

"Relax, Holt, I'm messing with you." She yawned and stretched. "So, we ready for this?"

"This?" Oren echoed, and she raised an eyebrow.

"It's mom. You know it's a big deal for her when we come home." She glanced at Rin. "Brace yourself. It's hot and humid out there."

"Sounds like my old summers," she offered with a small smile to try and ease her nerves. Sprit just grumbled, reaching for Rin's hair and tying it in a bun for her. "Uh…"

"Trust me, you'll appreciate it when we go out there."

"How is she?" Oren asked softly, subtly pointing to Mara, and Holt looked down at her as she hid her face in his chest.

"Mara?" He waited a moment and then regretfully looked to his captain. "I'm afraid she's scared of you, sir."

"Of course," he chuckled and smiled at the girl. "I called your aunt, Mara. She'll be here in three days to pick you up." Holt glanced at the child, and a small smile played at his lips.

"She's happy to hear that, sir."

There was a sudden loud hissing of air, and *Horizon*'s loading ramp slowly lowered, the sticky heat of the outside hitting them like a wall. Rin coughed a little bit as her lungs hurried to adjust to the new air, and she jumped as two figures clad entirely in white and black respectively came up beside them. The shorter one in black deliberately moved a few steps away while the taller one in white took a few steps closer, clearly giving his counterpart the cold shoulder.

"Hey, Avery. Anthia," Sprit greeted. "You two getting along?"

Avery made a noncommittal, disgruntled noise that was really all the answer Sprit needed while Anthia shrugged and addressed their captain.

"Better than before," she replied simply, voice slightly muffled under her opaque veil. "We'll be getting out of your sun as soon as we can, sir."

"Of course. Take care of yourselves."

The ramp finally settled in its fully lowered position, and Rin was met with the sight of what looked like an entire village gathered before them.

Oren smiled, heaving a sigh of respite, and led the way, Tzo and Sprit flanking him on either side. The captains' crews were completely mixed together at this point, not that either really cared. They were sister ships. This came with the territory. Rin made sure to stay close to Sprit's side as they went, knocking shoulders with her nearly every step.

"Uncle Ren!" a young voice shouted, and the moment Oren's boots touched Trozeran soil, he was swarmed by kids and teenagers, all of them clambering over him, giving him hugs and kisses as they welcomed him home. Instantly, the captain's weary face broke into a big grin, and he picked up one of the smaller children pulling at his pant leg, spinning her around in a circle before setting her back on dizzy, unsteady feet.

"Are they really all his family?" Rin asked in wonderment, trying to count how many Trozeran youths were gathered around Oren, and Sprit smiled.

"Everyone's family." She put an arm around Rin's waist, helping her stay a little closer as they walked. "That's how Trozer works."

Rin watched the people of Sahmot guide *Starlight* crewmembers away from *Horizon*, greeting friends and family from both ships as they went. A few adults had joined the fray around Oren, too, ushering the kids away so that two people could approach.

One was massive, built like a wrestler with large horns, long hair, a beard, thick brows, and severe claw marks along his shoulder and chest. Thick leather armor protected his left shoulder opposite the scars on his right—the stiff, heavy material buckled across his chest and fastened to his upper right arm. More battered leather armor encased his abdomen like a corset, and a dark, maroon wrap hung over shorts of the same color. He was barefooted, Rin realized, but his visible callouses were no doubt enough to protect him from the hot clay earth.

"Who's that?" she whispered, noting the decorative white paint on his face, legs, and right arm. He was a giant, easily six foot four.

"Oh, that's Khalo Whilden," Sprit answered, not bothering to keep her voice down as the men reunited. "He's Oren's husband."

Oren seized Khalo's horns and gently pulled his head down so their foreheads pressed together, and Khalo rested his hands on Oren's waist. They stood that way for a long time, the taller man quietly speaking to his husband before quickly kissing him and pulling him tight against him. And as Oren leaned into his partner's arms, Rin was hit with the realization that the captain had just lost so much with no one to confide in.

At this point, the second person stepped forward, and Rin frowned. This one was…harder to place. Their horns were longer, slenderer than the others she had seen so far, and their hair was tied back from their otherwise bald head in a ponytail mohawk. A couple piercings adorned the tips of their pointed ears, and they were clean-shaven, unlike Khalo and, to a lesser extent, Oren. But for the life of her, Rin couldn't decide if this newcomer was a guy or girl.

Though, they were clearly pregnant, and far along too, so that might be her answer.

"What about the other one?" Rin asked.

"Arzi Snow." Sprit paused, clearly struggling. "Arzi is…your language doesn't have words for *hir* gender, but *zie* also uses she pronouns if that makes it easier for you. *Zie* is Khalo and Oren's spouse."

As Arzi arrived at her husbands' sides, Oren quickly kissed her, running a hand over her belly before kissing the taut skin, too. She smiled at the gentle contact and laughed, putting her hands over her husband's and revealing the long leather cuffs encasing her forearms. Her brows were straight, like her nose, and three thin white stripes marked each of her cheeks. Her chest was encased by an armored band of leather and woven fiber, and a fur-lined, turquoise cloak hung about her frame, largely hiding her baggy brown pants and the heavy boots they were tucked into.

As Rin watched, Khalo swept a couple tears from Oren's cheek with a quick thumb, and Arzi ran a hand over their husband's horns.

And then, suddenly, everything went quiet.

The human hadn't realized how loud it had become until suddenly there was no noise at all, and Sprit quickly surged forward, pulling Rin with her until they were only a couple steps behind Oren. Slowly, the crowd of Trozerans and *Starlight* crew parted, revealing an old lady slowly walking towards Oren and his spouses, her pace clearly deliberate and not an indication of her age.

Despite her small, wrinkled stature, she bore the presence of a giant that made Rin think of Hanali'a. Her neck and wrists were laden with more jewelry than Morai, and she had bold blue markings on her face—a paint color Rin noticed no other Trozerans bore. Her horns curved tightly along her skull and were smaller than average, but her graying hair hung in long locks down her back. Her dress was simple, sleeveless and made of a rich red fabric that hung to her calves, and she wore a supple, ornately engraved leather vest over it. A finely knit shawl of that same blue paint color hung from her elbows instead of her shoulders, and her boots were made of some kind of animal skin instead of heavy leather, turning each step into a soft thud.

But where she walked, deliberate and tall, four hunters followed at all times—fully armored with massive spears clenched in their hands.

Oren immediately knelt and bowed his head, hands clasped over his knee. Khalo and Arzi silently stepped back.

Once the woman reached him, she held his scarred head around the bases of his horns and gently kissed his forehead.

"Welcome home, Galaxa, my son," she announced in a voice that was clear and powerful despite its aged, gravelly undertones. He slowly looked up at her, his eyes shining, and she released him. Her expression remained grave. "How I wish it was under better circumstances."

"Thank you for giving us safe harbor, Matzepo," Oren recited softly. "*Starlight* is in your debt."

Finally, her austerity broke, and her face turned warm and loving, a gentle smile spreading across her weather-beaten features.

"It is no debt for a mother to help her child." She quickly reached for her son's hands, pulling him to his feet and enveloping him in a bone-crushing hug. She sighed, eyes tightly shut as she somehow tightened her grip even more. "Oh, my boy." She pulled back and gently cupped his face with a leathery hand. "Come. We'll start repairs for your ship and crew." She waved her arm towards the village, and everybody started moving and talking again. "Your sister sent a list ahead of everything you need. We'll have you running again in no time," she assured him, linking her arm in his as they resumed walking. Her guards followed.

"Thank you, mother."

"Of course, my son."

Rin looked at the new world around her with wide eyes. Off to her left she could see massive shapes in the distance that looked like a forest of baobab trees. Some were smaller and thinner, but others had giant diameters and towering heights that Rin could barely comprehend. They made Earth's sequoias look small. Their trunks were vibrantly painted, and the human could see tree houses nestled in the top branches with ropes and platforms hanging from the sturdier limbs.

"Thrako trees, Miss Cooper."

Rin jumped at Holt's unexpected voice, and he muttered an apology.

"How'd you know that?" Sprit asked, genuinely curious.

"Foreign burial rituals are an interest of mine, ma'am."

The two women stared, taken aback and, in Sprit's case, disturbed.

"Of course they are," she said, perturbed expression bleeding into her voice. "I married a morbid creep." She patted Rin's hip where her arm was still wrapped around her waist. "There's Sahmot."

The village nestled up against the base of a mountain, and Rin looked up, following the jagged rock and gentle paths as the formation climbed ever higher. The soil was actually a little lighter than she'd thought from the ship, and the whitewashed adobe buildings bled into each other in a three dimensional maze of a town. There were a few large tents in the mix as well that seemed big enough to house the entire village beneath their multicolored canvas walls and ceiling. It was bustling with people, filled with the eager voices of children and adults as they hurried to help with arms laden with supplies.

And somehow, Rin felt like she'd just come home.

Sprit watched the human, half-human, closely and chuckled quietly to herself as the girl slowly smiled. Trozer, especially Sahmot, had that effect on everyone she welcomed home—even Jon Bledsoe once upon a time.

At Oren's side Matzepo stopped and held up a hand, bringing their procession to a halt, and she raised her voice to address everyone.

"Please, make yourselves at home. All of our doors are open to you, and if you need *anything*, do not hesitate to ask any of us. We will make sure you get what you need." Here, she grew somber. "We have set aside the town hall for your fallen." She bowed her head and sighed, weighed down by her sorrow. "We hope the space will let you find your loved ones and say goodbye."

She watched as the crowd slowly broke up, *Starlight* officers following Trozerans into dwellings and tents for rest and recuperation. But then she turned around, and her face lit up.

"My daughter!" she cried, opening her arms wide, and Sprit laughed as tears welled in her eyes.

"Matzepo," she grinned, running forward and throwing herself into the waiting embrace.

"Oh, my little one," the matron sighed, smiling into her girl's shoulder and holding her in the same vice-like hug she'd given Oren. "Are you okay, my dear?" She pulled back, worry suddenly clouding her wrinkled countenance as she cupped Sprit's bruised face.

"Yes, mama, I'm fine," the Ethonian assured her, gently pulling one of her mother's hands to her lips and kissing her palm. "I mean, I could be better," she admitted with a smile and rueful laugh, "but I'm fine."

"There is something different about you," Matzepo began, frowning, and tilted her daughter's face up a bit so she could look at her from a different angle. "I sense something...*other*." Her frown transformed into a gasp and then mocking disapproval. "Are you pregnant?" She pulled Sprit to the side and lowered her voice conspiratorially. "Don't worry, I won't tell your brother—"

"No!" Sprit protested, voice jumping an octave as she laughed and pulled her mom's hands from her face. "No, mama, I'm not pregnant." She stopped and shook her head, and Matzepo narrowed her eyes. Sprit winced. "I...got married. Sort of."

"*What?!*" Matzepo cried and swatted her daughter's arm. "How dare you get married without telling me? You know that was the one thing I asked of you, I wanted to be there for your wedding—"

Rin looked at Holt who was now much more uncomfortable than he had been moments before.

"I think you might've had better luck if you got her pregnant," she said, and Holt blushed, cheeks turning slightly blue.

"That is *not* helpful, Miss Cooper," he reprimanded tightly just as Sprit pointed back at him, and Matzepo started walking over. "Oh dear." He adjusted his hold on Mara, and Rin's eyebrows arched well into her forehead.

"Are you seriously using a child as a shield right now?" she whispered.

"Miss Cooper, Matzepo used to be High Matron of *all* of Trozer," he explained in quick undertones. "She is...terrifying."

"So. You are the one I have to blame for taking the simple pleasures in life from me," Matzepo greeted coldly, and Holt tensely cleared his throat. She crossed her arms over her chest and eyed him with a disgruntled gaze. "I'm an old woman, Lewis. I don't have very many pleasures left. My youngest daughter's *wedding* was one of them."

"I...um. Ma'am. It was not...I assure you—"

Rin subtly lifted a hand to her mouth, acting like she was rubbing her nose instead of hiding barely restrained laughter. She'd *never* seen Holt this flustered. A quick glance at Sprit told her the security chief was in the same boat as her. The woman was barely maintaining her straight face, biting her lower lip in an effort to keep it together. Matzepo let him hang there for a few seconds more, still struggling to find something to say while his face steadily flushed deeper blues before she caved.

"Oh my dear boy, you're really tongue tied, aren't you?" she laughed, expression torn between guilt and amusement. She bowed to him, and

Rin accidentally let a laugh escape at the way the lieutenant instead went white at the gesture of respect. "Apologies, Lewis. My troublemaker of a daughter explained the situation, of course." She glanced back at Sprit. "He's a good one, very polite. You should think about keeping him."

"Mother!" Sprit hissed, now the mortified one furiously blushing, and Rin actually laughed this time.

But then Matzepo turned to her, and instantly the girl went still. Holt was right. She was intimidating. Her stare slowly morphed from curiosity to wonder and then settled on intrigue with a flash of concern. The elder reached out for Rin and carefully took the not-human's slender hand in hers. Her skin was rough and calloused, and when she smiled, Rin felt a warmth break open in her stomach and spread throughout her.

"Hello, Rin Cooper."

CHAPTER 21

"Oh, y-you know my name," Rin stammered.

"Of course," Matzepo smiled. "Humans aren't very common out this way, much less half-humans. Welcome home." She reached out and gently chucked her under the chin. "We're delighted to have you." She turned to Holt once more and lightly ran her fingers through Mara's hair. "Hello there, little one. Would you like to go see some big, soft animals?" The little girl slowly turned her face from where she'd been hiding it in the cool fabric of Holt's shirt and nodded. "Well, then, let's go. If you don't mind, Lewis, this precious child and I are going to go on an adventure."

"She isn't speaking right now, ma'am," Holt began but passed the girl off to the matron nonetheless.

"Oh, that won't be a problem for us, will it?" she asked Mara with a twinkling eye, and the child giggled, running her fingers over Matzepo's necklaces and the engraving in her leather vest. She looked up at the much taller man she'd taken the girl from. "Go on, Lewis. Mother knows best."

He gave a small smile and inclined his head.

"Of course, ma'am."

"Sprit, you know where the guestrooms are in my home," she said as she walked away, engrossed by the Assidrian child in her arms. "Take your friends out of this sun." She looked up with that same easy smile. "It's not good for them."

"Yes, mama." Sprit sighed in contentment as she watched the elderly woman walk away. "Oh, it's good to be home. Alright, come on, guys."

Rin's attention was pulled in every possible direction as she absently trailed after the security officers, taking in everything from the outdoor, communal kitchen to the pool-sized trough some whilden were watering at; the beasts were even bigger than she'd imagined. The air was filled with so many smells like rich earth, spices, cooking fires, something that reminded her of vanilla and sage, leather, horses, so much she couldn't place and yet recognized like something from a dream. She stumbled slightly as the uneven earth turned into smooth, carved steps and quickly caught her balance, looking up as they entered a building that on the outside seemed nondescript, like an old missionary. But inside…

Inside, the walls were painted bright colors that seemed to be ubiquitous in Trozeran culture. They were decorated in tapestries, paintings, and carvings that Rin correctly guessed had been created by local hands. There were photos and holographic images like the one that had been on Sprit's bedside table of different people and faces she didn't recognize. Wait. She did know that one; it was Oren with Khalo and Arzi, all of them in fancy, ceremonial clothing.

Probably the wedding, Rin mused and then hurried to catch up to Holt and Sprit, her steps echoing down the vaulted halls and tiled floors. She glanced up to the unlit lanterns spaced along the ceiling as she went and wondered just how much light they provided in the evening.

"Here we are." Sprit pushed open a woven door that was more of a screen and presented the spacious room with a flourish. "Two beds, two baths, and a prayer room you can use for meditation, Holt. You need it." She walked over to the armoire in the corner and opened it. "We have some changes of clothes here, too, once we're cleaned up." She paused and looked her two roommates up and down a couple times. "Yeah, Holt, you should shower first. You look like…I don't know, but you look bad." She pointed to a curtained off room. "In there."

"Thank you, commander."

"Sprit, Holt!" she called after him as he limped behind the curtain. She sighed and muttered as she pulled her hair free. "It's Sprit."

She wearily sat on the edge of one of the cot-like beds and let herself slump over, elbows braced on her knees. In the other room, they heard the sound of water running, and the woman looked over at Rin.

"How are you handling the heat and humidity?"

"I always liked Montana summers," she said with a shrug and walked over to sit beside her friend. "This isn't so bad. It's a bit like a heat wave before a storm."

"Good…that's good."

Rin noticed how her gaze kept sliding to the curtain Holt was behind. "Is he okay?" she asked, keeping her voice deliberately quiet.

"Like I said, he was beaten into the deck plating," Sprit sighed, running her hands over her face. "I'm betting you saw his bruises?" Rin nodded. "Yeah, well, that was only his back. His stomach is worse." She cleared her throat and looked at her companion. "I should get cleaned up, too. You fine here on your own?"

Rin quickly nodded and watched as Sprit clapped her on the shoulder before heading to the other bathroom. Just as with Holt, there was a rustle of fabric followed by the sound of running water, and Rin got up and walked over to the balcony at the end of the room to kill the time. It was sealed off by another one of those woven screens like the bedroom door, and she was fiddling with the latch when somebody deliberately cleared their throat behind her. Rin jumped, knocking the lock open, and frantically steadied the wobbling door.

"Sorry, my dear," Matzepo apologized, tentatively entering the room. "I didn't mean to startle you. May I?"

Rin looked to where she was pointing with an open hand to one of the beds.

"Oh, uh, sure. It's your guestroom," she added with a brief laugh, but the matron just tutted.

"Nonsense. Right now, it is your room and Sprit and Holt's as well." She sat on the soft mattress and patted the empty space beside her. "Why don't you join me?" she asked and smiled disarmingly as Rin got settled.

"Where's Mara?"

"Oh, I left her with Khalo and Arzi to play with the whilden calves," she said with a dismissive wave. "They're really quite gentle."

"The calves or Khalo and Arzi?" Rin asked with a hesitant smile, uncertain if she was crossing a line, but Matzepo just laughed.

"Both, my child. Oh, definitely both." She patted the girl's arm. "But it meant I got the chance to talk with my son about you." She gestured to Rin's ears. "May I?" Rin nodded and shivered as the matron's cooler hands touched the sensitive skin behind her ears, examining the implants. "Incredible." She gently tucked the girl's hair out of her eyes. "Not the technology, my dear. You." When Rin blushed and tried to protest, the elder forcefully continued.

"No, no, no. You were rescued from a slave auction, thrown into the stars without a charted path, and look at you now. You're in the midst of sabotage and cloak and dagger politics in a world that you've no stake in, discovering that even you yourself aren't quite what you thought." She gave a good-natured shrug. "That's pretty incredible if you ask me." She paused, and that concern returned to her eyes as she peered closely at the girl's face. "Half-human...it was your father, wasn't it?"

Rin shifted back a little on the mattress.

"Uh, yeah. I-I mean, maybe. How did you—"

"You have a mother's face," Matzepo said simply, again waving away the question, but somehow the uneasiness didn't leave Rin's fluttering gut. "And you look human. The jump made sense." Matzepo folded her hands in her lap and sighed. "How are you doing, Rin, really? I know it's been a stressful time for you, bombs aside." Rin shrugged a little defensively, and Matzepo gave her a look of mild reprimand. "Come now, don't try to hide from me. I was the longest-serving High Matron, not to mention I am still the most respected diplomat on the Galactic Council. *And*," she playfully wagged her finger at the teenager, "I raised dozens of children. I know all the tricks, young lady."

Rin scoffed with a wry smile that slowly faded as she debated her response.

"I'm...I'm scared," she finally admitted, and Matzepo nodded sagely, head bowed as she listened. "*Apparently*, I glow purple when I'm stressed out, and I have whole organ systems I shouldn't...." Rin bit the inside of her cheek, trying to force her tears back where they were supposed to be. "I'm scared, because what happens when whatever's in me comes out all the way?" She forced herself to make eye contact with Matzepo, and the woman smiled sympathetically, reaching to gently cup her face much the way she had with Sprit.

And then she gave an answer Rin wasn't expecting.

"Revel in it, my child," she said earnestly, eyes shining. "You're a gift. Revel in your existence in whatever form it takes." She brushed a few of Rin's tears away before the girl even realized they'd fallen. "And, if that proves too much, go to Lewis."

"Holt?" Rin asked in confusion, clearing her throat a few times. The elder nodded.

"Lewis," she confirmed. "You didn't think the boy was *always* a communications relay with all channels open, did you?" She glanced at the two bathroom curtains. "The pair of them could really learn a lot from each other," she sighed. "I do hope they realize that."

"An everything happens for a reason sort of thing?" Rin asked with more than a hint of bitterness in her voice. Matzepo looked at her kindly.

"In my experience, everything does." She patted the girl's hand and rose. "Now, I have to go coordinate a welcoming meal and make sure my people are on schedule with repairs and caring for your new family. Why don't you relax? You've come a long way, and you've still far to go."

"Not really," Rin muttered as Matzepo headed towards the door.

The woman stopped at her scoffed words and turned back to her.

"What do you mean?"

"I'm staying here," Rin said uncertainly. "Oren said he was leaving me here while they caught the guy trying to kill them."

Matzepo drew herself up to her full height, which wasn't much taller than she already was, instantly indignant.

"We'll see about that, my dear," she said firmly and departed in a huff. "*My* son leaving passengers behind! I raised him better than that."

Rin smiled to herself as the irritated mutters faded down the hall and listened to the sounds of running water in the showers compete like dual rainstorms. It was relaxing in and of itself, and she returned to the balcony, pushing open the unlocked screens and stepping out into the open air. A nice breeze wove through the village, gently stirring the sheer netting enclosing the patio.

"I need to get used to this," she said firmly, sitting in the ebony chair to her left and marveling at the smoothness of the polished wood.

Sahmot stretched out before her, and Rin smiled as she saw a group of kids chasing after a dog-like creature in the dirt-packed streets below, weaving between adults as the taller people carried massive metal beams or expertly drove off-roading vehicles laden with construction materials. Others carried baskets of medical equipment or trays of medications that Rin had no doubt were bound for either *Starlight* or *Horizon* along with those big tents they'd passed on their way in.

The hairs on the back of her neck suddenly stood on end, and a fraction of a second later, she heard the sounds of bare footfalls on tile.

"It's great, isn't it?" Sprit grinned, joining Rin on the balcony and easing herself down into the chair opposite her. "Holt's meditating inside on one of the beds, so I told him we'd stay out here for a bit and give him some space. That okay?"

"Yeah, of course." They were quiet for a few moments, and Rin bit her lip. There was something bothering her, but she wasn't quite sure how to ask about it. All of these Trozerans seemed so open and compassionate, not to mention Sprit had said Matzepo's family adopted her, so they clearly liked interacting with other peoples. So why—

"I can tell you want to say something," Sprit said, eyes closed as she lounged in the chair with her feet kicked up on a small canvas footstool. "Spit it out."

"Why are there only Trozerans here?" Sprit cracked an eye open and looked at her. "I mean, they're all really nice, and you were raised by them so why isn't there more…"

"Variety?" Sprit smirked and closed her eyes again. "There is, just not here. Sahmot's a village, Rin. We have what, three hundred people?" She shrugged. "Really, the only ones who haven't been Trozeran here are the kids Matzepo takes in."

"How'd she find you?"

"Do you remember when I said I was from Ethonius?" Rin nodded. "Well, we had a bloody civil war that ran about seven years. We were *the* societal crisis poster child." Sprit sighed, and an iron curtain dropped behind her eyes. "My parents kept their heads down with it all. And then when I was eight, about five years into the war, they were coming home on a light rail that got hit by a rebel EMP." She mimed a crash with her hands. "Derailed the whole thing. I had no siblings, my extended family had died over the years, so I took care of myself." She gave a wry smirk. "Vanishers make excellent thieves and muggers. I was ruling my neighborhood by the time I was nine, had my territory marked out." Then, she ruefully laughed. "*Then* the Galactic Council sent a force of Peacekeepers in when I was ten, and I picked the wrong officer's pocket."

"Oren," Rin said, slowly smirking. "You picked Oren's pocket."

"I *tried*. Yeah, he wasn't too happy with me," she sighed, shaking her head wryly. "And after that...well, I just couldn't get rid of him. So, here I am." She smiled. "Best thing that's ever happened to me."

"Do you miss them?" Rin asked quietly. "Your parents and family, I mean."

"I do. Sometimes," Sprit admitted. "But I've had thirty-five years with Oren's family, his friends, his crew. Like I said, best thing that's ever happened to me." She reached out and lightly punched Rin's arm. "Who knows? Matzepo might adopt you, too."

"Wouldn't that be something?" Rin deadpanned and looked over the village. "You said 'the kids' Matzepo adopted. How many?"

Sprit's expression clouded, and she crossed her arms, looking forward with the half-human.

"She's fostered dozens until they located extended families, but she's adopted a few—six, I think, but only four were off-worlders. Myself, an Indegloan like Balok, and then one of the Madak People like Lucien. But they were before me, so I only see them on the few occasions we happen to visit Sahmot at the same time."

Rin frowned, adding up the names and coming up one short.

"Wait, you said four." She watched Sprit's arms cross harder over her chest, hands tightening around her upper arm like vices. "That was only three."

"Be careful, commander," Lewis' voice whispered in her mind.

"Go back to meditating, Holt."

"The fourth was her first adopted son," Sprit said once she'd pulled herself back from the link. "He was Alympan, just a few years older than Oren. They were inseparable, even through adulthood."

"Commander," Holt mutely warned, knuckles paling around his knees on the bed just beyond the screen.

A chill ran down Rin's spine despite the balmy breeze and hot sun.

"What happened?"

Sprit looked at her evenly.

"Well, he's spent the last couple days trying to blow us to pieces, so I think that sums it up nicely."

"What?" Rin gaped, and Sprit shrugged. "How did it go *that* wrong? Matzepo—"

"Oh, she's a great mom," Sprit hurried to assure her. "It had nothing to do with Matzepo. Rin, you have to understand. Jon Bled—"

"Commander, might I have a word?"

Rin jumped at Holt's sudden presence in the doorway and twisted in her seat to look at him. He was leaning on the screen's frame to alleviate some of the weight on his leg, and the bruises on his face were purple, turning black at their centers. But what made her feel small was his disapproving stare. Sprit sighed, rolling her eyes.

"Rin, you might want to stay out here." She got up and slammed her shoulder into Holt as she passed, and he stiffened, barely holding back a groan. "This could get ugly," she growled, clearly speaking to her deputy, but Holt ignored her, nodding once to Rin as he apologetically closed the screen behind them. It wasn't enough to block out their conversation.

"Commander, the captain gave us explicit orders."

"She deserves to know what's going on, *lieutenant.* She's just as involved as we are. I'll deal with my brother—"

"Respectfully, ma'am, he made that request as your superior, not your sibling."

"Look who finally grew a spine. Did Jhama knock some courage into you when she used you as a punching bag?"

"I'm not going to respond to childish—"

"Oh, because being passive aggressive is so much more mature!"

"Commander, there are too many variables in play to be so openly discussing our attacker!"

"Oh, good, Lewis. Raise your voice with me." Sprit's voice dripped with spite. "Because that solves *every* problem!"

"Ma'am, I am not trying to raise my voice with you, but you are making it very difficult."

"Oh, and we're back to the link! Whose fault was that again?"

Rin had enough and got up, violently pushing the screens open. Holt was towering over Sprit, the angry woman toe-to-toe with him, and they both went quiet immediately, guiltily frozen in their tense positions. The girl ran past them, fleeing from the room, and the officers listened to her footsteps fade down the halls.

"Dammit," Sprit sighed, uncrossing her arms and resting her hands on her hips. Lewis slowly let his hands unclench at his sides and looked at the ceiling. "Well, we screwed that up."

"Indeed," he said, leveling her with a stare that was nearly as cool as his words, and Sprit looked down as he stiffly turned away and walked off to the prayer room, the beaded curtain rattling in his silent wake.

"I'm sorry," she tried wordlessly offering.

All she got through the link in return was mental static.

"Cheater," she grumbled and dropped face-first into her cot, pulling a pillow over her head. He'd been right, as usual.

Man, guilt sucked.

———————

Rin wasn't sure how long she'd been walking. Well, no, that was a lie. She'd been walking long enough for the sun to start setting, setting the sky on fire with reds and oranges and yellows, even a few shades of pink. She'd wandered aimlessly around the small village the entire time, and at this point she was fairly confident she could navigate it all and never get lost. A few times, she'd climbed up to some parapets and sat down on the edges to watch the repairs on *Starlight* in the distance; the speed with which the Trozerans had patched up the hole in the hull was remarkable. But her view had grown unbearable after an hour due to the heat, so she had gotten up and moved again. Everyone she saw was working, helping with anything from setting up the meal in the communal kitchen to tending to the wounded in one of the larger buildings that must have been their village infirmary. A group of them, she noted with a heavy heart, stood guard at the town hall Matzepo had set aside for the dead.

Rin stayed away from that building, opting instead to linger near the tent at the other end of the village, the one they were setting up for a large meal. And she couldn't stop marveling at the people—how loving and open they were, ready and willing to help anyone who needed it.

But the sun *was* setting, so she decided that she had better return to Matzepo's compound. She smiled as she managed to find it quickly and without getting turned around, and as she started jogging up the steps, Khalo and Arzi exited the home's open door, loosely holding hands.

The two nodded to her with kind smiles that seemed a bit misplaced on the husband's grizzled features, and Rin returned the nod and smile she passed them on the steps only to stop in the foyer. She was suddenly unsure. While she had been exploring Sahmot for the better part of an afternoon, she'd never set foot back in the house. Oh, well. More adventure.

"Hanali'a would be proud," she muttered and set off down the hall.

She spent more time looking at the decorations this time around, losing herself in their beauty and intricacy. Everything had been created with so much thought and love and deliberate intention, and so it was that Rin found herself in an end of the house she wasn't familiar with. But just when she was about to turn back, a pair of voices drifted down the hall that she faintly recognized. Quickly glancing around to make sure no one was around, Rin inched closer to the half open door.

"Oren," Matzepo sighed, gently dabbing at her son's bruised eye with an herb soaked rag. "How many did you lose?"

"Between both attacks?" he asked tiredly. The question hung unanswered between them, and he looked down. "Thirty-six people. We only had a hundred and ten to start with, and that was including families."

Her hand stilled on his cheek.

"Children?" Oren nodded morosely, staring at his lap with unblinking eyes. "How many?" He held up three fingers, unable to speak, and Matzepo quickly pulled him to her so his head rested against her chest.

"They were having a playdate," he said hoarsely. "Their quarters were across from engineering. After the third blast...it depressurized."

She pulled a chair over and sat down in front of her son.

"Oren, *what* is going on?"

"I...mother, it's Jon."

In the hallway, Rin had that same, inexplicable shiver. Jon Bledsoe. It was the name no one wanted anyone to hear or repeat.

"Oh," Matzepo whispered, stricken. "Oh, Oren, no."

"He got to my crew. His ability...he's more powerful now, mother. His control is no longer restrained by time, possibly not even by in-person contact," he explained helplessly. "Omarik and Assora were two of my most promising ensigns, and he just..."

The matron gently squeezed the back of his neck, massaging the tight muscles.

"Does he want anything other than ruin and pain?" Oren shook his head and leaned forward to brace his arms against his knees. "Listen to me. Oren, look at me." She grabbed his shoulders, and he looked up at her, on the verge of tears. "You are stronger than Jon Bledsoe. You are *smarter*. You are *faster*." Her voice was firm and unwavering, her eyes blazing. "You've beaten him before, Oren. You *will* beat him again."

"Mother," he began despairingly, and she shook him hard, her voice taking on a tougher edge—a matron's edge.

"That is the truth! I know it. Hanali'a knows it. We *all* know it. But people are only as strong as their leaders, my son. So, toughen up." She squeezed his shoulders once, gently pulling him into proper posture. "Be strong. Be brave. Show no fear, no desperation." She reached out to tilt his chin up with a tender, yet firm, hand. "And no surrender."

"Yes, Matzepo," he whispered. His voice was soft, deferential.

"Good boy. Talk to your sister if you start to waver."

"Which one?" he asked with a weak smile, and she snorted, sitting on the bed beside him.

"Either one. By the way, Tzo won't be joining us. She's overseeing *Starlight*'s repairs. As for Sprit," she chuckled, "she *married* that poor boy, Lewis?"

Oren weakly mirrored her laughter and nodded.

"Yes, she did, albeit accidentally. Some entertainment came from this mess." She swatted his arm with the corner of her shawl.

"You are *horrible*." She let the moment of levity hang between them for a second more, watching her son smile, before returning to the more pressing topic. Her demeanor grew somber. "What are you going to do about Jon?"

"I don't know," he admitted, and she tried another track.

"What about Rin?"

Rin pressed closer to the wall outside, suddenly worried that the two could see her through the stone and plaster.

"I told you, mother. I want her to stay—"

"She can't stay here, Oren. She can't even stay on *Starlight*," Matzepo interrupted scoldingly, and something broke in Rin's chest. But then she continued. "Not without a purpose. She's lost right now, drowning, but she's so used to the feeling that she doesn't even notice it anymore."

"I...she's not human, mother. We can't let her out of our sight, yet. Not until we figure out her story."

"Her *story?*" Matzepo demanded, shocked and indignant as she stood up, and Rin felt a flash of warmth and gratitude towards her.

"She's half-alien—"

"Her *story* is she's a scared girl from a small world who just figured out the universe is bigger than she ever imagined," the matron lectured.

"Her *story* is that she's about to explore the stars and not as some slave girl living a waking nightmare until the day she dies, no. She'll do it as a free girl with a beautiful family aboard the ship that has made its albeit infamous name taking in people like her. *That's* her story." Oren looked down guiltily, and Matzepo drove her final point home. "All you have to do is teach her how to speak. You have to teach her how to read and write again. It's a new language out here, Oren. But once you do that, I think you'll find she fits right in with the rest of you. She has the fire in her. I saw it the moment I laid eyes on her."

There was a long pause, and Rin held her breath, praying that they weren't heading for the door.

"Now, go," Matzepo finished, patting Oren's knee. "Freshen up for the meal."

She left her son on the bed and fully opened the door to the hall.

Rin was already gone.

CHAPTER 22

Rin ran down the halls, heaving a sigh of relief as she finally found her way back to the guestroom door. But just as she reached for the door-knob, she stopped. Holt had wanted to meditate. Certainly, it'd been several hours, but she didn't know how long his people meditated, and she didn't want to disturb him. Sprit had really gotten under his—

"I can hear you lurking, Miss Cooper," Holt called, and she winced.

"He means get in here, Rin!" Sprit shouted after a few moments, and immediately Holt replied, voice wearing thin.

"Now who is reading whose mind?"

"Holt, you say that all the time."

Rin carefully opened the door with the sneaking suspicion she was about to walk into a warzone. However, she was instead met with a scene of the two officers tidying up their appearances, Holt actually helping his superior lace up the back of her colorful Trozeran dress.

"There you are," Sprit greeted. "We thought you'd fallen off a cliff or something."

"And you were so concerned you went looking for me," Rin returned dryly, taking pride in the small smile that flashed across Holt's face at her words. Sprit gasped in mock affront but quickly smiled and laughed.

"Get over here. Your hair needs tidying up." She waved the girl over and quickly worked on her hair, pulling it from its bun and running her fingers through it. "Holt, grab me a damp washcloth, will you? Our explorer streaked herself orange." As Holt headed for the bathroom, Sprit began braiding Rin's hair and wound it into another bun. "We'll head to the communal tent for dinner once you're presentable." She took the rag from Holt when he returned and passed it off to the girl. "Actually, is it fine if you two meet me there? I want to make sure mother doesn't need help with anything."

"Yep," Rin said with a small smile as she sat on the edge of the bed and started scrubbing the clay dust from her skin.

"Thanks." Sprit quickly hurried from the room, and Rin glanced at Holt.

He'd traded out his dirtied uniform for a pair of slacks that matched the white shirt he'd gotten from *Horizon*. His face didn't look any better if she was being honest, but he didn't look like he was going to fall over anymore. She offered him a small smile like the one she'd given Sprit and turned her focus back to the rag and her skin.

"You should try not to make it a habit, Miss Cooper," he said gently, and she frowned, glancing at him as he rocked slightly on his feet.

"Make what a habit?"

"Eavesdropping on the captain. He's a very private man."

Rin suddenly felt uneasy, guilt twisting her stomach.

"Stop reading my mind," she threw back bitterly, scrubbing away the orange dirt with a vengeance.

"Then stop thinking so loudly, and we'll both be happy," he returned just a note too sharply, and Rin flinched, clenching the rag tightly in her lap. The man suddenly looked ashamed. "I-I'm sorry. I...it has been a long week," he said softly, running a hand through his hair. "It's no excuse for my behavior, but please. I apologize."

Rin slowly finished cleaning herself up and set the folded rag on the bed.

"I understand. I'm sorry, uh, for your loss," she offered. He nodded his thanks as they walked into the hall together. "I-I'm sure you knew some of the people who died. Friends and...yeah," she finished lamely.

"Coworkers? Yes. Friends?" He gently scoffed, the ghost of a rueful smile playing at his lips. "I don't have very many of those. Mercifully, the few I have made it out alive."

"Oh," Rin said and looked down, unsure of what to say next.

"Thank you for your concern, Miss Cooper."

"We should catch up with Sprit," she said, and Holt inwardly winced at the note of discomfort and worry in her voice.

"You needn't be afraid of me, Miss Cooper," he assured her as they exited Matzepo's complex and walked down the stairs to the street. "Like I said, it has been a bad week." They walked in silence for a bit until Rin sensed the man stiffen beside her. "Oh dear." Rin glanced at him and then followed his gaze to the watering trough.

Oh.

Sprit was standing beside one of the massive dokori, running a hand over its rough hide and gently stroking its wet snout. It really did look like a huge water buffalo, and Rin bit her lip. This would be good.

"Commander!" he called, trying to keep his voice low enough that it didn't spook the creature towering over her.

"Oh, hey you two." She smiled at them over her shoulder and gave the beast one last pat on the cheek beneath its gentle eye before joining them. "I see you found me without a problem."

"They seem remarkably docile," Holt commented, still watching the dokori, and Sprit looked back at the animal.

"They are. You should go say hi! Rin and I can wait." She smirked and crossed her arms. "Oh, wait, that's right. Big animals scare you."

"I maintain it's a perfectly reasonable fear to have, commander," he said pointedly and walked ahead of them. "They can trample you."

Sprit snorted, and Rin smirked as the woman's expression softened while she watched the man walk away.

"You know, your mom *really* wants you two to stay together."

"Shut up, Rin."

"Before we begin, I would like to lead us in a moment of silence for our friends and family members who aren't sitting among us to share this meal."

Matzepo's voice carried easily throughout the enormous tent, and Rin glanced at the hundreds of people surrounding her. They were all cross-legged or kneeling on soft cushions and blankets, so their number was disguised, but the human estimated that there were probably a little over three hundred people present. The tables were big to match the tent and low to the ground so people could reach it in their seated positions, and at the head of the table that Rin and the rest of the *Starlight* bridge crew were seated at was Matzepo. She looked different. She was wearing far more gold this time, with clothing and jewelry that was much more intricate and ceremonial. She even had a gold headdress on that formed a crescent moon shape beneath her horns at the back of her neck. Her gray hair was pulled up into an equally elaborate bun above the metal arc, and Rin thought she could see gold filaments threaded into and around the detailed braiding. Her head was currently bowed, and as Rin glanced at her fellow diners, she realized they were all looking down as well and she hurried to follow suit. After a minute, Matzepo looked up.

"Thank you. Traditionally, we would perform a chant of protection and healing next, but we recognize that we have people of many different faith customs here today. So, we will leave these next couple of minutes for you to pray if that is your practice or to peacefully meditate on those present or gone."

Another long silence filled the tent, and Rin shivered at Sprit and Holt's whispers on her left and right respectively. The murmurs of those praying filled the tent with a sound like wind through the reeds, a stillness descending upon them and insulating them from the world outside. She glanced at whoever was opposite her to find herself staring at Lucien and Anthia. The young man's eyes were closed, a faint smile on his face. Lieutenant Acoua just met her gaze with her trademark coldness, and Rin got the distinct impression she didn't believe in a god of any sort.

"And now, relax," Matzepo intoned once the whispering had died away, voice calm and soothing. "Recuperate. You are in good hands here, safe hands. *Starlight* will be repaired by tomorrow. Galaxa has everything under control." She reached down to gently rest her palm against her son's bowed head. "You are all safe here among friends and family." She then spread her arms and smiled warmly at everyone. "Welcome home."

With that, the meal began, and everyone reached for the dish in front of them, lifting the lids free to reveal whatever was underneath.

"You trust me?" Sprit asked, and Rin nodded. "Awesome. Here." She took the girl's plate from her and quickly picked a few dishes for her to try before handing it back. "You'll love it. Don't worry."

"How's your time on Trozer been?" Lucien asked, and Rin looked at him uncertainly. "Oh, uh, sorry…if I'm bothering you—"

"Oh, it's no problem," she assured him. "I've, uh, liked it. I don't know if I could do the weather all the time, but it's nice in short bursts."

"See, I love the weather," he countered with that easy, eager smile of his. "Oh, did you know that the fruit of the thrako trees that they use for their cemeteries is actually a super food?" he asked excitedly, and Rin shook her head, amused at his enthusiasm. He was like a younger Balok. "It's actually incredible. It's got all the nutrients—"

"Luc!" Sprit scolded teasingly. "Let her actually eat the food instead of giving her a nutritional lecture about it."

"I don't mind," Rin tried, but Sprit just held up a hand.

"Cooper, Trinidore over there memorizes a list of facts for each planet he visits. It's his tradition," she explained. "If you get him going, he won't shut up for the rest of dinner. He's like a talking database."

Lucien just laughed.

"But they're such *good* facts, Sprit," he teased back, and she rolled her eyes good-naturedly. "Fine, fine."

"How's your back?" Rin asked, and Lucien grinned, twisting to look over each shoulder and then back at her. "Oh my god," she gaped. "How did they heal you so fast? That only happened yesterday!"

"I thought Balok and Morai were miracle workers, but then I met the Head Healer for Sahmot. I don't know what she did, but she fixed me right up. Her name's Marin Bonemender, and apparently, she's a *legend*."

"What did I tell you? Walking encyclopedia," Sprit baited and ducked with a laugh as Lucien threw a berry at her.

Rin laughed with them and let her gaze shift over to Anthia. She was picking stolidly at her food, methodical and orderly in her eating, and the half-human hesitated.

"Anthia?" The woman looked up at her. "I, uh…I just wanted to say that I'm not mad at you for knocking me out." She raised an eyebrow but said nothing. "I mean, it was a good idea, right?"

"I thought so." Anthia resumed eating.

Rin shifted on her knees. That'd gone about as well as expected.

"How's Avery?" Sprit asked around a mouthful of food.

"His hands are mostly healed," Anthia replied and jutted her chin at the other end of the table. "He's sitting with Balok and the other healers." A quick glance showed the engineer sitting over where his sister had indicated, in the middle of telling what seemed like an animated story.

"What about his shoulder?" Holt asked in concern. "He must have hurt it when he caught me."

Rin tuned them out as they continued talking and looked to the head of their table where Oren was sitting. Like Sprit, he'd chosen to forgo his uniform for native clothing like Khalo's. His spouses sat on either side of him, and as Rin watched, several little kids ran up to talk to him, holding onto his arms with wide eyes and eager expressions. Rin had the sneaking suspicion that they were asking about the stars, and Arzi smiled softly to herself, her hand resting on her stomach as she watched them. Khalo was grinning at the entire scene, and this time the smile seemed to fit the giant of a man perfectly. Maybe it was the warmer lantern light.

Meanwhile, Matzepo flitted from table to table, greeting some people and comforting others who needed it as she went. Rin wasn't sure if the woman was even planning on eating tonight or if she was just going to play host the whole time. The matron smiled kindly at Rin each time she passed, letting her hand run across the girl's shoulders as she went, and Rin was struck by the sudden feeling that the mother knew she'd been in the hallway during her conversation with Oren. After watching Matzepo for a bit, Rin tuned back in to the talking around her and smiled, easily rejoining the fray.

Throughout the evening, the matron continued to pass Rin with soft touches and equally kind smiles, and Sprit continued to introduce her to new and different foods while Lucien rattled off facts almost faster than Rin could keep up. It was chaotic, noisy, and perfect, and she glanced at Holt who'd so far been fairly quiet. He didn't return the look.

After two hours of dining and talking, Matzepo walked back to the head of the table and, with Oren's help, climbed up onto the lowered surface.

"If I could have your attention, please!" she called. The room quieted. "Thank you all. The meal has now concluded, but we have bonfires outside if you'd like to continue socializing. However, we won't scold you too much if you decide to retire instead. We know we're only fun in small doses for some people."

There was a ripple of laughter, and she dismounted the table, taking Arzi's hand as she stepped down.

People started moving, and Sprit stood up, pulling Rin with her.

"Come on. I want you front and center for this." She beckoned for Lucien to join them as they headed for an exit, and Rin snagged the back of Holt's shirt to pull him along, as well. "You, too, ensign. You couldn't shut up during dinner about Trozeran music."

"Awesome!" the young man grinned and slid under the table to join them on the other side, bouncing with excitement. "It's actually very similar to a lot of traditional, interactive chants that my people do, but I have to say Trozerans are better at harmonizing than the Madak—"

Rin reflected with a small smile that if she'd been raised here among the stars, she might've ended up a lot like the helmsman. As soon as they left the tent, she was hit with a front of cool air, and she looked up at the crystal-clear sky and yellow moon in wonder. It was like seeing the stars on a clear night in Montana, but tenfold in clarity and detail.

"Miss Cooper?" Holt asked, and Rin glanced at him as he gestured to her ears. "Music is best appreciated in its native tongue. If you'd like, I can turn off the translator function."

She turned to Sprit to check if he was right only to see Lucien nodding emphatically, and she laughed.

"Lucien says I should, so I guess I have to," she smiled and turned her head so Holt could reach her implants. Instead, though, he gently took her hand and guided it up to her ear.

"Do you feel the switch?" Rin nodded. "Just pull it down to turn the translator function off and push it back up to turn it on." She felt the small piece of metal click into place. "Dio vi povasdmi?"

"Uh…" Rin began uncertainly, and Sprit tapped her shoulder.

"Can you understand?" she said in broken, accented English.

"You, but not him," Rin said, pointing to Holt, and Lucien gave her a thumbs-up with a broad smile.

"I'll translate for you," the ensign said brightly and pulled her over to the bonfire where Oren and his family were gathered. "I learned English off Daniel's database, and then Avery helped me refine it," he explained as they sat on a felled tree trunk, Sprit taking Rin's other side. Holt remained standing in the shadows behind them. "It's difficult, but not the hardest language I've seen."

"Oh? And how many do you know?" she asked, joking, but then he responded.

"Right now? Seven. But I'm learning an eighth."

Rin gaped.

"How old are you, again?"

"I turned twenty last month," he said proudly and suddenly sat up straighter. "Shh! They're starting."

Sprit watched with a subconscious smile on her lips as the musicians gathered around the fire with them slowly mesmerized Rin. A few were using rattles made of hollowed and dried out dokori hooves; a couple others used flat hide drums. The two instruments started soft, like a distant rumble and the faint sound of rain on tin roofs. And then, after a few moments, the singing started, led by one of Matzepo's guards.

It was rhythmic, lyrical, and once he finished his line, the gathered Trozerans replied with their own verse, harmonizing perfectly with each other just as Lucien had said they would. The process repeated, drums and rattles punctuating certain moments but leaving most of the night air to the melody of burning, crackling wood and unaccompanied voices. There was a sharpness to Trozeran with a rolling smoothness beneath it all that tempered the occasionally shriller vowels, and while it was an unfamiliar language, Rin swore she knew the story they were telling.

The kids returned, this time with bowls of chalky paint and escorted by adults she assumed were their parents. Oren just grinned, laughed, and presented his arm to them, watching with loving eyes as they eagerly drew patterns on his skin. A few tottered over to Khalo and Arzi, and both acquiesced to their administrations, one child filling in Khalo's claw mark scars with yellow paint while her brother decorated Arzi's pregnant belly in green and blue handprints. A faint scent of incense, eucalyptus, and sage filled the air, and Rin laughed as Matzepo joined the fray and playfully smeared her son's face with a sloppy purple handprint much to his mock dismay and genuine surprise. But then the matron knelt beside the child she'd taken the paint from and whispered something.

Oh, no.

Rin stiffened as the little girl jogged over to where she was sitting and, laughing with the carefree nature of the child she was, pressed her purple-covered palm against Rin's broad forehead, leaving a large, lop-sided circle behind. She giggled lightly again and ran back to where Oren was sitting on wobbly legs. And as he picked up the girl and held her in her lap, Rin found she couldn't breathe.

"Rin?" Lucien asked worriedly as the human began shaking. Quickly, he switched back to common speak. "Oila, Sprit?" he called, reaching for Rin's ears and turning the translator on. "Something's wro—"

"I have to go," Rin said in a rush and quickly got up, hurrying across the bonfire circle and weaving through the singers and dancers to get back to Matzepo's complex.

Beside her son and his family, Matzepo frowned and quickly gathered her skirts in her hands.

"Rin!" Sprit called, starting after her, but her mother intercepted her.

"Stay. I will find her," she said firmly and set off after the fleeing girl.

Sprit reluctantly returned to where Lucien was waiting, concerned, and patted his shoulder.

"She'll be fine," she told him, and in the shadows Holt sensed her lie.

———

Matzepo beat the girl back to the complex despite her head start, and the woman thanked the backdoor for its existence for not the first or last time. Taking the route that she assumed the girl was, Rin would be back in a few minutes, so Matzepo took the time to start a fire in the massive hearth and string up her indigo hammock before it. She sat down and arranged her skirts before folding her hands in her lap and staring at the front door. Rin would be coming through any moment....

———

Rin ran up the stairs to the front door and quickly hurried through the foyer, wincing as she belatedly thought of the clay she was tracking across the floor. But just as she stopped and knelt to pull her shoes off, the hair on the back of her neck stood on end, and she turned around.

"Hello, Rin," Matzepo greeted with an apologetic smile, the hearth crackling with warmth and light behind her. The purple dye was smeared across half the girl's face now, and the matron had no doubt that she'd tried to wipe it away. She sighed and patted the hammock beside her. "Could I ask you to join me for a little? You don't have to."

Rin slowly joined her, and Matzepo sighed again. Neither said anything for a long while until the elder gently held her hand.

"You can trust yourself, you know?" she began, and Rin felt tears well in her eyes. "You can trust yourself—*all* of yourself. Even the alien parts." Rin turned to look at the matron, the dyed half of her face illuminated by the flames. Those eyes…Matzepo suppressed a shiver.

She knew those eyes.

"You are in control. Your father's genes, whoever he is, do not get to take that from you," she said firmly, reaching out and gently wiping away the paint stroke by stroke with her shawl. "Tomorrow, you're going back to the stars. And I want you to promise me you'll explore. You'll run. You'll climb every tree, venture into every cavern. Take note of every alien thing you see. Revel in it, child." She wiped the last of the purple from Rin's face and nodded once, satisfied with her work. "Because it's not alien anymore. It's yours, Rin."

"Yes, ma'am," Rin said softly, but Matzepo raised a warning finger at her. "Uh, I mean Matzepo."

"Good girl." She gently took Rin's head in her hands and kissed her forehead. "Off to bed with you. I'll let your friends know you're alright."

"Thank you," Rin whispered and slid off the hammock.

Matzepo watched her go and smiled as Rin stopped and pulled her dirty shoes off before vanishing into the dark hall.

But still that unease remained. She knew those eyes.

In her room, Rin walked over to the balcony and briefly stepped out to look down at the village. She could still hear the drums and the singing, could still see the bonfires. But she could also see *Starlight*'s shadow in the distance, moored beside *Horizon*, and she could see the sparks flying from her hull as the final touches were put on her damaged exterior. She could see the town hall where the dead were permanently resting. The shrill laughter of children drew her attention back to the bonfires and the tent where they'd shared a meal together.

There was something ugly coiled in her gut, waiting. Something dark had brought them here, and as she glanced at the stars she heard Hanali'a's words from what felt like months ago but was really only a couple days past.

"The stars may be beautiful, but monsters lurk between them."

Rin went to bed.

———————

Matzepo rejoined her people, nodding and hugging those who approached, but her intended target wasn't in the firelight or the festive groups of people. He was standing in the shadows a few feet outside the bonfire rings, and she shook her head as she walked over to him. *How typical.* Holt saw her coming and politely inclined his head, slightly bowing. She returned the gestures and then promptly got to business.

"What are your intentions with my daughter?"

"None, nothing, ma'am. Matzepo," Holt said, stammering in his effort to react to her intimidating tone. "I assure you, it was an accid—"

"At ease, lieutenant," she laughed, and Holt suppressed the urge to walk away. So, this was who Sprit got her humor from. "How are you?"

"Ma'am?" he asked, turned about by her sudden sincerity.

"I know it's been a long week," she said, "and my daughter is a handful even without sharing a mind."

Holt faintly smiled and scoffed.

"Is it that obvious, ma'am?"

"Come," she said sympathetically, pointing toward the mountain that towered above them. "Let me set you up with the Priestess' acolytes. I'm sure they'd open a room for you to meditate in properly—"

"Oh, ma'am," Holt interjected uncomfortably, "I couldn't intrude on your Priestess."

"You're my son-in-law, aren't you?" she asked playfully. "It wouldn't be intruding." When he still hesitated, she relented. "What do you need?"

Holt hesitated.

"Might I have a quiet place to pray?" he finally asked. "If I could use a place that is sacred or respected ground—"

"Say no more," Matzepo interrupted, waving her hand. "You can use my family's thrako tree."

"Ma'am, I couldn't—"

"My mother would love to hear your prayers, Lewis, or at least feel your spiritual presence," she assured him, touching his elbow with fleeting, gentle fingertips. "And if you'd rather have privacy, she'll leave you alone."

"I..." His protest died in his throat as he took in her sincere, yet set expression. He wasn't getting out of this offer. "Thank you, ma'am."

"You'll need incense and five candles, yes?" she asked as they walked off into the night. "I'm sure the crash destroyed yours."

"If it's no trouble—"

"No trouble at all, Lewis," she promised him and reached into the large pockets hidden in the folds of her skirt to produce the materials wrapped in a napkin. "I thought you'd need to pray, so I took the liberty of grabbing the supplies when I went after Rin." She passed them off to him. "I hope you don't find me presumptuous."

"Thank you, ma'am. Is she okay?"

Matzepo considered him in the yellow moonlight as they reached the path to the thrako trees, pebbles and dried flowers crunching underfoot.

"She will be. She got the short end of the stick with her family, but she'll be okay."

"Ma'am?"

"I won't say anything until the universe deems it time to confirm my theory." She looked somberly at her companion. "The eyes, Lewis. You can always tell someone's parentage through the eyes. Remember that."

"Yes, ma'am."

They came up before one of the biggest trees, and Matzepo stopped.

"This is where I leave you, my child. May you find peace." She bowed to him and unhurriedly made her way back towards the gathering.

Holt respectfully bowed to the giant of a tree before approaching and stepped around its gnarled roots until he was right against it. These were Trozeran graveyards. Each tree marked a family's lineage, and he closed his eyes as he realized he was standing over bodies and ashes of Oren's entire family. He quickly knelt and muttered a brief prayer for the tree's spirits to forgive him for his trespass. He opened the napkin bundle next, lighting each candle and assembling them in an arc in front of him. In the soft glow of lit wicks, he could see part of the silvery trunk before him. It was filled with paintings and carvings that Holt knew commemorated each new burial, told the story of the person being added to its roots. The funeral ceremonies were beautiful, he knew, and he looked up to where the trunk vanished into the night sky. He could see in his mind's eye the ropes and platforms that the children played in and the caretakers used to tend to the giants, and he turned his focus back to the burning candles.

He centered the incense in front of him and quickly spread out the napkin where he'd be kneeling. Once his setup was complete, he knelt on the fabric and bowed over the incense, hands flat on the earth beneath him. And then he started speaking, his voice low and subservient.

"Ama'hare ohn," he began. "Ama'hare aroh daretsk ande'oh. Sarame Ama'hare kalo oshem shantaloh. Ama'hare ran. Ama'hare ohn." He bit his lip before finishing. "Ama'hare aroh daretsk ande'oh."

He waited five seconds before sitting up, selecting one of the incense sticks, lighting it in the left-most wick, and pressing it into the ground behind that candle. One down, four to go.

He bowed again.

The Creator is just. The Creator has a plan for each of us. Celebrate the Creator with the whole of the spirit. The Creator is kind. The Creator is just.

The Creator has a plan for each of us.

———————

Sprit walked over to meet Matzepo where she was returning from the thrako trees, but before she could say anything, her mother grabbed her arm and pulled her aside.

"Mother, what is it?"

"Be gentle with him," she ordered in a reprimanding tone, and Sprit looked at her blankly. "Lewis," she elaborated as though it should be obvious, and Sprit groaned as her whole posture slumped.

"Mother, I'm *not* staying with him. It was accidental, nonconsensual," she whined in exasperation. "We're dissolving the bond as soon as it matures."

"Ah. I see," the old woman said, displeased, and Sprit rolled her eyes. "*Matzepo.*"

"The universe works in peculiar ways, my child," she warned, holding her hands defensively at her shoulders. "That's all I'm saying."

"I'll bear that in mind," she said dryly, and her mother's disapproval deepened at her lack of faith. "Anyways, is Rin okay?"

"Yes, she's fine. And Mara is sleeping in Khalo and Arzi's room, not that you asked about her." Sprit winced, and Matzepo's voice softened. "Everyone's okay."

"Good. Are you coming back?" Sprit asked, jerking a thumb over her shoulder to the bonfires. "Still plenty of people awake."

"Soon. There's one more person I have to see."

———————

Matzepo purposefully entered the back room of *Horizon*'s infirmary, brushing the beads out of her way with a sharp flick of the wrist, and Morai looked up in surprise.

"Matron. I-I wasn't expecting you."

"I didn't send word ahead, Morai," she said as she walked to the suspension tank and looked down at its occupant. "Relax."

"She's stable, Matron. We're just keeping her sedated right now so she finishes healing, but we'll wake her up tomorrow."

"Good." She looked up at the young healer and smiled. "You did a very good job, Morai. You have my gratitude."

"Thank you, Matron. I'll give you two a moment."

"My thanks." She waited until they were alone before grabbing the tank's edge with weathered hands. "Hello, Kowah'tlanti'omkatua-naloa. Gotten ourselves into a bit of a fix, haven't we?" Hanali'a continued to sleep on. "It's good you're waking up soon, old friend. My son...he's in another mess. Jon's back." Her voice took on a dark current, and her knuckles paled around the brass rim. "And I need you to blind the bastard's other eye. I don't care if he was my son. He's beyond redemption now." She swallowed hard and looked down. These decisions—she hadn't made a call like this for over a decade. "You know Oren has a soft spot for him, even now." She leaned over the vat, the aromas of herbal water overwhelming her, and she lowered her voice. "You and I aren't as forgiving. He needs you for this, Hanali'a. So when you wake up, pull no punches."

The beaded curtain rattled with someone's entrance, and she looked up to see Tzo.

"Matron," her daughter formally greeted, standing at attention, and Matzepo mirrored her stance

"Runner. Report."

"*Starlight* should be repaired by midday tomorrow. Capital provided its best when they heard Galaxa was the one who needed help."

"Good." Matzepo looked down at Hanali'a, and Tzo noted with some concern the furrow in her mother's brow. That was never a good sign. "He'll need to move on as fast as he can."

"Yes, Matron," Tzo agreed softly, and Matzepo looked up at her.

"You're a good girl, Tzo," she said, suddenly tired. "You know that, right?"

"Yes, mother, of course," Tzo replied, confused. "Are you alright?"

Matzepo beckoned for her to come over and enveloped her in a tight hug. The old woman was suddenly very unsure about everything.

"I'm worried about Oren. He's got a storm chasing after him."

"I know, mother." Her eldest child slowly pulled away. "I'll see if we can speed up repairs."

"Thank you, my daughter." Matzepo watched her leave and then looked back to Hanali'a. She reached into the lukewarm fluid and seized the giant's wrist. "Jon is to be caught dead or alive, Han," she said in the buzzing silence of the infirmary, and she could have sworn the first officer flinched in her sleeping state. "My personal preference is dead."

Matzepo withdrew her arm and left without a backwards glance, trailing water behind her.

CHAPTER 23

Rin watched the water swirl around her feet and down the drain as the showerhead above her continued to pelt her skin with warm droplets. She was the first one in her room awake. Holt had come back late last night, smelling like incense and clay earth. Sprit had returned even later, waking Rin up by accident when she climbed into their shared bed. But the upside to her roommates returning at the hours they had was Rin had woken first, rising with the sun as it filtered through the balcony screens she'd left open the night before. There'd been a pair of pants and a tunic folded on the ground on her side of the bed that she'd assumed were for her, so she'd taken them and headed to the bathroom for a shower. Sprit had been asleep in her usual sprawled fashion. Holt, she'd noted amusedly as she passed, was curled in the fetal position around a spare pillow, his battered face hidden beneath the corner of the sheets.

So it was that she found herself in the shower, listening to the sound of the water and imagining it was rain while the chirps of whatever bird-lizard hybrid creatures Sahmot had filtered through the window above her. Her skin was still crawling from the sight of the purple taint to the first burst of water that had run over her, and she closed her eyes, tilting her head back so the falling water struck her upturned face. Last night had been intense, to say the least.

Reluctantly, she turned off the water and stepped out of the shower. She thought she'd heard someone moving around in the main room, and if it was both officers, then freeing up the shower was the polite thing to do. She donned the dark green pants and tunic and returned to the bedroom, braiding her hair over her shoulder as she went.

"Morning," she greeted, and Holt looked up as she passed by on her way to the balcony.

"Good morning, Miss Cooper. I trust you slept well?"

"I did." She paused at the foot of her and Sprit's bed and looked over the still-sleeping security officer. "Should I wake her up?"

"I'll do it, Miss Cooper," he sighed. "She is not what you would call a morning person."

Sprit groaned warningly into her pillow and pulled it over her head.

"You were the one who stayed out late," Rin said and continued out to the balcony, taking her place in the chair she'd used yesterday. "Do you know how *Starlight's* doing?" she called over her shoulder, and Holt joined her on the verandah.

"Tzo's work crews completed repairs an hour ago. They're running tests now with the heads of departments to make sure everything is functioning as it should." He turned back to Sprit's bed. "Commander, do you want me to go in your place?" Sprit gave him a thumbs-up without moving from her prone state. "I take my leave then, Miss Cooper."

"See you, Holt." She looked back at the village and smirked as she heard him try to rouse his superior.

"Commander, might I suggest you get ready in case we need you for anything on *Starlight?*"

"Do your job right, and you won't need me," she grumbled and lifted her head from the mattress once she heard the door close. "Ugh, why is he right?" She pushed herself out of bed and sleepily walked over to Rin, rubbing at her eyes. "It's cooler than normal," she yawned.

"Yeah," Rin said absently. "The breeze is nice."

"Have you eaten, yet?" Rin shook her head, and Sprit started walking away. "Let me shower first, and we'll go find food."

Rin absently listened to the shower running and took in how quiet and sleepy the village seemed after the activity and noise of yesterday. It was like everyone was finally slowing down and taking a breath. But before she could appreciate the new atmosphere for very long, somebody else knocked on the door.

"Come in!" she called, twisting around in her chair and looking to the doorway through the open screens. "Captain Runner," she stammered as the woman walked in. "I didn't—are you looking for Sprit, because she's in the shower," Rin began, getting up and meeting Tzo in the middle of the room.

"No, I'm actually looking for you," she said with a look of pity in her eyes that vanished before Rin could be sure it had really been there. "My brother wants to speak with you. He's in the foyer." She stepped back and nodded her head towards the door. "If you'd like to follow me..."

————————

This wasn't going to be fun, and Oren knew it. It certainly didn't help that he knew his mother was going over paperwork in the next room, judging him beside the hearth with her every pen stroke. But it was for the best; he firmly believed that. Besides, it was only fair to the girl. She deserved a nice, quiet place to settle down with a loving support network.

"Miss Cooper," he greeted as he saw Rin approaching down the hall with Tzo at her heels. "How was your evening?"

"I had fun," Rin said after a moment of hesitation, her voice laced with wariness. "Everyone—well, everything, honestly—was really nice."

"Good, that's good. Rin, why don't we sit down?" he tried, but the girl crossed her arms over her chest, avoiding eye contact.

"I'd rather stay standing," she said softly, and in the other room, Matzepo drew a harder line than usual through an item on her list.

"Rin, I'm sorry, but I'm going to have to leave you here in Sahmot." Rin nodded tightly, biting the inside of her cheek hard enough that her mouth turned coppery. "It would be irresponsible of me to keep civilians on *Starlight* right now. Matzepo will take care of you."

"Is this because of Jon Bledsoe?" she asked suddenly, and Oren and Tzo exchanged a look. Rin recalled the light in Matzepo's eyes yesterday as she peered into her face, and her skin crawled again. "Or is it because I'm half-human?"

"It's both, Rin," he said apologetically. "You're a wild card in a high stakes game of cat and mouse, and you may be harmless. I hope to the ancestors you're harmless. I really do. But I've got a bad feeling you're not."

"I see," Rin heard herself say, and a chill ran down her spine at the coldness of her own voice. In the next room, Matzepo squeezed her eyes shut, pained. She knew that tone, too, the same way she knew those eyes.

"So, I'm going to have to ask you to stay here." Oren paused, taking in the half-human's statue-like stance, and sighed. "I'm sorry, Rin. Truly. But you're in good hands here. I promise." He turned and left out the front door without another word, and Tzo bit her tongue.

Rin's ears were ringing. No, they weren't ringing. It was that damn electronic buzz they kept telling her she'd get used to. They were leaving her. Holt had told her this would happen, but Oren thought she was dangerous, too. Once again, she thought about Matzepo's concern when the woman looked at her too closely, and in an instant, Rin felt very small. Without another word, she turned and left.

"Cooper," Tzo tried, but the girl just silently walked past her towards her room.

Beside the hearth, Matzepo set her work down and picked up the tray of food and tea at her feet. Her children could be so stupidly tactless.

The elder walked into the guest room and quickly spotted Rin sitting out on the balcony. She was too quiet, and Matzepo sighed as she joined the girl on the verandah. She could feel it simmering under Rin's skin, the anger and the betrayal, and she took a deep breath. It didn't do for people of Rin's bloodline to stay angry and hurt. She sat down in the other chair and offered the girl some tea.

Rin eyed the clay cup and silently accepted it.

"How are you doing, Rin?" she asked softly, but before the teenager could even begin figuring out an answer, Tzo knocked on the threshold. "Tzo, not now. I'm trying to undo some of the damage you and your—"

"Matron," she interrupted. "Hanali'a is awake."

"It's ok." Matzepo looked at Rin and felt hope at the sincere warmth in the girl's dark, almond-shaped eyes. "Say hi to Han for me."

The woman briefly touched the girl's cheek in thanks and left just as Sprit exited the bathroom, pulling her wet hair into a ponytail.

"Did I miss something?" she asked, nonplussed, and Rin scoffed.

When Matzepo returned to *Horizon*'s infirmary, she found Hanali'a sitting on one of the beds in the main room, talking with Oren. As soon as the first officer saw her, Hanali'a stood and bowed, ignoring Balok's disapproving hisses and gestures for her to sit back down.

"Matron."

The leader reached up, resting her open hand on Hanali'a's scabbed and healing skull. The giant alien closed her translucent lids and leaned her weight against her old friend's extended arm with a contented sigh.

"Are you well?" Matzepo asked, pulling back, and Hanali'a sat down.

"I should be able to return to my post soon." Balok cleared his throat pointedly, and she amended her statement. "With Doctor Balok's medical assistance, of course."

"Good, old friend." The Trozeran warmly grasped Hanali'a's arm. "I am glad. Oren, might I have a moment with her?"

"Of course. Balok, let's go."

"Oh, alright," the doctor reluctantly grumbled as he followed Oren. "But Hanali'a, please, for my sake, don't overexert yourself. I would much rather see you on *Starlight*'s bridge instead of in my medbay."

"Of course, doctor," Hanali'a said easily and waited until the two men left before allowing her pleasant demeanor to turn dark and somber. She looked back to Matzepo and found her expression mirrored in the aged face before her. "Oren told me what I've missed."

"Did you hear me last night?" Han nodded. "If my son wavers…"

"I will do what has to be done to protect my ship, my crew, and any innocents," Hanali'a said solemnly. "Nothing more."

"And nothing less," Matzepo added.

Her friend considered her a moment.

"And nothing less," she finally confirmed.

"I'm glad we're in agreement." Matzepo turned to leave, but stopped. "One other thing. The half-human, Rin—she must stay with you."

"With us?" Hanali'a echoed curiously. "Why?"

"Rin is part of something powerful, Hanali'a. There is nowhere better for her to be when it all falls into place than with you. You *know* this."

Hanali'a stared at her evenly before speaking.

"Oren won't change his mind," she warned.

Matzepo simply shrugged.

"Then, we'll change it for him."

The old women held each other's determined gaze for a long time until Han chuckled.

"I have missed you, Matron," she said, laying special weight on the title, and Matzepo smirked.

"I've missed me, too," she confessed. "It's been a long time since I've played this game. Now, get ready, old friend. *Starlight* departs soon."

"I will."

———

Sprit sighed as she dropped into the chair beside Rin, arms braced against her knees.

"I know this sucks," she began, and Rin scoffed. "But I promise we'll come back. I mean, we sort of have to; we're in charge of relocating you. But with what's going on with Jon, we've got to put everything else on hold."

"Because I'm a dangerous wildcard," Rin muttered bitterly.

"Did Oren call you that?" Sprit demanded, anger creeping through her voice, and Rin nodded. "Oh, I'll kill him," she growled and dragged her hands over her face. "Okay…look, Rin, I have to go. But I promise we'll be back. Here." She went back inside and returned a few moments later with a strip of paper. "This is my personal channel frequency so you can keep tabs on us." Rin accepted it with a wan smile, turning the thick material over and over in her fingers. "Can I get a hug before I'm off to chase a psycho through the stars?"

"I think he's the one chasing you," she returned but got up anyways, and Sprit rolled her eyes as she wrapped the girl in a hug almost as tight as Matzepo's. It helped, Rin noted as Sprit buried her face in her shoulder, that the two were the same height. Maybe she could pretend she was hugging Sprit each time she hugged Matzepo. "Keep out of trouble."

"I'll try."

Sprit pulled back and held up Rin's hand by the wrist, waving the paper in the girl's face.

"Any time, alright? I'm there, no matter the hour." Rin nodded, and the security chief sighed. "Okay, I need to go." She ruffled the half-human's hair and then quickly left the room, forcing herself not to look back. There was no need to make this harder on either of them.

Rin carefully tucked the paper slip into her pocket and returned to her chair on the balcony. Something unpleasant pulled at her chest and bubbled in her stomach, dark and oily. She watched the warming sky, the indigos and oranges as the sun finally breached the mountains in the distance and reflected off the dusty *Starlight* below.

Sprit's countdown started now.

"Are we good to go?" Sprit asked grumpily as she approached Holt at the foot of *Starlight*'s loading ramp.

"All systems are in order, ma'am," he answered and hesitated. "I heard what the captain said to Miss Cooper—"

"I'm dealing with him, Holt," she growled, crossing her arms as she stepped back to allow other crewmembers to board.

"Commander..."

"Hey, guys!" an excited voice interrupted, and the pair turned to see Lucien jogging over, grinning from ear to ear. "So get this, I was talking to Roiz, right? And..." He stopped as he saw the chief's irritated expression and Holt's downturned gaze. "What's wrong?" He did a quick head count and looked around them. "Where's Rin?"

"She's staying here," Sprit muttered, but before Lucien could protest, someone else beat him to it.

"What?" The trio looked to the loading bay ramp as Anthia and Avery walked down to them, the brother gaping. "Did I hear you say Rin was staying?"

"Oren thinks she's dangerous," Sprit explained, her disdain dripping from her words as she scowled.

"I agree," Anthia said simply and instantly drew glares from everyone except Holt. "And there *are* worse places for her to be."

"That's not the point," Avery snapped, but his sister ignored him.

"She's safer here," she pressed.

"Is she?" Sprit countered, hands on her hips, and Holt finally had it.

"Enough." Lucien looked at him in surprise at his firm command, and he continued. "It is not our place to challenge the captain's—"

"Oh, stop it, Lewis!" Sprit threw back, glaring. "You think it's a bad idea, too." She paused and darkly glanced him over. "Even if you're too cowardly to say it."

Lucien gulped in the silence that followed, nervously watching the security officers until finally Holt broke their staring contest and walked away without another word. Sprit resumed her original position of arms crossed over her chest and looked at her three friends, noting their uncomfortable—or in Anthia's case, unimpressed—faces.

"What?" she demanded, and Lucien quickly cleared his throat.

"Absolutely nothing, ma'am," he said a little too enthusiastically.

Sprit eyed them all warningly as she boarded *Starlight*, shaking her head as that mental static filled the space in her mind that now belonged to Holt.

"You're cheating *again*," she scoffed in disbelief but pushed it aside.

Getting angrier with Holt, no matter how appealing, wouldn't do anything for her now. She had to save some of her frustration for her dear brother, and just before she vanished into *Starlight*'s belly, she glared at where her sibling was approaching with Matzepo, Khalo, and Arzi. Holt, she noted, was joining them, and it confused her until she saw the blue-skinned child in her mother's arms. Figures.

"I see you've come to say goodbye," Matzepo greeted, hefting Mara on her hip. Holt bowed shallowly before responding.

"I have, ma'am."

"Holt!" the girl cried, reaching for him, and Lewis gave a rare smile as he took her from the Trozeran's arms.

"I see you're speaking again," he noted, and she giggled. "Be good."

"I will," Mara said dutifully and threw her arms around Holt's neck, seemingly uncaring of the spines that were no doubt digging into her thin skin. "Be good, too."

Holt chuckled softly, the sound heard only by the two of them.

"I will," he promised and reluctantly pulled her free so he could hand her back to Matzepo who accepted her with a warm smile. "And trust Matzepo. She's a good woman."

"I know," Mara said simply. "She's taking me to see momma today."

Holt's eyes clouded with pain.

"Say hello for me." She nodded at his request, clinging to Matzepo's side. "Goodbye, Mara." The girl smiled bashfully as he bowed to her.

"G'bye, Holt."

Matzepo watched as the deputy walked away and then glanced back to where her son was saying goodbye to his spouses and unborn child. Once she was certain the trio was finished, she approached and touched Khalo's arm.

"Could you take Mara, dear? I need to have a word with our boy."

"Of course," Khalo said. The child beamed when she saw who was reaching for her and immediately stretched her hands out to touch his horns once she was in his arms. "Come, Arzi."

His partner took his free arm in hers as they departed, and Matzepo waited until they, too, were out of earshot before turning to her son. She smiled softly and gently guided Oren's head down to press their foreheads together.

"Remember what I told you about a leader and his followers," she whispered and felt him nod. She tightened her grasp around his horns, running her fingers over the broken end in her left hand. "And Jon."

"I know, mother," he murmured, and she pulled him a little closer.

"He is nowhere *near* as strong as you."

"I know, mother," Oren repeated. "But...he's still my brother."

"He *was*." Matzepo pulled back and released him, and her voice took on her professional intonation. "Show him no mercy, Galaxa. For he will show you none."

"Yes, Matron." He slowly backed away, letting his mother's hand fall from his. "Take care of Rin for us until we get back."

"*I* will," she returned pointedly, and for a moment Oren paused. He knew that look in her eye, that dangerously stubborn look. He made it a rule to never trust that look. Reluctantly, he resumed boarding *Starlight*, and Matzepo slowly smiled to herself as her son moved out of view.

She had only a little time left.

––––––––––

"Rin!"

Rin jumped at the sudden call and turned in her chair as Matzepo ran into the guestroom, a heavy leather backpack in her arms. Her jewelry rattled together with a sound like the hollowed hooves from last night, and her bright, eager smile only furthered the girl's confusion.

"Oh, uh, Matzepo. What's—"

"No time, my dear." She threw the bag at the startled girl who barely managed to catch it. "Come." The elder breathlessly beckoned for her to leave. "You'll miss your flight."

Rin's heart suddenly started racing.

"My flight?" she echoed, slow smile spreading across her face.

"Oren changed his mind. You're going with him. Now, come."

Matzepo laughed as the half-human scrambled from her chair.

"Thank you!" she cried, tackling the woman in a hug that set all of her worries at ease. "Oh my god, thank you!"

"Of course, my dear," Matzepo said but quickly pried herself free. "But go on, now. Hurry." She unwound the shawl from her neck and quickly put it over Rin like a headscarf, making sure as much of the girl's face was covered as possible. "Hanali'a is waiting at the bottom of the stairs. She'll escort you aboard."

Rin laughed, still grinning like a kid on Christmas, and ran, finding her way through the house easily this time. Her chest felt ready to burst with excitement, and she laughed again as she ran outside and found, true to Matzepo's word, Hanali'a waiting for her. Not that she could tell it was Hanali'a by her face—like Anthia and Avery she was covered head to toe to protect her from the sun—but her height was unique.

"Hello, Miss Cooper. Ready to go?"

"Yeah. Yeah, let's go."

Beneath her veil, Hanali'a smiled and chuckled at the girl's eagerness. Yes, Matzepo had been right. This girl belonged in the stars, not planet-bound. As they quickly walked along, the first officer put her arm across Rin's bony shoulders to use her as a crutch, and the half-human's stomach filled with butterflies.

"I hope you don't mind me touching you," Hanali'a said between breaths as they passed through Sahmot. "This climate is a little harsh on my recuperating health."

"It's no problem," Rin said quickly, and her butterflies only intensified as *Starlight* slowly drew closer. "You, uh, got better fast."

"I'm told you never doubted I would," the giant returned smoothly, and Rin blushed beneath her headscarf. "Oren greatly appreciated your optimism. Thank you. He has the tendency to get in his head."

"Oh, uh, you're welcome."

They approached the loading ramp, and Hanali'a leaned a little more heavily on the girl's smaller frame as they slowly moved up the incline. The difference between the ship's interior and the air outside was instantly noticeable, and Rin shivered as the hair on her arms stood on end and her breath stuttered. It felt like she'd been dumped in a tub of ice. As soon as they were indoors, Han stopped and gingerly disrobed, revealing the now slightly damaged and stained outfit she'd been wearing when she'd gone through her computer display.

"Thank you for your help, Rin. I greatly appreciated it," she said sincerely, and the girl quickly nodded. "Sprit will be on the bridge for the next seven hours. If you'd like to join her, feel free. I'm sure Oren still wants to keep you under supervision."

Rin scoffed, her elation dying a little.

"Being the menace I am," she joked dryly, and Hanali'a echoed her nearly mirthless chuckle. "I, uh...I will though. Thank you."

"Good. I look forward to seeing you there once I change. It wouldn't be best for morale if I showed up bloody."

Rin smiled as she watched Hanali'a depart. Her pace was still a little stiff, but that didn't make her any less graceful. Rin pulled herself back into the moment, though. The bridge—she had permission go to the bridge, to sit there next to Holt and Sprit, and suddenly she couldn't wait to get to deck two. She pulled the headscarf down about her neck and set off at a jog for the nearest lift, waving to the few people who called her name in greeting. This felt far better than Sahmot had, and she increased her jog to a near sprint.

Might as well get a head start on Matzepo's request for her to run.

"What course heading do we want, sir?" Lucien asked, looking at his captain over his shoulder.

"Anywhere, ensign," he said, still filling out his report. "Just make it somewhere with minimal potential casualties." Lucien hesitated. "What is it, ensign?"

"Well, sir, how about Earth?" He quickly persisted when Oren went to dismiss the idea. "Not past the black site cordon, sir. But that general area is a dead zone."

Oren paused, considering it, and finally shrugged.

"It's actually not a bad idea, ensign. Set a course for black site cordon 001." He resumed writing on his tablet. "But make sure we are nowhere near the actual barrier." The bridge door slid open, and Oren glanced at the newcomers to see Sprit and Holt. "Ship's status?"

"All main systems are online and fully functional," Sprit reported as they took their seats. "But don't put us in any races. Avery's still wrapping up issues in engineering, and we only have level four traveling speed again. But he says we should be back to factory settings in a few days."

"Good. Has everyone boarded?"

"Yes, sir," Holt answered, checking the ship's manifest, and the door opened as Anthia entered the bridge and joined the others at her station. "We are ready to depart at your command."

"Alright. Let's take her up, Ensign Trinidore."

"Yes, sir." Lucien's brow furrowed in concentration as he started the takeoff procedures.

On deck four, Rin smiled to herself as the ship started to tremble around her and the engines changed pitch.

"Weigh anchor," she whispered and gave a dorky smile.

The door to her and Sprit's room opened, and she walked in just far enough to throw the leather backpack on the bed and looked at the window. She could barely see the sky through all the orange dust as they rose towards the waiting galaxy, and she resumed her trek to the bridge.

Oren sat back in his chair with a relieved sigh as they finally broke the atmosphere, and *Starlight* steadied with views of the stars out her windows instead of mountains and clay. He glanced briefly at his officers and for a moment let himself get lost in the feeling of being back in the air. But then he had to let reality settle back in, and he sighed.

"Takeoff went smoothly, sir," Lucien reported. "Permission to start our course for black site cordon 001?"

"Yes, ensign. Traveling speed four."

"Did he say cordon 001?" Sprit whispered to Holt, and her deputy nodded.

"Ensign Trinidore suggested it, ma'am. He had a fair argument," he told her in an equally soft voice as he looked over their internal sensors. "Don't worry, commander. We won't go near Earth."

"We'd better not," she grumbled, crossing her arms and turning to face the rest of the bridge as she continued ranting. With her back turned to Holt, she missed the way he tensed.

"Rin?" he whispered, perplexed, as Sprit distantly carried on her one-sided conversation. "Ma'am, Miss Cooper is here," he said, elbowing her to get her attention. "She's—"

The bridge door hissed open, and Holt inwardly groaned as Oren turned around, clearly expecting Hanali'a.

Instead he found himself staring at a specific half-human he was *positive* they'd just left on the planet in their wake.

"Miss Cooper!" he said harshly, and all eyes turned to the suddenly uncertain human.

"Um…hi?"

CHAPTER 24

"What are you doing here, Miss Cooper?" Oren asked slowly, voice perilously low, and Lucien winced at the hurt note to Rin's voice.

"M-Matzepo said—"

"I *told* her to keep you there," the captain interrupted and got up, walking towards her.

"I—"

Sprit quickly got up and closed the couple steps between her and her friend, gently grabbing her arm.

"Rin, go back to our quarters," she began, but Oren interrupted her.

"No. Come with me," he ordered and looked over Rin's head as the bridge door opened to reveal Hanali'a. She looked decidedly unsurprised that Rin was standing between her and her captain. "Hanali'a."

"Sir," she returned evenly, and a flash of anger ignited his chest.

"Take the chair. I'll talk with you later," he gritted out and waited for her to get out of his way before leaving the bridge. "Sprit, don't think about following us!"

The security chief reluctantly sat back down, and Rin hesitated on the threshold of the bridge.

"Sir, I'm sorry," she tried, but Oren just shouted his order back.

"With me!"

Head down and posture slumped like a kicked puppy, Rin wordlessly followed the captain into the hall and to his quarters. He hit the button on the wall and gestured for her to cross the open threshold first, his expression stony and unreadable. For a moment, he looked like Anthia, and Sprit sank in her chair as the bridge door closed, cutting off their view.

"Oh, he's really pissed off," she whispered, and at his station, Lucien mirrored her shrinking posture.

"Why are you here?" Oren demanded as soon as his quarters' door closed behind them, and Rin looked at him, confused.

"Matzepo said you changed your mind," she said, voice aching with betrayal, and Oren ran his hands over his face in exasperation.

"That's not…" He groaned and looked back at the nervous girl in front of him. "Why are you *here*? With us?"

What's your reason?

And Rin found her only honest answer rising to her lips.

"I don't know," she whispered, and Oren sighed.

"You have to give me an answer, Rin," he said, pinching the bridge of his nose. "Why are you here?"

"I don't know," she repeated, voice rising in pitch and frustration as tears burned her eyes.

"Oh, come on, Cooper—"

"I don't know anything!" Rin screamed, hands clenched at her sides, and startled Oren into silence. "I don't *know* where I am, I don't *know* how any of this works, I don't *know* anyone! I don't know who *I* am for God's sake—I know *nothing! NOTHING!"* She broke off to catch her breath and wiped furiously at her eyes as she cried. "Except you all saved me, and Sprit and Balok are nice, and they like me, and they make me feel at home," she continued, voice shaking, and she laughed in fragile disbelief. "In *space*," she sighed, gesturing at the world around them with shaking hands. "And Holt," she continued with another laugh, "Holt's nice, too, he makes me feel *safe*, a-and Hanali'a and Matzepo…. It's not home, but it's *something*. It's familiar, and I like…I think I could *like* it here."

Oren looked down as she broke off and rallied herself.

"But I can't get shipped off somewhere to be forgotten about! You all brought me out here!" she shouted, pointing at him. *"You* brought me, with your aliens and your black market auctions, and…and if I can't go home, I want to stay. *Please.*"

Her voice broke over that last plea, and Oren looked up at her, filled with shame. When he reached out to touch her arm, she jerked back, crossing her arms and turning her head away.

"You look like someone I once knew for a moment there," he finally said, and Rin slowly looked at him. "He felt betrayed, too. I'm sorry for how calloused I've been. You'd think I'd learn," he sighed and glanced at the ceiling as he chose his next words. "What do you think of me, Rin?"

"You care," she said bluntly. "About your crew, your family."

"You're part of that, Rin," he said, making eye contact. "That's why I wanted to leave you behind. It was safer for you."

"So, what does that mean you think of *me*?" Rin asked as she wiped away her tears, and Oren scoffed with a wry smile.

"I think you're a scared girl from a small world who just figured out the universe is bigger than she ever imagined," he said. She looked down at the familiar words. "I'm sorry you had to discover it this way, if at all." She nodded silently as he started pacing, running his hand over his scars as he moved. "What to do with you," he sighed, and Rin swallowed hard. "You do understand we're *not* a passenger ship, right?" he asked. "We're a defense force, law enforcement. It's not safe here. Certainly not as dangerous as it has been, but *Starlight* is never safe, not completely."

"I understand," she said softly. "I...I know."

"Okay, then," Oren said and gave her a warmer smile. "I suppose we should put a work order in to—" A knock at the door interrupted them, and he held up an apologetic hand. "I'm sorry. Enter," he called, and the door hissed open. "Ensign Ciarul."

"Sir," the young woman replied, walking into the man's quarters and holding a tablet out to him with her other hand behind her back. "Sorry to intrude, but Balok needs you to look over our medical supply levels."

"No worries, ensign," he assured her and took the device, habitually stepping in front of Rin as he did so. "I assume he wants me to restock this as soon as possible?" he asked, looking up from the manifest.

He went still. Very, very still.

"Oh. Oh, ensign," he exhaled, pained and pitying, and Rin frowned at the suddenly resigned slump of his shoulders. "I'm so sorry."

"What's going on?" Rin asked, trying to step around the captain, and he reached back in alarm, blindly trying to keep the girl shielded.

"Rin, stay behind me—"

Too late.

The half-human gasped, reflexively yanking away from Oren's hold and into the ensign's line of sight as she found them both staring down the end of a blaster. The ensign was sweating profusely, the only outward sign of her distress. Her hands were steady as stone, her aim unwavering as she switched the setting from stun to kill.

"Jon Bledsoe sent me," she announced robotically, her words cutting Oren to his core, and he closed his eyes. "I'm going to kill you."

Behind him, Rin couldn't breathe. That panic attack that wasn't a panic attack was rising in her chest, and she choked back a sob.

"No," she breathed, broken plea unheard as bright purple started to glow in spidery filaments deep within her hands, arms, and chest and only grow brighter. "No, no, *please, no.*"

Oren could hear Rin breathing raggedly behind him, and he reached back for her, touching only air. She was spiraling. Oh, *djienn,* her ability—

"He has a message for you," Ciarul continued. "Hello, Ren. This has been a long time coming…"

On the bridge, Holt froze, and Sprit was hit by overwhelming dread.

"Holt?" she asked, touching his arm.

He snapped out of his blanched reverie at the contact, violently shoving away from his post.

"Code silver," he blurted, running into the hall, and it took a fraction of a second to click for the rest of the crew. Sprit went pale and bolted after Holt, heart in her throat as she quickly overtook her deputy.

No. No, don't do this to me—

"Lieutenant Acoua, take the chair!" Hanali'a ordered as she sprinted after the security officers. Anthia purposefully took the captain's seat and sternly pointed a terrified, half-standing Lucien back to his station.

Code silver. Attempt on Oren's life.

"I've taken your crew, your ship, and now I'll…take you…" Ciarul's voice slowly trailed off, and Oren frowned as her eyes widened in bewilderment and fear.

And suddenly, the Trozeran was aware of a bright purple light in his periphery vision. He went numb, stomach plummeting to his feet.

"Rin," he breathed and, dreading what he was about to find behind him, slowly turned around.

Rin was frozen in utter terror, looking down at herself as she took in fast, ragged, gulping breaths. That violet light, that alien *thing*, had left the confines of her inhuman vessels—now swirling and curling in tight tendrils about her body like a caged beast just waiting to be let loose. Her skin crawled like static charge, and she let out a choked sob as she felt the overwhelming urge to scream and run push out against every inch of her skin, like she might burst with it all. No control. She had no control, nothing, just this light consuming her, blinding her, inescapable—

"Oren!" she cried desperately, filled with hysteria as her eyes blazed with the light, and Ciarul swung the blaster to face her instead.

"NO, DON'T!" Oren bellowed, lunging in front of the girl just as the ensign fired.

Rin screamed, throwing her arms up in a defensive 'x', and the purple energy exploded off her in a blinding shockwave. The blaster shot ricocheted back on Ciarul instantly, striking her in the chest just before she was thrown across the room with Oren. Everything caught in Rin's path was utterly destroyed. Furniture flipped, objects shattered, and the captain slammed back-first into the far wall, crumpling to the deck in an unmoving heap.

Rin collapsed and retreated in a frantic scramble along the wall until she backed into a corner against a chair, shivering and sobbing in brutal, hiccupping bursts. She couldn't breathe, couldn't think. She stretched her arms out as much as she could before her, whimpering and jerking each time the incandescent strands sparked off her body like electricity and scorched the plating and walls wherever it made contact. She had to get it away from her, had to keep it *away*, but it just kept getting *closer*—

The room's door opened, and Sprit ran in first, weapon drawn.

"Oh djienn," she gasped, looking at the demolished room as Holt ran in behind her, and her gaze was instantly drawn to the purple glow in the corner of the room. It took her a moment, but she knew the shivering, sobbing teenager in the midst of the chaos. "Rin!"

She sprinted for the girl, and panic seized the girl once more.

No. No, Sprit couldn't come over. She couldn't control this; she'd hurt her, too, she'd *hurt Sprit*—

"NO!" Rin screamed in warning, throwing a hand out to ward Sprit off, to keep her from coming any closer. But instead...

A tendril lashed out from her arm like a whip or a bolt of lightning, striking Sprit full in the chest and blasting her back across the room.

"No!" Rin wailed, sobbing as her friend crashed into a dresser and collapsed just like Oren and Ciarul. "No, I didn't mean to, I'm sorry! I'm *sorry!*"

"Rin," Holt called, holstering his weapon and forcing his voice to remain calm. Hanali'a ran into the room behind him, and he quickly motioned for her to check on the three officers while he tried to talk the hysterical girl down. "What happened?"

"I don't know," Rin sobbed, shaking her head. "I don't *know*. I didn't *mean* to."

"Stay calm," Hanali'a said gently, her hand resting protectively on the unconscious captain's head. "Sprit and Oren are okay, Rin. They're alive and well."

A smaller shockwave rippled off of her, dissipating before it hit either Holt or Hanali'a, and the mind reader's blood went cold as he saw the splintered wood it left in its wake.

"Make it stop!" she begged hoarsely, remembering Matzepo's words from earlier. Lewis. Trust Lewis. "Holt, please, make it *stop!*"

Her plaintive cry drove through his heart like a knife, and he swallowed hard. He knew this pain. He also knew how to make it end.

"Miss Cooper, look at Hanali'a." The girl continued to tremble and sob, and he tried again. "Miss Cooper, *look* at Hanali'a." She jerkily faced the first officer, and Holt took a deep, steadying breath to prepare for what he was about to do. "We will get you to Doctor Balok," he said firmly and carefully pulled his blaster from its holster, making sure it was set to stun and not drawing her attention. "He will be able to help you. We *all* will be able to help you. It'll be okay, Rin."

He quickly aimed and fired.

Rin's gaze flickered back to her friend just in time to see him pull the trigger, and her world went dark in a flare of panic.

Holt stowed his weapon and waited as the purple tendrils instantly retreated to the confines of her vessels once more, but did not fade away. He approached the unconscious girl slowly, gingerly stepping around the debris as he went. This was not good.

Hanali'a adjusted her headset and opened a comm channel.

"Anthia Acoua…lieutenant, send Balok to Oren's quarters. He's alive and non-critical." She finished the call and looked somberly to Holt and Rin. "I see you chose Sprit and Anthia's shoot first approach."

"No," Holt said softly as he knelt beside the half-human and took a risk, picking her up bridal style and holding her close to his chest. "I just did what I wish someone had done for me." He carefully walked through the wreckage, carrying Rin safely above it all, and paused in the threshold. "When the doctor gets here, ma'am, tell Balok I took Rin to the brig." He glanced at the teenager's now torment-free face and tightened his arms around her. "Tell him she finished manifesting."

Holt walked into the hallway, shifting his grip so Rin's head lolled to the side and hid her face against his chest. It was all the privacy he could give her right now. His skin wherever he touched her felt odd, like static charge coating his body, and he painfully closed his eyes as he remembered her voice as she'd begged for help, her face as she'd sobbed and cried. He distantly felt himself shaking and tried to force his grip to relax around her. She wasn't going anywhere. She was safe. He didn't have to hold on quite so tight.

He could see curious crewmates in his peripheral vision—whispering and pointing in shock, intrigue, and concern as he walked by. He ignored them, focusing instead on the weight cradled against him and replaying her fear and pain in his head. She'd called for *him* to make it stop, to help her. He focused on that, held onto that, as he walked into the brig.

"Lieutenant Holt," an ensign greeted, only to stop at the sight of the unconscious, glowing girl in his arms.

"If you could open cell A2, ensign," he said softly, and the on-duty guard quickly opened the glass door so Lewis could walk in. "Thank you. You can leave us." Taking care not to jostle Rin too much, Holt knelt on the padded white floor and gently set her down on her back, arranging her arms and legs so she wouldn't be in any discomfort. "You'll be okay, Rin," he whispered, fetching the blanket in the corner of the room and draping it over the girl's body.

The purple light had faded from her face and hands but not from the rest of her, so Holt reluctantly stood and left the cell, closing and locking the door behind him. Poor girl…he knew what came next in this process. It wouldn't be pleasant for anyone, but especially not Rin.

He walked back out into the brig anteroom, hands clasped behind his back and expression carefully composed, to await the others.

———————

"Holt?"

The deputy quickly turned around, instantly noting the way Oren and Sprit had their arms discretely pressed against their sides and stomachs.

"Captain, commander," he greeted and nodded once to the doctor as he brought up the rear. "I put Rin in cell A2, sir. She should still be sleeping. Are you two alright?"

"As alright as we can be. We'll have a few bruises," Oren grimaced as he pointed Balok through to the cellblock. "Go ahead, doctor. I'll join you shortly."

"Not *we'll* join you shortly?" Sprit asked, and Oren shook his head.

"Let us figure this out first. We'll call you back when we know more about the situation," he said hurriedly, walking backwards as he spoke. "Let it go, Sprit," he warned as he entered the cellblock and the door started closing behind him. "We don't have time to argue about this!"

Holt looked at his bondmate with veiled sympathy as she dejectedly backed away from the now-shut door, and he gently touched her elbow.

"Perhaps you should sit down, commander," he offered quietly. "We don't know how long they'll be, and you hit the dresser with impressive force." Sprit scoffed bitterly but let Holt guide her to the benches before the personal effects lockers.

"What is she, Holt?" she asked, wincing as she sat down. "I've seen a lot in my time, and I've never seen anything like that before."

"Nor have I," he agreed with a sigh, "which makes me almost certain about her heritage."

Sprit looked up at him in cautious intrigue.

"What?"

Holt sat beside her and mirrored her bent posture, forearms braced against his knees as he stared at the wall opposite them.

"I think I'll keep my thoughts to myself for now, ma'am, at least until the doctor and captain have their results." Sprit watched his fingers grind away at his knuckles, her stomach sinking. "False rumors won't do any of us any good at the moment."

"Are there any other kinds of rumors?" she asked in a weak joke as they settled in for the wait. Holt's reply was simple, sure in its veracity.

"Yes."

She joined him in staring at the wall. They said nothing.

Half an hour later, Balok opened the cellblock door and beckoned wordlessly for the security officers to join them. His expression did not bode well.

"I'm afraid we have the results," he said softly as the door closed, and he quickly glanced around for any stray security staff who might've been overlooked. They were alone, save for Oren who was facing Rin's cell, his arms tightly crossed over his chest and gaze unblinking.

Balok handed the genetic profile results over to Sprit, and Holt watched their captain carefully.

"Her unique abilities were her giveaway," the doctor explained. "We were able to run her genetics against Alympan samples, and her markers came back a match." Sprit looked up sharply as Holt looked down. So, he'd been right. But then he suppressed a shiver as he remembered that Matzepo had recognized Rin's parentage, and it all fell into place.

Oh. Oh, no.

"You're sure she's Alympan?" Sprit asked, practically begging for the doctor to give her some kind of reasonable doubt. But Balok nodded.

"I'm afraid so, commander." He was apologetic, voice heavy with the knowledge that the situation was actually much worse.

"What is she?" Holt asked bluntly, crossing his arms to mirror Oren.

"Holt," Sprit scolded, but he cut her off.

"You know what I mean, ma'am. What type of Alympan is she?"

Balok sighed and took the tablet back, glancing at their unconscious friend as he pulled up the records. Oren was still standing there, as silent and still as a statue. It was starting to get unnerving.

"The closest thing I could find in the Alympan Planetary Database was a shield maiden," he explained, pointing to the clearly old artwork on the screen. "It's about as rare as mind control. These are the only depictions of it I could find. Apparently, it hasn't surfaced in modern times."

"Her genes must be old," Sprit mused, taking in the old sketches and paintings of people with purple lightning and force fields around them.

"Ancient," Balok confirmed. "Ancient and from very high class families. I wouldn't be surprised if she's descended from one of the nobles."

"Who are not necessarily high class now," Oren muttered, speaking for the first time since his officers had joined him. His eyes remained fixed on the sleeping girl and her glowing veins, and Holt caught a flash of his captain's thoughts. And he couldn't help himself.

"You are joking, sir," he said with sharp disbelief, and Sprit looked at him in surprise at his uncharacteristically emotional reaction.

"Reading my mind *again*, Lewis?" Oren asked with no small amount of aggravation and half-turned to the man. "We talked about this."

"*Sir,*" Holt said firmly, unspoken demand for answers packed into the single syllable, and the captain relented.

"I'm not kidding, lieutenant, as much as I wished I was," he sighed, exhausted and for once looking his sixty-two years. "I had Balok run the DNA. It's a paternal match."

Holt's composure vanished as he ran his hands back into his hair and turned away, heart and mind racing in tandem.

"Creator," he breathed, and Sprit's eyes widened at his invocation.

"What am I missing?" she asked, now more uneasy than before.

Holt lowered his arms and turned back to her.

"What he's saying commander, is Rin's surname should be Bledsoe, not Cooper." Sprit went still. No, she'd been still before. She felt utterly frozen now. It was a new kind of stillness—that drifting, stunned quiet she felt whenever she got the news somebody died. Holt looked to their captain and continued. "Matzepo suspected."

"I figured," Oren sighed, massaging his temples. "I need to have a long conversation with my mother about what she keeps to herself."

"How?" Sprit interrupted in a hushed whisper. Speaking seemed to break the quiet, now leaving her with the urge to move constantly, and her skin crawled as her gut churned. She began pacing. "How could *he* be her dad?"

"He must've hid on Earth," Balok explained. "All things considered, he looks human. He would've blended perfectly with the locals."

"That's one way to put it," Sprit muttered darkly, and Balok gaped at the lewd insinuation.

"Sprit!" he scolded, and she instantly pointed at Holt.

"He was thinking it, too! Besides, Rin exists, so clearly that's what he was doing, doctor."

"Enough," Oren interrupted just as Holt began to protest Sprit's accusation, and the captain pointed at Rin. "What's coming off her?"

"It's some kind of energy," Balok answered, joining Oren at her cell. "But what it is exactly, I have no idea." The eagerness the doctor usually displayed in the face of a mystery was nowhere to be found.

"That's not comforting, Balok."

"Trust me, captain, it's not to me, either," he replied with mutual unease. "All I can tell is that it's reflexively tied to her adrenaline levels at the moment." He bit his lip worryingly. "I don't know if she can control it," he admitted. "If she were full-blooded Alympan, we'd know she'd be able to. But as half...." He trailed off, and Holt looked to him.

"If she wants to survive this, she is going to have to," he said simply, and Sprit looked down as he wordlessly challenged her to contradict him. "Alympans burn themselves out from the inside with unchecked abilities. For lack of a better and less crude comparison, Miss Cooper is a walking time bomb only she can diffuse."

"Don't you mean Miss Bledsoe?" Oren murmured under his breath, and Holt bit his tongue.

"Given Jon left Rin's mother with a brain aneurysm and an utter lack of executive function, I doubt she'd appreciate being called a Bledsoe," Balok said disapprovingly, casting the captain a baleful eye, and Lewis heaved an internal sigh of relief that the doctor had been thinking along the same lines as he had. "She's a Cooper until she says otherwise." He held up his tablet. "I'll return to medbay to look this over more closely now, if you don't mind."

"She's still a Bledsoe, too," Oren said once the doctor left and shook his head as Rin began waking. The tendrils started rising from her skin once more, and he crossed his arms a little tighter. "I need you two to leave."

"What?" Sprit demanded, and Holt was quick on her heels.

"Sir, I must object—"

"Your objections are duly noted," he said flatly, pointing to the door. "Now, if you would?"

But the security chief and deputy didn't move, and for the first time, Holt was actively glad for the link. Sprit's anger gave him the strength to stand his ground.

"Captain, I'm her closest friend here," Sprit said harshly, not bothering to hide her displeasure. "She trusts me!"

"And respectfully, sir, I have experience in the area of control and abilities," Holt added, hands clenching behind his back. "I can talk—"

"And *I* know Alympans," Oren interrupted, ending the conversation. "I know how they manifest, how they transform."

"As do I, sir," Holt returned with an eerie calm and professionalism that somehow didn't quite reach his eyes.

A chill trickled down Sprit's spine as she realized Holt wasn't backing down. She glanced at his battered and bruised countenance with a new light of understanding. This was it; she'd found his life issue, as Matzepo called it, the thing he'd defend to his grave, duty and rules be damned— defending people like him who were suffering like he had.

"I know *her* genes, Lewis," Oren pushed and sighed when he came to the same realization as Sprit. "You'll come in later, Holt. I promise. Now, this is not up for debate," he finished as he glanced back at Rin. She was getting closer and closer to consciousness. "You're *dismissed.*"

Sprit turned and left in a huff of frustration, but Holt lingered.

"Sir," he began, and Oren looked at him in exasperation.

"*What*, Lewis? She's waking up, make this quick."

Holt considered him for a few moments, and the captain realized the man was listening to noise only he could hear. A wave of dread hit him as all the possible worst case scenarios played through his head—another attack from a *fourth* sleeper or worse, Jon in person—until Holt spoke.

"Sir, Sprit wants you to remember," he began, and Oren instantly relaxed, "Rin is not Jon. She may share his genes, but we do not punish people for their fathers' sins."

Before Oren could tell him that wasn't his intent, the deputy left as he'd been instructed to. The cellblock fell quiet save for the unnatural electricity arcing from Rin's cell and *Starlight's* engine buzz. They settled in Oren's bones like an itch he couldn't quite reach.

The captain crossed his arms and waited.

"*Holy* djienn," Sprit said in a tense, awe-struck whisper as Holt joined her in the anteroom and gave a jittery, slightly spooked laugh. "Rin's a Bledsoe! She's *Alympan* and a powerful one, too. I got thrown around by an Alympan legend!"

"Indeed."

"Indeed? That's all you have to say? *Indeed?*" she said in disbelief as she followed her coworker into the hall. "And you! You just stood up to *Oren*. You put your foot down with him—"

"It seems you are a bad influence, commander," Lewis replied without looking, and Sprit threw up her hands in exasperation as she chased after him.

"Can't we just appreciate this for a moment?" she called. Once again, his reply was brutally short.

"No."

CHAPTER 25

Rin woke up suddenly, sitting up with a loud gasp that reminded her too much of waking on *Starlight* for the first time when she officially met Sprit. But this time—this time, there was so much more wrong. She felt like spiders were crawling over every inch of her skin, and she looked down to see that strange purple light and darker violet tendrils coiling around her limbs and torso, tapering off in spider-web strands about her fingers. That energy-sapping, horrible terror set in again, and she scurried into the nearest corner, hyperventilating and scratching helplessly at her skin.

"Hello, Rin," a voice said softly, slightly distorted by intercom static.

She jumped, cowering behind her arms as another one of those brutal shockwaves tore from her and slammed into every inch of room's interior like it was trying to break her free. A strange shudder ran down Oren's spine at the thought. For all intents and purposes, this strange energy was acting like some kind of sentient, symbiotic bodyguard.

"I'm *sorry!*" she cried, struggling to get a full breath. "I-I don't know what's happening, I…"

"It's okay," he said gently, his calloused fingers tracing the intercom panel's buttons. "I do." She looked up at him with such hope that it broke his heart. "You're half-Alympan, Rin. We figured it out."

"A-Alympan?" she repeated, struggling to place the word and then remembering her conversation with Sprit on the balcony. "Like that guy? Jon Bledsoe?"

The knife already embedded in Oren's heart twisted painfully.

"Yes," he said gravely. "Like him." He sighed and shifted his weight on his feet. This was going to take a bit. "Your father is from a planet called Alympa, Rin. They have a very strict caste structure that's stratified their people in…many ways," he finished diplomatically. "Mainly, they're divided by ability, their genetic codes. It's a societal and economic crisis we've been trying to address for nearly a century now, but they won't budge." He was stalling. He knew he was, and he was positive Rin did, too. But this...there was no good way to have this conversation.

"I don't understand," Rin whispered and gritted her teeth against a groan as another tendril lashed off of her, leaving a mark along the wall.

"Alympans are characterized by different abilities," Oren continued. "I'd say unique, but that's not true. People can make plants grow with a single touch, can set things on fire with their minds, can remember anything you put in front of them. Others can imitate any sound or physical feat, can see through certain materials like an x-ray." He stopped as the knife buried itself even deeper, impaling him now with even the hilt. "Some can control minds." Rin watched with another shudder and lash out as he ran his hands over his scars and broken horn again. "And some it seems can generate force fields and energy discharge of some kind."

"Me," Rin stammered, and Oren nodded, his expression unreadable. "S-Sounds like magic," she shivered. "Or something out of a...a comic book."

Oren gave a soft huff of laughter and looked down with a faint smile. "I suppose it does."

"So, I'm one of them?" Rin asked weakly, and he nodded.

"Half. That might explain why it took so long for you to manifest. You needed more stress, and, well, given what you've been through lately, it was only a matter of time."

Rin nodded, quick and uncoordinated as she wrapped her arms tighter around her body and closed her eyes. Maybe if she couldn't see the energy discharge, as Oren called it, it would go away. Instead, she just found herself hyper-focusing on the sickening sensations on her skin.

"Who..." She stopped and rephrased her question. "What was he? My dad?" She cracked an eye open and looked at the captain, hating her contorted, glowing reflection in the glass at his feet. "Do you know?"

"He was one of the elite bastards," he said, and Rin frowned.

"A *what?*"

"I..." Oren ran his hands over his face, sighing. If Rin was going to understand this, she needed a sociology lesson. "Alympan abilities are separated by class. The more powerful abilities tend to be associated with the elite—centuries of inbreeding and aristocratic marriages. You understand." Rin nodded. "The more mundane abilities are found in the poor and lower classes. Now, these two groups don't mix. The rich stay in their walled off cities, the impoverished in their slums."

"Sounds like Earth," she whispered with another sparking shiver, and Oren gave a sad smile.

"I'm sorry to hear that. Alympa's a sordid place." He paused. "Sometimes, though, there is an affair or a powerful family falls out of favor and is banished from the cities to the moats of shantytowns that surround them." His gaze turned distant, regretful. "And an ability that should be carefully monitored and trained ends up in the genetic code of a boy trying to survive in a world bent on stamping him out."

"That sounds like a Charles Dickens novel," Rin laughed, the sound frayed and threadbare as she struggled to keep herself together. Humor was as good of a glue as any. "My dad was a bastard child, that's…that's what you're saying."

"He *is*, yes." Rin looked at him with a disquiet that was different and worse than the fear already gripping her. "He's a mind controller of extraordinary power, Rin." He stopped. He'd been dreading this, but there was no way to avoid it. He met the girl's eyes with an apologetic, grave gaze. "His name is Jon Bledsoe."

First, there was disbelief, confusion. It wasn't computing, the words he'd spoken weren't fitting into any of the possible outcomes the girl had braced herself for, and he sighed as the tendrils started to pick up again, reflecting her agitation as it finally sank in.

"Wait. Wait, no, he's the one who's been…." She stopped, tried again. "The bombs, the—that ensign!"

"Yes. That's your father."

Oren took a half-step back as another shockwave burst from her and crashed against the walls, stronger than the last two.

"No. N-no, there's…that's…"

Bite the bullet, Oren, he told himself firmly. *Just get this over with.*

"His mother had an affair with a young noble from an old bloodline with a history of powerful capabilities. I'm sure you know the elite I'm talking about—the ones who adventure by playing with the lives of the poor." The words fell bitterly from his lips, a condemnation of their irresponsibility and callousness. "She ended up pregnant and gave birth to Jon." His expression turned dark, and Rin shivered. This was worse than a nightmare; there wasn't a word for what this was. "By the time he was a child, his abilities had manifested. You must understand; most don't until age eleven or so. His requests became godlike demands." A flash of pain filled his eyes. "When his father realized what his son was, he tried to take him back to the city for proper training. He knew the dangers. But Jon didn't want to go, and, at age six, he told his father to go away and never return. So, he did." Oren flinched as Rin gritted her teeth and another purple flash burned the glass to his left. "As for his mom…to this day, no one knows if Jon had a hand in it, unintentionally or otherwise. But when he was eight, she just started wasting away. In a few months, she was dead."

"Oh god," Rin moaned, taking deep, gasping breaths trying to bring herself back under control and failing miserably. *This* was her father. This horror story was her blood. She buried her head in her arms, clutching at her hair and pressing her shut eyes against her knees as Oren continued above her.

"Four years later, upper class authorities tried to track Jon down and get him into a training program, but he didn't need it. Twelve years old, and he'd already mastered his mind control. He'd gotten himself into the inter-planetary adoption system so he could leave Alympa and the people trying to find him behind."

"Didn't people notice?" she asked in disbelief, struggling to hold to the conversation as a distraction from whatever was happening to her.

"No, no," Oren said dismissively, shaking his head. "Jon's a master orator. You'd sooner think he was just a good debater than a mind controller," he explained, that dark, pained light still shining in his eyes. "He used his gift sparingly. That…was when Matzepo adopted him. He was only two years older than me, so we got along perfectly." A wistful smile touched his lips, grief pooling in his eyes. "The two of us were trouble-makers," he recalled, chuckling. "We never got caught." His amusement slowly faded. "We called him the boy with the golden tongue for that. So, when we were each eighteen, it only made sense that he'd pursue politics while I entered the Farpoint Peacekeepers Academy."

"Oh god," Rin choked out, suddenly feeling the urge to throw up for a few different reasons, not all related to their current conversation. A mind controller in office…it was nothing less than a recipe for disaster.

"Precisely," Oren said somberly. "We both progressed quickly. We were competitive that way, being brothers." He trailed off, his expression agonized. "I think it was a game to him," he admitted, words slow and sad, "how long he could stay just one step ahead of me. By the time we were in our forties, we'd both become prestigious in our fields. I was given *Starlight*," he said with a gesture to the air around them, "and Jon had positioned himself to become the Council President's chief adviser. That was when I started to question things." He looked down, and Rin noted how tightly his hands were clenched together.

"His dad," she croaked, and he looked at her in surprise.

"Yes. He contacted me." He began pacing a little bit before forcing himself to stand still again. "He'd been driven so far underground by his own son that…" His expression grew guilty. "Contacting me was probably what got him killed. Jon, it turns out, had used the shantytown crime rings to destroy his father's life. He'd been barely surviving over the decades, only managing it by keeping his head down. But when he saw that his son was going to become the next chief advisor…he knew he had to say something." Oren looked down, clearly not in the present but seventeen years ago. "Two days after contacting me, I received word that Jon's father had been found murdered in an alley. Jon's handiwork, no doubt, even if he did it remotely through manipulated crime lords. Absolute power…you know how the saying goes." Oren sighed, putting his hands on his hips and shaking his head. "Then, I did something stupid."

"You confronted him," Rin whispered, voice shaking with a painful shudder as more of the purple energy sparked off of her. She groaned and braced her head between her legs to try to quiet her nausea. "Rookie mistake," she bit out between clenched teeth.

"In retrospect, yes, it was." Now, there was nothing but pain and sorrow on Oren's face, and Rin imagined how he must have felt. Jon was his brother, his oldest friend, a boy he'd seen grow up into a young man. Her breathing grew more ragged than before. "I stopped him on a flight deck after a council meeting. I asked him if it was true, if he really could control minds. He just laughed at me with this…this *smile* on his face," Oren whispered, heartbroken as he touched to his own lips. "Like I'd just told him a funny story. And when he asked me who told me 'that wild theory,' I answered honestly. And that's when I knew." His eyes stared through Rin, lost in time, and she wiped away her tears. "I'd told Hanali'a what I'd learned before I left, that I was going to talk to Jon about it. She was smarter than I was, knew it wouldn't go well, so she followed me there to watch us talk from the shadows. And then…." He broke off again to rub his scars, and Rin suddenly knew exactly who'd given them to him.

"I told Jon he had to step down, to recuse himself from politics. And he got this manic look in his eyes." He looked at Rin, taking in her paled complexion, wide eyes, ragged breathing. This was cruel. He knew it, but he couldn't stop. Rin had to know where she came from, whose DNA she carried. "He started telling me he'd come too far and worked too hard to get where he was, and no red-skinned bastard was going to ruin this for him now. He hadn't changed the world, yet. I told him he'd changed it enough." Rin shuddered. "His power had consumed him."

Oren stopped and swallowed hard, nearly choking on the lump in his throat.

"That's when he drew the knife."

Jon, his brother, the boy he'd spent summer days side by side with, lunged at him with a feral howl, frothing at the mouth with fire in his eyes. Oren couldn't move. He couldn't defend himself, could only stare in incomprehension as the man he'd loved and grown with tackled him to the floor and slashed the blade down at his skull. The sight of the glinting silver plunging for his eyes finally broke him from his frozen state, and the Trozeran barely managed to knock the dagger to the side.

"I trusted you! I TRUSTED YOU!" Jon screamed, slashing over and over with the knife. Oren choked back cries of pain as he continued to barely block each strike with his forearms, a few getting through and gouging his forehead, and soon his blood was dripping into his face, blinding him. "I—TRUSTED—"

Somehow Oren managed to wrench the blade away with his weakening arms, and he briefly heard it skitter across the deck, useless to either of them now, before Jon grabbed ahold of his horns instead and started slamming Oren's head against the metal floor. Oren's vision went white with pain as he tried and failed to push the taller man off him. He could feel blood pouring into his eyes, and suddenly there was a loud crunching shatter. Horrible agony overcame him, and he screamed and clawed at his head instead of the brutal hands trying to split open his skull with nothing but visceral force.

His horn. Jon had snapped off his right horn. He was drowning in pain and blood, and he could hear someone screaming Jon's name, begging him to stop—oh. Oh, it was him, his cries leaving his throat raw. But then, a new voice penetrated his bleary mind.

"OREN!"

Oren's giant of a first officer was on them in an instant, tackling Jon back—

"Hanali'a charged us," Oren said robotically, his hand resting over his scars and damaged horn. "Picked up his own knife as she ran over and slashed his face as she tackled him. Kicked him off the loading platform. Just as he fell over the edge, though…" He made a poof gesture with his hands. "He vanished. Individual quantum jump device consolidated into a wrist cuff. They're excellent for quick getaways." He stopped as he relived the moment and cleared his throat. "We got a message from him a few hours later that I didn't see until I was out of surgery. Actually, that, uh, that was how I met Balok. He was the surgeon on call," he added in an absent aside, trying to buy more time before he had to immerse himself in the horrible memories once more.

"Jon was raving, bloody, furious. He'd been marked as a wanted man across the galaxy. There was nowhere for him to go. And he swore on his life that one day he'd take everything from me, too." Rin saw the captain shiver as he no doubt relived the message, that horrible moment.

"And then, quite simply, he vanished. We didn't know where to until you came along." He looked at Rin sadly, in pain. "You want to know why no one can tell you about your father? He told them to forget." Rin took in a shaking breath that quickly morphed into a sob on exhale. "Your mother, her mind was probably damaged by how often Jon used his ability on her. And as soon as he was able to, he left."

He's a monster, Rin thought to herself, now unable to hide her shaking. *Oh god, he's a monster.*

"Do you…can I see a picture of him?" she whispered, voice trembling almost as much as she was.

Oren hesitated but then pulled up a photo on his tablet and pressed it screen-first to the glass. Slowly, Rin got to her feet and stumbled over to the glass, bracing herself with a sparking discharge of purple energy on the barrier separating them.

"You have his eyes," Oren said softly as she looked at the 'Wanted' bulletin, took in the graying mousy hair pulled back in a ponytail from his pale, angular features. "I knew I'd seen them before."

This man, there was something in his eyes, something dangerous that said he would get his way no matter what. Something in the set of his shoulders that announced to the world no one would, no one *could*, stand in his way. She shakily reached out and covered the left side of his face, and before Oren could say anything, she wrenched away from the glass, landed hard on her hands and knees, and threw up on the floor. The tendrils and energy sparked off her like an electrical storm, and she looked up at the captain, eyes blazing purple.

"Why did you tell me this?" she demanded, voice and body shaking terribly. The lights in the cellblock flickered as she stood up, her hands clenched at her sides so hard her nails drew blood on her palms. "*Why?*"

"You have his temper, Rin." He kept his voice carefully neutral as she approached the glass, the energy somehow growing agitated about her. "And he?" He pointed to the picture on his tablet screen. "*He* is half your genetic code."

"I'm *not him!*" she shouted, and Oren took a step back as another, stronger shockwave pulsated from her, this time scorching the glass in some places and creating several cracks in the ceiling.

"Rin, calm down!" he ordered sharply, and suddenly the glow faded from her eyes.

Her legs turned to jelly and folded under her, barely giving her time to break her fall with her elbows as she fell backwards.

"I'm…not him," she breathed, and Oren sighed.

"I know you're not, Rin. But he's your history," he said softly, regretfully. "And if you're not careful, he'll be your legacy, too. He does this to everyone he touches."

Her father killed his own dad, possibly his mom. He tried to murder his own brother. He built an entire empire of power around himself for nothing but its own sake, a desperate urge to change the world in his image, and now he was killing innocent people, leaving pain and loss and orphans behind, and once again Rin saw in her mind's eye the town hall in Sahmot where all the dead lied. She saw Hanali'a's bloody head, Holt's bruised body, and Lucien's ashen face as she held his hands. She saw Mara in Matzepo's arms. She saw her mother's body at her funeral as her grandmother held her close. She saw her inhuman reflection in the glass, overlaying Oren's, and finally, it was too much.

Jon Bledsoe was her father.

Oren closed his eyes as Rin started screaming. It was raw and painful, and his earwig suddenly came to life as another ground-rumbling shockwave exploded off her. Wearily, he answered it.

"Lewis," he murmured, and there was a beat of silence.

"Do you want me to come down, sir?" Holt finally asked and prayed Sprit couldn't hear Rin's screams echoing from his earwig where she was sitting next to him on the bridge.

"Not just yet, Lewis," he said softly. "Right now, she just needs to scream. I know I would if I was her." He paused. "I know I *did.*"

"Yes, sir."

Rin's wails had finally died down into painful sobs, and the tendrils seemed to have joined her in her more subdued state.

"I know, Rin," Oren sighed, kneeling so he was at her level. "I know you're tired. You're hurting. You're scared." She looked up at him, eyes swollen and red.

"What do I do now?" she whispered, voice barely audible.

"We go forward. First night of a manifestation is always the worst, so you'll stay in here until you stop throwing off whatever that purple is," he said calmly, and Rin closed her eyes, struggling to take comfort in his steady, even voice. There was one question she needed answered first.

"Does he know I'm here?"

"Honestly, Rin?" Oren sighed, "I'm not sure he cares. People are pawns to him. At best, he'd see you as an oddity or maybe a weapon. At worst," he glanced at the cracked ceiling and the scorch marks, "he'd see you as a threat. And he only does one thing with threats."

Rin nodded, swallowing hard and clearing her gummed up throat.

"Will I be alone?" she whispered, still not looking at him. "I won't blame you…. I know I scare you."

Once again, the knife twisted hard in his heart, driving more of the hilt into his already wounded chest. The last thing this girl needed was to be alone.

"No," he assured her. "Of course not, I'll stay with you. I promise."

"Lewis Holt" the earwig interrupted again.

"One second. Your friends are insistently checking up on you," he said with a smile the girl didn't return. "Holt."

"Sir, Commander Matzepo needs to see you in headquarters. There's been a development."

"Alright, Lewis. I'll be there shortly. And Holt?"

"Yes, sir?"

"Are you doing anything tonight?"

"No, sir," the deputy replied after a moment's hesitation.

"Good man. Keep Rin company in the brig tonight." Jon's daughter gave him a tired smile for that, he noted in relief. "It's going to be a long evening." He closed the channel and slowly stood up. "Lewis will stay with you." He hesitated before departing, trying to think of something to offer to comfort her. "Jon was a brilliant man consumed by his abilities, Rin," he finally said. "But you have a pure heart."

Rin scoffed wearily.

"How do you know that?" she asked glumly, and Oren frowned.

"Look at me, Rin." He waited for her to lift her gaze to him, and he gave her a long, hard stare. "You saved my life with Ensign Ciarul. That's only *one* of the ways I know that." Rin looked down.

"I killed her, didn't I?" she whispered, and Oren sighed. He didn't have time to get into this. Sprit needed him.

"You saved my life," he repeated firmly. "Holt will be here soon. We *will* get you through this, Rin. I promise."

Rin continued to stare at the wall opposite her, expression flat.

"Okay," she whispered evenly, and Oren forced himself to leave.

Holt would have to deal with her guilt.

As soon as the captain left, Rin bowed her head and finally let the tension bleed out of her body, and the tendrils flared to life once more, the only outward betrayal of her internal struggle. She couldn't let them see. She could *never* let them see. She wouldn't be Rin *Bledsoe*.

———

"What did you find, Sprit?"

Sprit looked up at her brother as he walked in.

"I was looking over security camera footage of what happened in your quarters. Rin saved your life, by the way," she added pointedly as Oren joined her at her computer.

"Yes, I know."

"Anyways, Ciarul was doing something odd with her hand behind her back. Look at this." She quickly zoomed in on the screen capture of the ensign's back. "She's holding one finger up to the camera, see?"

"Sprit, that could be anything," Oren said sympathetically. "I know you want to find something to help us, but—"

"I think she's telling us one more," Sprit interrupted forcefully. "But one more what, I don't know. It could be a bomb, mole, sleeper agent, anything. But Jon's got one more something on this ship." She looked up at her captain. "I *know* it's a long shot. But it's all we've got, so I think we should take it seriously."

"Wonderful," Oren sighed and began pacing, Sprit watching him.

"How is she?" the security chief finally asked, not needing to be more specific.

Oren stopped moving and looked at her with a small smile.

"Strong."

"Hello, Miss Cooper," Holt said softly and got another pained moan and purple lightning strike in response. He set the chair down beside the intercom and quietly sat. "Don't fight it."

"I'm so tired," Rin groaned where she was lying in a shivering fetal position on the floor.

"I know." Somehow, Rin was pretty sure he actually did know. "You should eat something. Drink some fluids," he offered, and Rin scoffed, the sound quickly turning into another hurting moan as it pulled at her sore stomach.

"I can't," she gritted out between clenched teeth. "I'll just throw it up like before."

"Do you want to die?" There was no animosity or forcefulness to the question, just simple curiosity, and Rin looked up at Holt, noting the tray in his hands. "Fall into a coma?" She hesitated and then shook her head. "Then, you have to keep your body going."

He moved towards the cell door, and Rin immediately sat up, the quick motion leaving her dizzy and even more nauseous than before.

"No!" she blurted. "No, don't come in."

"I'm only opening the door, Rin," Holt said simply. "You won't hurt me."

It was said so matter-of-factly, that for a few seconds, Rin believed him. And that was all the time her companion needed to open the cell door, set the tray on the floor, and close the door again.

"See?" he said as he returned to his chair and sat down. "You didn't hurt me."

He pretended to read his tablet, watching out of the corner of his eye as Rin unsteadily made her way to the food. She was shaking so badly that for a moment, Holt was worried her legs wouldn't support her, but she reached the tray without falling and began eating. He smiled secretly as her hesitant pace quickly turned ravenous. He knew that hunger well.

"Good, Rin," he said, and she looked up at him as she used a corner of her blanket as a napkin. He'd set his tablet to the side, and Rin realized what was throwing her off about him. He was using more contractions, calling her Rin and not Miss Cooper—*informality*. "That's the first step."

"Eating?" she asked in confusion, and he shook his head, faint smile barely visible as he corrected her.

"Wanting to make it through this."

Nurse Gehmra waited with baited breath and heart in her throat for the reply on the static-filled channel. Ensign Ciarul had failed. She knew the price of failure with their employer, and it was often…extreme.

Finally, the voice came through.

"What do you mean Ren *isn't* dead?" Jon hissed. She winced as he continued, growing louder and angrier. "I told you *precisely* how to get to him. I told you *every single step!* This was foolproof! A *child* could have carried it out! How did you idiots mess this up?!"

"A girl saved him, uncle," she explained, hating how the familial term rolled so easily off her tongue. She hated even more how Anthia thought she was having a long distance call with her mother's brother, not…*him*. "Half-human, half-Alympan. I copied her file from Balok's computer."

There was a startled silence.

"Send it to me. Right now." Gehmra's hands trembled as she sent the medical file to her "uncle's" messenger account. A few tense minutes passed in silence. "I've gotten it. Let's see who…" He gasped, the sound a horrible mix of surprise and utter delight. "*Myra*…oh, your genes shone through. Do you have a copy of the security footage?"

He was excited now, and Gehmra could feel his feral grin.

"It's in the medical file. Balok requested a copy, uncle."

"Ah, yes, I see it." There was another pause and then a gleeful laugh. "Oh, she's a shield maiden! *Excellent!* Oh, excellent indeed. This changes the game." There was another wondrous, eager laugh, and Gehmra's skin crawled at his excited enthusiasm. "Oh, you're *magnificent*...." He seemed to forget Gehmra was on the other end of the line, and she wanted to cry at the way he was talking about the poor girl in the brig like she was an exotic pet. "Gehmra, my dear niece, we have a change of plans." She shuddered and squeezed her eyes shut. "I'm not going to kill Ren just yet." She heard a dull tapping sound across the audio channel and realized he was drumming his fingers. "He has something of mine. I'll be taking it back first."

"Yes, uncle."

"Where is she?"

"In the brig, uncle."

"Okay, here's what we're going to do," Jon said with far too much fervor to spell anything good. The nurse swallowed hard and picked up a stylus with a shaking hand.

"I'm ready, uncle. What are your instructions?"

"First thing's first—do *not* mess this up, or I will be very displeased. I'm coming to you. It's about time I handled this myself...."

CHAPTER 26

"What do you feel?" Holt asked softly, and Rin's brow furrowed in concentration.

"It's like my skin is crawling," she finally replied, voice tense. "Like static, like I need to throw up."

Holt gently shook his head.

"No. What do you *feel?* When it releases, when it charges—what do you feel?"

"*Terrified—*"

"Under the fear," Holt pressed, scooting the chair a little closer to the glass. "Put the fear aside. What do you feel?"

"I can't put it aside!" she snapped angrily and then instantly groaned as another tendril lashed out to accompany her irritation. Holt paused and re-evaluated his approach, leaving them in a long silence that Rin was beginning to interpret as she had hurt Lewis' feelings. "I'm sorry, Holt. I didn't—"

"For me, Rin, minds feel like an open frequency filled with unfiltered messages," Holt suddenly said, and she looked at him in surprise. He was actually telling her about himself. *Holt* was sharing personal information. He braced his elbows on his knees and slowly moved his hands together to a point as he continued. "Focusing is like singling that one channel out, that one voice, and making it crystal clear. It's...liberating," he said, and Rin frowned. "It's like finally being able to see. Colors are brighter, details sharper. In a way, I suppose, it's almost as comforting as it is exhausting and terrifying." He sat back in his chair and leveled her with an open, curious gaze. "So, how do you feel?"

Rin took a moment to think, playing over what he'd said to her and trying to apply it to herself.

"Tense," she began uncertainly, the word feeling more appropriate as she continued. "When it's building up, it's like that feeling when you have to run or scream, or like you're at the top of a rollercoaster." She took in a deep, steadying breath, as she continued to find the words. "Then, balanced, sort of calm when it—" Another strand of energy arced from her arm to the wall as if to prove her point, and she grimaced as it took a toll on her already strained body. "Was it like this for you?"

"Not precisely," Holt said, choosing his words carefully. "There was an incident when I was seven. My abilities became unhinged, shall we say? I couldn't turn it off, couldn't control it. So, *then*...yes it was like this."

"I can't make it stop," Rin admitted in a scared whisper.

"It is not an it," Lewis corrected. This was the hardest part of it all, accepting this concept. "It's a part of you. Look at it." He nodded for her to do as he said, and she shakily looked down at herself, grinding her teeth as she tried not to freak out over the ever-present purple. "That is *you*. You cannot make it stop. You can only control it."

She quickly looked at Holt, eager to face anyone except herself. "How?"

"Calm down," he said simply. She laughed like he'd just told her the best joke she'd heard in a long time. "Calm yourself, Rin," he repeated earnestly. "Focus on the balance, the calm between bursts. Hold onto it. Breathe into it."

"I can't—"

"Close your eyes," Holt ordered, bringing his chair even closer to the glass. "Breathe with me. Think about that balance. Focus on the balance and nothing else." He waited as she shut her eyes.

"Focus, Rin," he continued once she was settled. "Breathe in—one, two, three. Breathe out—one, two three..."

He repeated the cadence and watched as the tendrils returned to the confines of her body over the next several minutes, finally dissipating from the vessels into a fine diffuse across her skin. She looked like she was coated in a fine web of threads that shimmered when they caught the light correctly.

"Very good, Rin," he said sincerely. "Now, holding onto that calm and balance, open your eyes. You are in control."

"I am in control," she breathed to herself.

First Matzepo and now Holt had told her this, but somehow it wasn't convincing her. She slowly opened her eyes and looked down, that doubt eating away at the corner of her mind. And the moment she saw that that foreign light was still there, her breathing picked up again, the tendrils not far behind. Holt sighed and pinched the bridge of his nose. It seemed it was time for a more direct approach.

"What are you doing?" Rin asked nervously as Holt stood up and walked towards her cell door. "Holt, you can't come in! I can't make this stop! I don't—"

"You're going to have to," Lewis said simply and opened the door. Instantly, Rin sparked, and he looked down to the scorch mark not two feet in front of him on the floor. "Calm," he repeated to her. "Control."

There was nothing but complete trust on his face, and he stepped inside, closing the door behind him.

Rin took in a sharp breath and closed her eyes, turning her head away and bracing for everything to go horribly wrong. But instead…there was nothing. Hesitantly, she opened her eyes and slowly turned back to Holt. He was just standing there, waiting.

"I'm going to start coming closer, Rin. I will stop if you start arcing or if I see another shockwave forming. But I am not leaving."

Rin swallowed hard and took in a deep breath.

"What if I hurt you?" she whispered.

"That will be my own fault and not yours. I am in here willingly." He took one step towards her and instantly stopped as one of her tendrils marked the ground in front of his feet. "I see we are going to be here for a while."

"It has a mind of its own," she panted, struggling to force it down, and Holt shook his head.

"Don't tense up, Rin. It only makes you more strained, which in turn aggravates your ability. *Calm*." He paused. "As for it having a mind of its own, treat it that way. Convince it I'm not a threat." Rin closed her eyes again, breathing deeply and evenly, and Holt took another small, half-step forward only to stop again as her ability protested. Maybe it was time for another straightforward method.

"You could destroy this ship," he said suddenly, and she looked at him like he was insane. He took advantage of her startled silence to inch towards her, unhindered. "You could kill me and everyone else aboard."

"Why are you saying that?" she demanded, voice jumping an octave. "God, what's *wrong* with you, Holt?!"

"Because you haven't done either of those things, yet."

"I killed that ensign—"

"She killed herself. It was her own blaster shot that killed her, Rin," he said firmly. "You protected yourself and the captain. You did not kill her. If anyone did, it was Jon." She didn't respond, so he continued what he'd been saying before. "You have not killed me, and you have not destroyed the ship. You *are* in control. Stay that way."

He tried taking another step only to be brought up short by another discharge, though this one was smaller than the others had been.

"That's progress. You're already in control, Rin," he said softly and took another inching step forward. Nothing. This time, he tried a full step. "You're doing well—"

Holt broke off in a yelp of pain as one of the electricity-like bolts zapped his hand, and Rin pushed herself further into the corner.

"Sorry!"

"No, that was my fault. I took a bigger step than you were ready for." He sighed and tried again, barely sliding his foot across the cell floor.

Nothing.

"At this rate, it's going to take an hour to get over here," Rin joked a little deliriously, and Holt gave a quiet huff of laughter.

"Then, it will take an hour."

It took two hours.

Holt knelt before Rin at a painstakingly slow pace that the girl had no doubt was doing his injured leg no favors. She continued to breathe in a slow, even pattern and watched as Holt finally settled back on his heel.

"We done with this exercise, yet?" she panted, shivering sporadically, and Holt shook his head.

"Not quite." He gently reached out to her, and Rin tensed, watching with bated breath as his hand approached her knee at that same careful pace until finally his fingertips rested against the joint with an odd sense of finality.

Nothing.

Holt smiled gently at her—an actual smile, not one of his ghosts.

"Not dead," he said, and Rin laughed, closing her eyes and letting her head fall back against the wall. She was soaked in sweat, exhausted, but she grinned a blinding smile that Holt had never seen on her before.

"No, not dead," she agreed breathlessly. The purple, which had retreated to their vessels over the last couple hours, faded completely from view, and she looked down at herself. "Huh. Would you look at that?"

Holt sat beside her in a graceless fall and tiredly sighed.

"You're in control," he repeated for the last time as Rin let her head rest against his shoulder with a heavy sigh and closed her eyes. Once he was sure she was comfortable, he looked at the security camera outside the cell above the warden's desk.

"Commander," he thought, reaching out and touching the link. *"You can stop watching now."*

"You're insane," was Sprit's quick and yet still grateful reply, and Holt closed his eyes.

"And yet, ma'am, I know what I'm doing."

Sprit didn't respond, and Holt waited as, bit by bit, Rin leaned against him even more until the deputy had no doubt she was asleep. He didn't blame her. He was exhausted as well, and he wasn't the one trying to wrangle an ability on top of everything else. He opened his eyes and carefully moved Rin off his shoulder, laying her down on the floor much the way he had when he'd brought her in. He tucked her sweaty hair behind her ears before getting up and fetching a new blanket to drape over her. The original he then used to clean up the vomit from earlier and dropped it in the trash canister behind the warden's desk.

"Sleep well, Rin," he whispered as he closed her cell door and locked it again. He didn't need someone walking in, scaring her, and undoing all of the progress they'd just made.

He slumped down in his chair and let his head thump back against the wall. Now that he wasn't focused on Rin he could actually slow down and address the thoughts and memories that had been bubbling up over the course of the last few hours. It wouldn't be fun, but it had to be done if he was going to resume helping his young friend when she woke up.

It wasn't to be.

He looked at the door as it opened, and Sprit walked in.

"You look awful, Lewis. You okay?"

"Yes, ma'am," he said easily, forcing himself to sit up straight. "Just some bad memories." She nodded, quickly understanding what he meant, and then stood there, rocking back and forth on her feet.

"I hate to have to do this to you," she began apologetically, "but…."

Holt closed his eyes, face lined with discomfort.

"Jon may have another sleeper aboard," he finished, and she nodded.

"Last one," she said firmly. "Think you can find them?"

"I can do my best, ma'am." He pushed himself to his feet, unintentionally ignoring Sprit's offered hand. She awkwardly clasped her hands behind her back.

"I'll, uh, follow your lead."

Holt just nodded and headed into the hall as Sprit trailed behind him. He was unsteady on his feet, she noted, and she chewed her lower lip as he occasionally let his hand run along the walls for support as he walked. His head seemed permanently cocked to the side as he listened, and she crossed her arms nervously each time he paused for a few seconds before shaking his head and walking again. Nothing. And the longer they kept finding nothing, winding throughout one deck before going up or down a level to repeat the process, the less hopeful Sprit became.

Holt could feel her confidence waning, and he took in a deep breath.

Look for the mind that's different, he told himself. *Look for the one who is not behaving normally.*

And for each deck, he came up with nothing.

Finally, on deck three, he stopped and braced himself on the wall, his brow furrowing in pain.

"Holt!" Sprit quickly caught up, and he pushed himself onto his own two feet again.

"I'm fine, ma'am," he said automatically, and she glared.

"Liar. You can't pull that with me anymore. I'm inside your head," she scolded and pulled the back of his uniform. "Come on. I shouldn't have asked you to do this. You need sleep." It was telling that he didn't protest and instead just let her guide him back to deck four. "Nothing?"

"Nothing," he confirmed wearily, and Sprit shook her head.

"Jon must have coached them," she said definitively. "Told them not to think about what they're being forced to do so they can evade you."

"Except in the moment," Holt tiredly corrected, rubbing his eyes. "It's abstract...pieces with no context..."

Sprit looked at him as they stepped into a lift.

"Holt, you're worrying me. Don't go speaking in tongues, or I'll take you to Balok," she threatened, and Holt winced.

"I just need tea." *And prayer*, he added privately, and they stepped out onto their deck. "Thank you for your concern, though, commander."

They walked in silence the rest of the way to Holt's quarters, and she gently touched his elbow.

"Get some rest, Lewis. I'll go sit with Rin. Don't worry."

"Thank you." He bowed shallowly to her and limped into his room, the door hissing shut behind him. Sprit smiled to herself, pleased, as she walked back towards the brig.

"He didn't call me ma'am or commander when he said thank you," she told the empty hall and lopsidedly grinned.

In his quarters, Holt made his way to the decorated memorial shrine in his sitting area. He painfully knelt on the prayer rug that permanently resided before it and bowed three times before preparing the same prayer he'd performed in Sahmot at the thrako trees. But this time, before he began, he turned his attention to the silver placard at the center of the candles and incense and read the two names engraved on its surface.

Amos Holt. Evrae Holt.

Heart aching, he bowed his head and began to pray.

———————

Five hours had passed when Oren came in to check on Rin. Sprit had been called to her post, and she'd brought Holt with her, so the girl was unfortunately on her own except for an on-duty warden.

"Lieutenant," he greeted, and the officer nodded to him from behind the desk. "Has she woken up, yet?"

"I think she's awake now, sir."

"Thank you." The captain walked over to the girl's cell. She was lying on her side, back to the room, and he gently knocked on the glass to get her attention.

Instantly, Rin jerked awake and lashed out with an arm at the sound, leaving a scorch mark on the glass in front of Oren as the purple energy flared to life and then died back to that spidery webbing over her skin—there, but waiting.

"I see we're still adjusting," the captain said dryly, and Rin blinked sleepily, peering at who was talking to her.

"Oh...sorry, captain..."

"No, it's my fault. I startled you." He looked back at his lieutenant, and the officer blushed. "*Somebody* said you were awake."

"Guess I'm staying here for a while, then," she said, ruefully pointing to the damaged room around her.

"It *is* one of the more reinforced parts of the ship," he said with a crooked smile. "But it's only until you get your abilities under control. Did Holt help while he was here?"

"Yeah, he...he helped a lot."

"Good. He's a good man for these sorts of situations. He's a good man in general." Oren trailed off, suddenly looking uncomfortable, and he cleared his throat as he shifted on his feet. "Miss Cooper, I've been thinking about our conversation," he began, "and I realized I may have given you an unfair image of Jon."

Rin scoffed bitterly as she got up and joined him at the glass barrier.

"I really don't think so."

"Jon's...he's not a bad man at his core, Rin."

"Are you *kidding* me?" she gaped, on the verge of laughing in the captain's face.

"I'm not saying he hasn't done terrible things, Rin, by no means. But he was a free spirit as a child. He just...didn't have the right guidance. He didn't have *any* guidance—not when it mattered. But I believe he still has the potential for good in him."

"How can you think that?" she demanded, truly confused. "Look at everything he's done! He's killed your people. He as good as killed my mom. *How* can you believe he has the potential for good?"

"To survive out here, you need to hold to a truth," he said. "We all have them, these creeds. Mine is all people have the capacity for good."

"Seems naïve," she muttered, turning away from him and going back to her spot against the wall.

"I suppose," he admitted as she sat down. "Are you comfortable?"

"As much as I can be," she said with a shrug, keeping an eye on the purple tendrils out of the corners of her vision.

"Do you want more food? Water?"

"No, I'm...I'm fine. Balok's going to bring some when he stops by later."

"Alright." He nodded once to her as he turned away. "I'm going to get some rest now. I'll leave you to it."

"Goodnight," she called after him, and he looked back as he kept walking, amused.

"Night? It's morning, Cooper." He faced forward again as he left the cellblock for the anteroom, and Rin caught a faint "hello, doctor" before Balok took the captain's place.

"Miss Cooper!" he beamed, noting the tamer state of her ability. "I see we're doing much better today than we were last night."

"A bit," she agreed with a small smile. "It's more the 'your dad is a raging psychopath' that's taking a little more effort to get used to."

"I'm sorry," Balok sighed and shook his head as he approached. "I'm afraid you drew the short straw with your parentage. Fortunately, absent parents rarely shape their child's personality with their own. May I come in?" Rin nodded, and he joined her. "I have a few scans to run to see how your body is holding up to the strain of its newfound abilities."

"Non-invasive?"

"Have they ever been otherwise?" he asked playfully as he waved the familiar scanner at her. "May I come near you?"

Rin looked down at her body and stretched her arms out before her, fingers splayed. The violet threads encasing her skin were barely visible still, and she smiled.

"I think you're good," she said and spread her arms so Balok could take his scans. "Will I ever be able to fully control this?"

"Seeing how well you're doing, I'd say there's a good chance." He tousled Rin's hair and then grimaced. "Oh. I should get you a hairbrush when I come back with food...."

"I'm offended," Rin said with playful indignation and looked curiously to the door as someone walked else walked in.

"Lieutenant Acoua," Balok greeted in surprise as he continued taking his readings. "How can we help you?"

"I'm just here to tell you Sprit and Holt are working overtime, so they won't be able to come," the communications officer said bluntly to the girl, and Balok felt her deflate slightly beneath his hands.

"Thanks, Anthia." The short woman nodded to her and turned to leave when Rin caught sight of something. "Your wrist…"

Anthia stopped and glanced at the raw patch of skin peaking from under her sleeve.

"Sunburn," she said impassively, looking back up at the two people. "I wasn't careful enough in Sahmot."

"It looks painful," Balok said, moving towards the cell door with his kit in his hands that Anthia eyed with open distaste.

"I barely feel it," she said curtly. "Good day."

Balok made a wry, displeased sound in the back of his throat as she left, and he turned back to Rin.

"I have a feeling I'll need to look at her later," he said with a sigh and patted the girl's shoulder. "Whatever you do, don't turn into her. I can only chase so many nosocomephobic people around on this ship."

"Noso-what?" Rin asked in confusion, and Balok laughed.

"Fear of hospitals." He hummed as he looked at Rin's scans. "Well, it seems you need some more electrolytes in your system. I'll be back with food and some supplements."

Rin sighed and flopped down on the padded floor as Balok hurried out, and stretched her arms above her head. She focused on keeping her breaths deep and even and was relieved when the purple remained quiet.

"I should name you," she muttered to the empty cell and held her luminously decorated hand before her eyes. "I mean, if I'm going to be stuck with you and if you're still planning on being this temperamental, I should really give you a name." There was a beat of silence. "What about Jupiter? You're a bit Zeus-like, aren't you?"

At the warden's desk, the security lieutenant cleared his throat and turned his focus to his reports. That human was a little off…no wonder Balok liked her so much.

CHAPTER 27

Holt eyed Sprit with quickly fraying patience as she got up from the table and began pacing again, muttering and burning through personnel files and the security footage they'd salvaged from before Talik and Jhama's attacks. Nothing and more nothing, that was all they seemed destined to find. And the more nothing they found, the more frustrated Sprit got, the more she focused on the unknown clock counting down from an unknown time, and the more her anxiety and anger passed on to Holt. And by now, it was well over his tolerance threshold.

"We need to restart from the top with our profile," Sprit announced, and Holt fought back a groan as he set his tablet down with a little more force than was necessary or characteristic. "We're missing something—"

"Get out."

Sprit looked at her partner in surprise.

"Holt—"

"I cannot concentrate, so please, either stop pacing and spiraling or calm down!" he ordered and instantly grimaced, squeezing his eyes shut and clenching his hands on the tabletop.

"I've *never* seen you snap this much, Holt," Sprit said after a moment of silence, and he sighed, avoiding her gaze.

"I am deeply sorry, commander."

"It's me," she said finally, looking down. "Isn't it?"

"You do have a fiery disposition," Holt conceded. "But it suits you. For myself, it…"

"It just turns you into a jerk?" Sprit said flatly with a raised eyebrow, and Holt gave a faint huff of laughter.

"Yes. That is a generous way of putting it."

She smiled apologetically and spun her chair around so she could sit in it backwards.

"I'm sorry. I'll try to think nice, proper thoughts from now on."

And just like that, a light went on in Holt's head.

"That's it," he said, slowly standing, and Sprit frowned.

"What's it?"

"Proper thoughts," he repeated, a note of almost-excitement entering his voice. "I'm not looking for the abnormal mind. I'm looking for—"

"The too normal mind," Sprit finished, quickly catching on, and Holt nodded.

"Yes, precisely. We are looking for the one that's trying not to get my attention by overly acting like there is nothing wrong in the first place."

Sprit grinned as they lapsed into eager silence. It was not a nice smile.

"Let's catch ourselves a sleeper," she said and quickly began clearing their table so they could start all over again. This time, they had the right angle to work from.

"So far," Sprit began loudly, frustration palpable in her slightly higher than usual voice as she brandished her tablet, "we have caught a below-decks gambling ring, confiscated an illegal plant, and found not one, but *two* affairs. With *each other's* partners." She slumped forward and plowed her head into her folded arms on the table. "Since when did we become internal affairs?" she asked, voice muffled by her sleeves and limbs, and looked up at her deputy. He didn't return the gaze, instead keeping his elbows firmly planted on the table and his forehead propped on the heels of his palms. "And why does everyone seem to think you're just sitting around waiting to bust them on this stuff? Do they *seriously* think you've got that little of a life?"

"I am trying, ma'am," he said tiredly, voice tight, and Sprit sighed.

"Do you need a break?" she asked as she sat up, nothing but concern behind her words. "We've been at this for three hours, and I really doubt that two hours of rest was enough for you after what you did with Rin."

"No," Holt said quickly, shaking his head and reassuming his proper posture. "No, ma'am, I have to find them."

Sprit watched sympathetically as he pressed his hands flat against the table, took a deep breath, and closed his eyes. Maybe the fiftieth time would yield results, she thought sarcastically and stood up. Combing through the crew was a one-person job she wasn't biologically equipped to help with, but she could do one thing for her partner. She picked up his empty mug and the kettle between them.

She could give him another cup of that awful tea he liked.

She set the cup carefully by his hand so that he could feel the heat and know it was there, but not close enough to distract him. Unable to sit still for another ten minutes at the least, she got up and slowly paced the length of the room, taking care to keep her thoughts calm and even. But even that quickly grew old, and she stopped behind Holt, noting the tense line to his shoulders and the faint furrow of discomfort to his brow. Uncertainly, she reached out to the link and found a shadow of soreness permeating his thoughts. Oh. Migraine. Not to mention some seriously tender muscles.

She sighed scoldingly as she looked down at him.

"I told you to take a break," she muttered and without really thinking about it, reached down to massage his aching muscles.

She forgot about the spines.

Holt jerked out of his trance as Sprit grabbed his shoulders and then yelped in surprised pain, yanking her hands away from him like she'd been burned. He sighed and shook his head.

"Commander," he began in exasperation as he turned to her, and she hissed, sucking a little blood from the small puncture wounds on her palms.

"Oh, ease up, Holt. All I wanted to do was loosen your shoulders a bit," she muttered, scowling at her hands. "You're way too tense." She made a disgruntled sound and started walking to the door, distracted by her stinging skin. "I'll go get some antiseptic from Balok."

Holt fought the urge to roll his eyes.

"They *are* clean, ma'am."

"You should get something for your migraine, anyways," she said and beckoned for him to join her, "or at the very least your back and shoulders. Besides, we need the break. We've interviewed at least a dozen people." She paused expectantly in the doorway, and he finally relented, getting up.

"Very well, commander."

Sprit watched Holt as he passed and smirked.

"You know, one of these days I'm *really* gonna get on your case about the whole commander-ma'am thing." She playfully sauntered after him. "If you don't start calling me Sprit, I'll make your life very difficult."

"I'm sure you will, *ma'am*."

"Dammit, Holt."

By Rin's estimate, Balok hadn't been gone two minutes before the cellblock door opened again, and she frowned at the ceiling. It was too quick to have gone to the cafeteria *and* medbay *and* come back, so it had to be someone else. But who, she couldn't guess. She propped herself up on her elbows to see who her visitor was and immediately grinned.

"Wow, you're not all…glowy," Sprit said in genuine surprise, and Rin snorted as Holt got a look on his face that the half-human knew was his formal equivalent of an eye roll.

"What are you two doing here? Anthia stopped by and said you were working overtime."

"Medbay run," the security chief said, holding up her hand. "We're in the middle of some chaos right now, so we can't stay for long."

"Commander, perhaps I can go ahead and get the appropriate medication," Holt said easily. "That way, you can spend some time with Miss Cooper."

"You sure?" Holt nodded, and Sprit smiled. "Thanks, Lewis."

"I'm glad to see you are doing better, Rin," the deputy said with a small smile and shallowly bowed to the girl before departing.

"Okay, spill," Sprit said as soon as he'd left, entering Rin's cell and sitting on the floor across from her, back against the glass. "How did you get him to start calling you Rin? And how'd you get him to *smile* at you?"

Rin laughed and rubbed at her eyes.

"Oh, I turned out to be half-Alympan with a psychopathic dad and threw a few officers around with weird, unknown energy that acts like telekinesis with purple lightning," she said dryly, playful indifference a mask for the fear and insecurity burrowed deep in her bones. Sprit saw right through it. "I'm thinking of calling it Jupiter, actually."

"Rin—"

"Are you okay?" she interrupted, concern burning in her eyes.

"Yeah, I'm fine. A little bruised, but nothing I can't handle."

"I knocked you out, Sprit," she pressed.

The woman scoffed, crossing her arms defensively.

"A one-time event, I can assure you," she returned testily, and Rin smirked at her pretend indignation. Suddenly, though, Sprit seemed to zone out, and the girl's smile softened.

"What did Holt say?" she asked once Sprit blinked a few times, and the officer rolled her eyes.

"You can tell, too, huh?"

"You space out when he talks to you. What's he saying?"

"He said to think of your ability as a living thing within you," she said with an expression that mirrored her friend's. "Think of it like a guardian, a protector that answers to you and you alone."

If at all possible, Rin's smile grew even gentler.

"It's a little better to think about it that way." She gave a quiet huff of laughter. "He's good at phrasing things, making them less scary."

"He grows on you that way," Sprit agreed, interlocking her fingers behind her head. Rin's eyes took on a mischievous twinkle.

"Oh, really?" Sprit narrowed her eyes warningly. "Is Matzepo going to get some good news about the future of your marital status?"

There was a beat of silence.

"I hate you, Rin Cooper."

Rin just laughed.

———

"Lieutenant Holt. It's surprisingly been a while," Balok teased as the man walked in, and Holt raised a tired eyebrow.

"Yes, and I want to keep it that way, doctor. I've been having some migraines, aching muscles. It is…distracting, to say the least. I would like to get ahead of it before it becomes something worse."

Balok raised an eyebrow as he grabbed a few items from his medicine cart and approached the officer sitting down on one of his stools.

"And I suppose it would be expecting too much to hope you've been getting rest and not using your ability nearly constantly for long periods of time?" he asked dryly as he handed the Xanidian some pills.

"Yes, I suppose it would be," Holt said reluctantly, and Balok tutted disapprovingly. "We're racing against a ticking clock, doctor. If we had time to spare, I would be more discerning with my abilities."

"You're not invincible," Balok scolded as he headed for a sink, and Holt quickly took the tablets, swallowing them dry. The doctor stopped and turned to him, hands on his hips. "Now why would you do a thing like that? I was getting you water!"

"As I said, doctor, we are working on borrowed time."

Balok's expression darkened.

"I take it we've found another problem?"

"Of sorts," he said vaguely. "Before I go, could I get some antiseptic cream for Commander Matzepo? I'm afraid she pricked her palms on my spines a few minutes ago."

"Oh?" Balok asked suggestively, and Holt leveled him with a dangerous stare. "Oh, alright. I'll get her cream, calm down."

As the doctor moved off, Holt closed his eyes and sighed, leaning back against the edge of the desk behind him. Medbay was always a good environment for him. It was clinical, methodical, and he let the space's equally systemic thoughts wash over him and soothe his worn nerves.

Methodical.

His heart instantly started racing, and he carefully opened his eyes, looking around the busy space with a perfectly collected expression while internally he was anything but. One by one, he took in each nurse's face, the physician's assistants, the doctors, the surgeons....

Any one of them fit their new profile. He glanced at the ship's chief medical officer as he returned. Except for Balok, he decided. The man's mind was all over the place, far from methodical and nearly incapable of keeping a mental secret. The doctor frowned as he approached, noting Holt's sudden pallor and his abnormal stillness as he took in every part of his surroundings. Hypervigilant—it was the way he got when he was on to something.

"Lieutenant," he said softly, taking care to look unconcerned to any outsider as he handed the man the cream and fussed with some reports on his desk. "Is something the matter?"

"Has anyone's behavior suddenly changed?" Holt asked, still looking at the people surrounding them with piercing scrutiny.

"Everyone's has, following what we've been through," Balok replied under his breath, still maintaining his buoyant, nonchalant air.

"No, before that," Holt elaborated, trying to keep his breathing even despite the breakneck pace of his heart. "Did anyone suddenly become much more absorbed in their work—clocking long hours and late nights? Perhaps they requested more lab time?"

Balok's heart skipped a beat as he calmly signed off on a patient's chart.

"Now that you mention it," he began cautiously, checking that they wouldn't be overheard, "Nurse Dalia has become quite industrious." He turned to Gehmra as the furred nurse walked over and handed him another patient's updated chart. "Thank you, Gehmra." She flashed a quick smile at him, her elongated eyeteeth catching the overhead lights as she returned to work.

"Send her to security headquarters, doctor," Holt murmured. He stood and headed for the door at a casual pace, raising his voice slightly to allay suspicion. "Thank you for the medication."

"Of course, lieutenant," Balok said in veiled reply to both statements and gave the man a smile only the two of them knew was fake.

As soon as he was out of the medbay, Holt reached for Sprit's link. *"Jon's agent is a part of medical. Possible suspect found."*

In the damaged cell, Sprit immediately tensed, and Rin felt her skin begin to crawl in that way that spelled nothing but trouble.

"I have to go," the security chief said and abruptly stood to leave.

"What's wrong?"

"It's nothing, Rin—"

"Don't lie to me," the girl protested, standing and following Sprit to the door as the woman closed it in her face. "Sprit, what's going on?"

"I'll tell you once I know," she promised, briefly touching her hand to where Rin's was pressed against the glass before running for the exit. "Just stay there and keep your head down!"

"I *can't* leave," Rin called after her. "You guys locked me in here!"

The teenager watched Sprit vanish through the door and shivered as she backed up to the wall and let herself slide down it to the floor. Horrible, suffocating dread crawled about in the pit of her stomach, its slick tendrils coiling around her insides and tightening until she felt ready to throw up, and she watched as the purple energy did the same, lifting once more from her skin in a visible manifestation of her fear.

She closed her eyes and breathed deep. *Control. Keep control.*

———

Holt looked up as Sprit ran into their security headquarters, slightly out of breath. When she spoke, she was blunt, to the point.

"Who?"

"Nurse Dalia."

"Are you *sure?*"

"As much as I can be, ma'am," he reported, and she nodded curtly. "Balok is sending her here now. She's just down the hall."

"Okay. Okay, let's do this."

Sprit released a long, slow breath as she undid and redid her ponytail, hating the way her hands minutely trembled. They possibly had him. Just this once, they were possibly ahead of Jon Bledsoe's game. She sat beside Holt and composed herself just as the door opened, and Dalia walked in, galaxy-filled eyes wide with guileless curiosity.

"You wanted to talk to me, commander?" she asked, looking to Sprit, and the woman gestured to the chair opposite them.

"Yeah, Dalia, we did. Please, take a seat."

The violet-skinned nurse sat down a little nervously.

"Is something wrong?"

"Well, that's what we're trying to figure out." Sprit paused. "Dalia, I need you to tell us everything you did during the refueling run on Othlu's far moon."

———

"Doctor, I'm stepping out for my food break now," Gehmra called, and Balok waved from his microscope, not looking up from the sample he was studying.

"Have a pleasant meal," he said absently, not even registering the fact that the nurse's lunch period wasn't for another two hours.

In the hallway, Gehmra quickly took out her earwig and surreptitiously crushed it under her heel. It was time. She set off down the hall at an unbothered pace, anxiously fiddling with the button and circuit board disguised as her necklace's pendant as she went.

"Hey, Gehmra!" someone called, and she smiled and waved. "You still on duty?"

"No, I just got off," she lied. "But I need to check something out in auxiliary control for Balok's life support status report before I'm free."

"I swear the man doesn't understand the premise of shift hours," her coworker laughed, and she rolled her eyes.

"With how often he forgets to go home, I agree. I'll see you around, my friend." She continued on her way, turning the piece of jewelry over and over in her fingers.

It's time.

"And nothing else happened, Dalia?" Holt pressed, and the medical officer shook her head.

"N-no, sir. Does this have to do with Talik and Jhama? People have been talking—"

"Maybe we should move on to extracurricular activities," Sprit interrupted and slid her tablet across the table. "What it is you're working on that requires so much overtime in auxiliary control, Dalia? Life support systems haven't been malfunctioning since Sahmot, so I must admit Holt and I at a bit of a loss to explain it ourselves."

Dalia's face contorted in genuine confusion as she picked up the device.

"I...I have no idea what this is," she stammered, looking up at them in fear. "I haven't been working in auxiliary control."

"Dalia," Holt said gravely, "we can easily confirm these records with security footage. Lying to us will not help you."

"I'm *not* lying, though! I have a strict routine, I-I work my hours and then I go to the gym, then to the cafeteria, and then my quarters."

Holt walked over to one of the room's computer terminals and did a cursory check of the last day, following the itinerary Dalia had given them. And sure enough, there she was in each place she'd said she'd been. Sprit glanced at her deputy in confusion as he spoke through their link.

"She's telling the truth, ma'am."

"How is that possible?"

Holt's stomach suddenly dropped out, and he turned off the monitor in tense silence.

"Dalia," he began, far too calm and collected for the intense distress Sprit could feel through their link, and he returned to the table, his pace deliberate in a way that told the security chief he was shaken to his core. "Whom did you give your personnel code to?"

Dalia blinked in shock, struggling to grasp what he was suggesting. "W-what?"

In her cell, Rin began trembling. The dread was choking her now, and she couldn't shake the ghastly feeling crushing down on her. There was a knife hanging, invisible, above her head, held at bay by nothing more than a slowly fraying string. Something was coming. She braced herself on her hands and knees and groaned as she tried not to throw up.

Behind his desk, the lieutenant nervously stood, eyeing the barely-contained energy storm eddying about his charge.

"Hey, you okay?"

"Your personnel code," Sprit repeated, quickly grasping where Holt was going with this. "Someone has it. They've been using your credentials to sign into auxiliary and work overtime on something."

"Who?" Dalia stammered, shaken, and Holt stepped in again, sensing Sprit's mounting frustration.

"That is what we're asking you," he said, and the nurse looked at him helplessly. "Did you give your code to *anyone*, Dalia?"

"No!" she cried, shaking her head vehemently. "No, I keep it secret, as per protocol. I—"

"Someone had to get it somewhere," Sprit pressed, missing the way her partner tensed and spaced out beside her, lost a deck below them.

"Oh, Creator," Holt breathed and grabbed his bondmate's arm in a sudden vice-like grip. "I know who it is."

Gehmra pushed the small button at the center of her pendant as she brushed past auxiliary control.

It was done. Now, there was only one thing left to do….

On the bridge, Lucien froze, lifting his hands away from his console.

"Whoa," he said sharply, confused and alarmed, and everyone on the bridge quickly looked at him.

"What is it, ensign?" Oren asked, and Lucien hesitated, struggling to explain what was happening.

"Our shields dropped," he said in disbelief, quickly trying to bring the vital device back on line and failing. A second later, the pitch of the engines changed, and *Starlight* very obviously began slowing down.

"Ensign—"

"This isn't me, sir!" Lucien replied, voice cracking with anxiety as he tried and failed to restart their vessel. "I don't know what's happening, but this isn't me!"

"Avery Byrone."

Oren quickly accepted the incoming call.

"Captain, what are you all doing up there?" the engineer demanded, clearly annoyed. "All of our engine coils just went cold. You *know* that's not good on the components—"

"Byrone, that wasn't us," Oren interrupted sharply. "If it wasn't us and it wasn't you, then it was auxiliary control. Get over there and figure out what in the galaxy is going on."

"Sir, we just lost weapons, too," Lucien reported in a panic, and the captain's hands clenched around the edges of his chair.

No, he thought to himself, staring out at the empty expanse of stars before them as *Starlight* came to a stop. *No, no, no, no.*

A vessel came out of traveling speed just outside weapons range off *Starlight*'s starboard bow. Her new captain smirked, steepling his hands over his nose and mouth as he stared at the defenseless ship.

"Bring us right up to her nose," he ordered, small smile turning into a savage grin. "And drop the cloak on my order."

"Yes, sir."

"Sir, we have an incoming message," Anthia reported quickly.

"From where?"

"A ship," she replied as she worked, and the captain fought the urge to lecture her on her deliberate terseness.

"*Where*, Anthia?" he repeated, fear only making his frustration worse. "There's no one out here except us—"

"What in the…sir, I just lost control of my communications board," Anthia interrupted, turning to him. "The whole system just shut down. I have no access to anything."

A new voice suddenly spoke, oozing from every single speaker on the bridge, and Oren's blood went cold.

"Hello, Ren."

Hanali'a went still at her station, her hearts beating in rapid tandem. That voice—she and Oren hadn't heard that voice in so long, had prayed they would *never* hear that voice again.

"Anthia, turn it off," Oren said before he could help it, before he could remember that Anthia was just as helpless as he was, and the voice on the other end of the line sighed dramatically.

"Sorry, Ren, she can't do that. I had Gehmra recode and rewire your core systems." Lucien felt the last remaining shreds of hope in his heart slowly disintegrate as he watched his captain slowly cave in at his station, his expression numb and...and *powerless*. The taunting voice continued. "Shields, bridge communications, weaponry, engines—I control it all."

Oren closed his eyes, shakily inhaling and exhaling as Jon Bledsoe laughed, the sound a bone-chilling chuckle.

"Unfortunately, only for the next ten minutes," he conceded with a lamenting sigh. "I only had so much time to put this together, but we both know ten minutes is enough for me to do irreparable damage. You *see*, Ren, I *was* planning on killing you. That's what Ensign Ciarul was for. But she failed, as we both know, and that was when I uncovered something of mine." The lighter lilt to his voice vanished, replaced by a note far colder and more dangerous. "I'm going to take it back now."

Rin.

"She's not an it, Jon," Oren said to the room, voice shockingly steady and bold. "And you're not taking her."

Jon gave another theatrical sigh and began lazily counting down.

"Three...two...one...*zero*."

Oren flinched at the way he growled the last number.

Oh djienn, Jon, what have you done?

"Gehmra just shot herself in the head, brother dear," Jon announced, and Lucien let out half a sob before he could stop himself, hand clapped over his mouth. Oren went as still as Hanali'a.

"Acoua, verify that," he ordered flatly, completely unreadable. Anthia ran over to Sprit's station, checking internal scanners and security camera feeds. He looked over his shoulder, and she met his gaze with somber black eyes.

She nodded.

Oren looked back at the empty viewscreen, seething.

"Jon, *stop it*," he ordered.

"Give me my shield maiden, and I will," he returned patronizingly, and the captain's grip tightened even more around his chair.

"Not. Going. To. Happen," he growled between clenched teeth and let his voice rise to a near-shout. "She is a *child*, Jon! She isn't part of your game—"

"Our game, Ren," Jon corrected like he was speaking to a toddler. "*Our* game. Don't forget it was *your* guard dog that blinded me the day I…redecorated your skull," he finished with an unseen smile that made Oren's skin crawl, and Hanali'a looked at him gravely.

Her captain was unraveling, falling apart.

"Jon," Oren tried again, nearly begging, but Bledsoe cut him off.

"I think I'll let you have your communications array back, brother," he mused, taunting and overly considerate. "I wouldn't want our reunion to be deprived of a welcoming party, now would I? That gets rid of the fun." He gave that chilling laugh again and sighed. "I'm taking what's mine, Ren, whether you allow it or not. See you soon."

"Jon!" Oren shouted, standing, but the channel went dead, filled with nothing but static.

"Sir, we have communications control again," Anthia called, but he didn't respond. "Sir!"

He couldn't breathe, couldn't think, couldn't speak. The breath had been knocked out of him along with everything else.

And then Jon's ship de-cloaked right in front of them.

People are only as strong as their leaders, my son.

"Acoua," he ordered, shaking himself free of his momentary freeze, "sound the boarding alarm, all decks. Tell them it's Jon Bledsoe and to approach with extreme caution. Also, tell Sprit she needs get Rin out of the brig and someplace safe, and you need to coordinate with Lucien, Avery, and aux control to restore power. We can't give Jon ten minutes."

"Yes, sir."

He took a deep breath as the sirens started once more, and the room descended into a chaotic flurry of talking. He touched his scars and slowly took his seat, staring down the vessel before him. His black uniform stood out starkly against the stainless white of his chair, and he grounded himself in the ridges of paler, healed skin beneath his fingertips and the jagged end of his broken horn and glanced at Hanali'a. The giant met his tormented gaze with her calm, centering one and nodded once.

He turned his focus back to Jon's waiting ship and clenched his jaw.

So, toughen up.

CHAPTER 28

"We're putting a team each at the fore and aft of every deck. Try not to let Bledsoe speak. If you've got protective auditory equipment, use it," Sprit ordered, walking quickly past the gathered officers. "I'm staying here in headquarters as your director, and I'll notify you the moment we've been boarded. Any questions?"

"Are we shooting to kill or incapacitate, ma'am?" Holt asked softly, and Sprit glanced at him.

"Captain hasn't said which, so I'm making the call. Shoot to kill." She adjusted the setting on her own weapon. "If Oren changes that call, I'll let you know. If he doesn't and gets mad at us afterwards, I'll take full responsibility."

"Yes, ma'am."

"Now go." Everyone left at a jog, but Sprit caught Holt's arm before he could lead his team out. "I need you to take your group and get Rin out of the brig. Do not let anyone know he's her father," she whispered, and he nodded.

"Yes, ma'am. Where do I take her?"

"Anywhere. Just make sure she's hidden."

"Jon will not get his hands on her, commander. I promise."

Sprit watched Holt lead his team off at a run and quickly went to her command computer, pulling up top-view maps of every deck and tracking the teams as they split up. She turned her earwig to the conference setting and cleared her throat.

"This is Matzepo. All teams check in." She took a deep breath as one by one, the team leaders stated their names. "Okay, let's do our jobs."

"What's Avery's status, Trinidore?"

"Uh, they're trying to reroute power and reboot the ship's wiring and coding," Lucien reported, quickly reading off the report in his hands. "It doesn't look good though. We may have to give Jon his ten minutes."

"That's not good enough, ensign—"

"Someone just quantum jumped onto deck four," Anthia called from Sprit's station, harshly cutting through the chatter. "Single person jump device, no signs of other uninvited guests."

Oren and Hanali'a quickly looked at each other.

The brig.

"It seems he still has that clever gadget, captain," Han said softly, and Oren quickly touched his earwig.

"Sprit Matzepo."

"Oren, someone jumped onto deck four—"

"Sprit, that's Jon. Send a security team to intercept and get Rin out of there now." He hesitated, glancing guiltily at Hanali'a. "Shoot to incapacitate and capture."

"*Sir,*" Sprit tried to argue, and he cut her off.

"Give the order, Sprit. He's killed too many people to not be held accountable." He closed the channel and frowned as his first officer got up to leave. "Han, where are you going?"

She looked back at him evenly, not breaking her pace.

"Fulfilling a promise, sir," she said, and Lucien watched nervously as she left without another word.

He had a bad feeling about whatever she was going to do and a quick glance at his captain told him he did as well.

———

"What is going on?" Rin shouted after the seventh security officer to run by and swore as he gave her the same answer the other six had.

"Nothing for you to worry about, miss! It'll be fine!"

The door closed behind him, and she squeezed her eyes shut, arms wrapping tightly around her stomach as she dropped to her knees and forcefully subdued another potential shockwave.

"*Intruder on deck four,*" the computer announced in its empty tones. "*Armed and dangerous, approach with extreme caution. Intruder on deck four—*"

Rin looked up at the ceiling and felt a wave of nausea and fear sweep over her as she realized she was on deck four. She couldn't get out. She was trapped in here, she couldn't get out, what if the intruder came in here and tried to kill her—

She gritted her teeth as the tendrils increased in size and number, and doubled over.

"Please," she wheezed. "Please, don't. I've been doing so well, don't do this—"

"Rin!"

She looked up with a gasp, and Holt's stomach turned as he saw the purple light in her irises and the coiled arcs of energy sparking around her.

"Holt," she whispered, taking in the team of six people behind her friend and the drawn weapons in their hands. "What's going on? No one will tell me what's happening."

"Bledsoe's here. We're getting you somewhere safe," he explained as he quickly unlocked the cell door and opened it.

"What? N-no, I can't leave here," Rin protested, retreating from the open door. "This—this is safe. Oren said this was safe, he said this was the most reinforced part of the ship."

"Rin—" He stopped, and the girl instantly recognized the spaced out look on his face. Sprit was talking to him. "Rin, he's coming for you right now. We *need* to go." He held his hand out to her, and she fearfully shook her head, pressing herself against the wall. "Rin, *look* at me."

"I'll hurt you," she whispered. "I can barely control it in here. Out there, I'll hurt all of you."

"You control it," he pressed, voice admirably calm given the person closing in on them. "It listens only to you, so *make* it obey, Rin!"

She looked at his hand in open anguish, and Holt glanced over his shoulder. He could feel him coming. Could feel the anger and malice and *desire*, and he looked back at Rin.

"Rin," he breathed, taking a few quick steps into the cell and keeping his hand extended to her. "You will not hurt me. But the man coming for you right now? He will *kill* me. He'll kill all of us. I need you to take my hand." Holt swallowed hard, pushing the terror of his crewmates down the hall out of his mind. "You *will not* hurt me."

Rin looked up at him with glowing eyes, and he held his breath.

Jon looked around as he walked purposefully towards the brig. It had been so long since he'd seen this ship, since he'd roamed her halls, and he scoffed. She hadn't changed a bit—just like her master.

"Stop!"

Oh, there's so much you can do in a heartbeat. Behold.

In the span of a second, Jon lazily looked at the voice, smiled at the six security officers and the weapons trained on him, glanced at their ears, and, seeing that only two had protection, smirked.

How cute. I'm about to have some fun.

"Kill the two with hearing devices and then sleep for an hour," he said off-handedly and without breaking pace.

"No, *wait!*"

Jon closed his eyes with a blissful smile and listened to the startled shouts of the doomed officers as their friends killed them without hesitation, followed by the thud of six bodies hitting the floor. He could have just told them to *all* kill each other, he noted as he brushed past the fallen people. But where was the fun in not having to live with the memory of killing one's friends and coworkers without question?

He glanced at the security camera as he rounded the corner and gave it a big smile. Little Matzepo was no doubt watching; all the more reason to put on a show. But before he could continue, he heard fabric rustling behind him, accompanied by the soft footfalls of someone who knew how to move quickly and silently, and he spun around.

"STOP!" he bellowed, and Hanali'a came to a skidding halt not one foot behind him, looming there in the perfect freeze frame of the instant before she would have tackled him. He gave a breathless, nervous laugh as he looked up at her and suppressed a shiver at the murderous light shining in her eyes and lining her massive body.

"I'm afraid you were too slow this time, guard dog," he sneered as he caught his breath and gestured to his blind eye and scarred face. "Appreciating your handiwork?"

"Greatly," she muttered, eyes blazing, and he scowled.

"This is your lucky day, Hanali'a, because I want to save this particular payback for when I actually have time to break every bone in your body. So, *sleep.*"

He walked away, not waiting for her collapse but taking pleasure in the sound her body made hitting the floor anyways.

He had places to be.

Sprit sat before her computer and stared in open-mouthed horror at the screen, at the bodies strewn in Jon's wake. Some were asleep. Others were dead by each other's hands, though their foe only seemed to resort to that command to take out those with auditory protective devices.

Once she'd recognized the pattern, Sprit had told her people to take the devices off, and she prayed it'd been the right call. She looked back at the cameras following Jon and shuddered as he flashed her another feral grin over the streams. He was taunting her, playing with them all, and she frantically reached out to her link as Jon brushed through another team with ease and, she hoped, no casualties before rounding the corner of the last hall before the brig.

"*Lewis, you need to go. You NEED TO GO!*"

Rin took Holt's hand.

The tendrils instantly retreated up her arm, dying away as if aware of who she was touching and not wanting to cause him any pain.

"Not dead," she whispered, wide eyed.

"Not dead," he agreed. "Now, come on." He quickly pulled her along behind him, setting off at a run that she struggled to keep up with as they rushed out of the brig and into the hall. "Close ranks around us," he told the team quickly and squeezed Rin's hand as he took the lead, keeping her squarely behind him and holding his gun at the ready. "We'll keep you safe, Rin. Just stay close and stay behind me."

"Lewis?"

He looked back at her and gave her a quick, reassuring smile as they hurried down the hall. She was breathing heavily, fighting to keep her ability in check and, so far, succeeding.

"You're doing very well, Rin." She shakily returned the smile, looking more like she was about to cry than anything else, and he squeezed her hand again. "Keep it up."

"Okay. I can—" Her eyes widened as she looked past Holt, and she paled, coming to a stop and clutching his arm, pulling him back. "Holt!"

He quickly faced forward and stopped, his team lifting their weapons beside him and adopting a defensive stance around him and Rin.

A man clad in all black and a heavy coat stood in the middle of the hall directly in front of them. He was tall, probably as tall as Holt, and Rin dug her nails into her friend's arm as she took in the long, jagged scar blinding his left eye and the damaged skin around it. Ragged, graying hair framed his gaunt face, and Rin whimpered as she saw her own eyes staring back at her, soulless and cruel.

Jon.

"Run," Holt ordered, trying to push Rin away without looking at her, but she only hung on tighter.

"No, Holt—"

"*Run!*" he shouted, tearing his arm from her grasp so he could hold his weapon with two hands. "We'll hold him off, run!" He felt his friend unsteadily back away, far too slow, and he glanced back at her, letting her see his fear and grim resolve. "Rin, *run!*"

Finally galvanized into action, Rin turned tail and ran, sprinting as fast as she could back the way they'd come, and Holt faced the Alympan before them. He had to buy her enough time to get away. He nodded to his team, and they started forward slowly.

"Jon Bledsoe," he began, "you're under arrest—"

"Stop moving," the man said, nearly yawning with disinterest.

Holt's heart stuttered in his chest as his team froze, and he bumped into the officer in front of him. Even from this distance, he could see the twisted smirk on Jon's face as he nonchalantly walked towards them.

In headquarters, Sprit was frozen in her seat, hands pressed over her mouth. She couldn't do anything. She was helpless, could do nothing but *watch*—

"Normally, I'd have some fun, but I have something to chase down," Jon said as he passed them, matter-of-fact in his voice and pace. "So, set your guns to kill and shoot yourselves in the head."

The security team obeyed in a unified motion without hesitating, and before Holt could even react, his vision went white and his hearing drowned in a loud bang as he jumped out of his skin.

"NO!"

Holt could feel Sprit's scream and her anguish in his very bones, and he was suddenly alone, his breath as loud as a hurricane in his ears. Why was he alone? He reached for his face with violently shaking hands, aware of a strange sensation on his skin, and his fingers came away wet and sticky. Why was his face wet and sticky? Why was he trembling?

He slowly lowered his hands, and suddenly the numb, buzzing bell jar that had descended over him shattered.

Blood—not his blood and not just one kind of blood. He looked down with a shaky, nauseated groan to see his team lying in a gruesome, hapless mess on the floor around him, their eyes open and empty, and bile surged up in the back of his throat.

Dead. They were all dead, they all just shot themselves because Jon Bledsoe told them to—

Jon.

"What the…"

Holt turned to see the Alympan standing there in shock, looking at him like he was a bomb, a monster, some horrible anomaly of nature. He wasn't dead. It hit Holt like an asteroid. He wasn't dead. He could move.

Jon hadn't controlled him.

The realization seemed to hit the Alympan at the same time, because the man began running. After a few dazed moments, Holt lunged after him. His pace was shaky, slow, and he forced himself to forget the dead and focus instead on Rin. He had to get to her. He had to stop Jon.

"Lewis! Lewis, holy djienn—" Sprit's voice came over the earwig.

"Commander, the other teams must stay away," he panted. "Jon's on the warpath. He will kill anyone who gets in his way to Rin now, and we cannot lose any more people."

"Lewis, are you okay?" she asked, voice shaking.

"Commander, give the order. I'm not important right now."

"Lewis!"

"I'm fine, ma'am," he lied. "Now, please, give the order. I'm the only one who can get near Jon safely."

In headquarters, Sprit glared at the computer screen, rage turning her chest into a furnace.

"Not the only one," she growled and ran from the security offices, booking it for the nearest lift and turning invisible as she went.

Jon wouldn't know what hit him.

Rin sprinted for her life, energy arcing off her and leaving scores on the plating and walls as she went. She couldn't keep control for much longer. She didn't even know where she was running, and all she could think of was the auction, running with no direction and finding nothing but dead ends with something horrible on her heel—

"Rin, stop!" Jon shouted as he crashed around a corner behind her.

Rin screamed as she came to a stumbling halt, her arms bent at her elbows and palms facing her chest. The Alympan jogged over to her, eyes gleaming as he took in the way her ability was rapidly spiraling out of control, lashing around her in an attempt to protect her.

"Stop that, too."

A false, forced sense of calm came over her, and Rin groaned as the light quickly returned to her skin, pulsating beneath its thin barrier like a caged animal. She felt helpless, trapped, and she forced back tears as Jon slowly circled her, taking her in as he went. She wasn't about to give him the satisfaction of crying. He came to a stop before her, peering at her like she was a rare gem.

"You look like Myra," he finally said, and Rin shuddered at the sound of her mother's name on his lips, the greedy light in his eyes. "She was a pretty young thing, too."

"She died," Rin said accusingly. "Brain aneurysm."

"A pity," he replied, tone saying it really wasn't.

The girl squeezed her eyes shut, clenching her jaw.

"After you left, she was a zombie," she continued, shaking. She had to know the truth about this part of her story. "Was that your fault?"

"Probably," Jon admitted with a shrug as he examined Rin, especially the purple embedded in her skin. "I did tell her to forget quite a lot."

"How often?" she whispered, fury creeping into her voice.

"Oh, easily twice a day," he answered absently like a cruel version of Balok. "I had to rant about what my brother had done to me somehow." He looked at Rin, smirking at his own humor, but frowned when he saw the quiet rage filling her eyes. "I've offended you."

"You *killed* her," Rin spat, trembling in anger now. Jon just shrugged.

"A regrettable side effect." The girl gaped at him and slowly the tears started to fall. He was unbelievable. The sheer *callousness*... "You are the perfect blend, you know," he said, reaching out and lifting a handful of her long, straight hair and admiring the dark color. "Myra's looks, my Alympan abilities..." He leaned a little closer to her face. "Though, those are my eyes and mouth, aren't they? How fitting."

Oh, I definitely want her. The raw might and potential...it's unparalleled.

"Please," Rin begged, wanting nothing more than to pull away from him.

"Look at you, Rin!" he laughed as he grabbed her arms and grinned. "You're powerful, immensely, *beyond* measure. You could rule anything you choose. You're invaluable. Untouchable." An eerie light touched his eyes. "Don't you like that? After everything you've been through? To be untouchable?"

"Jon," Rin tried, refusing to call him by his familial title, but he continued speaking.

"If you come with me, I can show you how to *use* your abilities," he pressed, voice growing eager and his eyes more feverish, "not cage them. You'd be *free*." His expression became darker, his voice conspiratorial. "Tell me...have they treated you the same here?"

"Yes," Rin said immediately, and he snarled.

"The *truth!* Tell me the *truth*, Rin!"

"*Yes*," she repeated, eyeing the man with barely veiled disgust. "It was to protect me—"

"THEM!" Jon roared, and Rin flinched, closing her eyes and hating her tears at his sudden shout. "It was to protect *them*," he hissed, pointing his finger in her face, and she slowly opened her eyes to look at him. "Even a half-born like you...you're a world above and beyond. I can give you a life where you'd *never* answer to anyone. Never have to feel scared that you were going to hurt someone or *guilty* if things went wrong." He tapped her forehead, and his voice lost its wonder to bitterness. "*Ren* can't give you that. All *Ren* thinks about is *himself*—his crew, *his* family. He doesn't see you for your own wants and ambitions." His speech was growing less and less controlled. "He sees you only as a tool to be harnessed. If you come with me—"

"You are insane!" Rin shouted, finally unable to stand his tirade any longer. "That's *you!* That's *you*, not Oren—"

Rin cried out in pain, unable to flinch or hide, as Jon backhanded her.

"How dare...you are mine!" he shouted back. "*My* daughter!"

"I'm *no one's!*" she screamed, not caring about her tears now. "I'm *not* your pawn!"

"SILENCE!" The hall fell quiet save for their ragged breathing, and Rin shivered as the fear began to set in through the anger. Jon started circling her again, this time like a shark instead of an admirer. "I see Ren has corrupted you already," he said, his voice dangerously even and quiet, "filled your head with his righteousness. We are gods, *demigods* among mere mortals, Rin," he growled, alarmingly close to her now. "We are the new order. We can shape whole planets. We could change the *galaxy!*" She flinched at his half-shout in her ear, and his voice dropped back to calm and controlled. "But with *Ren* in the way..."

Jon stopped. A sudden light of *laughter* was growing in Rin's eyes, and he glanced around them at the empty hall. He didn't trust this.

"What are you laughing at?" he demanded. "Speak!"

Rin giggled a little deliriously, closing her eyes.

"Ren," she echoed and opened her eyes, her giggle transforming into a laugh at his baffled expression. "That's what you call Oren. And you ranted to mom about him almost twice a day for a whole year."

She laughed again, long and hard, and broke off with a watery smile, eyes filled with tears. But she was sure they weren't bad tears.

"Mom said she named me after *your* friend. She named me after *him.*" It took a moment, but when it finally clicked, Jon's face contorted in rage, and Rin began laughing again. "Your only child is named after the man you despise," she snorted.

"ENOUGH!" Jon bellowed, and she went silent, staring at him with an indomitable light in her eyes now that left him unsettled. "Now, you will come with me whether you like it or not," he growled, grabbing her arm and yanking her after him down the hall. "Move—"

"Stop."

Rin heaved a sigh of relief at the familiar voice, and Jon momentarily tensed before recovering himself. He turned to face Holt, tutting at the weapon aimed at him.

"Ah-ah, Mister Holt. I may not be able to control you, but I do control her." To emphasize his point, her jerked Rin around to face her friend, and she paled at his ghastly appearance.

That blood…none of it was his.

"Let her go, Jon," he ordered softly, burning with quiet strength, but Jon just laughed. Rin meanwhile, took in her friend's ashen complexion, his haunted eyes, and her rage only grew. Subtly, she curled her fingers into a fist

"You are in *no* position to demand anything," Jon said incredulously. "We're leaving now. Rin—"

You will never touch me again.

Rin howled in pain and wrath and brought her fist slamming into her father's chest, her tendrils coalescing about her arm like armor before discharging, and Holt took a startled step back as Jon was hurled into the wall so hard he dented it and crumpled to the floor.

A few stray arcs of Rin's energy crackled across his body before dissipating, and the stunned girl spun around, gaping, to look at Holt. Her arm was still encased in the mesh of tendrils, and she held it up between them, breathing heavily.

"This is new?" she said weakly.

"Rin, come on. Let's go!" he called, beckoning for her to join him, and she started forward, only for Jon to grab her ankle and yank her leg out from under her. She cried out in pain as she landed awkwardly on her hip and looked in terror at the man lunging for her.

"You think you can throw me around like a *ragdoll*—"

"Get away from her!" Holt shouted, starting towards them, and Jon snarled.

"Oh, shut him up!" he spat, and, against her will, Rin threw an arm out at her friend.

Her energy bolt struck him full in the chest, throwing him across the hall and cracking his skull against a beam with a loud snap.

"Stop!" Rin begged as Holt collapsed, unconscious, and Jon got up, standing over her. He was seething, livid with blood dribbling from the corner of his mouth, and for a split second, Rin could see the message he sent Oren after the captain had confronted him eighteen years ago.

"You think you can stand up to *me?*" he hissed, voice growing louder. "You can throw *me* around?"

Rin looked up at him from the floor, recalling Oren's words. He'd said she had Jon's temper.

Time to give him a taste of it.

"Yes," she hissed, letting go of her control, and her eyes turned completely, inhumanly purple. "You hurt my friends. And you killed mom."

His face contorted into something ugly, indescribable.

"Kill—"

His command was cut off as something body slammed into him from the front, leaping over Rin to lock its legs around his neck and painfully and brutally slam him into the ground. Once he was down, it quickly straddled his torso, yanked the Alympan up by his coat lapels, and head-butted him so hard his nose shattered.

And just like that Rin knew exactly who it was.

Vision red, Sprit grabbed Jon's head and slammed it against the plate floor a couple times, swearing at him in Trozeran with each strike. This was for Oren. This was for their brother who he so brutally attacked, for every person he took from them, for Jhama, for Talik—

"Filthy war brat!" Jon shouted, mouth bloody, and clocked Sprit in the head with a harsh strike from his quantum jump cuff. The security chief cried out in pain, falling back as she clapped a hand over her brow and briefly flickering into view. Jon scrambled to his feet, lunging for his sister, and Rin saw her opening.

"Sprit, move!" she shouted and stood up.

Sprit rolled to the side, leaving Jon open, and Rin quickly threw her arm out at him, blasting him back the way he'd forced her to attack Holt. The Alympan crashed to the deck plating at the other end of the hall in a sparking heap of battered bones and scorched clothes, and he struggled to his feet, breathing heavily and groaning in pain. He glared down the corridor and bared his teeth with a snarl.

The half-Alympan stared him down, standing between him and her friends with her hands clenched at her sides.

Her tendrils had finally decided on a pattern, coalescing over most of her arms and legs and her torso like plate armor with a few coils reaching up to frame her face, and he met her glowing eyes. There were no irises, no pupils—just light and one emotion that he knew his own bore.

Fury. Abject rage.

He'd lost this round.

As Rin watched, Jon took an uncertain half-step back before pressing a button on his metal cuff and vanishing in a blinding flash. The ship's alarms that Rin hadn't even noticed were still sounding shut off, and her symbiotic companion quietly departed, the colorful force arcing around her slowly fading back beneath her skin where it belonged.

And everything was peaceful.

CHAPTER 29

"Holt!" Sprit called, hurrying over to her deputy's side as he groaned and slowly tried to sit up. "Easy. Easy, just take it slow."

"No, Rin," he muttered, blearily reaching for the threshold of the quarters next to them and grabbing ahold of the doorjamb so he could pull himself into a sitting position. "Go help Rin, ma'am. I'm—"

He broke off, startled, as Sprit wrapped him in a hug that was no less crushing for its brevity, and she pulled back, looking into his eyes.

"Do *not* do that again," she growled, and he blinked.

"Do what, ma'am?" he asked, and Sprit gave a delirious laugh.

"Anything you've done this whole affair, okay?" she said with an only half-joking grin. "No more bombs, no more getting blown into space, no more near-forced-suicides, no more getting knocked out, just...no more, agreed?"

Holt gingerly touched the back of his head and winced in pain. That would leave yet another bump.

"I agree, ma'am," he groaned, and she rolled her eyes as she got up and went over to Rin.

"Rin, you okay?" she asked, gently putting a hand on the girl's shoulder, and the half-human looked at her with a strange, glassed over look in her eyes. Sprit quickly turned concerned and grabbed her other shoulder as well, holding her steady. "Rin?"

The girl didn't answer, instead looking down the hall to the sound of approaching footfalls, and shortly Oren rounded the corner, surrounded by his security team. They all had their weapons free, and as soon as they saw their fellow crewmates, they fanned out to inspect the area.

"What happened?" the captain asked, holstering his weapon. "Anthia was getting abnormal energy readings."

"What's Jon's status?"

"He's gone, Sprit. Now, what happened here?" Oren repeated, and she gave a short bark of laughter.

"Captain, you'd have to see it to believe it." She gently shook Rin's shoulder and gave her a lopsided grin. "I'll show you the security feeds."

"Rin saved our lives, sir," Holt clarified, wincing as he stood up and the world spun a little.

"I'm afraid you can't show us security feeds, Sprit. Whatever Miss Cooper did fried the cameras," the captain said, looking at Rin appraisingly. "I suppose I'll just have to see it myself some other time."

"I didn't…" Rin trailed off, missing the captain's good-humored tone in her tired state. "I'm sorry…."

"Oh, no, he's just joking. You did great," Sprit assured her, gently squeezing her shoulder, but Rin stumbled away, struggling to walk back towards the brig. Sleep. She needed sleep.

"I'm…" Her already ashen complexion turned haggard as she passed out, and Oren quickly lunged forward, barely managing to catch her and cradling her close. He scooped her up easily in a bridal carry and looked at his security officers.

"Medbay, all three of you," he ordered. "You both look like you got some pretty nasty blows to the head."

"Yes, sir," Holt confirmed wearily and readily accepted Sprit's offer to help him walk, letting his arm drape across her shoulders as she firmly supported his waist. "Sir…we lost more people."

Oren shifted his hold on Rin, focusing on her sleeping face.

"I know."

"Half of our crew is gonna need to be replaced," Sprit whispered and tightened her arm around Holt's body in search of comfort he couldn't give. Oren sighed and looked at his sister and her bondmate over Rin's head as they continued down the silent hall save for their shuffling footfalls and uneven breaths.

"I know."

"You know, captain, I could do without medbay being this busy again for a very long time," Balok said as he looked over Rin. "Though I suppose we're lucky most of the people here are just sleeping and not dead or critically wounded, though we have too many of those as well."

"I'm aware of how lucky we got, doctor," Oren muttered, massaging his temples. His migraine was back. "How is she?"

"Miss Cooper, it seems, suffered from an electrolyte imbalance and dehydration," the medic explained as he set up the IV drip. "It's to be expected. She doesn't yet know how her body's needs have changed, and from what Sprit told me, she was doing some impressive tricks."

"She'll be okay, though?" Sprit asked from where she was sitting on a stool beside Holt's bed, and Balok clicked his tongue at her.

"Commander, leave your bandage alone!" She sullenly lowered her hand from her temple. "I'm not redoing that dressing before it's time," he scolded before answering her question. "But yes, your roommate will be back tomorrow, Sprit. I'll just keep her overnight for observation."

"Good," the security chief said, crossing her arms and resting them on the edge of Holt's mattress so she could prop her chin on them. "You know, Lewis, this mind link thing has been kind of useful," she began, and Holt raised an eyebrow, the gesture hampered slightly by the bandage wrapped about his head. "See, like right now, I can tell you you're actually smiling on the inside."

"I'm glad to know that is what you have learned from our experience, Sprit," he said tiredly but with a note of amusement in his words, and he let his eyes drift half-shut.

Sprit snorted and let her head rest on her arms, only to sit up almost immediately and poke his leg with a blunt finger.

"Hey!" He looked at her, and she grinned her massive, lopsided grin. "You called me Sprit."

Holt gave a quiet huff of laughter and let his eyes close.

"I suppose I did."

Oren walked over to one of the curtained-off beds and took a deep breath. This wasn't going to be a fun conversation.

"Oren," Hanali'a called, and he winced. "I can feel you out there."

He pushed open the curtain enough for him to step inside and closed it behind him. His first officer watched him with discerning eyes as he sat on the stool beside her bed and sighed, looking down. She knew that he knew he'd messed up. He was fully aware of the depth of his mistake.

"He needs to be eliminated, Oren," she said firmly, no less kind for her words. "This cannot happen again."

"I know." He looked up at her, pained. "He left you alive?"

"He said he wanted to have the time to break every one of my bones. Today wasn't that day," she recited impassively, almost unimpressed, and Oren bowed his head, sickened.

"We got lucky," he whispered, and she nodded.

"*This* time. Why did he leave?"

"It would seem his trophy was a bit more powerful than he was expecting," he sighed, looking in the general direction he knew Rin was in. Hanali'a followed his gaze as if they could see through the curtains.

"Will she be alright?"

"Physically? Today, yes. Mentally? We'll see." He groaned and wearily got to his feet. "For now, I have to go report this mess to Lokar. And…I have a lot of families to contact with bad news." Hanali'a looked down, somber and pained. "I'll see if I can set up a support group for everyone who got a notification throughout this whole affair. Hopefully they can find some comfort in each other." He walked to the curtain and paused. "I…I'm glad your wife isn't one of them."

If Hanali'a had had an eyebrow to raise, she would have.

"I am, too." She paused before drolly continuing. "Kalo'a would've killed you."

"Yes," Oren agreed wryly and opened the curtain to leave. "And I've had enough of *that* this past week."

The next morning, Holt found himself in Oren's quarters. He wasn't sure why the captain had requested his presence, but the sooner he got this over with the less uncomfortable he'd be. At the moment, they were standing before a window, looking out at the stars, and the deputy tightened his fingers around the cup of tea his captain had made him.

"I'm sorry for everything you've been through this last week, Lewis," Oren finally said softly. Holt glanced at the floor and his captain before looking back to the stars.

"Thank you, sir," he replied. "But…I am not made of glass."

"No, of course not," Oren hurried to say, looking up slightly at the man beside him. "I just…I'm sorry."

"Thank you, sir."

The captain waited as the lieutenant took a sip of his tea.

"So. You're immune to Jon's mind control?"

"Yes, sir," he replied, acutely aware of the scrutinizing eyes on him.

"Any theories?"

"A few, sir," Holt said vaguely. "I'm exploring them."

"Good…good." An awkward silence dragged out between them, and Holt took a deep breath. He had to have this talk with Oren, and this was as good a time as any.

"She should stay with us."

"Excuse me?" Oren asked, nonplussed, and Holt clarified.

"Rin, sir."

"Holt," Oren sighed and crossed his arms. "She's an inherent magnet for Jon, and I can't put my people in that kind of danger again. This is…the Bledsoe family is *not* what they signed on for."

Holt looked at the Trozeran, brow furrowed in confusion.

"Captain," he began hesitantly, shifting his hold on his cup, "it's *space*. The universe. None of us knows what we signed on for. If I can be so bold, sir, that is somewhat the point of it." Oren chuckled, and Holt continued. "She should stay with us because she *is* dangerous. She has the potential to become a weapon of mass destruction, sir. She could tear us all apart."

Oren's eyebrows traveled further up his forehead.

"You're supposed to be convincing me to *keep* her here, Holt."

"I'm getting there, sir," Lewis replied, holding a hand up in a request for patience. "She is immensely powerful. But she's also very powerless. She is vulnerable out here. In the wrong hands, she could become just as dangerous as she would have been in Jon's. Or Jon could get to her some other way. Under our supervision, that is less likely to happen."

"So," Oren began slowly, eyeing his crewman in his periphery as he spoke, "you want a WMD to stay with us—people who you have already pointed out know nothing about her—instead of the experts?"

"We are the experts, sir."

"Lewis," Oren scoffed, "you're a prodigy, not a weapon of mass destruction. There's no compari—"

"Sprit can turn invisible, sir," he countered. "Lucien can see in the dark. Avery can climb on walls and ceilings. If you think we've not asked them to do terrible things with those abilities on a job..." He trailed off and let the implication speak for itself. "Adjust the grav settings on this ship to mimic the buoyancy of water, and Hanali'a could incapacitate an entire deck before we got a shot off. As for me," he paused with a bitter laugh, "I could strip your mind of everything you know and leave you in a coma without breaking a sweat."

"Holt..."

"We're all weapons, sir," Holt continued, staring out at the stars. "We all have the capacity for something monstrous. We *are* the experts." He went quiet, tea growing cold in his hands. "May I be dismissed, sir?"

"Yes," Oren said after a few moments, not looking at the man. "You have given me quite a bit to think about." He listened as Lewis set the cup on his table and opened the door. "Goodnight, Holt."

"Goodnight, sir."

Sprit smiled as she watched Rin walk up to the massive glass wall of the observation deck. It was about time they did this, and since they'd been near the sector anyways, Sprit had convinced the captain that they owed the half-human this much. Rin had actually cried when she saw it, and Sprit knew the feeling—that ache for your first home.

In the distance was Earth.

"I ran some recon. That Internet of yours is quite useful. It's like the hive mind of humanity," the security chief finally said, waiting to see if the joke landed. It didn't, and she sighed. There was no easy way to say this. "Rin, I'm sorry, but your grandmother died two months ago."

"What?" the girl whispered and turned to her, stricken.

"Manda Cooper?" Rin nodded, and Sprit's heart ached. "I'm sorry. The obituary didn't specify how, but...they said it was peaceful." She watched sympathetically as Rin turned back to the glass. "She never gave up on you, you know?"

The girl didn't say anything for a long time.

"I'm really never going back, am I?" Rin finally murmured, and Sprit gently put an arm around her waist, pulling her close.

"You can't," she said with a wan smile. "Besides, you're not human."

"Not Alympan, either," Rin said absently, lost in the view before her. She glanced at Sprit and saw her space out briefly before giving a small smile. "What did Holt say?"

"You can stay with us," Sprit said with a smile. "He'll call for you in the morning to offer you a job as a civilian asset." Her smile turned into a smirk as she looked at the stars. "Our boy managed to convince him."

"What for?" Sprit looked at her, confused. "Why a civilian asset?"

"We could use your help," the officer said with a shrug.

"My *help?*"

"You pack a punch," Sprit said, elbowing her slightly. "And with Jon still out there..." Instantly, Rin darkened.

"He makes me sick," she muttered, shifting on her feet and scuffing her boots against the floor. "He—it's like he just wanted to *collect* me."

"Jon's a psychopath, Rin," the Ethonian sighed and rubbed the girl's back. "It's not you. He only sees things through how he can use them. So, when you stop being useful or get in his way..."

Rin recalled his hatred, how he'd changed at the drop of a hat. And she made her decision. She looked at Sprit and took a deep breath.

"How can I help?"

"We have a squad of ability-possessing crew," Sprit said with a smile. "It's only a handful of us, and we operate as first responders of sorts. We call ourselves Strike Team Leo."

"Who's in it?" Rin asked, intrigued.

"Myself, Holt, and Lucien. And Avery, if we can spare him."

"Lucien?"

"Yeah, he can see in the—"

"See in the dark, right," Rin finished, remembering the detail.

A few moments of silence passed, and Sprit glanced at Rin.

"We could really use your help," she needled and smirked. "Besides, we kinda like you." She elbowed the girl playfully. "Well, when you're not raining mayhem down on us."

"But I really am volatile," Rin protested. "I'm dangerous—"

"We'd train you," Sprit hurried to reassure her. "We *are* the best, you know."

Rin raised an eyebrow.

"I thought you said you guys were the hottest mess in space."

"Shhh," Sprit hissed, and Rin laughed. The adult waited a moment before grounding the conversation again. "You want to do some good?"

"Yeah," Rin said after a few seconds. She gave a twisted smile. "One of the Bledsoes has to turn out alright, yeah?"

"Rin, you're already alright," Sprit scolded. "You've saved a couple of lives, haven't you?"

"I guess I have," she said softly, and the two looked out at the stars for a bit. It was a wall of light with Earth in the middle of it—a marble of blue and green and white nestled in a sheet of glitter. Without the light of the sun, an atmosphere, or other filtering agents, Rin could see all of the stars, billions of shining points. It was overwhelming, colorful, heavenly.

"When I was little, I used to press my hands against my eyes when I couldn't sleep." Sprit looked at Rin as the girl continued, unblinking gaze reflecting the cosmos. "I'd make galaxies behind my eyelids—nebulas, supernovas, solar systems…. I mean, really, I just put so much pressure on my optic nerves that they freaked out, and I shouldn't have done it, but…I always liked to see the stars. Or at least imagine I was."

"How's it working out for you now?" Sprit asked. "Feel the way you thought it would?"

"Can't say that it is, no. It's better, but worse…you know?"

Sprit nodded. She knew all too well what Rin meant.

"Pretty soon, it'll just be better. Trust me."

The two women turned to leave, and Sprit pulled Rin a little closer by the waist as they went, sweeping her thumb in small, comforting strokes along her hip as they departed. As they left the dark room for *Starlight*'s brighter halls, the almost-human spared one last glance over her shoulder to Earth, so beautiful from this distance.

And in the blink of an eye, it vanished behind the closing door.

EPILOGUE

Jon sat in his quarters, staring out the window into space. No, not *his* quarters; they were commandeered, like the ship. It wasn't a good vessel. Its climate control was always on the fritz, leaving it either burning hot or freezing like it was now. He watched his breath fog before his lips, took in the way it caught the starlight from outside, trapping it in its grasp.

Someone knocked tentatively on his door, and Jon listened but did not turn his chair around as his deputy came in, every step cautious and scared.

"Is—is there anything I can get you, sir?" he asked, teeth chattering from a dizzying mix of blood loss, cold, and fear.

"My daughter, Svent, would be an *excellent* place to start."

The man shuddered at the cold fury and glanced at the holographic image currently projected on Jon's desk. It was a woman who looked a lot like the aforementioned daughter, except older and with different eyes. Maybe it was the mother. Jon finally turned his chair enough so he could look at his deputy. The man was nervous, sweating despite the freezing cold, and the Alympan snorted.

"Relax, old man. That's not an order. Yet." He looked back at the stars. "We need to re-evaluate the situation. Rin is far more powerful than I anticipated. And her *humanity…*" He spat, disgusted. "They are so malleable, and yet so stubborn at the same time. Whoever convinces them of the 'truth' first gains their undying loyalty. And Ren, well, he and his *merry* band of cast-offs and the never-should-have-succeeded got there first. They're…" He broke off in a hiss and ran his hand over his scarred eye. Oh, how long it had been since his vision was complete. "They've turned Rin into a threat," he growled, "made her unusable."

"Do you wish for us to kill her, sir?" Svent asked quietly, wringing his mangled hands.

"No, you'll never get close enough, not now," Jon said dismissively, waving him away. "And she's still smaller picture. *I want Oren,*" he hissed, continuing to run his fingers over the scarred side of his face. "I want to take everything from him as he took everything from me. I want him betrayed, gutted, cast away to some backwater, backwards planet populated by *beasts*." He slashed his hand through Myra's image as he furiously spat the last word, and it barely managed to flicker back into focus.

He considered the hologram for a moment.

"Though...Myra was beautiful...." Svent watched him reach for the gray scale figurine of light before thinking better of it. Jon's hand curled into a fist, and he pulled it back into his lap as he looked at the stars. "Rin is a threat. Now, she stands between me and Ren, her and her damn *friends*. That war orphan brat Matzepo adopted and that..." his voice dropped to a spiteful whisper, "that Mind Reader. He'll be a problem, too. The bastard's immune to me." He went quiet for a few moments and seemed to remember that Svent was still there. "Deputy!"

"Yes, sir?"

"Find out more about Lieutenant Lewis Holt. I want to know what makes him tick," he growled, fingers drumming methodically on the arm of his chair.

"Yes, sir. Anything else, sir?"

"We have to come up with something big, deputy," Jon breathed, drumming growing quicker and more intense. "Something so massive that Ren and my blasted daughter and their damned attack dogs won't be able to hold it together."

"Do you have an idea, sir?" Svent asked uncertainly, wondering if the man was asking him to come up with possible solutions. His answer came in the form of a leering grin and viciously glowing eyes.

"Oh, deputy," Jon purred, "I have *several*."

Svent shuddered and prayed his boss thought it was just the cold.

"Yes, sir."

"Dismissed," Jon said, waving his hand vaguely towards the door, and the old man hurried for his exit. "Oh, and Svent?" He stopped and looked back to Jon.

"Yes, sir?"

"Mention anything we spoke about to anyone, and I'll ask you to cut off another one of your fingers," the Alympan said lightly, and a new cold settled in the man's bones. "Understand?"

"Y-yes, sir."

"Good boy, Svent," Jon praised as if talking to a dog. "Run along."

The door clanged shut, and the mind controller sighed, turning back to his desk and the holographic projector. He reached out for the small device and clicked to the next image in the album. He chuckled and ran his hand over his scars. This one was of Rin, the screen capture Gehmra had sent him in her medical file—his daughter in the middle of a shockwave, throwing Oren and Ensign Ciarul through the air and shredding everything in her path. He considered her for a moment, head tilted to the side.

"So like Myra," he muttered. "Such a pretty thing." A long silence filled the space until Jon's face contorted into a bestial, fervent snarl. "A pity."

He brought his fist smashing down on the small holoprojector, shattering it. Rin's image vanished.

Jon turned back to the stars and steepled his fingers over his nose and mouth. His hand steadily bled where he'd cut it on the holoprojector, crimson dripping down his palm to his wrist and trickling into his sleeve uninterrupted. He either didn't care or didn't notice.

He gave the smallest smile, eyes gleaming as he stared into the nothing between the stars.

A pity, indeed…

ABOUT THE AUTHOR

R.L. Stanley splits her time between home and family in California and school in Washington. She's an irritated introvert who's loved reading and writing since she was little and has been writing non-stop from the moment she could put pen to paper. She's written one other book called *Valor* about a gay couple in the military of a dystopian society in the final year of a thirty-year war.

Starlight is the first book in *The Alympa Chronicles* series. The next book will be called *Ash and Dust*.

The Alympa Chronicles: Ash and Dust

Book 2

Read a sneak peek of the next book in the series

ASH AND DUST

Almost Two Years Ago

Breathing sounded like sandpaper. Each inhale was a long, rhythmic stroke that moved with the wood grain, pushing out, only to turn into an exhale, pulling back in. It was slow, even, methodical, rasping and grating in her heightened hearing like a woodshop and leaving no rough spots behind.

She'd never noticed how much breathing sounded like sandpaper.

Something somewhere sounded like slow-motion rain or water falling from the corner of a gutter. Her heart pulsed, muffled beneath her ribs, its valves opening and closing in time with its contractions and rushes of blood, and she counted out the clicking tattoos that composed each singular beat. It shared her lungs' tempo, precise and metronomic with not a shadow of distress or adrenaline to be found. Cool. Mechanical.

"DANIEL!"

The pitch of Avery's wail set her teeth on edge in a physiological response akin to nails on a chalkboard. Its eeriness only added to the static surrounding her—the white noise her thick, black hair created as she moved and it rubbed together; the rustle of every stitch of fabric that folded at her joints or rubbed against her skin as she walked; the soft thuds of her boots on *Starlight*'s diamond plate floors and the squeak of their leather as she shifted her weight from heel to toe in a fluid, certain gait, unstopping, firm—

Her brother's haunting, wordless screams broke off in a gasping, shuddering breath before resuming again.

"No!"

Footsteps rumbled against the deck like thunder as crew sprinted towards Avery's drawn-out, sobbing cries in the brig. His voice was hoarse, wracked with pain she couldn't comprehend. There was anger there, too, hatred if she wasn't mistaken, and helplessness. Hysteria. Her calloused palm and fingers tightened around the sullied saber in her left hand, the leather-encased hilt creaking in her merciless, bloody grip. Bright red coated the entirety of its silver surface, running down its hardened body with the faintest hiss only she could hear to come to a pooling stop at its razor-sharp edge until gravity pulled it free. The blood dripped from her blade in a steady trickle, and she listened to it splatter on the cold deck like rain—so that's what that sound was—shadowing her unwavering steps.

"Get Captain Oren and Doctor Balok." Holt's voice was falsely calm, somehow controlled in the face of what she'd just done. "Tell them we have a casualty in the brig."

"Danny!"

Avery's howling lament touched nothing in her. She continued to walk, to breathe at that deep, unbothered pace like sandpaper and rolling tides as her heart kept up its relentless beat, as unmoved as time.

Step.

People ran past her with horrified glances, gathering at the brig to see what was wrong and shouting orders to each other.

Step.

She kept her eyes fixed ahead, her bloodied complexion devoid of all emotion. She could feel the gore seeping through her clothes now.

Step.

Blood continued to fall like rain.

Step.

"I'll kill you!"

She knew Avery's new howls were directed at her, his shrieking voice cracking with its rage and agony. Its desperation to be heard, responded to, twisted his normally playful lilt into a frothing mess. She didn't break pace; didn't blink. She kept her head tall, and her grip remained tight on the saber in her tacky hand.

"I'll kill you!" he screamed again.

Holt's voice was a barely audible mumble, trying and failing to bring Avery back down. She kept walking, entering the open lift before her and facing the doors as they closed.

"ANTHIA!"

The elevator fell quiet, save for the steady drip of falling blood, and Anthia glanced down, sidestepping the growing red puddle beneath her. Her bloody, distorted reflection stared back at her in the metal doors of the lift, and she exhaled matter-of-factly.

I need a shower.

Made in the USA
Columbia, SC
14 October 2017